She once lost his heart on a bluff. Will she risk everything to win it back?

Beautician Tracy Quinn spends her days making the women of Colton, Texas beautiful, while living down the nickname of Olive Oyl, given to her by the only man she has ever loved--Zack Cartwright. She spends her nights alone, despite what her ex husband wants their friends and neighbors to think.

Ex-rodeo cowboy. Ex-bad-boy. Ex-Marine. Widower and single dad Sheriff Zack Cartwright can describe his life in exes. One ex in particular reminds him of what's missing in his workaholic life: Tracy Quinn. For years since she broke his heart, he's practically made avoiding her a second job. He still wants her, but can never go after her.

When cattle rustlers target her brother's ranch, Tracy and Zack are stuck working together. Her son could use a positive male role model, and his daughter is wild for a chance at a "substitute" mom. But Tracy's ex threatens to sue if she lets Zack near her son, and the Colton grapevine is abuzz with rumors about their past relationship. Is it worth the gamble to see if what they have is more than lust?

Books by Sara Walter Ellwood

Colton Gambers Series
Gambling On A Secret, Book One
Gambling On A Heart, Book Two
Gambling On A Dream, Book Three

Heartstrings

Published by Kensington Publishing Corporation

Gambling On A Heart

Colton Gamblers Series

Sara Walter Ellwood

LYRICAL PRESS
Kensington Publishing Corp.
www.kensingtonbooks.com

Lyrical Press books are published by
Kensington Publishing Corp. 119 West 40th Street New York, NY 10018

All Kensington titles, imprints, and distributed lines are available at special
quantity discounts for bulk purchases for sales promotion, premiums, fund-
raising, and educational or institutional use.

Special book excerpts or customized printings can also be created to fit
specific needs. For details, write or phone the office of the Kensington
Special Sales Manager:
Kensington Publishing Corp.
119 West 40th Street
New York, NY 10018
Attn. Special Sales Department. Phone: 1-800-221-2647.

Kensington and the K logo Reg. U.S. Pat. & TM Off.
Lyrical Press and the L logo are trademarks of Kensington Publishing Corp.

First Electronic Edition: July 2013
eISBN-13: 978-1-61650-482-3
eISBN-10: 1-61650-482-X

First Print Edition: July 2013
ISBN-13: 978-1-61650-986-6
ISBN-10: 1-61650-986-4

Printed in the United States of America

To D'Ann Lindun, amazing writer, fantastic critique partner and good friend. Thank you.

Acknowledgements

Thanks to everyone who has helped make this book possible.
My friends and critique partners, D'Ann Lindun and Martha Ramirez, thank you for your wonderful critiques.
My amazing editor, Piper Denna, thank you for believing in me and for your guidance

Foreword

The Colton Gamblers

In 1865, three disillusioned first cousins return from the battlefields of the defeated South to find their home in East Texas a shambles. Determined to make a new start, they head west. In the cowboy town of Dallas, Texas, they decide to pool the few silver dollars they have between them and enter into a poker game. With their gamble, they win over 100,000 acres of good grassland in Central Texas. Over the next century and a half, their descendents build a fortune in cattle and oil, but as time goes by, greed erodes their family bond.
These are the stories of the eighth generation gambling on love and bringing back the bond of family…

Chapter 1

"Have either of you seen Bobby?" Tracy Parker all but barked, and immediately lassoed the irritation. She might have a ton to do, but taking her crappy mood out on her brother and father wasn't fair. "Lucinda needs him next for pictures."

She dragged her feet up the wide front porch stairs of the Victorian house at Butterfly Ranch, feeling like the whole state of Texas was on her shoulders. And everyone knew Texas was bigger than the world.

She glanced at the groom, her brother Dylan, who sat in a cane rocker beside their father. Each of them had a glass of sweet tea--the drink of choice in Central Texas on a hot August Saturday--in their hands.

"Check inside. He has to be around here somewhere." Dylan looked too at ease to be getting married in less than an hour, with his Stetson pulled low over his forehead and his legs stretched out and ankles crossed, showing off his custom crocodile boots. He pushed his Stetson back and smiled. "You need to take a chill pill, sis. You're more nervous than I am."

She narrowed her eyes on him. "Someone has to take the wedding seriously."

"I am. I'm marrying the woman I want to spend the rest of my life with, and in February, I'm going to be a father. It's the happiest day of my life."

The sudden burn in her sinuses didn't surprise her. She was so not going to start bawling. Today had to be perfect for Dylan and Charli, the type of wedding she would never have. Not wanting to think about her own messed up life, she hugged Dylan and smiled at her father. She shook her head at the picture her cowboy brother and city slicker father made sitting together drinking tea.

As she entered the coolness of the house, she heard the television on in the living room and headed in that direction.

Bobby sat on the couch flipping through channels. The shirttail of his Western shirt hung outside his creased new jeans. His vest and bolo tie were nowhere in sight.

Her eleven-year-old son looked up as she entered, and scowled. "I wanted to go with Dad this weekend. He was gonna take me to the Rangers game."

Tracy took the TV remote from his hand and turned off the flat screen. She tossed the controller into the basket on the coffee table, then clasped her hands in front of her. "It's more important to be here at Uncle Dylan and Aunt Charli's wedding. Your dad can take you to a baseball game any time. What's going to happen today will only happen once."

He rolled his eyes and gave a longsuffering sigh. "Right. If you say so. But I still think it's all dumb. Dad doesn't think they'll last longer than a year."

She took another deep breath to calm her temper. Losing it now would only prove disastrous. Damn her ex-husband. Why would he say such a thing to a boy? "Bobby, this wedding is not stupid. Uncle Dylan and Aunt Charli love each other and want to share their special day with the people they love. Which includes you. Now, let's go out before they wonder where we are."

His jaw was set in the irritating reminder that he was Jake Parker's son through and through. His hazel eyes flashed with defiance. "I still think all this wedding crap is stupid. You and Dad didn't stay married and neither did Uncle Dylan and Aunt Brenda."

She put her hands on her hips and glared at her son. "Robert Allan Parker, if you don't get off that couch right this minute, I'm grounding you for a month."

With a glower, he slowly pushed himself up to get off the couch, mumbling, "Dad wouldn't make me do this."

"Well, I'm not your father."

"Tracy, the photographer is getting impatient. She needs Bobby ASAP," a familiar deep voice drawled behind her.

She turned to Zack Cartwright standing in the doorway, unsmiling, handsome and tall. He seemed taller than he had been back when he was eighteen. As a saddle bronco rider, he'd stood loose and relaxed. Now, he was all perfect posture. The Marines. The same thing had happened to Dylan after he'd joined the Army.

She forced herself to meet the midnight blue gaze of the only man she'd ever loved. "Thank you."

Zack wore the same Texas tuxedo as her brother--tight new blue jeans, white Western shirt, vest and custom boots. But the silver belt buckle was his own. A trophy from his rodeo days. He held his tan Stetson in his hand at his side. She tried not to notice how the stubborn curl of his golden blond hair fell over his tanned forehead. He'd always had that lock, but back when she'd run her fingers through his thick hair, it had been a lot longer.

She slammed a lid on the memories. The past couldn't be changed.

Bobby sulked beside her. "I hate getting my picture taken."

Zack turned with the thumb of his free hand hooked on a belt loop. "Today isn't about you, now is it? Today is your aunt and uncle's day, and they want pictures of you." He nodded his chin toward the archway. "Now, go out there and do what Mrs. Hudson tells you to do."

She shooed Bobby toward the door. "Go."

Zack put his hand on Bobby's shoulder to stop him as he passed. "Where's your tie and vest? And tuck in your shirt."

He looked over his shoulder at Tracy, then up at Zack. "You ain't my boss."

"No, I'm not, but we are on the same team out there. You have to walk your grandma down the aisle and stand beside me with your uncle. That's a pretty important job. And I can't imagine you'd want to embarrass your uncle and aunt or your momma."

Her heart stumbled over a beat when his gaze connected with hers.

With another glare at her, Bobby huffed and crossed the room to where he'd dumped the tie and vest. After tucking in his shirt, he headed out of the room.

Once the front door slammed behind Bobby, she flopped down on the couch with an exasperated sigh.

Zack tapped his hat against his lean leg and looked everywhere but at her. "He's got quite an attitude."

She laughed, but didn't feel any mirth. "You don't know the half of it. Things have really gotten worse the past couple of months."

"Want to talk about it?" He sat in the overstuffed chair by the windows. She imagined him doing the same thing in a small room at the sheriff's office with a victim of some crime.

Oh, great. Was he wondering how soon her son would end up with a rap sheet? She rubbed her suddenly damp palms together in her lap. "Let's just say his major problem is Jake and I have very different ideas about parenting."

Zack squared his shoulders and was all perfect posture--just as one would expect the ex-Marine sheriff to do. Where did Zack Cartwright, cowboy, go?

"So, Jake still lives by the motto rules are bad, while you try to lay down the law and set a good example?"

She forced a smile and met his gaze. "You got it. Neither Dylan nor I would have *ever* thought of trying to get away with half the stuff Bobby tries to. Sometimes I'm at my wit's end. Dad has given him a talking to, but it only worked for a few days."

He laughed and the deep rumble tickled along her senses. "The general losing his touch?"

She matched his smile. He'd had a few run-ins with General Robert Quinn back when she and Zack had dated. Her father had taken an almost instant dislike to Zack, a rodeo champion, especially after he'd kept her out all night Christmas Eve their senior year of high school. Of course, he absolutely hated her next boyfriend, Jake Parker.

"Maybe." She tugged on her short skirt. "I'd better make sure Charli doesn't need me. She chased Mom and me away, but Mom's back in there fussing."

"I think your mother should have been a bullfighter instead of a chef."

"A head chef is more tenacious than a bullfighter. But she could be the bull."

He chuckled again, and her heart pinched painfully. God, how she missed his easy laugh.

She had to escape him. Being expected to spend the rest of the afternoon with him at her side was hard enough. She stood, pulling on the short skirt of her dress again. Why had she let Charli talk her into wearing this scrap of silk? When she spared a glance at Zack, he was staring at her.

"I like the dress." He stood in a fluid motion that defied his six foot, three inch frame.

Subtle heat prickled her cheeks. "Thanks. Charli picked it out." The slip dress was nothing she'd ever choose to wear on her six-foot, stick-figure skinny body.

"Well..." He cleared his throat and looked down at his hat. "You look good. See you later."

As he put the hat on his head, he turned toward the doorway. Her heart galloped away. Had he just given her a compliment? "Yeah, see you soon."

What had just gone down between them? She shook her head and walked to the master bedroom.

She knocked at Charli's door and couldn't keep from smiling when the bride opened it, spearing Tracy with an impatient look. Someday she hoped Bobby understood when marriage happened between two people who truly loved each other, it would last a lifetime.

Charli tapped the toe of her strappy, ski-high sandal. "I want to be married already."

* * * *

A massive rental tent set up in the backyard protected the reception from the hot afternoon sun. Fans at either end helped circulate air to further keep the guests cool. Zack performed his duty of toasting the bride and groom with a bit of humor and serious admiration. Caterers served a delicious meal of spit-cooked barbeque, potato salad, baked beans and a dozen other outdoor foods. The atmosphere was a mix of old-fashioned cattle roundup and church picnic.

His six-year-old daughter sat beside him at the head table. He helped Amanda cut the tender beef and buttered her roll. She ate with such grown up tenacity, carefully making sure she didn't make a mess on her flower girl dress, his heart ached with pride. She was such a little lady.

He glanced over at the other end of the table. Tracy leaned over and whispered into her son's ear. Bobby sat at the end of the long table with his arms crossed over his white shirt. The kid was missing his vest and bolo tie again, and he'd undone his top pearl snap.

He was definitely Jake Parker's boy. Zack clenched his hand around his fork at the shot of pain in his heart. He wasn't ready for the memories.

The August after high school graduation, he'd driven over to her grandfather's ranch hoping to drive Tracy to their favorite spot at the secluded lake on the CW Ranch. He'd planned everything perfectly, down to the picnic supper, including a bottle of his granddad's best homemade wine.

The prior weekend in Houston, he'd won the saddle bronco event and had decided to go pro for a while. He and Tracy had already talked about his dream, and she'd seemed so supportive, while he'd encouraged her plan to become a doctor.

At the time, he'd never considered them too young for marriage. The prize money he'd won in the last two rodeos plus a good chunk of his trust fund had bought a three-carat diamond ring he'd planned to give her that evening. Then he'd make love to her half the night under the stars.

Although they hadn't ever told each other how they felt, he'd thought he'd known her well enough to know she loved him.

He'd never been so wrong. When he'd found her in the barn on Oak Springs Ranch, he'd watched all his dreams die in the arms of his best friend since kindergarten. Jake had Tracy against the back wall of a stall with her arms and legs wrapped around him. There was no mistaking what they were doing.

Zack tried to shake off the rest of the past, but he couldn't. Staring down at the plate of half-eaten food, the painful memory crashed over him, threatening to drown him.

He punched Jake Parker hard enough to lay him out. Jake played football, and as a result, was muscle-bound, but Zack had the element of surprise and raw rage on his side.

Tracy screamed and fell to Jake's side as she groped for her clothes, attempting to cover her breasts with the tank top she'd picked up from the straw-covered floor. The fly of her denim shorts lay open to reveal hot pink bikini panties. He looked at Jake, and acid rolled in his stomach when he saw his nakedness where his jeans hung open.

Afraid he'd throw up, he turned around and staggered toward the door.

Tracy ran after him, pulling on her top as she followed, and grabbed his arm. "Zack, please, I'm sorry...I thought you and..."

"Save it," Zack hissed through clenched teeth.

Sharp pain tightened his chest. Not only had Tracy betrayed him, but Jake had been his best friend. He'd known Zack intended to ask Tracy to marry him.

"I never thought you'd turn out no better than a whore, Tracy." With his chest constricted, he fought to breathe. "I wanted to spend the rest of my life with you. Now I don't ever want see you again."

He pushed past her and left the barn.

"Zack! Please, I love you."

He couldn't look at her. If he did, the tears burning his eyes would fall. "You have a peculiar way of showing it."

The next day, he'd left town and joined the rodeo circuit, never looking back.

"Daddy?" Amanda tugged on his sleeve. "Daddy?"

He squeezed his eyes closed and sucked in a breath through burning sinuses. He shoved the memory of the woman he'd once loved into the cobwebs of his brain where it belonged.

When he looked at his daughter, he realized despite the pain Tracy had caused him, he hadn't been ready for marriage then. Hell, he hadn't been ready when he'd asked Lisa Foster to marry him four years later.

Forcing a smile at the concerned pucker of Amanda's brow, he laid a reassuring arm across her small shoulders. "What is it, Mandy?"

"Why aren't you eating? Don't you like the food?"

He patted her shoulder, then picked up his fork with his left hand. "I was just thinking."

"Oh." Mandy picked at her potato salad and looked at him again. "What about?"

He glanced at Tracy. She met his gaze over the plates of the obliviously happy groom and bride. How many times had he lain awake under his Humvee in Afghanistan or Iraq and wished things had been different with Tracy?

As he met Mandy's big blue eyes, he sighed. If he had the power to change the past, it would be Lisa's fate he'd want to change. "I was thinking about your momma."

Mandy tilted her head to the side. "Was your wedding like this one?"

"No, not exactly. Your momma and I got married by the minister of your grandma's church in the living room of her house. The only guests were close family."

"Then you went to the war as a Marine?"

He forked up a bite of barbecued beef. "Yep."

Two days after marrying Lisa on her parents' Wyoming ranch, he'd shipped off for boot camp in San Diego. He'd joined the Marines after Nine-Eleven, giving up the rodeo forever.

"Do you still miss Momma?"

He looked into his daughter's face and his gut twisted. "Yes."

"Is that why you don't have a girlfriend?"

Mandy was too young to come up with that on her own. "Who says I need a girlfriend?"

She turned back to her meal and shrugged. "I heard Grandma and Aunt Winnie talking. They said you should get a girlfriend."

Locating his parents, uncle and aunt among the guest tables, he narrowed his eyes. "Well, maybe I don't think I need a girlfriend."

Mandy grew quiet, and he thought the topic had run its course. Despite the solid rock of pain and guilt filling his stomach, he finished his food and sipped his lemonade. There were champagne and beer for those who wanted it, but besides being pregnant, Charli was a recovering alcoholic and Dylan had stopped drinking months ago.

Zack didn't drink much alcohol these days, and he never drank it when he had to drive. Besides being the county sheriff, he knew firsthand how driving drunk affected a family--even a shattered one.

"Daddy?"

He set his glass down and turned to Mandy. "Yeah, baby girl?"

Her violet eyes met his with guileless innocence. "Momma isn't ever comin' home, is she?"

He looked away and swallowed. For the past two years, Mandy had believed her mother would come home from heaven when she missed them enough. He'd sit by every night while Mandy said her prayers and asked God to send her momma home. After all, He didn't need any more angels. He already had lots.

And every evening Zack would go to his room with his heart shredded all over again.

"No, baby girl, she isn't," he said gently and wrapped his arm around her shoulders again. "Heaven isn't a place you can leave once you go there. But your momma is always watching out for you, don't you ever believe she isn't."

She nodded and sniffed. "Would she mind if we got another momma? You know, someone who could be here for us since she can't?" Mandy must have seen the surprise register on his face. "Like my friend Kayla's grandma found her a new grandpa when her real grandpa died. A new momma could fix my hair for school and teach me girl stuff. She could play dolls with me." She looked down at the roll she was picking apart. "I know you hate it when I ask you to play with me and my Barbies." She glanced across her shoulder at him. "And a new momma could keep you company, too. Maybe she could give me a baby sister."

God, he hadn't known she was that lonely, but he couldn't give her what she wanted.

She reached for her lemonade with both hands. "Things like that. Kinda like a substitute teacher."

To her, it was probably that easy. Mandy didn't understand the complications and disastrous outcomes of adult love, but his heart swelled with love and pride for his little girl. She was making a step in the right direction of accepting her mother was gone. But he wasn't ready to find a substitute wife.

He swallowed the lump sticking in his throat. "Who says I don't like playing with you and your dolls?" She gave him a yeah-right-dad look, and he squeezed her shoulders. "Okay, I'll admit playing with your Barbie dolls isn't my favorite thing, but we're doing okay, aren't we? Just you and me."

She didn't look convinced. Before she could spew out the words reflecting what he saw through her eyes, he said, "I think we should get ready for wedding cake, don't you?"

When he looked up, Tracy watched him, and not for the first time, his body reminded him how the tall, slender brunette had always affected him. She was downright sexy in the short cornflower blue dress that made her gray eyes take on the hue of a bright summer sky. Her long, brown hair curled softly and fell around her bare shoulders.

He may not be ready for a substitute momma for his baby, or the complications of falling in love again, but he'd really like to find a woman who could keep him *company*. He already knew who he'd like that woman to be. She was the last person on Earth he should want. And the last woman on Earth he could have.

* * * *

Tracy watched her brother hold his wife so close they seemed like one person as they moved out on the dance floor to Logan Cartwright's cover of Alabama's *Feels so Right*.

As Logan finished the song, she dreaded the next dance. When she looked over her shoulder, Zack peered at her from behind a group of wedding guests. His dark blond brows lowered over his intense blue eyes. He didn't look too happy about their turn on the makeshift dance floor.

She swallowed and waited for him to walk toward her. Zack's younger brother announced the next dance, and Zack stepped before her. When she placed her hand in his, heat tingled up her arm. She looked at his face, but if he felt anything, he didn't feel the same thing she did.

His eyes narrowed into slits. "Let's get this over with."

She swallowed hard and nodded.

All eyes were on them. In a community as close-knit as Forest County, Texas--where everyone seemed related in some convoluted way--not many people didn't know Tracy and Zack's sordid past. A past she had never lived down.

He didn't smile. His expression didn't change from the angry contemplation she'd seen more than once on his face.

They reached the middle of the dance floor, and he dropped her hand and reached for her waist. Heat from his light grasp immediately flowed through her, and she sucked in a breath. She had to get a grip. He was making it clear he wanted nothing to do with her. Didn't she want as far away from him as she could get, too?

She rested her hands on his broad shoulders. His grip tightened slightly over her hips, and their gazes touched only briefly before she looked away.

Logan sang a cover of John Michael Montgomery's hit, *I Swear*. Why did Logan pick this song for their dance? She was trapped like a calf with a pack of coyotes nipping at its flanks. She wanted Zack to pull her closer, but on the next shallow breath, she wanted him to push her away. He moved her over the floor with several inches between them.

His heat warmed her, and his muscles flexed under her hands where she touched him. He avoided meeting her eyes, but she caught him looking at her as Logan sang about giving everything and hanging some memories on the wall.

Was Zack thinking about what could have been between them, or was he missing his wife?

He looked over her head. A muscle twitched in his jaw and his movements seemed hurried, like he wanted to get the dance over with. So different from the first time they'd danced together at a cattle roundup two weeks after their senior year of high school had started. A week later, they'd begun dating.

His icy, penetrating eyes locked on hers when Logan sang the chorus. Had this cold man given her a compliment earlier? Was he the same man who lovingly cut up his little girl's barbecued beef and buttered her roll?

Desperate to break the tension between them, she said, "Logan's doing well these days, it seems."

The muscle in his jaw twitched again as if he had to unclench his teeth to respond. "I guess."

That was the extent of their dance floor conversation. The moment the music ended, Zack dropped his hands and stepped out of her grasp. He didn't say a word, only turned and walked away.

She watched him make his way toward her parents, his back straight as a branding iron. He was so damned handsome he made her heart flutter.

Dylan took Tracy into his arms and kissed her cheek. With her heels, she was two inches taller than her brother. "Hey, sis, it's my turn with the third most beautiful woman in the world."

She playfully glared into his gray eyes and forced her trouble with Zack Cartwright to the back of her mind. "Third?"

Dylan shrugged. "My bride is the most beautiful woman in the world. I know better than not to call my mother the second. So, that leaves third place for my busybody little sister."

She laughed and hugged him close. "I love you, you jerk."

"Hey, have you and my bride been swapping endearments for me?" He swung her into a two-step to a countrified love song that Zack and

Logan's mother had originally made a hit when she was a rock singer in the '70s.

"That and a few stories." She let him spin her around.

When she faced him again, he cleared his throat. "I guess I owe you."

She leaned back. "Why's that?"

Dylan chuckled, but it was like a hawk's call over the grassland, deep and echoing. "I know you and Cartwright have been working together to get me straightened out. Without you, I wouldn't have ever found Charli."

She followed his stare to the woman dancing with their father. Charli laughed at something he said. Zack swung their mother into view. He smiled with an ease making him a stranger to the man Tracy had danced with.

"I don't know where I'd be without her." When Dylan's voice grew soft, she focused on her brother again.

"Have you two figured out a name for the baby yet?" she asked, turning the conversation away from the emotional cliff before she fell into the blubbering abyss below.

"Yep."

"You know the sex?"

He grinned and swung her into the last strains of the song. "I never could keep a secret from you. But all I'll admit to is we'll need both."

"You're having twins?"

"Shhh." Dylan glanced around. "We'd like to keep that off the Colton Grapevine. According to the ultrasound, we're having a boy and a girl."

Her eyes burned. She blinked, but a tear slipped by anyway. "Oh, Dylan. So, what are their names?"

He shook his head and wiped the drop of water off her cheek. "Not telling you. That's a surprise for the family."

As the music ended, Dylan drew her close and spoke huskily near her ear. "Tracy, I want you to be careful, but don't over-think things where Zack's concerned. Follow your heart. You may be surprised where it leads you. I know I was."

He kissed her on the cheek and left her standing in the middle of the dance floor. When the hell had her big, hard-assed brother started sounding like a Hallmark card? No, actually, he sounded more like a fortune cookie.

She hated fortune cookies for a reason. In her experience, they never boded well.

Chapter 2

God, Tracy was happy to see the evening end. She'd waited for the last of the catering help and Logan's band to pack up their equipment. The guests had left a half-hour ago after the groom whisked the bride and their soon-to-be-adopted teenage daughter, Annie Larson, off in his new pickup truck, a wedding gift from his bride.

Tracy parked in the five-car garage beside her parents' rented car. She and Bobby got out of the old Taurus. Now that she could afford a new car, she should consider buying a replacement. Then again, she was waiting for someone to tell her the millions of dollars she'd inherited from her grandfather was all a joke. She still couldn't believe the man she'd considered an uncle would have been so devious as to forge her grandfather's will to cheat her mother, brother, and herself out of their inheritance.

She and Bobby entered the massive Antebellum-styled house she'd moved into almost a month ago. As she kicked off her shoes by the coat closet in the mudroom, she ruffled Bobby's hair and kissed his cheek. He usually squirmed and made a face when she cuddled him. Tonight, he let her smooch him without so much as an *Eww, Mom.* He had to be tired.

She ruffled his dark brown hair. "You should have left with Grandpa and Grandma. You'd be in bed by now. Go on up and get ready."

"Do I have to shower?"

"Yes. You and Mandy were playing in the lake, which we'll have to talk about tomorrow," she said with a firm tone. "You're filthy. And brush your teeth." When he didn't argue, she hugged him close one last time, her heart so swollen her chest hurt.

What happened to the days when she'd played with him in his bathwater and helped him brush and floss his teeth? Jake had never let a single time go by without accusing her of coddling the boy, but she'd ignored him.

With a deep breath, she let her arms relax. "Good night, sweetheart. I love you."

"'Night, Mom. Love you, too," he said, stifling a yawn.

Bobby trudged through the kitchen, stopping long enough to accept a kiss from his grandma, then went through the swinging door leading to the front hall of the mansion to the stairs. He didn't allow her to tuck him in anymore--another thing his father made him believe was babyish--but how she ached to follow him up the stairs.

Her mother sat at the kitchen table with a cup of herbal tea. Tracy made herself a cup and joined her. "Where's Dad?"

With her graying blond hair cut to a chin-length wedge, and dressed in a cream-colored linen pantsuit, Eileen Ferguson Quinn cut a stylish figure. At six feet tall and with her runway model body, her mother didn't look her sixty-three years--or much like a world-class chef.

Her mother smiled. "He just took the pooches out."

After sipping her tea, Tracy sat the cup on the table and grinned. "Ah."

Her mother's two Yorkshire terriers had joined the family when she had left her grown children in Texas to follow her husband on his first assignment after returning from Bosnia. The big bad general claimed the dogs were only her mother's, but Tracy knew he loved the yappy rats-with-fur as much as her mom.

Her mother sipped her tea. "You and Zachery Cartwright seem to be getting along."

The last person Tracy wanted to talk about, after spending all day with him, was Zack. She sighed. "It was a wedding. Of course we'd be on our best behavior."

Mom shrugged and studied her with summer blue eyes. "You two made such a lovely couple on the dance floor."

Tracy groaned. The dance they'd shared was still excruciating. The awkwardness of the slow dance had been worse than anything she'd ever experienced as a gangly teenager.

Her mother pushed her hair behind her ears. "Winnie and Jackie told me Zack doesn't have much of a social life."

"I doubt Zack has time for one. He's the county sheriff and raising his little girl all by himself. Besides taking over his share of the CW." Crap, she'd said too much. Was it too much to hope her mother wouldn't pick up on how much she knew about Zack Cartwright? "So, Dad is really retiring and moving to Texas?"

Mom raised a brow and smiled. "As soon as a replacement is found for his position. We decided we want to be near our grandkids. Thank you again for letting us move in here with you."

Tracy didn't mind having her parents around--*really*. "The house would have been yours if Dylan hadn't inherited the ranch. I'm glad you're here. This is a big house for just Bobby and me."

"You've been avoiding us." Her mother took a deep breath. "I know you think your daddy and I are still disappointed in you. Honey, we love you very much and are proud of you."

"I know you love me, Mom." Whether or not they were proud of her was a different opinion altogether. There were plenty of times Tracy wasn't so proud of herself. "I guess it's admitting to Daddy that he was right about everything that's the real problem. I should never have stayed with Jake after the miscarriage." She picked up her teacup and stared down into the dark liquid. "Hell, I shouldn't've gotten involved with him again after we broke up the first time. If I hadn't, I wouldn't've gotten pregnant in the first place. Then I should've joined the Army and got my training to be a doctor away from here like Daddy wanted me to."

"Then you wouldn't have Bobby." Her mother reached over the table and laid her hand on Tracy's. "I can't imagine life without my grandson, and neither can Bob. Besides, you never wanted to join the military any more than Dylan had. Doing so would have been just as disastrous for you as it was for him."

"Bobby's my life." Tracy sipped her tea. She actually couldn't imagine being a doctor now at this time in her life, either. But there were times she felt like she'd settled.

"What are you going to do with his attitude problem?"

Tracy straightened her spine and clenched her teeth. "Can I wring Jake's neck? He's the reason there was a problem today. He's known about the wedding for two weeks, and that jerk had Bobby believing he wanted to take him to a Texas Rangers game. I'd bet my paycheck, he had no intention of taking Bobby anywhere. Jake was playing him because he knew Bobby would give me a hard time."

"Which he did. If Zack hadn't intervened while Dylan and Charli exchanged vows, he wouldn't have stopped fidgeting. I think he was doing it only for attention, too." Her mother sipped her tea. "But he wasn't expecting Zack to bring him into check."

Tracy's stomach flip-flopped when Bobby started tapping his foot in clear impatience and obstinacy during the ceremony. Then her heart had done an answering back flip when Zack snuck his hand over and laid it on Bobby's shoulder. He'd looked up into Zack's stern face, immediately stopped his agitation, and spent the rest of the service behaving himself. Later in the ceremony, Zack winked at Bobby and patted him on the shoulder. With that caring move, Tracy saw what kind of man Zack had turned into--loving, supportive, and understanding.

She ached with the knowledge Jake couldn't be anything but manipulative, demanding, and demeaning.

"What are you doing about Jake?" Her mother drew Tracy out of her thoughts.

Tracy shrugged and hugged the mug between her hands. "I have no idea. I've tried talking to him, but he won't listen to me. And now, he's threatened me with another custody battle. We go to court in three weeks."

Her mother took a deep breath and let it out slowly. "What does your lawyer say?"

Tracy snorted and set her mug on the table. "I'm looking for a new one."

"So soon before the court date?" Tracy nodded in answer, and her mother's lips compressed into to a thin line. "You should sue *him* for full custody."

"I can't take Bobby away from his father."

Mom leaned back in her chair. "In this case, no father would be better than a bad one."

Jake wasn't anybody's saint, and compared to Zack, he was severely lacking, but he wasn't necessarily a *bad* father. He wasn't a deadbeat dad. He never hit their son, nor had he lacked interest in Bobby. Sure, Jake lost his temper and said things that hurt him, but in Jake's mind, he was better than his old man. Jake's father had been physically abusive and cruel.

Her mother shook her head and lifted her cup to her lips. "Jake Parker has been bad news ever since you let him into your life. What in God's name did you see in him to make you do what you did? Zack has turned into such a wonderful young man. He's such a doting father too."

Tracy tightened her grip on the mug until her knuckles whitened. Her mother knew the story, every disgusting detail. She didn't need to be a mind reader to know her mother wished Zack was her grandson's father.

Tracy set her cup down with a thump, angry at her own stupid foolishness as much as her mother for bringing up the past. "I don't know, Mom. I thought Jake loved me."

"But you never loved him. Just like you probably didn't love the man you left Jake for."

She pinned her mother with a glower. "You really haven't a clue, do you?"

"About what?" She lowered her mug.

Tracy stood and fisted her hands by her sides. "I didn't leave Jake for another man."

"But everyone knows you lived for almost a year with someone in Waco before moving back. You haven't even told me his name."

"That's because I wasn't living with anyone!" When her mother's brow puckered, Tracy sighed and relaxed her hands. "It was Logan."

"Zack's brother?"

Tracy would have laughed at her mother's widened eyes if her total lack of faith didn't slice right through Tracy's gut. "Yes. Logan gave me a loan to move away from Jake and helped me get a job with a friend of his at a salon in the city. Over the years, Logan became my best friend." Tracy shook her head and looked away. "At first, we kept our friendship secret because he was Zack's brother. Now we do because of the hideous rumor I left Jake and shacked up with some guy in Waco. We never wanted people to wonder. If Winnie Cartwright didn't like me so much, I'm sure that little rumor Jake and his mother put out there would have flamed as out of control as a brush fire in August." She faced her mom again and winced. "I've never slept with Logan. It would be like being with my brother."

"I had no idea."

"Of course not." Tracy crossed her arms. "You haven't had much interest in anything concerning Dylan and me since high school. And the fact you'd believe a rumor started by my ex-husband to drag my reputation further into the dirt really hurts." She spun away.

"Your father and I have always cared about you and your brother."

Tracy faced her mother. "Right. If it hadn't been for Maddie--"

"Stop right there." Mom scowled and held up a finger. "I'll admit I wish I'd been here when you found out about your first pregnancy, but you were supposed to be a responsible adult by then, too. You were supposed be working toward your medical degree. Not--" She swallowed and shook her finger. "Don't you dare compare me with my stepmother."

The French doors opened and her father, following two noisy ginger-colored Yorkies, stepped into the kitchen. Retired General Robert Quinn looked from Tracy to Eileen. "Am I interrupting one of those mother-daughter talks?"

"Yes." Her mother glared at her.

"No," Tracy said at the same time as her mom.

"Okay," her father drew out in his East Coast accent and started moving across the kitchen. "I've been a soldier long enough to know to stay out of no-man's-land. Goodnight, ladies."

"Sit down, Dad." Tracy looked at her mother. "Mom and I are finished."

"Alright then." Her father looked again from her mother to Tracy, obviously unconvinced. "Where's Bobby?"

"Sleeping. He's worn out." She retook her seat across from her mother.

Tracy cringed when her dad chuckled and took a chair beside her mother. A team of interrogators couldn't be more intimidating than her mother and father. "He and Cartwright's little girl seemed to get along well."

She jumped out of her chair and headed for the teakettle on the stove. Was there no escaping the topic of Zack Cartwright and his little girl? At first, Bobby hadn't wanted to have anything to do with Amanda when she'd approached him while the adults danced and mingled after the wedding dinner.

"I think it was a combination of boredom on Bobby's part, and Amanda's determination in showing Bobby she wasn't a sissy." Tracy went about making her father a cup of the god-awful instant coffee he drank from the hot water still in the teakettle.

She returned to the table with the cup of the so-called coffee and asked her mother if she wanted more tea. Despite their tiff, Eileen was still Tracy's mother, and she'd been raised to respect her parents. Her mother declined. Tracy refreshed her cup, set the kettle back on the stove, and returned to the table.

Her father took a sip of his coffee. "I enjoyed watching the kids. Amanda's definitely a tomboy under the lace and frills."

Once her mother finished her tea, she raised her brow and smirked at her husband. "*You* and Zack seemed to get along well."

Dad shrugged and lifted the lid on a cookie jar in the middle of the table. "Zack's came a long way from the days he played cowboy. He's a good man."

He removed five chocolate chip cookies, and her mom held up three fingers. He sighed and dropped one of the cookies back into the jar. "Damn shame about his being wounded, then losing his wife, but he seems to have bounced back and settled into civilian life. He told me he and his cousin Lance are seriously getting into the cattle business." He dunked one of the cookies into his coffee and popped it into his mouth. "I guess when it's in the blood, the ranching bug can't be fought. Look at my own son. The Quinns have a military history going back to an aide de camp to General George Washington, but Dylan's damned Texas blood is too strong. I'll never understand the whole cowboy allure."

"That's because you're a damned Yankee," her mother teased in her best southern drawl and leaned toward him. She kissed him on the lips and winked. Then she took one of his remaining cookies, but he took it back by grabbing her wrist and plucking the cookie out of her fingers. She narrowed her eyes at him. "But I've never held that against you."

He held up the cookie and popped it into his mouth around his smile. Her father's gray eyes twinkled. He loved his wife with his entire being.

What Tracy wouldn't do to have a man--*have Zack*--look at her that way, especially after thirty-eight years of marriage.

He swallowed the cookie with a sip of coffee. "Well, I'm glad that's the only thing you haven't."

Tracy groaned and covered her ears with her hands. "Ugh! I'm gonna be scarred for life soon." She loved her parents and admired their relationship. It hadn't always been easy for them, not with her father away for months at a time and moving every few years when he was in the Army.

"Sorry, sweetie, I guess your daddy and I need to learn to behave ourselves." Her mother bent and ruffled the fur of the two Yorkies sitting by her feet. "I think Ginger, Cinnamon, and I are going to bed." She stepped in behind Tracy. "Goodnight, sweetheart." With her eyes full of sorrow and her smile rueful, her mother patted Tracy's shoulder.

Tracy smiled her forgiveness. "Goodnight, Momma."

Her mother nodded once and headed out of the kitchen with the little dogs padding along on either side of her.

Several minutes of silence passed until her father asked, "So, what's going on between you and the good sheriff?"

What was with her parents? Back when she and Zack actually had a chance at a future together, Mom and Dad hadn't wanted them together. Now, they were all but planning their wedding. She looked down at the cup between her hands. "Nothing."

"Why not?"

"You know very well why not." She narrowed her eyes on her father.

He raised a brow and set his mug on the table. "I don't think I do. You aren't married. He's a widower. And there's no one who attended that wedding today who doesn't know Zack Cartwright and you would've preferred to have been somewhere else instead of on the dance floor."

She leaned back in the chair and laughed. "Well, you've got that right. We wanted to be on opposite sides of the state."

"I meant somewhere *alone--together*."

"Huh?" Zack had treated her like a leper.

Her father leaned over his arms with a mischievous gleam in his eyes. "Do I really have to spell it out?"

"I have no idea what you're talking about. I don't know what you and Mom think you saw, but I know Zack, and I know now that Dylan is okay, we'll go back to avoiding each other. He has made it pretty damned clear what his opinion of me is."

Shaking his head, her father sat back. "Tracy, I'm going to give you a piece of advice."

"Why bother? You know I'm not going to take it." She stood and carried her cup to the sink.

"This time I hope you do," he softly said, and she looked over her shoulder at him. "I know you think there's no future for you and Zack, but I think differently."

She hurried toward the door to the hallway. She'd had enough of her parents thinking they knew something when they didn't. Neither one of them had seen her since last Christmas when they'd come to Texas for a few days to celebrate the holidays. "Well, good for you, but I know better. Goodnight, Dad."

"Tracy," he said as she reached the door.

Against her better judgment she stopped. She drew in a breath and turned. Why had she been raised to obey that particular tone in her father's voice? She crossed her arms.

He picked up his cup and her mother's, and headed for the sink. "So, you've made mistakes. But if you're given a second chance, don't screw it up."

"That's your advice?" She clamped down on the rest of her retort. *Nice that you're such an expert on my life.*

Her brother's final words, as he left her on the dance floor, eerily echoed her father's statement.

Depositing the mugs in the sink, he shrugged, then strode across the kitchen to her. He patted her on the shoulders and looked her in the eye. How could she be an inch taller than her father, even without her shoes, but still feel insignificant?

"Yes. I suppose it is, but I also think that advice could be taken for a lot of things. Not just concerning Cartwright. Are you really happy, Tracy Caroline?" Before she could process an answer, he kissed her on the cheek. "All I want is for you to be happy. That's all I've ever wanted for both of my children. Sweet dreams, Pixie."

She watched him leave through the swinging door into the hallway.

The last time he'd called her by the pet name had been when she'd clung to him before he boarded a plane headed to the first war in Iraq twenty-two years ago when she was twelve years old.

* * * *

Zack pulled the extended cab Ram truck into the two-car garage he'd built onto the log and limestone house. The old homestead had seen six generations of Cartwrights come and go. Cutting the engine, he looked over his shoulder at his daughter sleeping in her booster seat. It wasn't incredibly late, but she and Tracy's boy had played long into the evening.

He got out and opened the back door. After unbuckling the belt over Mandy's seat, he lifted her into his arms.

"C'mon, baby girl," he murmured and held her close to his chest. She moaned and wrapped her arms around his neck.

The house was dark and quiet as he carried Mandy down the hall to her bedroom. He pulled off her sodden shoes, laid her down onto the frilly pink comforter, and left her to fetch a damp washcloth from the bathroom.

When he returned, he wiped the worst of the grime from her face, arms, and legs. Her black hair tangled around the limp sleeves of her blue dress. The scuffed and wet white patent leather shoes were unsalvageable. He didn't have much hope for the filthy frilly dress either.

While the adults had been enjoying traditional dances and the whole garter and flower throwing silliness, Mandy and Bobby had played in the water of the lake at the edge of the front yard. If he hadn't wanted to escape after he'd caught the blue garter Dylan deliberately tossed to him and after Tracy had caught Charli's bouquet, he might not have found the two kids to get them the hell out of the water.

Besides her newfound friendship with Bobby, Mandy had attached herself to Tracy in a way he'd never seen her do with any other woman. Not that Mandy had much opportunity to become close to women outside of his family. Other than her babysitters and Deputy Dawn Madison, Mandy wasn't around too many females.

With the worst of the dirt off her and on the washcloth, Mandy awakened enough to help him remove the dress and slip a nightgown over her head. He took her hand and led her into the bathroom across the hall where he helped her brush her teeth, then attempted to untangle her snarled hair with a brush.

Giving up on the hair, he carried her back to her bed and tucked the blankets around her small body. She yawned and folded her hands over her chest. With her eyes closed, she murmured the age-old bedtime prayer recited by children everywhere. "Now I lay me down to sleep..."

He sat on the edge of her bed and smiled as she asked God to take care of every member of her family, including her pony and horse.

"And let Momma know I love her, and me and Daddy miss her."

He prepared for the twist in his gut when she asked God to send her mother home soon.

"And finally, Baby Jesus, keep Miz Tracy and Bobby safe. Amen." She opened her eyes and smiled lazily up at him.

He swallowed past the thickness in his throat.

"I thought I should stop asking God to send Momma back to us, since I know now she can't come home. It might make her sad because she can't. But I thought it would be nice to add Miz Tracy and Bobby to my list."

His smile grew stiff. He remembered their conversion over the wedding dinner. The little wheels in Mandy's head were working. She hadn't included Tracy and Bobby into her prayer without considering possibilities Zack didn't even want to think about.

"That's nice. Bobby is your friend," he said past the dry tongue sticking to the roof of his mouth.

She yawned and shrugged under the hideously pink bedspread. The ruffle must have tickled her chin, because she pushed it away. "I like Miz Tracy, too. She's your friend, isn't she?"

Tracy and him friends...fat chance. He hoped he never had to deal with her again. "I suppose." He patted her covered chest. "Nighty-night, baby girl. I love you."

"Nighty-night, Daddy." She grinned at him. "I love you more."

He leaned over her and kissed her forehead. "I love you 'til the cows come home," he whispered, and into her arms placed the stuffed bunny Lisa had given to her when she was a baby.

"We aren't missin' any cows." She giggled and hugged the raggedy stuffed animal. "So, none of 'em needs to come home."

It was an old ritual. He chuckled and stood, giving her one last kiss on her forehead and feathered back her black hair. "Then I'll have an even longer time to love you. Now go to sleep."

She nodded, yawning again. He tucked the sheet and comforter around her. For several moments after he'd turned out the light, he stood by the door until her breathing evened into sleep.

He snagged a beer from the fridge, then made his way into the big master bedroom next to Mandy's room. His grandparents had built on the master suite when they'd married. He'd completely gutted the bathroom and modernized it, much as he had the kitchen, when he'd moved in almost two years ago. He'd never be as good at carpentry as Dylan Quinn was. Dylan had practically rebuilt the old house on Butterfly Ranch, but Zack had learned from trial and error and called in the experts when he got in over his head. The work had helped him come to terms with living in a house he'd always dreamed of sharing with Tracy.

Like the rest of the house, the walls of the room were off-white and the wood trim aged oak, but the flooring was plush forest green carpet, which his feet sunk into as he crossed to the sliding glass door leading out onto the patio. He looked out over the darkened land. A horse whinnied in the distance, and from somewhere out on the ridge, a coyote howled for its mate. Stars twinkled overhead and the last of the season's fireflies flickered in the tall grass, which he really had to find the time to mow.

He drank from the longneck bottle. How many times had he and Tracy lain on the bank of the lake out in the pasture with fireflies dancing around them?

He gulped down more beer and turned away from the yard. What the hell was wrong with him? She'd cheated on him with his best friend. Regardless of what Mandy was planning in that precocious little mind of hers, he was never falling in love again. It hurt too damn much when it all fell apart.

Setting the bottle on the patio table, he pulled his smart phone from his pocket and checked his voicemail. The only message was from his mother-in-law wanting to know if he'd considered coming to Wyoming for Thanksgiving.

He supposed he should think about it. The Fosters had only seen their granddaughter a half-dozen times since Lisa's death two years ago, and for all of those times, they'd come to Texas. But he wasn't ready to go back. He'd sworn he'd never set foot in Wyoming again after Lisa's death.

Surprised not to have a call from his second in command, he dialed Dawn Madison's cell number. She answered and he asked, "Madison, what's going on?"

"Sheriff, it's your day off. Why the hell are you calling me?"

"Because I *am* the sheriff and figure it's my duty to know if the people who elected me are safe."

"Well, other than watching Simms get fatter with each creampuff he stuffs into his mouth and listening to Grant complaining about not getting any, all's well in Dodge."

He winced and looked up at the starry heavens. Larry Simms was on his way to clogging his every artery. Zack tried to promote good health among his deputies, but Larry didn't care. Zack only prayed the man didn't croak on county time. The paperwork would be a bitch. Doug Grant wasn't the only one not getting any, but Grant's reason--his wife had just had a baby--was a temporary one. There was definite light at the end of his forced celibacy tunnel. Zack's was a black hole.

"So, are Kennedy and Timmons out on patrol?" he asked, even though he already knew the answer. "Those cattle rustlers are getting bold."

"Boss, do you take me for an idiot?"

"Of course not."

"Good. I wouldn't want to think you doubted my abilities because I'm a woman."

He laughed and shook his head. He was sometimes slow on the uptake, but he got the point this time loud and clear. "Madison, you and I both know I don't think that."

"Then why the hell are you calling on your night off?"

He sighed and picked up the beer. *Because, besides my daughter, my ranch, and my job, I don't have a life.* "Take care, Dawn. Call me if you need backup."

"*Goodnight*, Zack." She hung up.

He slipped the phone into his pocket and finished off the beer.

As he glanced out over the last of the summer fireflies, Tracy drifted into his mind like a phantom. The huskiness of her voice, the sexy whisper of her laughter, the way she bit her lip when she was unsure of herself. With her heels, she was almost as tall as him. Could he still fit his hands the entire way around her waist as he had back when they'd dated? He clenched his hand at the surge of desire to try it sometime.

The dance they'd been obligated to share had been pure torture. The short blue dress showed off her long, long legs and the flawless, creamy skin of her shoulders. She smelled like sunshine and honey. He'd purposely held her away from him and refused to look at her. If he hadn't done both, he honestly wasn't sure what would have happened.

He'd convinced himself he hated her. Then, last year, he'd called her to come down to the jail to pick up her brother after a drunken binge. As they'd contrived ways to help Dylan, he'd been exposed to the side of Tracy he'd fallen head over heels for when they were thirteen--her inner beauty, her tenacity, her compassion.

Qualities she bestowed on him, even though he'd given her a nickname she'd never outgrown: Olive Oyl.

Zack's mind returned to her skimpy dress and the way it showed off her body. He'd always loved her long legs. He sucked in a breath at the image of the low-cut dress that made her breasts seem bigger.

Tracy had been self-conscious of how small she was back when they'd dated. However, once he'd discovered how sensitive her nipples were, he couldn't get enough of them. He'd never known a woman who could almost orgasm with just having her breasts stimulated. Had Jake, or the man she'd left Jake for, been able to push her over the edge?

"Damn." He shook the question from his head and re-entered the bedroom. Remembering his time with Tracy was as sadistic as thinking about his and Lisa's last fight.

He tossed the bottle into the garbage can by his dresser and headed for the shower.

Four in the morning came too damn early. Tonight was going to be one of those nights. He was strung as tight as his brother's guitar strings.

Chapter 3

"How was the Rangers game?"

Jake Parker looked across the console of the semi-truck cab at his brother. Younger by five years, Brent still reminded Jake of a baby with his round face and potbelly. "How the hell am I 'posed to know?"

Brent beetled his flabby brow as they neared Highway-6. "Didn't you go to the baseball game?"

Jake geared down the truck when the intersection came into view. No one was out at this hour in the morning. "I didn't even have tickets."

"But Bobby told me the other day you were going." Brent chuckled and folded his hands over his gut. "The kid was mad as a hornet he couldn't go 'cause of Dylan's weddin' to that pretty little filly who bought Uncle Jock's place."

Jake snorted, stopped at the stop sign, and turned left to head north on Highway 6. "I only told Bobby I wanted to take him to the game to mess with the bitch. I knew he'd cause Tracy all kinds of hell at the wedding."

Brent shook his head. "You're one hard bastard, bro. I hope I never get on your bad side."

"Then don't ever double-cross me."

In the side mirror, Jake watched their cousin Johnny Blackwell head south.

"Don't worry. I won't." Brent reached for the radio dial and turned it on to a classic country station. Soon the cab was filled with harmonica and guitar music and the voice of Willie singing about blue eyes crying in the rain. "So, are you still determined to try to get full custody of Bobby?"

"Damn straight. I'm suing Tracy for support, too." Jake glanced at his younger brother with a smirk. "I know just what to do, too. She's rich now that she inherited all that money from her grandfather. I deserve to have some of it, don't I?"

Brent shrugged and fiddled with the seatbelt over his paunch. "I don't know how you survived being married into that family. Her brother and father are two arrogant assholes."

Jake glanced at his brother. "Fortunately, General Dickhead and GI Prick were off saving the world when me and Tracy were married."

They approached the town square and stopped at the red light. He tapped the steering wheel, looking out the side window at the old courthouse and the massive tree in the front of it--the Tree of Justice, it had been dubbed over the years. A shiver slithered down his spine at the sight of the old oak tree where his forbearer Elijah Blackwell, along with his cousins Cole Cartwright and Dylan Ferguson, had hanged anyone who broke the law in their county a century and a half ago.

"Well, Tracy's still always been too damned skinny," Brent said. "I can't imagine what you saw in her."

Jake shifted the truck into gear, thankful the light turned green. The town was too damned spooky in the dark. "Tracy might be skinny, but she's sexy skinny--all long legs and tiny waist. I'd still fuck her if she'd let me."

Brent shook his head. "She has no ass or tits. Huh-uh. Not me. I want some meat on my woman. Hell, she doesn't even have anything to hold onto. Popeye can have Olive Oyl."

Jake laughed and shifted the trunk into a higher gear. He wasn't about to tell his brother just how wild in the sack normally shy, sedate Tracy Quinn was. At least, she was until she found out he didn't love her.

"Speaking of Popeye and Olive Oyl." Brent fiddled with his seatbelt. "Is it true Tracy is seeing Zack Cartwright again?"

Jake spared Brent a glace. He'd almost forgotten who gave her that nickname.

Brent's blubbery gut jiggled from laughter. "Don't you get it? Tracy is Olive Oyl and Zack was a Marine--Popeye was a sail--"

"I get it. I'm hoping she is screwin' Sheriff Asshole because that's how I'm gonna get Bobby. I refuse to let that prick anywhere near my son."

Brent held out his hands. "Whoa. Bro, you need to get over this anger you have with him."

"I'd be playing professional football right now if it wasn't for high and mighty Zack Cartwright. I'll never forget what he did to me."

"You know that almost sounds like crazy talk, Jake." Brent sucked in a deep breath, bent over his belly and reached down between his legs to get the plastic grocery sack at his feet. He pushed his hair back from his fat face before he pulled a bag of pork rinds and a bottle of Dr. Pepper from the sack. He held the bag toward Jake, who winced and shook his head. Brent shrugged and stuffed one of the disgusting deep fried pieces of pig skin into his mouth.

"Speaking of crazy people," Brent said around the crunching of the fried fat. "You know, I'm still a little freaked by the fact Leon Ferguson was Uncle Jock's son--and that Leon killed his own father."

Jake shrugged and let some of the tension leave his shoulders. They'd cross the county line in another few miles. The closer to Fort Worth they got, the easier it was to get lost within the metropolitan morning traffic. The eastern sky was beginning to purple with predawn light.

As a van passed them, he said, "I'm not surprised about Leon killing anyone. He was one sneaky, cold-hearted sombitch, but him being a blood relative of mine makes me wonder about our gene pool." Jake frowned as he glanced at Brent again. He was still shoving more lard into his already fat body. "Then again, look at Johnny, Darryl and Talon. The three of them are the hardest men I know, and not all of that comes from being Jock Blackwell's bastards. They have Jock's crazy genes. Mom missed getting those from Granny Blackwell, I guess."

"I agree. 'Cause I sure as hell ain't crazy. But I don't know 'bout you," Brent mumbled.

"Ha, ha. You're a fuckin' comedian tonight." Jake glared at his brother. How the hell could they possibly be related? Jake was stocky and muscular, while Brent was mostly blubber. "If you'd lay off the junk, you might actually find a woman."

"Don't want one." He crunched on more deep-fried fat. "Nuttin' but trouble."

"Keep tellin' yourself that, baby brother."

Brent settled back into his seat and took a deep breath. "It's just a shame Mom didn't inherit Blackwell Ranch when Granddad died. We'd be rich bastards right now with all that oil still under the place. I could buy myself a woman. Maybe one like that stripper that just married Dylan Quinn. She's one hot number, and rich."

Jake met his brother's eyes and grinned. "Shut the hell up. I'm not listening to you yack the whole way."

He turned the radio up and settled into the seat as Hank Williams, Sr., crooned out *Hey, Good Lookin'*.

* * * *

The aroma of bacon and blueberry pancakes wafted up the stairs to meet Tracy as she stumbled down the second floor hall. Her belly growled, and she scowled at the treacherous sound.

She never ate a heavy breakfast--a bowl of Cheerios or cornflakes was as elaborate as she got. And always with copious amounts of coffee. She didn't smell the morning liquor and sighed. Her mother could make a breakfast she really didn't want, but wouldn't make the coffee she needed. Mom didn't drink the stuff and Dad preferred the instant crap--probably because that's what he was used to drinking.

Tracy turned at the bottom of the stairs. As she headed down the hall toward the kitchen, she overheard Bobby squeal, "Mom never makes me pancakes! Blueberry! Thanks, Grandma, you're the best."

The sound of her father's deep chuckle and her mother's laugh grated over Tracy like the tines of a rake. "Your mom needs to learn to cook." His words were salt rubbed into the scratches. "A growing boy can't live on chicken nuggets and cold cereal."

"Mom says she hates to cook." Bobby spoke between slurping sounds. He must have drowned the light and fluffy pancakes with syrup. His mouth sounded full. "I swear only Dad is worse."

Her belly growled again at the memory of her mother's special homemade blueberry pancakes. This time she slapped her hand across her middle.

"As long as I'm around you won't be eating that processed junk." Her mother's voice was soft, but her words hurt like a punch.

Mom made it sound like Tracy didn't take care of Bobby. So what if she couldn't cook? She hated it and never understood what her mother found so fascinating about it. Who in their right mind wanted to slave over a hot stove? But Tracy didn't just feed Bobby junk. They ate salads, and she made spaghetti. She baked chicken breasts and pork chops and served them with rice from a box and bag of frozen vegetables--just like every other working mom out there in the world.

She didn't slave over a simmering pot for hours, but what she made was good and quick. Unlike her mother, Tracy worked for a living.

When she'd been in high school, her mother had tried to equate the mixing of ingredients with chemistry, a subject Tracy had always found interesting, but she just didn't get it. Now, she only found cooking tedious and something she had to do, like cleaning the toilet.

As she allowed the stress of having her parents in the house continue to boil over, she assured herself that she was a good mom by thinking of the things she did do for Bobby. She'd taken time to play with her son. Bobby never wanted anything, and she'd easily lay her life down to spare his. She'd saved her tips and maxed out one of her credit cards two years ago to take him to Disney World, SeaWorld and the Universal theme park. He still talked about the two-week trip.

Bobby had never complained about her cooking until his grandmother moved in, and suddenly Tracy wasn't a good mother because she didn't make blueberry pancakes--from organic wholegrain flour, buttermilk and fresh blueberries.

What does Zack make Mandy for breakfast? Did he make her pancakes and cook up fantastic meals? Or did Zack serve the same things like cereal, canned spaghetti sauce, and boxed mac and cheese?

Zack had cooked for Tracy a few times. She remembered the first time he'd surprised her with a picnic basket full of homemade potato salad and fried chicken. The image of him watching her with anticipation in his blue eyes as she took those first bites still burned in her psyche. After she'd assured him the meal was delicious, he'd blushed and admitted he'd made it himself.

Tracy squashed the memory in its sneaky tracks. Hadn't being up half the night thinking about the man been enough?

Sucking in a deep breath, she entered the kitchen and kissed Bobby on the forehead. Bobby squirmed in his seat but didn't fuss. He was too busy stuffing pancakes into his mouth.

Tracy went to the granite-topped counter and began making coffee. Her mother was dishing up more pancakes and bacon. "Tracy, you really shouldn't drink so much coffee. All that caffeine isn't good for you."

Closing her eyes, Tracy breathed through her nose and held the breath. As she let it out, she opened her eyes before turning to face her mother. "I beg to differ. There is absolutely no concrete evidence on whether caffeine is good or bad for you. In fact, that bacon is probably worse to eat than drinking two cups of coffee in the morning is."

Tracy took the plate her mother held out toward her.

Mom pursed her lips and turned back to the stove. "I hope Dylan and Charli have a nice time in Hawaii. I still don't understand why they wanted to take that girl with them."

Tracy took a seat beside Bobby at the big center breakfast island and picked up a fork to dig into the pancakes. "I'm sure they all are having a great time. And that *girl* has a name. Annie. Charli and Dylan took her along so she could get away from here for a little while. You know her mother was just murdered by her biological father."

"I think their wanting to adopt her is a lot to take on." Her father turned the page of his morning newspaper. "Have you heard from them yet?"

"Maybe it is a big responsibility, but I personally think it's noble of them." Tracy spread butter on her pancakes and dumped her mother's special blueberry syrup over them. "Charli's going to text me when they get to the resort."

"There was another cattle theft." Dad laid the paper on the island top.

"Where?" Bobby swallowed the bite around which he'd spoken. "Was it close?"

"A ranch called W bar T."

"The Westcotts, distant cousins of Zack's--and ours, too, I guess. Over near Gambler's Lake on the other side of the county." Tracy wiped the syrup off her mouth with the paper napkin her mother handed her. Mom also placed a cup of the freshly brewed coffee with cream already added before Tracy. "Thanks, Mom." She picked up the mug. "That makes the seventh rustling since the end of June."

Dad shook his head as he scanned the news report. "It says, *The Texas and Southwestern Cattle Raisers Association--TSCRA--are assisting the Forest County Sheriff's Department in determining when the raid occurred. According to Sheriff Zachery Cartwright, the forty-three Herefords were reported missing Friday, but may have been stolen as many as four days ago.*" Her father looked up and removed his glasses. "I'm surprised Cartwright didn't mention this yesterday at the wedding."

"Maybe he didn't want to cast a shadow on the day." Her mother bustled about, cleaning up empty plates. "Which was the polite thing to do."

Bobby, now finished devouring his breakfast, glanced up at Tracy. "The newspaper always makes everything sound so boring. Can I go outside?"

Tracy nodded and sipped her coffee. "Yes, you *may* go out, but don't get dirty. We'll be going to church in a couple of hours. And stay out of the ranch hands' way."

Bobby's response was his usual roll of the eyes. Why she bothered warning him was beyond her, but she had to try. Bobby missed living in town where he had friends, and she was secretly thankful the workers Bobby attached himself to didn't mind having the boy around.

When Dylan had invited them to live in the mansion on Oak Springs Ranch, she'd been thrilled to get Bobby out of town and on the ranch. She'd always loved the old house, which had been in her mother's family for six generations. It was a replica of the original plantation house where her great-great-great grandfather had been born before the Civil War. When he'd returned from the War Between the States, he and his two cousins headed west.

Tracy picked at her pancakes. "Zack sure has his hands full. He's still helping the Texas Rangers and the FBI investigate Leon's crimes, and now this."

Her mother stopped wiping the counter. "I heard yesterday from Winnie Cartwright that Leon's trying to plead insanity. He's pulling in doctors from all over to give credence to his claim because his father and grandmother had bi-polar disorders." Her blue eyes flashed and she huffed. "I'll tell you I can agree that Leon's crazy, but if my stepbrother tries to use that crock of classic bull crap to get off murdering his grandfather, his father and the mother of his daughter... *Plus*, the forgery of my father's will." She slapped a hand against the counter. "*And* he threatened the lives of my son and the mother of his unborn child. If he gets off, I'll--I'll..." Her face flushed red as her shrill voice trailed off. She released her death grip on the dishcloth in her hand and ran the fingers of both hands through her short hair.

Her father grinned and raised a dark brow. "You'll what?"

"I'll raise Cain," her mother drawled with a jut of her chin.

Both Tracy and her father laughed. Picking up his empty mug, he stood and went around the island and kissed his wife on the cheek. "I'm sure you will do just that."

Tracy averted her eyes and focused on eating the now-cold pancakes on her plate.

"Mom! Mom!" Bobby ran into the kitchen from the mudroom with her mother's two yapping Yorkshire terriers on his heels. "Mom!"

Tracy winced as Cinnamon and Ginger barked very time he called for her. "What?"

While her mother calmed the excited dogs, Bobby looked up with widened eyes from her to his grandfather. Before he could explain what the hullabaloo was all about, Tom Miller, the foreman of Oak Springs Ranch, and Zack Cartwright followed the boy into the kitchen.

Zack stood in the doorway, dressed in a tan uniform that looked too damn good on his lean frame. He took in the entire room with one sweeping glance as he removed his Stetson. His eyes burned with something Tracy couldn't name when they settled on her. "Someone rustled forty-five Angus steers out of the southeastern pasture of Oak Springs last night. Who wants to break the news to the newlyweds?"

* * * *

"Oh, no!" Eileen and Tracy gasped at the exact same time and both women covered their mouths.

Zack almost smiled at the reactions of the mother and daughter. He looked from Tracy to Bob and couldn't help slipping into a military stance with his arms at his sides. "Morning, General Quinn."

Bob's lopsided grin surprised Zack. "Relax, Zack. Last time I checked I'm not wearing a star on my shoulder. Good morning, Tom."

When the retired Army general moved around the counter to stand by Tracy, Zack blinked. The tough old general wore a pair of running shorts, a wife beater, and a pair of flip-flops.

"No, I suppose not," Zack said.

"Bobby, go up to your room and start getting ready for church," Tracy said.

Bobby started to protest, but when she arched a delicate dark brow, he huffed out a breath and headed out of the room.

She stood from the stool, the long pencil skirt hugging her slender figure as she moved. She tugged on the flouncy sleeves of her white blouse and looked from Zack to Tom. "Would the two of you like some coffee?"

Tom shook his head, but Zack could use a cup. He hadn't had more than a couple hours of sleep, and now his mouth was dry. "That'll be good. Thanks."

As Tracy headed for the coffee maker across the kitchen, Zack's gaze followed the sway of her slender hips.

"How do you know the cattle were stolen?" Bob broke into Zack's memory of what Tracy looked like without her clothes.

Zack cleared his throat and focused on business. "I saw the cut in the fence on my way to work this morning. The thief didn't close up the fence, and a few steers were out on the road. I stopped and got them back in and called Tom."

The foreman shuffled his feet and twisted his hat in his hands. "I drove out there with a few hands and verified forty-five of the steers are missing. I have the hands driving the rest into another pasture."

"How can you be so sure the fence didn't just break and the cattle got out on their own? Daddy used to have that problem all the time along that road." Eileen placed a creamer pitcher and sugar bowl near Zack.

Tracy returned with Zack's steaming black coffee. He set his hat on one of the stools by the bar and reached for the sugar bowl. "I already added the sugar." Their eyes locked as he took the mug from her. She smiled and shrugged. "Four heaping spoonfuls, just as you've always liked it."

Was she flirting with him? "Thanks." He took the cup from her. His fingers brushed hers and awareness buzzed through him as surely as the caffeine and sugar would, once he drank the coffee.

"It was cut," Tom said, reminding Zack that he had a job to do. "Dylan checked those fences Wednesday."

"I really don't want to ruin Dylan and Charli's honeymoon with this news." Eileen took a stool beside her husband.

Tracy glanced at her mother. "I agree. I think we shouldn't tell them unless something else happens."

Zack rubbed his chin and shook his head. "I can't do that. They own this ranch, and it was their property that was stolen."

"True." Tracy slid onto the stool beside him and leaned against the edge of the island, facing him. "But I live here, as do Dad and Mom. Dylan and Charli both left it up to us to make any decisions regarding the place while they were gone."

Zack considered her words. He knew they were true, but he also knew the law. As Tracy regarded him with big gray eyes, he gave in. He didn't want to ruin his friends' honeymoon any more than she did. "Okay. But if there's any other trouble, I'll have to call them."

She pushed off the stool and smiled at him. "Good. Now, I have to make sure Bobby is getting ready for church. See you around, Zack. Tom."

Tom nodded. "Have a good day, ma'am. Ah, tell Bobby I have a job for him when he comes home."

She smiled. "I will. Thanks, Tom, for putting up with him."

He shrugged and shuffled his feet. "Not a problem. He's a good help around the barn."

As she passed Zack and headed toward the door, he glued his gaze to the swish of her long brown hair and the sway of her behind until she pushed out the swinging door.

"Cartwright, if you're done lusting after my daughter, why don't you tell us exactly how you plan to catch these cattle thieves."

Tom Miller's chuckle punctuated Bob Quinn's amused words.

Damn, he needed a woman.

But *that woman* couldn't be Tracy, no matter how much he wanted her.

Chapter 4

Tracy smiled at Henrietta Parker as she shuffled across the wood floor toward the salon sink, her cane making a jaunty tap-tap with each step. Although she was now stoop-shouldered and aged ninety-one, Henrietta was still famous around town for being a pilot during World War II. And up until six years ago, she'd flown her crop duster. Only her eldest son's taking the engine out of the old thing grounded her.

Henrietta pointed her cane at Tracy as she sat in the chair in front of the sink. "Haven't I told you a thousand times to get rid of those granny clothes?"

As Tracy took the old woman's cane and leaned it against the wall, she looked down at her favorite peasant blouse and long denim skirt. "I happen to like this outfit, Grandma."

Henrietta narrowed her sharp green eyes on her and shook her head. "Yeah, well, it makes you look like you're wearing a gunnysack. I don't get you, Tracy Caroline. There are women out there who starve themselves half to death to look like you. And make big money for their efforts." She pointed a knobby finger at her. "Just the other night I was watching a television show about girls who want to be models and what they have to do to stay skinny." She looked Tracy up and down and frowned again. "How the hell do you expect to catch a husband dressed like that?"

Tracy sighed and helped the woman lean back into the sink. "I'm not looking for a husband. I had one, remember?"

With a snort, Henrietta settled her head back. "And you did the right thing by dumping him. Now, you need a new one. That great-grandson of mine needs a steady hand. Jake is too much like his daddy. God rest Allan's soul, but he was the poorest excuse for a father put on God's green Earth."

Tracy sprayed the thin white hair with warm water. "Now, Grandma."

She turned in her seat and shook a finger at Tracy again. "Don't you 'now, Grandma' me. It's the gospel truth. If my son had been any kind of man, he wouldn't've beat his boys, and they may have turned out halfway decent."

Tracy grabbed a towel as water dripped from the woman's hair onto her embroidered Western shirt. She wasn't about to get into an argument about Allan Parker's parenting skills or those of his son, Jake. She grabbed a drape and put it around her ex-grandmother-in-law. "Jake isn't like Allan, and you know it."

Henrietta harrumphed and leaned back against the lip of the sink. "Maybe not, but it still burns my ass that I've reached this age, and instead of my grandsons taking care of me, I'm still taking care of them."

Tracy lathered Henrietta's hair and worked her fingers through the thin strands to massage four days worth of hairspray off the woman's scalp. Henrietta came in to the shop twice a week, Monday and Thursday for a wash and set and trusted Aqua Net and a sleeping cap to keep it looking good between those days. "Now, what did Brent do?"

"Well, let me tell you." She huffed and folded her hands over the drape. "He's been laid-off since the tire factory packed up and moved to China and has been freeloading off me or his mother ever since. But last week, he shows up with a brand, spanking new Silverado. I can't even get him to help me buy the grub he shoves into that big mouth of his, but he has money to get himself a fancy pickup truck." The many wrinkles around her mouth pulled down as she scowled. "Hell, what does he need a truck for? All he does is sit on my couch eating my food and watching my television set."

Tracy furrowed her brow. "Did he get another job?"

Henrietta threw up her arms. "Hell, no! Although he's been riding along with Jake in that truck driving gig he's got going, but he ain't makin' any money at it. Or so he says."

Tracy rinsed Henrietta's hair and patted the excess water out of it. "Did Sandy buy the truck for him?"

Tracy didn't care what her ex-mother-in-law did, but she sensed Henrietta needed to vent her frustration.

The old woman stood, and Tracy helped her shuffle across the floor and settle into the seat at the workstation. Henrietta waved her hand in a dismissive gesture. "You know Sandy doesn't have any money to buy a truck like that." She wrinkled her nose in disdain. "She may have been born with a silver spoon in her mouth, but that was taken away when that son-of-a-bitch John Blackwell disowned her for marrying my Allan."

Tracy retrieved a comb and picked out the knots in Henrietta's thin hair. Swallowing, she watched the woman's reflection in the mirror above the counter. "You're not giving him money, are you?"

Henrietta's green eyes narrowed again. "No. And before you go asking 'bout my savings. No one but my oldest boy, Charles, has access to 'em. I made sure my clock hadn't been cleaned, the moment Brent showed up with that truck." The old woman chuckled. "Hell, I know better than letting either one of those grandsons of mine know how much damn money I have getting moldy over there in the Cattlemen's Bank and Trust."

Tracy smiled. Henrietta didn't get rich on her crop dusting service by not being a shrewd businesswoman. "Are you coming to Bobby's game Wednesday?"

"Wish I could. But that's my poker night with the Cartwright sisters. Those two old biddies swindled me out of five bucks last week and I want it back. Plus interest."

Tracy laughed and reached for the styling gel. Zack's great-aunts were in their eighties and two of the sweetest old ladies she'd ever met, and she couldn't imagine the spinster twins swindling anyone. "So, they take after the famed Cole Cartwright, do they?"

Henrietta *tsked*. "Hardly. Oh, they like to think they take after their great-granddaddy. But neither of them can beat me when I'm in my game."

Tracy applied styling gel to Henrietta's hair. The old woman watched the action through the reflection in the mirror for a few moments. "So, when are you gonna get yourself some help around this place? You don't need to be doin' hair now that you inherited all that money from your granddaddy."

With a shrug, Tracy reached for the tray of rollers under a cabinet. "I like what I do. Sure, I may not need the money, but I can't imagine not working."

"No one said you had to give up working, but if you hired another girl to work here, you'd have more time to do other things. Like go back to school. Get the education that no-good grandson of mine denied you of."

Tracy sectioned Henrietta's thin hair and then rolled the wisps onto the rollers. She'd love to have more time to spend with Bobby, but not being here every day for the women who depended on her?

Go back to school? She hadn't even considered the possibility before Winnie Cartwright mentioned it last week, then her Aunt Janet said the same thing at the wedding. Maybe now she should think about getting her degree. But in what? Going to medical school seemed as much a pipe dream as it always had.

Tracy smiled, but it was slippery and soon slid off her face. "I'm beginning to think nobody wants me anymore. A few other people said the same thing to me."

Henrietta turned and looked over her shoulder at Tracy. "You know better. You're ten times better at doin' hair than Sandy Parker ever was. But now, you could go to school. Become a doctor like you always wanted. Lord knows you've got the smarts for it. Besides, you've always said, if you could, you'd go back to school. Now's your chance."

Tracy shook her head and looked down into the tray of curlers. She gripped the comb in her left hand until her fingers hurt. "I have Bobby to consider."

"True. But think about how much your going to school will mean to him. Right now, all he wants to do is play football because that's what Jake's pounding in his head. The boy needs an education if he's ever gonna amount to anything."

Her new sister-in-law had been a drug addict, a teenage runaway and ended up serving a year in prison for a crime she'd been duped into committing, and now, she was happily married, pregnant and adopting a teenage daughter. But she was still taking classes at the local college.

Danm, was that envy she felt? She licked her lips and rolled the last curler into Henrietta's white hair, suddenly anxious to get her out of the shop. "I'm too old to go back to school."

"Poppycock. You're what? Thirty-two? If I was your age, livin' in today's world, I'd be doing everything I could to be a pilot in the Air Force. Maybe even join NASA. Can't you see me flyin' one of those fancy Space Shuttles?" She laughed, but her misty green eyes betrayed more than a wistful dream as she stared at their reflections in the mirror. "You're too young with too many opportunities to just give up on your dreams, Tracy Caroline."

* * * *

Zack read the report and looked up at the Texas and Southwestern Cattle Raisers Association agent standing in front of his desk. "Not a single clue."

Agent Herbert Milroy caressed his graying mustache. "Nope. Damned frustrating, is what it is. But I haven't seen a rustler yet in my twenty years of being a TSCRA agent that didn't suffer the same disease: cockiness."

Tossing the sheet of paper onto the jumble of traffic tickets and deputy reports covering his desk, Zack leaned back in his chair and tried to ignore the ache springing up in his temples. "I sure as hell hope so. The Westcotts were already on the verge of bankruptcy. Losing forty-three prime steers didn't help them. And I'd hate for someone else as bad off to be hit next."

Milroy rubbed his hand across his nose and sat in the chair in front of the desk. He glanced at his hands before looking up at Zack, and cleared his throat. "I need to talk to the owners of Butterfly Springs Cattle Company."

Zack straightened in his chair. "They're on their honeymoon and left Tracy Parker in charge. If you need anything, she's the one to ask."

The agent seemed to consider his words before nodding. "Alright. I'll do this your way. I suppose Quinn and that sassy filly he married deserve to have a little peace after what happened at the Independence Day Charity Ball."

Herb Milroy was a local man and had been at the Gambler's Lake Country Club for the annual shindig when Leon Ferguson had held Charli and Dylan at gunpoint. Zack still remembered the adrenaline rush when he'd pulled the trigger of his Glock from twenty yards away. He hadn't shot a man since his last tour in Afghanistan over two years ago. Although he hadn't wanted to kill Ferguson and had aimed for his shoulder, he now wished he'd saved the state of Texas and himself the trouble of wanting to try him for his various crimes. The businessman's lawyers were making Zack's life a living hell. The thought of the meeting with the DA earlier that afternoon weighed on him, threatening to drag him under.

The slight ache in his temples turned into a bonafide throb.

"Thanks, I know Charli and Dylan will appreciate it." Zack focused on the puzzle currently in front of him and stood. "Want some coffee?"

With a wrinkle in his bushy brows, Herb glanced at the old, stained coffeemaker in the corner. "How old is it?"

Zack shrugged and poured himself a cup of the brew. It smelled as strong as it looked. One step up from road tar. "I made it at lunchtime." As he stirred four heaping spoons of sugar into the cup, he looked over his shoulder at Herb and caught his grimace. With a chuckle, Zack turned. "That was only four hours ago."

"Thanks. But no thanks," Herb muttered. "My ulcer hurts just thinking about drinking that swill. Do you know where I could find Miz Parker?"

Zack sat in his chair again and sipped from the cup Mandy had given to him for Father's Day last year. The old coffee hit his empty stomach with an unpleasant thud. Maybe he shouldn't drink the stuff. "She's probably at her hair salon. I'll follow you over there."

Or was the fluttery feeling from the prospect of seeing Tracy?

* * * *

Tracy pushed her glasses up her nose and stared at the list of classes she'd have to take to complete her bachelor's degree. If she could go full-time, she'd be done in three semesters. But since she couldn't quit her life and devote every second to studying, it would take her at least five.

She sighed and clicked the exit icon at the corner of the University of Texas at Austin website. It was foolish to entertain the idea of going to medical school. She'd be forty before she'd graduate.

With a sniff, she opened her email, deleting junk mail and spam until she landed on a subject line that read, *In response to your ad.*

Tracy leaned back in her chair. Was it possible someone had already replied to her advertisement she'd placed that morning on the local paper's website after Henrietta had left? She clicked it open and read the note.

Hi, not sure if you remember me. I'm Melissa Blackwell. I'm back in Colton to take care of Buck, my dad, who recently was diagnosed with lung cancer. Anyway, I saw your ad this morning and would love to meet with you to talk about the job. I worked for six years in LA at LaSalle's. I've attached a copy of my resume.

I'll be waiting to hear from you.

Melissa Blackwell

Tracy didn't remember Melissa, but she knew who she was. Melissa and her identical twin sister had lived in Los Angeles with their mother since they were little. Their father, Buck Blackwell, owned the Broken B Ranch across the road from Butterfly and Oak Springs.

As she opened the resume, the bell above the front door twinkled its cheery warning that someone entered the shop. No other customers were scheduled. She glanced at the clock on her computer and frowned.

"Tracy?" Zack's voice sounded from the front reception area. "Are you here?"

She gasped, pulled the glasses from her face and reached up to touch her hair. Messy strands stuck out of the butterfly clip. She hurriedly took it out, twisted her hair, and put the clip back in, calling, "I'm here. I'll be out in a minute."

After she jumped from her chair, she rushed into the small bathroom and peered into the mirror above the pedestal sink. Her makeup had long ago disappeared and the mascara had smudged under her eyes. She rubbed at the marks and sighed.

Figures, he'd show up when I look my absolutely worst after a day of making others look beautiful.

Giving up, she headed out to the front of the converted Victorian to the front room. Zack bracketed his waist above his service belt and stood next an older man she recognized as Herb Milroy.

Zack turned as she entered the room, and removed his hat. He stared at her with those new-denim blue eyes for a moment as if he wondered why he was there. "Tracy, I think you know Agent Milroy."

Tracy rounded the antique desk she used as a reception counter. Holding out her hand, she smiled. "Herb, it's been a long time."

Herb shook her hand. "Ma'am, I'm hoping you can answer some questions regarding the cattle your brother and his wife lost the other night."

She glanced at Zack, who was busy looking everywhere but at her. "Sure. What do you want to know?"

One side of Herb's lips twitched up, and he took out a notepad. "What can you tell us about the cattle that were stolen?"

Tracy folded her hands and shrugged. "According to Tom Miller there were forty-five taken. Ah...I'm not sure what you want me to tell you."

Zack stopped avoiding her and met her gaze. "How long were they in that pasture?"

Sweat gathered at the back of her neck and she rubbed it. "They were moved over into the pasture about two weeks ago. I think they were going to be rounded up after Dylan and Charli come back from their honeymoon, and put into the feedlot."

"What can you tell us about their brands?" Herb looked up from his pad.

"They are the last of the cattle that were owned by Leon. Their brands are the old oak leaf with an *F* inside. The Oak Springs brand, rather than the B bar OS brand."

"Thanks, Miz." Herb put his notebook away and bobbed his head. "That gives us something to work on. Have a good day."

"You, too. Tell Ellie hello from me," she said, referring to his wife.

"Will do." Herb smiled as he settled his hat onto his head. "See you tomorrow, Sheriff."

Tracy expected Zack to follow Herb out the door, but he hung back. After the door closed, Zack looked down and turned his hat in his hands. "Have you talked to Dylan and Charli?"

"I got a text from Charli letting me know they arrived in Hawaii okay. But if you're asking if they know about the cattle, the answer is no."

He nodded and met her gaze. "Are you okay?" Quickly, he added, "I mean sometimes when a theft happens so close to home, it can shake you up some. Especially with everything else that's gone on with your family."

She shrugged and rubbed her arms. "I'm okay. It isn't like my house was broken into. But I can see how something like this could bother a person."

When he put his hat on, getting ready to leave, Tracy was both glad and disappointed. Without meaning to say anything at all, she said, "I got an interesting email this morning."

Zack puckered his brow in askance.

"It was from Melissa Blackwell. She's back in town."

He rubbed the side of his face in thought. His beard was coming in as a dark shadow on his angular jaw. She could imagine the sinful sensations it could cause on her skin in certain forbidden places.

She shivered as a blush heated her neck. *Don't even go there.*

"You heard about Buck?" he asked.

"Yeah, apparently she's here to take care of him. She answered the ad I placed this morning for help."

He swung his sharp blue eyes to hers. "You're looking to hire someone?"

She moved behind the desk and pretended to rearrange her pens and pencils in the lace-covered jar in which she kept them. "I'm thinking about it."

"So, you're expanding. That's good."

Tracy shook her head. "Not really." A short snort of a laugh escaped her lips. She had to be crazy for even thinking this, let alone telling Zack, but something deep down needed his approval, or maybe it was his acceptance. "I'm going back to school to finish my degree."

He raised a brow, and his lips turned up at the corners. It wasn't much of a smile, but it made Tracy's heart soar. "Good for you. Well, I gotta go and pick up Mandy from daycare."

Still recovering from the thrill he'd given her, Tracy swallowed hard and nodded. "Have a good night."

At the door, he looked over his shoulder at her and tipped his hat. "You, too. See you around."

For a long time after he left, Tracy stood there in the reception area. What the hell had just happened? When had she actually decided to go back to school?

She laughed aloud and shook her head. "I guess I decided two minutes ago."

Damn. She rushed to her office and clicked on the website for the university. She'd better get registered.

Chapter 5

Zack held onto Amanda's hand and looked over the crowd gathered for the first game of the Colton Junior Cowboys and the Hamilton Broncos Wednesday evening. Football always drew a large crowd in this part of Texas. And the Pee Wee Flag Football League wasn't an exception. The limited seating offered by rickety bleachers was filled to capacity and blankets and lawn chairs lined the sidelines. Every available space seemed to be filled.

If he hadn't promised Mandy they would come to the game, he wouldn't be here. That morning, Zack got the news that another rustling happened in a neighboring county. Herb Milroy was convinced the same thieves hitting up ranches in Forest County were involved.

Later in the day, Zack had been stuck at the office longer than his shift for a meeting with the Texas Rangers and FBI investigators involved in Leon Ferguson's multiple murder case. When he'd gotten back to the ranch, one of the foremen cornered him with information that a strip of fencing between his share of the CW Ranch and a neighbor was down. His neighbor's stud ended up on Zack's side of the fence with his recently purchased thoroughbred mares. Lord only knew what damage to his mares that big paint stallion ended up doing.

As he tried to shake off the bad day, he looked over the spectators. The game had already started and the Junior Cowboys had scored the first touchdown.

Mandy tugged on his hand. "Hey, there's Miz Tracy. She has plenty of room on her blanket. Let's go sit with her."

Before he could protest, Mandy let go of his hand and weaved her way around the other cheering spectators. She stopped beside the worn blanket on which Tracy lounged with her arms braced behind her and her long, bare legs crossed at the ankles. She'd kicked off her sandals and they lay beside her slender feet. The early evening sun played in the long hair flowing over her shoulders, picking out golden highlights from the brown. Tracy had no idea just how sexy she was with her lean body dressed in denim shorts and a t-shirt.

When Tracy looked over her shoulder at Amanda, he watched a winning smile light up her sculpted face. She said something to Mandy, but Zack was too far away to hear. However, as Amanda sat next to her, he assumed it must have been an invitation. A knot formed in his throat as Tracy put her arm around his daughter's shoulders, hugging her close. Mandy smiled at Tracy and said something that made her laugh. Even from the distance, he heard the husky whisper of her laughter.

Tracy looked over the heads of those sitting behind her and greeted him with a tentative smile of invitation. Every brain cell still holding an ounce of reasoning screamed at him to grab his daughter and sit somewhere else. Unfortunately, he didn't seem to have enough of those brain cells left.

Zack sat on the blanket beside Mandy and looked out over the field as a kid from the opposing team ran the football until a Cowboy deflagged him, downing the ball.

He looked at Tracy and smiled. "Hi. Thanks for the seat."

"You're welcome." Tracy pulled her legs up to sit in an identical pose to his six-year-old. Something Mandy called *crisscross applesauce*. He knew it as Indian style, but he supposed these days everything had to be politically correct. "You making an official appearance? Or are you here to watch someone in particular?"

"I guess it's an official appearance, and I promised to bring Mandy. She wanted to see Bobby play." Zack suddenly found himself tongue-tied. Looking for something else to say, he asked, "Your parents aren't here?"

"Nope, they decided to take a drive down to Fort Hood for a few days to visit the general in charge. Dad's friends with him." She shrugged and a clump of her dark hair fell over her face. She pushed it back and held it there for a few beats as if that would make it stay in place. "I'll be glad when they get home. Those two furballs they call dogs are driving me nuts. I'm so not looking forward to watching them when they go back to Washington in a couple of weeks."

Zack laughed and followed the movement of the lock of hair as it fell over the side of her face again. "Dog sitting?"

She nodded and pulled one of those big fabric ponytail things out of her pocket. As she pulled her hair back and secured it with the thing, she said, "Now that I have more room, I'd love to get a dog, but I want a real dog, not a yapper."

"We have an Austrian herder." Mandy looked up at Tracy. "Daddy says they are the best dogs alive."

Tracy smiled and squeezed Mandy's shoulders in another embrace. "I like them, too. I'd really like to have a Labrador, but convincing my mom might be hard, and she lives at my house, too. She doesn't like bigger dogs."

"Really? Why not?" Mandy asked.

Shrugging, Tracy let go of Mandy to fold her arms into her lap. "I'm not really sure. I think she was bitten as a kid and is afraid of them. She wouldn't have Cinnamon and Ginger if my dad hadn't gotten them for her before he went away to the war the last time."

"We should bring Bailey over for your momma to meet. She's a great dog."

Tracy glanced at Zack and then returned her attention to Mandy. "Maybe that would work."

Zack had sensed the tension between Tracy and her parents at the wedding. "That's going to be a big change for you. Living with your parents, I mean."

"Yep."

"I can't imagine living with mine again either."

She pulled her knees up and hugged them. When she sucked in her bottom lip between her teeth, he knew she was unsure about something. At last, she said, "You always had your house to come home to. Even when your grandparents were alive, the old house was always earmarked as yours."

And it could have been yours, if you hadn't cheated on me.

Mandy's voice broke through the painful thought. "Which player is Bobby?"

Tracy looked at Mandy, her pride in her son obvious in her smile. "He's number ten. The quarterback."

"Wow. He throws the ball, right?" Mandy looked at Zack.

He gently yanked on one of Mandy's pigtails. "He sure does."

Just like his father did.

But Tracy's not with Jake anymore.

"Bobby has to be really good, I guess." Mandy came up on her knees and fidgeted a few moments as she watched the next play on the field. "He said his daddy is the coach."

"Yes, he is." Tracy's voice had an edge to it.

Everyone in the county knew Jake Parker had been a rising high school football star. He'd earned a football scholarship to Texas A & M his junior year of high school by leading the Mavericks for two straight years to the state championships. He'd been touted as the best quarterback the school had ever seen before and since. But Jake lost the scholarship and the chance to make something out of himself when a riding accident took it all away.

Many people in the county would have loved having Jake coach the high school team if he'd been qualified, meaning if he had a college education. However, there were just as many who didn't think Jake was fit to coach anyone, especially a group of impressionable young boys who would do anything to please Coach Parker.

Zack looked back at Tracy, but she had her attention on the plays on the field. He wasn't even sure who had the ball. "I get the impression you aren't thrilled about the choice of coach?"

When Tracy took a deep breath, the blue and white Junior Cowboy Logo of her t-shirt stretched over her chest. Did she ever go without a bra as she had when they'd dated?

Dear God! He had to get a grip. He forced his eyes to the nine- through twelve-year-olds on the football field and off speculating about Tracy's underwear. Hell, he was acting like a hormone happy fourteen-year-old!

"Not particularly." She raised a brow, and he realized she'd probably caught him ogling her chest. "So, Mandy, do you play any sports?"

"Not really." Mandy shrugged and shook her head. "Daddy's teaching me to barrel race my pony. He won't let me try on Holly, my horse--*yet*. He's being a big stick in the mud. Says I'll get hurt." She punctuated the statement with a dramatically exasperated huff.

A corner of Tracy's lips twitched upward as she looked at Zack. "Really."

"I want to ride in the rodeo at the fair next summer."

"Imagine that. I'm sure you'll do well."

Zack had to put a stop to where this was going, and fast. "I told you we'll see about the rodeo."

Mandy's eyes turned to his, and she lost some of the cheerfulness. "Just because Momma didn't like you doing rodeo doesn't mean she won't like me to."

If Tracy noticed his tensing at the mention of his reason for quitting the rodeo, she ignored it. "Your daddy was a really good rodeo cowboy. I still remember the thrill he'd give when I watched him."

Mandy's eyes got big as she looked from Tracy to Zack and back again. "You saw Daddy ride broncs?"

"Yeah. Many times."

Zack couldn't look away from Tracy's gray eyes. He knew she'd seen him ride locally, but had she seen him ride professionally? "Miz Tracy and I went to high school together."

"Wow. That was a really long time ago."

"Oh, ages ago, for sure." Tracy chuckled and broke the sudden spell Zack was under by looking at Mandy. "I saw him on TV a few times, too."

Mandy twisted around, incredulity beaming from her in glowing energy as volatile as a grenade. Tracy had pulled the pin with her words, and he could almost see the energy expanding within Mandy as she bounced up and down until she exploded. "You were on TV!"

Several amused, and not so amused, folks turned and peered at the trio. Tracy laughed, and Zack scowled at her, muttering, "Thank you, oh, so very much."

But inside he couldn't contain the flutter of excitement that Tracy had watched him.

"She didn't know?"

"No." He'd never told Amanda much about his rodeoing days. He had DVDs of the broadcasts he'd been in, but he'd never shown them to her. It was bad enough she'd conned him into teaching her how to race around barrels. Showing her the DVDs of him riding broncos and winning big silver belt buckles might put it in her little head that she should try it.

"Daddy! You never told me you were on TV!" The aftershock of Mandy the Grenade had him wincing. Several of the onlookers laughed and there were even a few comments that Zack chose to ignore.

"Sorry," Tracy mouthed and then turned to Mandy. "Well, it's not like he was on a TV show, Mandy."

Amanda looked crestfallen and confused all at once. "He wasn't on a TV show? But you said he was on TV."

Tracy shook her head. "Have you ever seen rodeo on TV?"

Mandy nodded, her attention rapt.

Zack stared at his daughter. "Where did you see rodeo?"

"Uncle Logan and Uncle Lance were watching it one day when I was over at Uncle Lance and Aunt Audrey's when you were working," she said. A local TV station often played broadcasts of some of the Central Texas events, but Zack never let Mandy watch them.

"When was this?"

Mandy shrugged and fidgeted again. "A while ago. I wanted to watch the barrel racers." She puckered her brow. "I didn't see much of the riders, though. They're too fast."

"That's how your daddy was on TV. When he competed in the National Finals Rodeo, they showed the events on ESPN. But he wasn't on very long. Only a blip, really." Tracy added a snap of her fingers to illustrate her meaning. Tracy smiled at Zack. "It could have been anybody being thrown off the bucking horse."

Several onlookers snickered. Tracy was lying through her teeth and she knew it. Winning any of the NFR events was a huge deal. The two times he'd won the saddle bronc title, he'd become an instant celebrity--interviewed by EPSN sportscasters, plus many of the Las Vegas and dozens of Texas news programs.

Mandy's whole body deflated. "Oh," she muttered. "That's all?"

As she nodded, Tracy's smile was the sorriest he'd ever seen. "That's all."

Zack wasn't sure if he wanted to wring Tracy's neck or kiss her silly.

Kissing her silly had a definite appeal, but not because she made his winning the NFR bronco title seemingly no more significant than being caught on camera crossing the street during a news report of a mass murder.

Before Zack could respond to Tracy's smirk, Mandy's friend Kayla and her older sister Malinda ran up to their blanket.

Malinda smiled tentatively. "Hi, Sheriff Cartwright. Kayla and me were wondering if Mandy could come with us."

"We're getting corndogs," Kayla chirped and pointed in the direction of the concession stand. "Our mommy runs the Chow Wagon. There's cotton candy, too."

Mandy bounced and turned to him. "Daddy, I'm still hungry. Can I go with them?"

"May I go with them?" Zack corrected automatically, and Mandy rolled her eyes. "Please."

With another of her increasingly irritating huffs--God help him when she was a teenager--she repeated resignedly, "May I *pretty please* go with Kayla and Malinda?"

"I guess no harm can come of it. Here, get me a corndog, too. And a bottle of water. But stay away from the cotton candy. You don't need any sugar."

She rolled her eyes again in response.

Zack shifted onto one hip and pulled his wallet from his back pocket. "People are going to start thinking I never feed you, girl." He glanced at Tracy. Her cocky grin had melted away and her eyes seemed wistful. "Would you like a corndog?"

"No thanks, I'm fine."

Mandy jumped to her feet, defusing the sudden awkwardness. She plucked the ten-dollar bill from Zack's outstretched hand and rushed off with her friends. "I'll be back!"

"You'd better bring back the change!" he called after her.

Tracy's soft laugh had him focusing on her. "I'd be more worried about her bringing back the corndog and water."

"Oh, I'm sure I'll never see either of those. She'll forget about even wanting a corndog. Instead, she'll end up eating cotton candy and will be bouncing off the walls half the night." Zack returned her chuckle and relaxed. "Heck, she had two bowls of chili before we left the house. She can't be hungry."

"You know she's bound to figure out just how famous you were at one time."

"Yeah, I know."

Tracy snorted and covered her mouth.

"What's so funny?"

Her laugh turned into a mischievous grin. "What will even be funnier is when she finds out about that calendar spread you did."

"Shit," he breathed and dropped his chin to his chest. "I forgot all about *that*."

Tracy laughed again, the sound settling somewhere better left forgotten. "Oh, Zachery James, you should be happy I'm not out to blackmail you. Amanda will be quite surprised at how naughty her daddy was in his younger days."

He slid a glance at her from under his hat brim. "Have you seen that spread?"

She looked down at her crossed legs and fidgeted slightly. "Who hasn't seen it? *Ride in the Millennium* was a big deal when it came out in 2000. At least, around here it was."

Zack couldn't hold in the groan. "Can you imagine the ribbing I got at basic training over that calendar?"

She laughed so hard she bent over. "Oh, yes, I can! How many times was your underwear stolen?"

"Enough for me to keep a few pairs somewhere no one could get to them." An overwhelming sense of homecoming settled on him when their eyes met. He lost his smile, but couldn't look away. "Tell me, did you have one of those calendars?"

She cleared her throat and looked back onto the field. "I was married then."

"Of course." He looked up and saw that the Cowboys had scored two more touchdowns. Bobby passed the ball and the crowd cheered when the intended receiver plucked it out of the air.

"I'll never think of March in quite the same way, however." She looked across her shoulder at him with a wry smile.

That calendar had seemed like such a good idea at the time, coming off the high from winning his first NFR and heading for his second. Only about half of the guys in the spread were even cowboys, the rest were male models. Four of them were straight from New York City and had never touched a live horse before, let alone ridden one.

He remembered the photo to which she referred. The pretty New York photographer had taken many shots, but only one was picked. He still had the pictures--somewhere. In the one that became the pinup for March 2000, he was leaning against a corral fence with his Appaloosa stallion, Wild Aces, standing behind him.

He was shirtless and dressed in a pair of custom black cowboy boots, faded jeans, one of his big rodeo silver buckles, and a black Stetson. He grinned at the thought of the jeans he'd worn for the shoot. They were so tight he could hardly get his fingers into the pockets further than to his first knuckles. No way could he have mounted the horse. He'd been hard-pressed to hide the nice response in the jeans as the female photographer posed him against the fence rails, making sure he got an eyeful of her cleavage.

He'd repaid her skill with the camera later that night by inviting her to his hotel room. He'd almost let her talk him into going back to New York with her and try modeling for a while.

He smiled at the thought of what *that* kind of life would have been like. Zack Cartwright, underwear model and pinup poster boy.

Naw, he couldn't even imagine it.

"Nice sock, by the way."

He cocked an eyebrow as her meaning dawned on him. His best slow grin--one he hadn't used for a long, long time--curled his lips. When was the last time he'd flirted with a woman? He leaned over and whispered, "I think we both know *that* is no sock stuffed down my jeans."

The choice of the present tense was very deliberate and Tracy had to know it. Her face turned red, and he couldn't explain the burst of joy it brought him. She elbowed him in the chest and took a deep breath as she squirmed in her shorts. And that action sent his burgeoning hard-on to full mast, especially when he found himself glancing down at the logo on her t-shirt. Two distinct points were slightly visible. So, he was affecting her the same way she was him.

Thank God his jeans weren't as tight as those in that calendar had been.

Swallowing hard, she blessedly changed the subject. "I registered for classes at UT."

"You got in this late?"

She shrugged and nodded. "I'm only taking two classes and they're on-line. They start tomorrow."

He laughed and shifted into a more comfortable sitting position. "I'd call that cutting it close."

Tracy laughed and the breathy sound of it settled over him. "Definitely, considering before Monday, I wasn't even thinking about going to school."

"What made you decide to go back?"

"I really don't know." She met his gaze and held it. "I think I realized I settled where my life is concerned. On a lot of things."

He didn't miss the heat in her steady gray eyes.

Amanda came back then, surprising Zack with his change, water and corndog. She immediately scampered off to play on the swings with her friends--besides Kayla and Malinda, three other little girls trailed behind her.

Once she was gone again, Tracy said, "She's very outgoing."

"Mandy's very much like her mother. We couldn't go anywhere without Lisa knowing someone, even on a new base. I remember being stationed in Japan between my first tour in Afghanistan and deployment to Iraq." Talking about Lisa was like someone dumping a bucket of ice water over him. "We weren't there three days when she'd already befriended all of our neighbors and began volunteering at the hospital on base. Hell, I hadn't even met my sergeant yet."

"Mandy's a very special little girl." Tracy averted her eyes, and he got the impression she'd have rather hidden the sentiment.

"Yes, she is." Not for the first time in the past year, he sensed a loneliness about her.

But he had to be mistaken. He knew Tracy Parker was never without a man in her life for long. She dated prolifically. There was also the rumor of her living with the man she'd left Jake for in Waco until she bought her hair salon in Colton. He'd never heard what happened with that relationship. Her sadness must stem from a broken heart.

A heart I'd like to fix.

Where the *hell* had that come from? He quickly ate the lard-fried processed meat byproducts and cornmeal on a stick that masqueraded as actual food. The last heart he ever wanted any part of was Tracy Parker's.

Right?

The next series of plays on the football field kept Tracy's attention riveted. Zack's focus was completely on her. Peripherally he was aware of Bobby tossing the ball to another player, who ran it in for a touchdown.

Tracy jumped up, cupped her hands over her mouth, and yelled, "Way to go, Bobby! Yahoo!"

Zack followed her to his feet, but he felt like he was somewhere else and not part of what was happening around him. Only the woman and his unadulterated desire for her mattered.

* * * *

Tracy glanced at Zack, taken aback by the raw fire in his deep blue eyes. She'd seen desire in his eyes before when they were talking about his photo in the calendar. She'd even surreptitiously noticed how tight his jeans had become. No, Zack didn't need a sock. But what burned in his eyes now was powerful and unguarded, catching her on fire, and would have consumed her if he hadn't looked away.

Searching for some kind of handhold to steady herself, she looked out over the field. With a dark scowl, Jake watched them across the sea of green and spectators. Her ex didn't look like a man winning a football game. Soon after they were married, she'd discovered Jake hated Zack. Why, she hadn't ever found out. Would Jake try to use her friendship with Zack against her in their custody battle?

Friendship. Hell, she and Zack weren't more than enemies bound by treaty to make nice with each other. It was the Cold War all over again. The accord had been made a year ago in his office when he convinced her he wanted to help with getting Dylan's life back on track. Jake was delusional if he thought there was something going on between them.

But Dylan is fine now. Married to the love of his life. Happy, with twins on the way and a pending adoption of a girl who needs a family.

She looked up at Zack. If he really hadn't wanted to sit with her, he'd have left when Mandy did. Not only was he still here with her, but he was actively flirting with her.

If you're given a second chance, don't screw it up. Her father's words whispered through her mind. Was Zack considering giving her a second chance?

After reclaiming their seats, Zack said, "Bobby's good with the pigskin."

Tracy shrugged, needing to find her center again. "The first toy Jake gave Bobby was a football. The nurses all laughed at him when he wanted them to put it in his nursery crib after he was born."

Zack turned away. He shifted to sit on the heel of his cowboy boot and drank his water. He looked so sexy and capable of anything in the worn jeans, chambray shirt and leather vest, complete with an old tan Stetson. She'd glimpsed the Glock in a shoulder holster under the vest earlier when he'd sat down. He also had his Sheriff's badge clipped to his belt, as he did when he wasn't officially on duty.

He twisted on the top of his bottle. "Jake would have probably played professionally if he hadn't torn his knee to hell that summer before our senior year when that horse stumbled. I'm still sorry it happened. Without the football scholarship, he didn't want to go to college. He hated school."

Jake gathered his team around him. When they broke up to execute whatever football magic he had up his sleeve, her ex-husband found her again with a glower. A shiver quaked down her spine, thoroughly cooling the heat Zack had ignited in her only seconds before.

She looked at Zack's profile. "He hated that you were doing so well riding rodeo after his injury ended his chance at playing football in college. You'd gone professional, and he was stuck working for his dad."

Zack looked at her, sharp and penetrating. She probably shouldn't be telling him any of this, but she'd gone too far not to tell him something.

"What do you mean?"

Sighing, she folded her hands in her lap. "Jake saw you as having it all." *Including me.*

"He was my closest friend since kindergarten."

She couldn't hold back the snort. "Yeah, well, Jake has only ever taken care of number one. Trust me, I know."

Tracy didn't want to talk about Jake. She'd called her lawyer, but didn't get much satisfaction from him. If she didn't think of something fast, she could lose her son. But right now, Zack didn't need to know her problems with Jake.

"Do you have any leads regarding the cattle thieves?" she asked.

Zack cleared his throat and shifted his weight onto his other boot heel. "No. There was another one sometime last night over in Hamilton County."

"Crap. Neither your office nor TSCRA has any leads?"

Zack shook his head and dropped his voice to a husky whisper, which did all sorts of crazy things to the fluttering in her lower belly. "Nope. I have some ideas, but no concrete evidence."

She had to get her out-of-control libido corralled. "Wanna share?"

"You know I can't do that."

"Why not? Unless it's me you're considering hauling off to jail for stealing cattle, I don't have any intention of telling anyone. I want these thugs caught as much as you do. They stole my brother's steers."

Zack stared at her for a long time, then sucked in a deep breath. He leaned closer, and in that low, rumbling timbre, he said, "Have you noticed the new Silverado Brent Parker is sporting around town? I thought he was still laid-off."

She furrowed her brow and flashed to her conversation with Henrietta just two days ago. "Yeah, I have. And I think he is still officially out of work, but Granny Parker said he's been riding shotgun with Jake driving truck."

Zack's brow wrinkled as if he was in thought. "Well, keep your ears open, will ya? I know the government is extending unemployment benefits and from what I hear Jake's making out good hauling cargo, but I doubt Brent's making enough sitting on his butt to buy a thirty-thousand-dollar truck."

* * * *

In the second half, the Hamilton Broncos rallied and tied up the game. Mandy returned to sit between Zack and Tracy during the last quarter. Her excitement was contagious as she bounced up and down. Was it solely due to the game--or the sugar she'd no doubt consumed?

While the Broncos had the ball, she looked up at Tracy and asked, "Do you like to ride?"

Tracy smiled and looked into the girl's bright upturned face. Her pigtails were askew and wisps of uneven dark hair fell around her heart-shaped face. Tracy's fingers itched to fix the wayward hair, but she wouldn't dare. It wasn't her place. "Yeah. I don't have a horse of my own anymore, but I can use one from the stable. Dylan and Charli have a lot of horses."

"Daddy has lots, too. He just bought a bunch of mares that he wants to have babies. We also have lots of cows. Do you have any cows?"

"Like the horses, they belong to my brother and his wife, but I live on a ranch."

"Oh, that's right. Miz Charli and Mr. Dylan have the cows. Anyway, we have big ugly cows. San--Sana Ger--Gert--"

"Santa Gertrudis," Zack supplied and shook his head. He gazed upon his daughter with an emotion shining in his eyes that couldn't be called anything but love and pride. "And they are not ugly."

"Yeah, they are. But Daddy said that he wants to make the CW into a cattle ranch again. And not just raise horses like Pappy and Uncle Paul did." Mandy prattled on while Tracy regarded Zack with a sideways glance. "He and Uncle Lance--well, he's not really my uncle, he's my cousin, I guess. Uncle Paul's son. Anyway, Daddy said they want to get on the ball because Mr. Dylan and Miz Charli are gonna corner the market."

Tracy grinned. "Really? He said that?"

Mandy vigorous nodding sent her pigtails bouncing. "Uh-huh."

"I think Miz Tracy has heard quite enough about my adventures in ranching, Amanda Jean." Zack quelled his daughter's tell-all with a note of amusement in his voice.

Tracy looked at Zack and crossed her arms. "So, what do your dad and uncle think of your ideas?"

"They already know my opinion. Cartwrights have been raising cattle since Cole Cartwright won this county in a poker game."

She laughed and shook her head. "Well, if it hadn't been for his first cousins Elijah Blackwell and Dylan Ferguson talking him into playing in the game, you wouldn't have that land."

Zack scowled at her. "Why do the Fergusons and the Blackwells always bring that up? Jake always claimed we somehow cheated his side of the family out of something."

She groaned. "Please, I really try not to think about the fact that you and I and Jake are cousins, considering all that happened between us and...well, Jake and I were married, for goodness sake."

"Distantly--very distantly. Eight generations. I wouldn't even call us related anymore, in fact."

Mandy wrinkled her nose and looked from Zack and Tracy. "Wait, you're cousins? That means y'all can't get married."

Tracy didn't miss the wince Zack couldn't quite hide. She took a deep breath. "No. I mean. If your daddy and I wanted to get married, we could. Like he said, we aren't really cousins anymore."

"That's good." Mandy pointed toward the all but forgotten football game and squealed. "Oh, look! The Cowboys got another touchdown!"

The crowd cheered, but Tracy and Zack stared at each other.

Once the celebration calmed down, Tracy cleared her throat. "I didn't realize you were so interested in the CW."

Zack's shoulders were stiff as they moved in a shrug under his light blue shirt and black vest. He plucked a piece of grass and studied it as he played with it between his fingers. "There was a time I wasn't. Now, it's all I have."

Mandy chirped, "You have me."

Tossing the blade of grass, he smiled and then tugged on one of her pigtail. "Yes, I do."

As the Cowboys got the ball back after the Broncos fumbled it on the first down, Mandy turned to Tracy again. "Daddy really misses Momma. I think we need--"

"Mandy..." Zack's voice was full of gentle warning and underlying sadness. "I don't think Miz Tracy cares whether I miss your momma or not."

But he was dead wrong. Tracy was extremely interested in how much Zack still cared for his dead wife. "So," she said and forced herself to redirect the topic. "Mandy, how'd your first couple of weeks of first grade go?"

Mandy nodded enthusiastically. "Good. I already can read lots."

"That's great. I bet Daddy reads to you." Why did that assertion hurt so much?

"Yeah, he does almost every night when he puts me to bed before my prayers. When he's not working, anyway."

Words from her constricted throat wouldn't be possible even if someone held a gun to her head. She turned away and found her son among the boys battling over the football. He was her life, and she'd never give him up, but how she wished his father wasn't the man who had sired him.

Bobby threw an interception on the next play, giving the ball right back to the opposing team with only a few minutes on the clock. Jake called a timeout and pulled his son over to the sideline. Bobby's head hung low as Jake berated him. The evening sun glistened off the silver-colored helmet as it bobbed in curt little nods.

When Bobby went back onto the field, she looked at Jake. His face was a mask of calculated consternation, his feet apart, his fists on his hips. He called out to his team and they rallied behind their quarterback. Jake would be a bear if the Cowboys lost the game, making Bobby feel as if he'd lost it for his team. Bobby never saw the wrongness of his father's actions and words. To him, he deserved the cold shoulder and the criticism he'd get later if they lost.

"Do you like fixing hair, Miz Tracy?"

Mandy's question reined her attention back to the little girl stealing her heart. She worked to paste on a smile. "I feel like I'm helping people. I can make someone feel pretty if I can do their hair in a way they like. Sometimes folks just want someone to talk to and that helps them, too.

But I'm thinking about going back to school. I've always wanted to be a doctor. It will take me forever, though."

"I don't like the doctor." Mandy wrinkled her nose. "I always get shots when I go there."

Tracy laughed and looked up at Zack. Surprise seemed to register in Zack's widened eyes as he studied her. Did he remember a similar conversation? They'd talked most of one night prior to graduation. He'd made love to her for hours, but when they'd rested, he'd held her close and asked her why she'd wanted to be a doctor.

Her answer seemed as idealistic now as it had when she'd told him. *I want to help people, make them well again and heal disease.* For as long as she lived, she'd never forget the awed expression that had come to him looking up into her face as she'd leaned over him.

The same expression that was on his face now.

"My momma was a nurse," Mandy said dragging Tracy back to the present.

"Yes, I've heard." Tracy forced her smile to reappear.

Zack cleared his throat. "Mandy..."

Bobby was getting his team ever closer to scoring the winning touchdown. People around them jumped to their feet, but Zack and Tracy remained sitting.

"I wish I had someone to show me how to do my hair. Can you show me?" Mandy's words were almost lost in the sudden cheering erupting around them when another Cowboy ran the ball to just inches from the goal line before being deflagged.

Zack's intake of air was a warning, but Tracy couldn't look at him. This was between her and his little girl. "Sure. You'll have to talk your daddy into bringing you over to the shop sometime. We'll have a girl's day."

Zack's smile was borderline grimace. "I think we need to watch the game. Our team is about to win."

The crowd around them went wild. Her son and his team had pulled off a win. Zack's gaze connected with Tracy's, and something monumental churned deep within the dark blue fire.

Was it hatred?

Or was it something else entirely?

Chapter 6

Friday after school, Tracy drove Bobby to his father's automotive service station, which Jake had taken over when his father died five years ago with cirrhosis from years of alcoholism.

She always felt like she was abandoning her baby when she left him with Jake on his weeks. They shared joint custody of Bobby, which meant he spent every other week with his father.

Jake lived beside the business in an old trailer that couldn't quite be considered ramshackle, but definitely needed some TLC. Tracy remembered the day Jake carried her over the threshold. His parents had given them the former rental as a wedding gift. And never allowed her to forget that, in their eyes, her parents had given the newlyweds nothing. They'd never considered the small fortune from her parents that Tracy sunk into the place to make it livable worthy of mentioning.

Across the street, Jake's mother, Sandy, lived in an old two-story, which also needed a date with the handyman. The house had probably been beautiful once upon a time, built by one of Jake's Blackwell ancestors. In contrast to the overgrown grass in front of Jake's house, flowering pots and a flock of pink flamingos filled his mother's yard. In a small carriage house beside the house, Sandy had her beauty parlor. Tracy had worked there until the day she'd announced she was leaving Jake.

"Dad will take me to my game tomorrow," Bobby said as she parked next to the curb, bringing her out of her ponderings.

Tracy looked over her shoulder at her son in the backseat. "Okay. But I'll be there, too."

Bobby shrugged and concentrated on gathering up his backpack. "Can we all go out together? Dad said if we win again, he'd take me out to eat."

She turned in the seat. "Bobby, you know that isn't a good idea."

"Why don't you like Dad?"

She resisted the urge to close her eyes. Tracy wished she could tell him the truth about her relationship with his father, but he was too innocent to understand. Even if he hadn't been young, she couldn't tell him. Destroying Bobby's belief in his father was beyond her ability to do. Someday Jake would do it himself.

"He said it's your fault you're not married anymore."

Tracy swallowed her retort and took a deep breath. Ah, Jake was at it again. He'd been making her out to be the bad guy in their divorce since the day she'd packed her things and moved out. Most people in town still believed she'd left Jake for another man because she'd moved to Waco for a while. After all, once a cheater, always a cheater.

"Sometimes people just can't get along, sweetheart."

He watched her with imploring eyes, and it broke her heart that the standard answer wasn't enough anymore.

As he opened the door to get out, Bobby mumbled, "I don't understand why you married him. Or why everyone made such a big fuss about Uncle Dylan's wedding. Nobody stays married anyway."

How could she tell her son that love makes the difference?

When Jake came out from one of the open bay doors of the garage, Tracy exited the Taurus and came around to watch Bobby stop in front of his father.

"Hey, T-Rex." Jake smiled as he ruffled Bobby's brown hair.

"Hi, Dad." Bobby moved in a step and lifted his arms as if he wanted to hug Jake. But he didn't; instead, he stepped away again and crossed his arms. "Are we gonna go fishing tomorrow before the game? You promised."

Despite all of Jake's faults, he loved Bobby. They were buddies. "You bet. Tonight I thought we'd go out for supper and rent a movie. I'm even closing up early. I just need to get the fire chief's truck done."

"Can I see whatever I want?"

"Anything." Jake glanced at Tracy. "Say 'bye to your mom and then go see Grandma over in the big house. She's got somethin' for you."

Bobby turned toward her. "'Bye Mom."

"I love you, sweetheart."

For a moment, Tracy thought he was going to hug her as he had when he was little. Instead, he mumbled, "Love you, too."

"I'll see you tomorrow at your game," Tracy reminded him.

He nodded, gave her a quick wave and then turned away. With almost everything within her, she wanted to gather him up in her arms. She watched Bobby look both ways before sprinting across the street and up the steps of his grandmother's front porch.

"We need to talk." Jake's even voice jolted her into turning toward him. "And time's a-wasting. Marlin McPherson won't be too happy if I don't get that water pump done on his bucket of rust and bolts."

"Yes, we do need to talk." Tracy bit on her bottom lip and fidgeted with her keys in her hand. "We have to do something about Bobby's behavior. He copped a terrible attitude Saturday at Dylan's wedding."

Jake put his hands on his hips and scowled at her. "I had tickets to the Rangers game for weeks. As soon as your asshole brother decides to get married, my plans have to be thrown out the window. Last weekend was supposed to be mine. He never acts up when he's with me."

"He never 'acts up' when he's with you because as long as he plays football the way you want, he can do whatever he wants. You never set any rules."

He stepped closer and leaned into her face. "By the way, I will not allow your latest fling to yell at *my* son. No wonder he has a bad attitude when he's with you if you let your flavor of the week abuse him."

"What are you talking about? No one yelled at Bobby, and no one ever abused him. I don't have a 'latest fling' or a 'flavor of the week' as you so gallantly put it."

"Zack."

He couldn't be serious. "What does Zack--"

"You may be screwin' your old flame, but I will not allow that sombitch anywhere near my son. You got that?" Jake looked Tracy over from head to toe. She was dressed in jeans and a baggy t-shirt, nothing remotely sexy, but his eyes flared with a lust that disgusted her. Giving her a slow grin, he said, "You know if it's just sex you want, I'm always available."

"Damn it, Jake, we're divorced. We can't stand each other."

He moved close enough for her to kiss him if the thought didn't make her gag. "Don't worry." His voice was low and husky. "I'm not talking about a walk down the aisle again. But the sex was always good."

Huffing, Tracy smiled as smugly as she could muster. "Not always. Believe me, I've had better." She enjoyed the irritated narrowing of his eyes way too much. "I had blinders on. I believed your bullshit and fell for your charm. Not again, Jake. Now, let's talk about your constantly making me out to be the heavy where Bobby is concerned."

"Ah, yes, I was never as good as dear old Zack Cartwright." He spoke in a low hiss. "I heard that either the Marines or his beauty queen wife neutered him. Glad to hear that was all vicious lies."

"Goodbye, Jake." She turned away and headed back to her car.

"Does Zack know you screwed me over for his brother?"

She jerked to a stop and spun around. "I never slept with Logan and you know it. He helped me get away from you. Without him, I probably never would have. He helped me see your true colors and how you cheated me out of the life I really wanted. He's my friend, nothing more."

"If I remember correctly, that's all you considered me when you fucked me for the first time." He moved toward her and smiled. "I remember that first time, Tracy. I remember how you came on to me after the roundup at the McPherson place. You couldn't even wait until we got off the ranch. You told me to pull into the pasture, and we went at it on the bed of my truck."

Tracy flinched and took a step back. "You manipulated me into thinking the man I loved was cheating on me. You were supposed to be his best friend. In my stupid, naive way of thinking, I was getting back at him. Not to mention you had me believing you actually loved me. I just didn't realize, until much too late, *I* was no more than a pawn in some sick game."

She glared at him and snarled as she fisted her hands. God, she wished she could punch that cocky gleam out of his eyes. "If there is a chance for Zack and me to find what we've lost, it is none of your damned business. But you will not use my son in your games."

"I'll raise my son any damned way I see fit. But I will not allow Sheriff GI Joe to verbally bully him."

Tracy pulled into her full height, putting herself a good two inches taller than him, which she knew infuriated him more than her words. "Zack didn't yell at Bobby. He needs someone to show him some authority and that he can't get everything he wants just because he wants it. Bobby didn't like being reminded he's a kid and the world doesn't always turn at his will. God knows he would never learn that from you. In the end, Bobby had fun, and if you were to ask him, I'd bet he'd even say he enjoyed being part of his uncle's special day instead of going to see his favorite baseball team lose."

Jake snorted and leaned back on his heels. His shirt tightened across his shoulders when he folded his arms over his chest. Clenching his fists, he sneered. "Zack Cartwright is not the boss of my son, Tracy."

As she reached for the handle of her car door, Jake's next words halted her. "Do you know why I'm suing you for full custody?"

"Because you're a royal jackass?"

"Not any more than you're a two-bit whore."

She spun on him.

"The company you keep has become increasingly bad news. The men you parade in and out of your bed have gone from bad to worse. Not to mention having your alcoholic, suicidal brother living with you in your small apartment. Exposing Bobby to his craziness."

"Dylan was never suicidal and he isn't crazy."

Jake shrugged. "Post-traumatic stress disorder. Google it. One of the symptoms is suicidal thoughts. So is violence. I heard he put Brenda's new husband in a chokehold in the Longhorn back in March," he said, referring to Dylan's ex-wife, her husband, and an incident that happened before he started working for Charli.

"You can't be serious. What was I supposed to do, Jake? He's my brother. Dylan was never suicidal or dangerous and you know it!"

Jake looked at his watch. "My lawyer sees things differently."

He turned away and headed toward the open garage bay.

Dear God, what was she going to do?

* * * *

When the bell jingled above the door, Tracy glanced up from the reception desk and smiled at the woman standing inside the entry. "Melissa?"

The petite woman tentatively returned Tracy's smile and pushed golden blond hair behind an ear. She held out a small hand and nodded. "Hi. Yes, I'm Melissa Blackwell. You must be Tracy."

Tracy stood to shake the small hand. She towered over the shorter woman by almost a foot. Heading around the desk, Tracy gestured toward the couch by the double window. "Please sit. Can I get you anything? Coffee? Tea? Soda?"

Melissa shifted the strap of her bag from her shoulder. She was dressed in black slacks and a white clingy sweater, which did everything to emphasize her curves. "Coffee would be fine."

Tracy went to the commercial coffee maker on an old sideboard and poured them each a cup. After she settled on the wingchair next to the couch, she took a deep breath and clutched her cup between her hands. She'd never conducted an interview before and hadn't had time to prepare as well as she'd have liked.

Melissa appeared to be nearly as nervous as she was. She sipped her coffee as she looked around. "This is a really nice place."

"Thank you. I'm sorry to hear about your dad."

"He's not doing well. Although he doesn't let on he's as bad off as he is." She looked down into the cup between her hands. "I wish I'd known how sick he was sooner. I would've been here before now."

At a loss for what else to say, Tracy asked, "So, how long have you been in Colton?"

Melissa shrugged. "About a week." A sheepish smile touched her full lips. "I'll admit I'm not sure how long I'll be in town." She lost a smile and took a quick sip of her coffee. "It's a lot different than LA."

Tracy laughed. "I can't disagree with that. I've lived all over the world. But I wouldn't want to live anywhere but here."

"Colton has its own kind of charm." She glanced around again. "Sometimes I wonder if it's because it's..."

"It's home."

Melissa's eyes sparkled. "Yes. I guess that's it. I mean, I'm living in the same house my great-great-grandfather built."

"I understand perfectly."

They shared a smile. She and Melissa would get along perfectly.

The rest of the interview went smoothly. Tracy was impressed with Melissa's education and her work history. After a quick tour around the salon, they returned to the reception area.

"How would you like to start tomorrow?" Tracy held out her hand.

Melissa's smile dazzled as she took Tracy's hand and squeezed. "Sure! I'd love to. Thank you."

"Then we have a deal. I'll see you tomorrow at ten."

At the door, Melissa tilted her head to look up at Tracy, again reminding her of the difference in their height. "Is Logan Cartwright still in town?"

Logan? "Ah... He actually lives in Dallas, but hangs out at one of the smaller houses on the CW when he's in town, which is a lot."

She smiled, but it never reached her eyes. "Thanks. I'll have to look him up."

"I'm sure he'd like to see you. How do you know Logan?" Tracy couldn't keep the question from popping out. In all the years that she'd know him, he never mentioned knowing the Blackwell twins. Once their B-movie actress mother hightailed it out of Texas, she'd never set foot in the state again. As rumor had it, the only way Buck had gotten to see his daughters was by going to California to visit them.

Melissa looked at the floor, but not before Tracy noticed her frown. "I don't know him--not really. But my sister does. They sang together when he was in college."

Actress Olivia Blackwell and Logan?

Before she could ask any more questions, Melissa smiled and reached for the doorknob. "I better get home. Thank you again, Tracy."

* * * *

Zack woke up before dawn Saturday. He dressed and ate a breakfast of eggs, bacon and toast, washing it all down with a pot of black coffee with way too much sugar. After kissing a still-sleeping Amanda, Zack left her in the care of Amy Jackson, the seventeen-year-old daughter of his head foreman. She babysat Mandy when his mother wasn't available and the daycare in town was closed.

He wasn't on duty today, and his cousin had promised to help him replace the patched fencing between him and his neighbor. It was too early to determine if old man Estrada's stud had bred any of Zack's mares, but after the stallion had broken through the fence his men had patched again yesterday morning, there was a chance the paint would be a proud papa in eleven months.

Zack should have made better precautions to keep Estrada's stud on his side of the fence. Besides the wood and barbed wire fencing, a fencerow of thorny mesquite acted as a barrier, but that wouldn't keep a determined stud away if he smelled a mare in heat.

Zack laughed at the comparison and headed out the back door and down the path to the barn. Estrada's Thunderbolt wasn't the only stud with a female on the brain. Tracy was never far from his thoughts these days. Last night he'd dreamt about what he'd like to do to her--again. He was playing with fire by getting involved with her. She'd hurt him eventually if he ever let himself care too much. As he fed and watered the two dozen horses he had stabled at the barn, he realized he'd never wanted a woman as much as he wanted her.

And there laid the crux of his dilemma. If he gave in to the desire, he'd rediscover the things he'd fallen in love with before, qualities time hadn't erased or changed. Qualities like her gentleness, her compassion for others, her naive belief in the good in everyone, and her feistiness that always managed to surprise him.

Not to mention time had only made her sexier; a fact he wasn't so sure she understood herself. There were too many times when he'd gotten the impression, by the shy way she'd pushed her hair away from her face and had bitten her lower lip, that Tracy still saw herself as a skinny, awkward adolescent.

As Olive Oyl.

In the gray dawn, Zack got busy loading the back of his Dodge with tools from the shed, and attempted to push thought of the only woman he'd ever fully loved to the back of his mind.

He was dog-tired from another hell week at work. The rustlers had hit again and Leon Ferguson's attorneys were starting to cause trouble. According to the lawyers, Zack had forced an incriminating confession from Leon's accomplice, Kyle McPherson.

Which, of course, was a load of bullshit. Kyle eagerly ID'd his boss when he realized he faced charges of not only arson, but also for the attempted murder of Dylan Quinn, livestock poisoning, and the murder of Ella Larson all by his lonesome.

Okay, Zack had neglected to share with him that some of the evidence pointing Kyle's involvement in these crimes was circumstantial at best, but that was a horse of another color.

He finished loading the back of his pickup with the supplies he and Lance would need to fix fences all day and glanced back at the log house. He'd rather spend a relaxing day at home with his daughter. But that wasn't the life of a rancher.

The CW was the second largest ranch in the county and employed several hands, but on the weekends, only enough workers were around to do what was needed to keep the cattle and horses fed.

Zack waved at Tate Jackson as the foreman passed the barn.

"You sure you don't want any help?" the African American man said from the doorway of the tack room.

Zack shut the tailgate and shook his head. "Nope. I think Lance and I have it covered." He paused at the driver's side door. "Can you stick close to the house in case Amy needs anything? I know Mandy can be a handful for her, and I'm not sure how long I'll be."

"I thought you liked me, boss. I'm not sure which is worse riding herd on--your little girl or my big one."

Chuckling, Zack opened his door. "Riding herd on Mandy, for sure. I have my cell phone if you need me."

"Fair 'nough." Before Zack stepped into the truck, the foreman added, "Those mares you have out there in the west pasture are worth a pretty penny. Better get the fence fixed before they wander off."

"Or Estrada's stud gives himself a heart attack."

Tate snickered. "Oh, but what a way to go. Well, if you were a stud, that is."

Grinning, Zack touched the brim of his hat in salute as he climbed in behind the steering wheel.

There was another reason he insisted on fixing the fence. He'd been thinking about his roots, and the events that had changed his life, such as why he'd moved away to begin with. If he denied Tracy's cheating on him had been the main reason he'd left Texas, he'd be lying to himself. He would have rodeoed even if they'd married, but he'd always known rodeo was a temporary thing. However, after her betrayal, he'd wanted nothing to do with the CW. Every dream he'd ever had about the place had included her.

He'd already decided he'd never come back to Texas when he'd met Lisa. After he'd been thrown during a rodeo in Cheyenne, he'd been taken to the hospital where she worked as a brand new nurse--fresh out of college and fresh off her reign as Miss Wyoming. Lisa had been super-model beautiful and they'd instantly clicked. And had instantly ignited into flames. He hadn't lived as a monk in the two years after he'd left Texas, but he'd never been so in lust with a woman besides Tracy as he'd been with Lisa.

Although she'd been a beauty queen, she'd lived a sheltered life. Zack still remembered his shock when they'd made love the first time on their second date and discovered she was a virgin. He'd proposed two weeks later, and after only two months of dating, they'd married. Their parents had thought they were making a huge mistake, and Logan had come to Wyoming to talk him out of it.

Zack had met Lisa in August 2001. When the terrorist attacks on the US happened in September, he knew what he had to do. He'd signed up at a recruiting station in Cheyenne and had been immediately processed through. Two days after his wedding in October, he'd shipped off to a tearful goodbye that had been on the local news. Due to his status as a professional athlete, not to mention being married to a former Miss Wyoming, and being the oldest son of former rock star Jackie McGinnis, he'd been lauded as special.

He'd hated the reporters who'd shoved microphones in his face asking stupid questions about why he'd felt compelled to fight in the war. He'd never forget Lisa's response, *"My husband is an American. We all should stand up and fight."*

The war and her death had changed everything again. His drinking had gotten worse, and he'd quit his job on the Cheyenne PD. When his in-laws had threatened to take his little girl from him, he'd sought out help for the depression that wouldn't leave him. And then he'd moved his daughter home to the CW where they belonged.

By helping Dylan Quinn through his issues with the war and his possible role in the deaths of the men under his command, Zack realized he had to work through his own issues concerning Lisa's death.

But there was one thing for which he'd never forget or forgive himself--Lisa's death wouldn't have happened if he'd been able to forget the past and Tracy.

Driving over the rough ranch roads crisscrossing the pastures and crossing an old wood bridge straddling Oak Springs Creek, he made it to his cousin's half of the ranch in a fraction of the time it would have taken by main road.

Lance Cartwright had built his house as a wedding gift to his wife twelve years ago. It dwarfed all of the homes on the twenty-thousand-acre ranch. Modeled after a Spanish hacienda, it boasted natural stone and stucco exterior walls, a four-car garage, a portico and an interior courtyard.

Lance leaned against the railing of the corral by his barn with his hands in his pockets. Dressed like Zack in old jeans, work shirt open over a t-shirt, work boots and an old brown hat over his unruly blond hair, Lance could have passed for Zack's brother rather than first cousin.

"Hey, cousin." Lance wore an easy grin as Zack got out of his truck. "I was beginning to think you weren't going to show up until dinnertime."

"I was thinking about it, but I don't want Luis Estrada to start charging me for Thunderbolt's stud service."

"Audrey fixed us enough food and drink for a week." Zack turned at the sound of his brother's voice. From the back of the house, Logan Cartwright ambled toward Zack and Lance carrying a red cooler. "But she refused to send along any beer. Said we wouldn't get a lick of work done."

Zack didn't bother hiding his surprise, or his irritation. "What are you doing here?"

As Logan placed the cooler onto the back of Zack's truck, he grinned. "Nice to see you, too, big brother. I'm coming to help with the fence. Lance said you could use some help. Or is this a first-sons only party?"

Lance slapped Logan on the shoulder. "It's a we-can-use-all-the-help-we-can-get kinda party. Let's get going. Audrey and I have a date later." He winked and gave them a cocky grin as he headed for the passenger side. "Timing is everything."

They got in the Dodge--Zack behind the wheel, Lance beside him in the passenger's side, and Logan in the back next to Mandy's empty car seat.

Once they settled and Zack shifted into gear, Logan drawled, "You know, Lancelot, all that clock watching can take the fun out of the doing."

Zack chuckled at the old nickname as Lance looked over his shoulder. "Not really. But the pressure can get to me at times."

The fact that Lance let slide Logan's teasing him with his hated childhood nickname cued Zack into just how much stress his cousin was under. Zack glanced at him. Lance and his wife had been trying to have a baby since a riding accident caused her to lose her first pregnancy over a decade ago. Zack drove the truck through the gate into the pasture, heading back the way he'd come earlier. "When's that appointment with the fertility specialist y'all want to see?"

Lance shrugged and looked down at his hands, which, Zack noticed with a glance, were curled into his thighs. "At the end of the month. But I know what he'll say. Two years ago, when we saw that other specialist, he didn't know why we aren't able to conceive and suggested we're trying too hard. How can we not try when the timing's right? Besides, Audrey and I never had a problem in the bedroom. I don't consider loving my wife 'trying too hard.' But I'll be thirty-seven in October. Audrey just turned thirty-five. We just want a baby before we're too damned old. If the specialist can't help, or she miscarries again, we're going to look into adoption."

Zack made a U-turn in the pasture and Lance asked, "What are you doing?"

"Taking you back to your wife." Zack looked at his first cousin again. "You and Audrey need a day away from this place. I suggest you pack a lunch and ride over to that little grove of trees by the lake on my side of the ranch and get busy."

"Or better yet, drive down to Crawford and use that hunting cabin on your uncle's ranch." Logan laughed and cuffed Lance on the shoulder. "Get going, Lancelot. Why should Estrada's Thunderbolt be the only stud making babies?"

Lance smiled and opened the door when Zack stopped the truck by the back of the house. He looked from Logan to Zack and bobbed his hat brim before jumping out.

Zack waited until his brother climbed in the front seat before driving off again. An uneasy silence buzzed the air. They both were avoiding the subject of their cousin's problems. Audrey had been pregnant twice early in their marriage. The first one she lost in an accident, the second one she miscarried. For the past six years, she hadn't been able to get pregnant at all.

"Would it really be all that terrible if that paint and those princesses were to mix?" Logan asked, breaking the silence by referring to the stallion and Zack's thoroughbred fillies.

"How about it's the wrong time of the year, and I would've liked to wait until next spring when the fillies were older before breeding them?" Zack glanced at Logan. "I'm sure that stud would throw some nice looking foals. He's a beautiful horse. I won't deny he looks like he's from good blood. Do you know where Luis got him?"

"I heard that stud was a rodeo bronco."

Zack spared a glance at his younger brother. "Really? Local or national circuit?"

"Don't know. I just know Luis bought him hoping to use him for breeding."

"Interesting. I drew a stallion I swear was possessed by demons in the last NRF I was in."

Logan fiddled with the radio and chuckled. "I remember."

As Alan Jackson's *Livin' on Love* came streaming out of the speakers, Zack flashed Logan a grin. "That was the longest eight seconds of my life." He'd won the saddle bronco title that year and walked away with more cash than most people made in a year in prize money, and a silver belt buckle. Zack lost the cockiness as he remembered the ride that ended his career. "I drew that same horse again in Cheyenne the following year. That monster must have remembered me, because he showed me in a big hurry that he was the boss. Five seconds out of the chute, he had me in the dust and cracked two of my ribs."

"Thus, the end of Zachery Cartwright's rodeoing days."

Zack could sense his brother watching him.

"Why'd you give it all up so easily?" Logan asked. "It's not like you hadn't eaten dirt or gotten kicked in the ribs before."

"You know why." Zack looked at Logan. "I met Lisa. She hated everything to do with rodeo."

"Yet, you weren't willing to give it up for Tracy."

"That's different and you know it." Zack tightened his grip on the steering wheel as he fought to keep his voice level. Logan knew exactly which of his buttons to push. "Tracy was supposed to be going to college, then on to medical school. Instead she was screwing my best friend."

Logan sighed and shook his head. "Ever wonder about why she'd do that?"

"Hell, yes!" Zack focused on the rutted trail. "For over two years, I wondered. I still wonder," he added a little subdued as he remembered their evening together watching her son's team win the football game.

"Zack," Logan said calmly, "have you ever asked her?"

"No."

"Why not? It's all over town that you and she are seeing each other."

Zack glared at his brother. "We aren't 'seeing each other.' Being forced together for her brother's wedding and sitting together at a Pee Wee football game isn't dating."

"Mandy likes her."

"Mandy likes everyone. She takes after her mother. But even if I did want to date Tracy, I couldn't. Mandy is too--"

"Bullshit."

Zack stopped the truck beside the patched fence and snapped his attention on his brother as heat climbed his neck.

Logan didn't give him a chance to explode. "You're still blaming yourself for Lisa's death. Why is that? She's the one who got mad, walked out, and chose to drive on a snow-covered mountain road."

"I should've realized how hard my PTSD was on her."

Logan huffed. "Lisa was a nurse. She would have understood how watching your buddy getting shot after he saved your life had affected you. If I had to guess, I think you fought about something a lot more personal than your drinking whiskey instead of eating her cooking."

Zack wouldn't talk about the fight that ended with Lisa losing her life. He pushed the door open with more force than it required and got out, then slammed it for good measure.

Logan followed him at a much more leisurely pace.

Zack lowered the tailgate and started unloading tools. "You never did tell me why you're here."

Logan grabbed the cooler he'd put on the truck bed back at Lance's barn. "I wanted to talk to you."

After depositing the crate of hand tools on the ground beside the bundle of barbed wire and cedar fence posts he'd brought out yesterday, Zack straightened and narrowed his eyes on Logan. "Since when have you ever wanted my opinion on anything? You're the one with all the answers."

"I don't want your opinion. But I hope I get your support." Logan sat the cooler down and faced Zack. In jeans, plaid cotton shirt, boots, and Stetson, Logan looked every bit like the cowboy he pretended to be when he was up on stage singing before an audience. Zack knew his brother had no interest in the ranch or working on it. He didn't have much interest in being a lawyer either. Logan rubbed a hand over the dark growth of beard on his chin. "Thanks for coming to my shows over the past few months. It means a lot having you out in the audience."

Zack shrugged and grabbed a posthole digger from the truck bed. "I never said you couldn't sing, Logan. But, I think sometimes you're putting too much energy into a hobby."

"What if singing and songwriting weren't hobbies anymore?"

Zack met his brother's green eyes. "Logan, you had your chance, and it didn't happen. Let it go."

"No. One lousy summer in Nashville when I was eighteen doesn't count. Sure, I fell on my face. I didn't get a record deal, but I never gave it a chance either. I expected to blow into town and sing in a couple of bars and get picked up in a few months. To be honest, I figured Mom's fame would have opened doors for me. It didn't, and I was too impatient and let one *no, thank you* discourage me. I came back to Texas and headed off to college like Dad wanted me to. But I'm selling songs I've written to big name singers. Seth Kendall's latest number one single is one of *my* songs, and Nate McConnell's got one climbing the charts." He tapped his chest. "I have a CD full of my own music that's selling locally and a couple of demos making the circuit in Nashville. Plus, I'm a hell of a lot smarter now."

"That's giving up a lot for a dream. You're a lawyer, too. A damned good one. What's Lance think of you leaving the firm?" Zack put his hands on his hips and assessed the job in front of them.

"I've already talked to Lance. He's willing to cut me loose from the firm, but I can come back if things don't work out again. My only pending case goes to court in a couple of weeks. After it's settled, I'll be set."

No one could talk reason into Logan once he had his mind set on something. So, Zack let the subject slide. He glanced at his brother. "By the way, why the hell haven't you ever given me a copy of your CD?"

Logan shrugged and turned away. "Because I figured you wouldn't want it."

Zack shook his head and looked down at his scuffed work boots. "Well, I do want a copy. Logan, it's not that I don't believe in you, but I hope you know what you're doing. I'd hate to see you fail again."

Logan sucked in a breath and glowered. "Why are my mistakes always failures, but yours are always someone else's fault?"

Zack faced Logan. "What is *that* supposed to mean?"

"I think you damn well know what it means. You and Tracy.

"What--"

"Have you ever considered if you would've told her that you loved her, she might not have ever done what she did?"

Pinning Logan with a scowl, Zack took a step forward. "She knew that I loved her!"

"How?" Before Zack could answer, Logan said, "Tracy came to Colton as a shy, gangly, cross-eyed girl that had only one boyfriend before you. You were the catch of Colton High. How many girls had you dated before Tracy? Ten, fifteen? What if Tracy figured she was just one more statistic? Holy hell, Zack, you're the one who gave her the god-awful nickname of Olive Oyl."

"I..." Zack paused and remembered. He'd never told Tracy he loved her and had no real good reason as to why he hadn't confessed his feelings for her. "That still doesn't excuse the fact I caught her in the middle of the act with my best friend."

Logan stepped over to Zack and put his hand on his shoulder. "Ask her about that, will ya? And if y'all do have a shot at an encore, don't assume she knows how you feel." Logan stepped away and grabbed a pair of work gloves from the crate of tools. "Let's get busy. I have a gig tonight, and we're burnin' daylight."

Chapter 7

Zack pulled his official Tahoe in behind the brand, spanking new Chevy Silverado and called in the license plate, which was standard procedure, but a waste of time. He already knew who the driver was.

"Morning, Brent." Zack pushed his Stetson farther back on his head to allow him a better look at the speeder through his mirrored sunglasses.

The youngest Parker brother looked over the star pinned on Zack's uniform before meeting his eyes. With a what-can-I-do-for-ya grin, Brent said, "Howdy, Zack. Is there a problem?"

"Sure is." It never failed to amaze him how often drivers breaking the law asked that question. "A big problem. You were going fifty-three in a twenty-five mile per hour speed zone."

Zack was waiting for the rest of the script, where Brent would play coy and deny that he knew he was driving excessively. Instead, he said, "S'pose I was goin' a little too fast."

"Speeding in this part of town isn't acceptable, especially with the elementary school on this street." *The school my daughter attends.* "I'll need your driver's license, registration, and proof of insurance."

Brent chuckled, but it sounded a tad shaky. "C'mon, Zack, you aren't really gonna give me a ticket, are you?"

A passing driver honked, so Zack turned to see a Ford Escape. He waved before looking back at Brent. "Yes. I'm giving you a ticket."

"Boy, those Marines made you a hard-ass, huh?" Brent dug around in his glove box. He straightened with a grunt and pushed his lank dark hair from his face. "Here."

With a curt nod, Zack took the information, went back to his SUV, and wrote the citation. Handing the ticket, license, registration and insurance card to Brent, Zack made a show of looking over the truck. "Nice wheels. Your driving gig with Jake must be paying well."

Brent didn't even glance at the slip of paper and cards before tossing them onto the seat beside him. From behind his sunglasses, Zack watched him closely. He'd known Brent as long as he'd known Jake, which amounted to Brent's entire life. The air conditioner was working overtime, if the cool air escaping the open window was any indication, but Brent had sweat beading on his forehead. He also drummed his fingers in a fast tattoo. Brent looked out the windshield and said, "Yeah, it is."

"Good. You've been out of work for a long time."

"I've heard you're seeing Tracy." Brent looked back at Zack.

"What?"

"Jake mentioned he'd seen y'all at Bobby's ball game. He said you and her looked pretty chummy."

Zack wasn't about to discuss Tracy with Jake's brother. "I don't know what you're talking about."

Brent's smile rounded his already pie face even more, and he shrugged his wide shoulders. "Oh, maybe that's why she's back with Logan, then. Are you done, here?"

"Yeah." Zack stepped back and touched the brim of his Stetson. "Slow down."

Brent glanced at Zack, nodded and put the truck into gear. Zack watched him ease away from the curb. "Oh, Brent, my boy, you're such a tool."

As Zack got back into the SUV, his mind suddenly replayed a snippet of Brent's last comment. *Back with Logan?* What the hell did that mean? Tracy and Logan were never together--or were they? He knew they'd become friends over the years. He remembered the few times Tracy showed up at honky-tonks where Logan's band played. The first time had been back in April down in Waco where she'd dressed to turn heads. Had it been Logan she'd hoped to impress? The bitter twist in his gut reminded him of the feelings he had when Tracy had cheated on him. He didn't care what Tracy did. He couldn't care. She meant nothing to him. They were barely friends.

Then why did he suddenly want to see her?

Why had she been at the forefront of every thought he'd had since her brother's wedding?

He stopped at the intersection and took a deep breath. As he let it out, he corralled his conflicted feelings for Tracy into a corner of his mind and focused on Brent. Something was up with him. He'd asked Tracy to keep her ears open. Maybe she'd heard something he hadn't.

When the light turned green, he circled the block and headed to Tracy's salon.

* * * *

After Tracy removed the glasses she only wore to do computer work and to read, she sat back in her office chair. The letter from Jake's lawyer, informing her of his intentions to reopen their custody case, came to mind. She wasn't ready for a battle. Her father had advised her to dump her crappy lawyer and get a real one; after all, she could afford one. And she knew who she wanted to handle the case. Hopefully, she hadn't waited too long. They were due in court in less than two weeks.

She wasn't the type to cause waves, though Lord knew, she'd caused more than her share indirectly. Shaking her head, Tracy put her real problem aside to think of a less painful one. She couldn't afford to become a sobbing mess for the afternoon. Her schedule was too full--one color, two perms, and two cuts and styles. Then she'd have to concentrate on the calculus class she'd been crazy enough to sign up for.

Melissa was doing well, and she'd cover the Thursday evening hours, but she was new and it would take a while before the women Tracy serviced trusted her with their hair.

She sipped her coffee and thought about what Melissa had asked earlier. What was she going to do with the apartment above the shop? *That* was much more conducive to getting through her day than thinking about living without her baby.

Renting it out made the most sense, but she couldn't bring herself to do so. She'd bought the old Victorian house on College Street a few months after her divorce became final. The downstairs had been a mom and pop store that had gone out of business. The upstairs had been remodeled into a two-bedroom apartment. It had been perfect for her and Bobby; they lived in the apartment, and she'd set up her styling salon on the main floor.

She understood her attachment to the apartment stemmed from it being the first and only place she could ever call truly her own. The big ranch house was beautiful and she could redecorate it in any way she wanted to, but it wasn't hers. Dylan owned it.

Besides, her parents lived there as well. She had no idea how long that was going to work. Her parents hadn't been around since she was eighteen, when her father had been assigned to Pennsylvania, and her mother had left to be with him while Tracy entered college in Colton.

"Oh, stop stalling." The small place would be perfect for college students. A great many of her clientele came from the college at the northeast edge of town, just up the street. Making up her mind, she decided she'd call Mrs. Pratt, who owned a boarding house a few blocks away. She'd know how to go about having her place listed in the college housing office.

With that problem solved, her mind was again free. However, it wasn't the pending custody battle with Jake that came to mind. She closed her eyes and replayed her evening with Zack at the football game last Wednesday. He'd actually flirted with her, though what had touched her more was his treating her like a friend.

The bell over the front door tinkled, and Tracy glanced at her watch. Her ten o'clock appointment had cancelled at the last minute, and she wasn't expecting anyone until one. She moved down the short hall into the reception area of her shop.

The smile she'd pasted on to greet the potential customer became genuine the moment she noticed Logan Cartwright closing the door. "My goodness, I know certain people call me an artist, but I'm not sure anyone could make you beautiful."

"Well, since I'm already drop dead gorgeous, it's a good thing I'm not here for your services." He laughed and embraced her in a tight hug.

"Is that what all the groupies are telling you?" Tracy stepped away from one of her best friends in the world. "How many times do I have to tell you not to believe them?" Although she was partial to only one of the Cartwright men, Logan was considered by most of the females in town to be as sexy, if not a little sexier than his cowboy-turned-Marine-turned-sheriff brother. She figured it had more to do with the fact he was a successful lawyer in his cousin's law firm and just happened to be a fantastic singer.

"A few more times, at least." He lost the smirk. "How's college treating you?"

"Okay. I guess. But I still think I need someone to pound sense into me."

He laughed and looked around the reception area. "Here I thought someone already had done that." He met her gaze, and in typical Logan directness, asked, "What's going on with you and my big brother?"

She groaned. "Please, tell me your aunt Winnie isn't already ordering the china for our wedding."

"Not quite, but she is as happy as a lark. Mom, on the other hand, would like to hire a hit man. You aren't one of her favorite people."

"Tell your mother she can save her money and avoid jail time because nothing is going on between Zack and me. We're friends. If you can call barely tolerating each other a friendship." She leaned her backside against the antique desk in her reception area.

"But you'd like to be more?" Logan sat his designer suit clad, six foot, two-inch frame on the replica of a Victorian couch in front of the windows. He outstretched his arms over the back of the sofa and rested a custom-booted foreleg on his knee. He was totally relaxed as he watched her squirm.

Other than their last names and the above average height and good looks, Zack and Logan were polar opposites. Zack had blond hair and blue eyes; Logan's hair was brown and his eyes were green. Zack was more serious, while Logan didn't take much seriously--unless it dealt with domestic and estate law or music. Many considered Logan the more successful of the two brothers in spite of Zack's rodeo wins, military service, being the county sheriff, and his substantial bank account. Tracy knew Logan's dream wasn't about battling it out in divorce court for the Dallas rich. Logan wanted to sing his way to the top. Every Friday and Saturday night and every chance he got, he played guitar and sang lead with his band Texas Justice. And looked absolutely nothing like the wealthy lawyer sitting in her salon at this moment.

"You know I'd like to be more." Lying to Logan was impossible. "But he's still in love with a dead woman. Also, Jake's trying to make it an issue."

"Are you so sure he loves Lisa?"

His question gave her pause, but she refused to let the implication cause her hope. "It doesn't matter. He'll never forgive me."

"I forgave you, and so will Zack."

"You forgave me for breaking your brother's heart. It was his heart I broke. I think that's a little different, don't you?"

Logan shrugged and straightened to peer into her eyes. "Maybe. But I know my brother thinks about you. At the Fourth of July ball, he couldn't keep his eyes off you. And then, there was the wedding. The man was in torture with that dance. Just as I planned him to be." She narrowed her eyes at him, and he chuckled. "He wanted you, T.C. He wanted you so damned bad he was afraid that touching you would be the match to the fuse."

Logan's words reassured her a little, but she also knew Zack. He'd never forgive her because he still believed the worst about her, that she was a cheater. "I know he wants me. There's no denying the sparks flying between us. But I want more than just sex." She closed her eyes. "God, if

I'd only known what he'd felt for me, Logan, our lives would have been so different."

"Sure." He didn't seem convinced. "You'd be saving lives and Zack would be risking his on some half-crazed horse. But neither of you would have your kids. And I, for one, wouldn't ever wish Mandy away. I'd bet you wouldn't Bobby either."

The sigh she thrust out was from her soul. "You're right, of course. Can I wish Jake away, then?"

Logan chuckled, and then became serious. "Let me see that letter you got from his lawyer. Preston Tilley, right?" Tracy nodded, and he let out a disgusted huff. "Yeah, he's a shark, but Lance and I are the best family law attorneys in the Big D. And I *do* mean Dallas," he sang the last, causing her to laugh.

She left him to return with the letter from Jake's lawyer. As she handed Logan the overlarge envelope, she said, "The court date is next Friday. Can we be ready?"

"Shouldn't be a problem." Logan read the letter and then looked up at her. "Since when have you been promiscuous and not a good judge of character?"

With her hands pressed into her hips, Tracy paced again. "That's what burns me up. The last man I had sex with was Jake Parker. Before him, your brother took my virginity when we were both seventeen, and then I got involved with Jake. I haven't slept with any of the jerks I've dated since him. Sure there's been quite a few, and I'll admit the last few men were a bit shady, but Bobby hasn't ever met any of them. I only go out when he's with Jake. Dammit! I'm tired of being considered the town floozy because I made a mistake--when I was eighteen!" She slapped her fists against her thighs and faced Logan. "And then there's that whole business about you and me having an affair... Ugh!"

Logan stood, took her by the shoulders, and spoke gently. "Tracy, listen to me. Jake can't win."

She wanted to believe him. "Jake told me he won't tolerate Bobby being around Zack. He plans on using Zack's PTSD to prove his thing about the men I dated not being safe, just because he reprimanded Bobby at the wedding. He also brought up my taking in Dylan."

"Have you talked to Bobby about any of this?"

"No." Shaking her head, she said, "Besides, he's with Jake this week."

"That's not what I meant. I'll have to speak with him. If anyone has ever been destructive around Bobby, it's been Jake. I've seen that bastard when he's coaching. Jake will not win, Tracy. Not if we bring up all the lies he's told you and how manipulative he is."

"Logan, you know that's water under the bridge." Tracy averted her gaze and rubbed her hands over her dark denim skirt. "I could have left him long before I did. I should have when you came to me, before Zack married Lisa, but I just had Bobby." She sighed and turned away. "Hell, I could have said no when he wanted to have sex the first time."

"Why didn't you?" There wasn't any censure to his tone; oddly, it was gentle understanding.

"You know why." God, how many times had she asked herself that question?

Logan sat back on the couch. "Yes, I know as your friend. Now, tell me because I'm your lawyer."

Heaving in a breath, she sat down beside him and folded her hands in her lap. "He tricked me into believing Zack was sleeping with Dawn Madison. He told me he went to your parents' house and walked in on him and Dawn having sex. Dear God, he even explained exactly what they were doing." The sting of tears burned her sinuses as the memory replayed. "I didn't doubt him because I knew your parents were away. And..." The angry fire was dying, extinguished by pain and shame. She swallowed hard. "Zack was known for being a player. I just figured he was tired of me and decided to move on. I thought he was cheating on me. Zack was my first serious boyfriend, and I never understood what he saw in me." The sob was out before she could stop it. "I could never compete with someone as beautiful as Dawn. Jake wanted me, and I guess I lost all perspective. He told me he loved me." Logan wrapped her up in his arms and held her to his chest.

"I'm sorry, T.C.," he murmured into her hair.

She pulled away and stood again. "Damn, I was so stupid!"

He regarded her for a long time before he said with a note of incredulity, "Tracy, you really believe that, don't you?"

"What? That I'm stupid? I know I am."

"No, you are not. And that wasn't what I meant. I was talking about Zack not possibly loving you and having a fling with Dawn because you think she's prettier than you."

Now she was puzzled. Logan knew she didn't believe that lie anymore. Not after Logan showed Tracy the ring Zack had bought her with his rodeo prize money. Prior to Zack's first National Finals Rodeo, he'd given the ring to Logan to sell to help him pay for college, even though he already had a college fund that sent him to Stanford University. Tracy had just given birth to Bobby and had been sucked totally into Jake's lies. Logan had helped her realize the awful truth--entirely too late.

He stood and took her into his arms again. "Tracy, when you finally figure it out, you'll understand. But no one can explain it to you."

She looked up at him and pressed on a smile as stiff as Mr. Potato Head's. "Have you taken up fortune telling, too?"

Logan touched her nose with his index finger in such a brotherly way her heart ached. She loved Logan with the same bone-deep affection she felt for her brother. "No, but I know this for certain. Jake's hoping to use the past to his advantage, and his sudden interest in Bobby has everything to do with you becoming a rich woman. Tracy, according to that letter, Jake wants you to pay him child support and alimony if he wins custody."

The cold lump in her belly expanded. "I know."

With a gleam in his green eyes, Logan said, "All of Jake's antics stink of opportunism at its lowest. May I make a suggestion?"

"Yes." She was still reeling. Jake only wanted to take Bobby away from her for her money?

"I suggest the first thing we do is convert your name back to your maiden name. Otherwise, it seems like you still want to be married to him."

She opened her mouth to protest his observation, but shut it again. Why hadn't she ever changed her name back to Quinn? The reason she explained to her family and friends seemed so lame now. Was it really because of Bobby? Or had she kept the Parker name to punish herself?

Smiling, she asked, "When can I start signing your checks as Tracy Quinn?"

He sniggered and raised a brow. "I'm not cheap."

"I know, and I expect to pay you whatever your going retainer is. I didn't let you to take my case before because, one, I couldn't afford you, and two, I didn't want Jake spreading gossip that we're lovers."

"Not a good image." Logan winced.

"I agree. No offense, but you aren't my type."

"No, tall, blond and crazy is more like it."

She shook her head. "Always a comedian, aren't you?" Logan shrugged, and she laughed. "Now answer my question. How soon can we get my name changed?"

He flopped back down on the couch, dwarfing the thing. "I have to go back to Dallas for a meeting, so I'll put in the paperwork later today. We'll have to wait on the Social Security office. But if you want to start using your maiden name as soon as I get the papers filed, go for it. It will be legal soon enough."

"You're the best," she proclaimed and hugged him again. "Thanks, Logan."

"Hey, we Cartwrights stick together."

She sat beside him. "I'm not a Cartwright."

He waved his hand and puffed air between his teeth in dismissive gesture. "Technicalities. You will be soon enough. Then we'll be changing your name again."

She couldn't help but laugh. "You're a dreamer."

"That's me." He lost some of the good-natured cockiness. "Before you hear this through the infamous Colton Grapevine, of which Aunt Winnie is the president, I want it to come from me."

"Whoa! Don't tell me someone has finally lassoed the heart of Logan Cartwright."

He shook his head and smiled. "That'll be the day. After I win your case, I'm moving to Nashville."

"Wow. When did you decide to do this?"

"After the second song I wrote went to number one, but I'm not the singer singing it. Before I get too damned old to take the plunge, I'm closing my eyes and jumping in the deep end with the alligators."

Logan had been her best friend for years. They didn't advertise their relationship, mainly because the rumor mill would start churning out untrue stories about them. She was happy for him, but scared for him, too.

"Oh, don't look so glum," he quipped, and she let out a laugh at the face he made at her. "I've already got the lecture about how stupid this is from my ever practical big brother and father. The only one who isn't banning me from the next family photo is Mom."

Tracy folded her hands in her lap. "It's not that. I know you'll make it. I guess that's the problem. I'll miss you."

Suddenly it hit her that both of her best friends--Dylan and now Logan--were moving on with their lives. Dylan had found Charli and was about to become a father. Logan had his music. But her life was still a mess. She tried to swallow the lump in her throat. "Is the band going, too?"

"No, I'm going alone."

"When are you leaving?"

He smiled. "I told you, after we win your case. Listen. I'm not disappearing. I'll be around." He winked and added, "Besides, Zack's here and looking for a friend."

She made a face, which included sticking her tongue out at him--the identical one he'd made earlier. He laughed and stood. After glancing at his expensive watch, he said, "I've got to get to Dallas. I have a meeting in three hours with one of my other clients. We're headed to court on Monday. And her case isn't as cut and dry as yours will be."

"Just sing to the judge. That should put him right where you want him." She was hugging him again when the bell rang above the door.

"Am I interrupting?" Zack said with a clear edge to his voice, and she jumped away.

Logan headed for the door, cuffing his older brother on the shoulder as he went. "Nope, she's all yours. Later 'gator."

"'Bye, Logan. Thanks." The tinkling of the bell above the door echoed in the silence as she stared at Zack. Her heart raced at the sight of him, and for one desperate heartbeat, she thought she'd conjured him. "Hi."

"Hey." He removed his hat and twisted it in his hands as he looked around. Finally, he said, "I just pulled Brent Parker over for speeding."

"I hope you really socked it to him."

Zack nodded and regarded her for a moment. She became very aware of him searching her eyes. Was he looking for something in particular? "Oh, I did."

"Too bad it was the wrong Parker brother."

"Speaking of brothers, I didn't realize you and Logan were close." The sharpness of his clipped words surprised her.

"He's a friend."

"Well, then." He glanced around again and his jaw set in what she suspected was irritation.

What right did Zack have to come off like the jealous boyfriend? Tracy propped her hands on her hips and narrowed her eyes. "I don't know what you're thinking, but Logan and I are just friends. I've asked him to take over my custody case with Jake. The asshole is taking me to court again."

"What was I thinking?"

She lost the fire and dropped her hands to her sides. After tugging her lower lips between her teeth, she shrugged. "I don't know. I just don't want you to get the wrong idea about Logan and me. That's all."

Zack looked away. "Jake didn't take long to make a move."

"What do you mean?"

He met her puzzlement with something dark and dangerous clouding his blue eyes. "You're a rich woman now, Tracy. Surely, you can smell this skunk a mile away."

"Logan said the same thing." Sighing, Tracy leaned against the desk and folded her arms over her chest again. "Thank God I can now afford Dobbs, Cartwright and Cartwright. My old lawyer is a bumbling idiot.

"So, Logan's taking on your case?"

"Yeah, but I don't want to talk about it."

They stared at each other for a long moment. Zack didn't seem to be in any big hurry to leave, but it was easy to see he had no clue what to do or say next. He twisted his hat in his hand and then put it on his head. She figured he was on his way out. Instead, he asked, "Hey, are you free for lunch? I was heading over to the diner when I saw Brent taking the turn at the intersection of Ferguson and Austin Streets like a bat out of hell."

Her heart skipped a beat. Whatever had brought Zack into her shop, she wouldn't question it. "I don't have an appointment until one. Besides, Melissa will be here by then. So, yeah, lunch sounds great. Did you want me to meet you there?"

His deep laugh warmed her clear through. "You can come with me, if my ride isn't too intimidating."

"I don't mind." She couldn't tear her gaze from his, and before she thought about what she was saying, she asked, "Are you gonna handcuff me?"

The instant darkening of his eyes forestalled her embarrassment. His slow Texas drawl set her insides on fire. "Would you like to be handcuffed?"

She swallowed back her response to him and the X-rated image his husky tone created. "Ah...let me grab my purse from the office."

His reverberating laughter followed her down the short hall. No, doubt about it, Zack wanted her body, but did he want her heart?

Chapter 8

Although Leon Ferguson had murdered Ella Larson back in July, her sister and brother kept her diner open. They ran Ella's Diner during the day and the Longhorn Saloon at night.

The interior was reminiscent of a 1950's soda shop in bright red and white. The faux red marble- and chrome-edged bar filled the front of the dining room. The alternating red and white stools, along with most of the booths, were all filled with folks who regularly patronized the diner. Zack became very aware of the woman beside him as they entered.

He removed his hat, but kept his mirrored sunglasses in place.

As he searched out an empty table, every eye in the place seemed to turn toward him and Tracy. He returned the greetings he received, but he was cognizant of the curious looks. Many of these same people had attended the football game the other night.

Zelda Marion, an older woman who usually was his waitress at lunch, hurried past loaded down with plates of food. "Hey, Zack, you want your usual?"

He glanced at Tracy. "No, not today."

When Zelda noticed Tracy, her eyes widened with surprise. Everyone knew his and Tracy's ugly history, if for no other reason than because he was a Cartwright and she was part of the Ferguson clan. Both families had been favorite topics of gossip for over a century.

Zelda glanced at Zack again and said with a smile, "Oh, I see you've got company today. Sit anywhere. I'll be right over."

Tracy seemed as anxious as he was about the overly interested audience as they found a booth and sat across from each other. No doubt, he would be fielding phone calls from his mother and aunt that night regarding his *date* with Tracy Parker. He wouldn't be surprised if his aunt didn't have him married by the end of the week. Thank God she liked Tracy and he was her nephew, or his life could become a cesspool of rampant rumor very quickly.

He retrieved the plastic covered menus from behind the napkin dispenser and handed one of them to Tracy. She smiled her thanks and took it from him. He had a hard time concentrating on the billings for the lunch rush as Tracy adorably scrunched up her nose and squinted down at her menu.

"Forget your glasses?" Zack put the menu aside. He decided to order his usual anyway.

His heart skittered over several beats at the pinking of her cheeks.

She pushed her long hair behind her ears. "I only need the darned things for reading. I don't even wear glasses to do hair. I should get Lasik surgery, but I can't seem to justify the cost, and my insurance won't pay for it. But I've been doing a lot more reading lately with school."

"You could afford it now."

She shrugged and the corners of her pink lips twisted into a smirk. "I suppose I can. I forget that I'm a rich woman these days. Heck, the interest payment on my inheritance alone almost gave me a heart attack. No wonder everyone wants a cut."

"How're classes going?"

Tracy closed her menu and wrinkled her nose. "Okay. I guess. It's gonna take some getting used to. I mean, I've taken classes before to get my associate degree in business, and of course my technical training to get my license to do hair, but I'm still wondering if pre-med isn't a pipe dream."

"You'll do fine."

"Tell that to my crazy nerves."

Zelda saved him from commenting by stopping to take their orders. After she returned to the workstation behind the counter, he broke the sudden awkward tension and asked, "Have you heard from the newlyweds?"

Tracy laughed and visibly relaxed. He'd always admired the relationship of the Quinn siblings. Growing up with a father who moved around every few years had made it difficult for them to make lasting friends, especially since they both had been loners. Dylan was as loyal as they come when it came to those who he cared about; however, it took him a while to form that kind of relationship. Tracy had been shy and introverted as a kid.

Zack still remembered the gangly, cross-eyed girl who had walked into his sixth grade class. She'd looked like she was being led into the bullfighter's ring--and something about her overwhelming vulnerability had stolen his heart. And scared him shitless.

Still did.

"You've got to be joking, right?"

He shrugged and leaned back against the red leather of the booth. "I wasn't, but I can deduct from your response the answer is no. I was hoping you'd told them about the theft."

Zelda returned and placed their drinks before them. He thanked her, and once the older woman was gone again, Tracy sipped her sweet tea. "I told you I'd only tell them about it if something else happened. Nothing has, so why ruin their time together? They deserve this. But to answer your question, Charli sent me a message when they arrived, a picture of her and Dylan posing on the beach in Maui. No message, only the picture taken with her cell phone."

"We did good setting them up."

"That we did." Tracy matched his grin and lifted her glass in toast. He clicked his glass against hers, and they both drank. "Although I never expected them to fall in love. But thanks again, Zack, for telling me about Charli's newspaper ad. I kept thinking Dylan would be good in security or something like that because of his Army background. I never considered ranching."

"I'm just glad I saw the ad. I knew, from all the work Dylan had done on your granddad's ranch and his own place down in Killeen, that managing a place would be perfect for him."

Again silence engulfed them, and he found himself gazing at Tracy. He should swing the conversation back to Brent, but he had time. Despite her coming a long way from the shy little girl she'd been in junior high, there were times when her pewter eyes seemed insecure with the world around them. She was no longer cross-eyed, which one last surgery had corrected, leaving behind minor farsightedness. The braces she'd worn their early high school years were gone, leaving behind a bright, sincere smile in a face sharp with angles. But she'd grown into her once pointed features. Her lankiness remained, but pregnancy and maturity had rounded her body ever so slightly, making her less waiflike and more willowy. She still was practically flat-chested, but today she obviously wasn't braless. Her once short dishwater brown hair was now long and streaked with becoming natural-looking highlights of golden brown.

Jolted by his desire to kiss the disconcerted pucker from her lips, he had to look away. He turned to look out the window above the short Coca-Cola themed curtain.

Tracy sucked in a breath. "Logan told me he's moving to Nashville."

Zack met her eyes across the table. He didn't want to talk about his younger brother and his crazy dreams. He didn't want to make small talk with her at all. Or any other kind of speech. He wanted her in his bed, with only the soft moans and mewls of a woman in the throes of passion coming from her.

To hide his growing desire, he busied himself with drinking his Coke. "Actually, he informed the family last night. I personally think he's being a fool. The kid's a lawyer, and a damned good one. He makes a seven-figure salary that's closer to eight." He shook his head and pursed his lips. "I hope he can make it, but out of every hundred hayseeds who fly into that town thinking they'll sing their way into fame and fortune, only one makes it. And he's already had that chance."

"Who knows? Logan might be that one out of a hundred this time around."

Something about the tone of her voice had him meeting her gaze.

"But I'd suggest you never call him a hayseed to his face."

"Whether he likes to admit it or not, Logan Cartwright is a hayseed as much as I am. He might make it big, but I'm not holding my breath. I'll bet in six months, instead of making record deals, Logan is back making cheating husbands and gold-digging wives wish they had never crossed paths with attorney Logan Cartwright." When she narrowed her eyes at his obvious doubts concerning his brother's talent, he said, "I'm not saying that he can't sing, because I know he can."

Tracy's ruffled feathers settled, and she smiled. "Unlike his brother."

"Hey! I can sing."

She raised a perfectly arched brow. "I remember your attempts at singing, Zack Cartwright. It's a wonder I didn't run in the other direction."

He grinned at the mention of a particular date when he'd attempted to sing a Garth Brooks song to her. "Okay, I can't hold a tune in a bucket. I guess I take after my old man. In my defense, *Ain't Going Down 'Til the Sun Comes Up* isn't an easy song to sing, though I remember getting the results I was aiming for."

Zelda took that moment to deliver their hamburgers and fries, but he didn't even acknowledge the woman. He was too busy fighting the image of him and Tracy tangled together in the soft grass by the lake on his ranch. From the intensity of the storm clouds in her eyes, he got the impression Tracy remembered the same wild encounter.

When Zelda left, Tracy reached for the ketchup--the exact same time he made a grab for the bottle. His fingers brushed hers. The soft satin of her warm skin was like touching an electrified fence.

She pulled her hand away and cleared her throat. As she tucked her hair behind her ears again, she cooled the rising heat by asking, "Any leads in who's stealing the cattle?"

Swallowing hard, he set the bottle before her with a smile.

She tentatively reached for it and murmured, "Thanks."

Once she finished with the ketchup, he dumped some on his own french fries. "Actually, that's what I wanted to talk to you about."

"Oh."

He looked up from his plate.

Tracy put down a fry and quickly averted her eyes. "What did you want to know?"

"Do you know anything about Jake's truck driving gig?" Zack picked up his burger and took a bite.

Tracy took a deep breath and picked up her fork. "Henrietta Parker was in the shop yesterday for her bi-weekly wash and set. I asked her about Brent, and she wasn't too nice in her comments. But she never is, concerning her grandsons."

Zack set his burger back on the plate. "What did she have to say?"

"Henrietta doesn't know how he can afford that truck either. He apparently is still mooching off her and his mother. He lives at Sandy's until his mother gets fed up with his lazy butt, and then he goes to Henrietta's for a few weeks. Promises to help her out around the house, but he never does. As far as I can tell from what Bobby has said, Jake must be doing well. He's been buying new furniture for the trailer and can afford to sue me for custody. But what I don't get is, if it's so lucrative, why is he still running the garage?"

Zack leaned back in the booth seat and crossed his arms over his chest. "Do you know where Jake's cargo is coming from?"

She popped a french fry into her mouth. "Maybe Waco or Killeen. Or even Austin."

* * * *

They ate in silence for a few moments, and Tracy couldn't keep her eyes off Zack, while everyone in the diner seemed to be watching them. The rumor around Colton was Zack never dated. According to his aunt Winnie, he claimed he didn't have time for a woman in his life. Nor did he want to confuse Amanda, who still believed her mother would come home someday. Tracy remembered her conversation with the little girl at the football game.

Wait, you mean y'all can't get married?

What did she mean by that? Surely, Amanda wasn't implying she *wanted* Zack and Tracy to get married.

She shook her head and smiled.

He wiped his mouth with the paper napkin, and his brow wrinkled into a frown. "What's so funny?"

She met his intense blue eyes and decided to throw everything down. "I was thinking about what Mandy said about us...ah...getting married the other day when we were talking about how...our families are connected."

His bewildered expression turned hard. "Mandy is going through a stage. She overheard Winnie and Mom talking about me needing a girlfriend. Now, Mandy got it in her head that I need another wife."

Tracy blinked at the idea and laid her hand over her chest. "And she picked me?"

Zack stared at her with cold, unforgiving eyes as he said, "Yes, but it isn't going to happen."

She looked away and swallowed her heart along with her pride.

"But I'm still a man in need of a woman. I'm just not looking for a wife."

His voice was so low she wondered if she'd heard him correctly. Tracy brought her gaze back to his and the fire had melted the ice in his eyes. Unless Zack Cartwright had changed in the past fourteen years, she knew he was a man with a very healthy sex drive. He didn't want *her;* he wanted a woman. Any woman would do.

Was she willing to risk her heart if Zack never forgave her? Could she deny him if he wanted her to be the woman to appease his lust?

She had no answers, but the way her body ached for his touch made her want to find out. "I was wondering..."

He raised a brow in quiet question, and she forced herself not to look away. She sucked in her lip and wasn't sure she wanted to ask.

"Yes?" he prompted when she didn't continue.

"I was wondering if you and Amanda would like to come over to Oak Springs tomorrow evening for dinner. Mom and Dad have to go back to Washington for a week or two and are leaving in the morning..." When his lips flattened out, she realized she couldn't push him. He had to come to her. Reaching for a possible explanation for wanting him to have dinner with her, she added, "Bobby and Amanda seemed to get along so well at the wedding, and I thought they might like to see each other again. She could bring along her bathing suit and the two of them could play in the pool." When his expression didn't soften, she averted her eyes to her half-eaten burger and murmured, "Oh, never mind. I don't--"

"What time?"

Her jaw went slack as she looked up. She could barely force words past her suddenly dry throat. "Is five okay? That way the kids can play for a while before we eat."

"Sounds Good. Should I bring my trunks?"

"Trunks?"

He picked up his glass of Coke and the air buzzed with electricity as he pinned her with his gaze. "You said something about swimming."

* * * *

As soon as Tracy got home, she found her mother in the kitchen. "Mom, what was I thinking?"

Her mother laughed and continued stirring something delicious smelling in a large pot on the stove. "Hello, to you too, sweetheart. So, now what have you done?" Then she lost all the amusement. "Is Bobby okay?"

"Bobby's fine." Tracy plopped onto a barstool and huffed.

Her mom faced Tracy. "Logan can't take your case?"

"No. I mean, Logan is all gung-ho about it. He's convinced we can win."

"Then what's wrong? Is school going okay?"

Tracy fought the impulse to roll her eyes, but barely. What was it with everyone's fascination with her going back to school? "Yes, school is fine. I invited Zack to dinner tomorrow night."

"That's wonderful!"

"No, it's not!" Tracy pushed a lock of hair from her face, deciding in that second she was cutting it. "Mom, you know I can't cook. I wish you would be here to whip something wonderful up."

With a wistful smile, her mother said, "I wish I was, too. I'd have made my cranberry glazed pork chops." She shook her head and laughed. "Actually, I'm glad Daddy and I won't be here. This is a great opportunity for you."

Her mother opened the oversized refrigerator and pulled out a pitcher of lemonade--fresh squeezed with lemon slices floating on top. She poured a glass and set it before Tracy.

"Mom, what am I going to do? I can't make a meal like your pork chops."

Her mother pursed her lips and opened her mouth to speak.

Tracy cut her off. "And no, I won't have you cook for me so all I'll have to do is warm the meal. This was my brilliant idea. I guess I could make spaghetti or bake some chicken. With my luck the noodles will be soggy and the chicken dry like they always are."

"How about steaks on the grill?"

"I can't grill steaks." Tracy jumped up from the bar and paced the kitchen. "The last time I even tried cooking steaks, one of them was raw and the other one was burnt." She wasn't at all sure what she wanted her mother to do about her situation. "I shouldn't have been so impulsive. But we were having lunch together and...Mom, I think we might actually have something going for us. I just wanted to do something that didn't happen by chance. Like lunch today or the football game the other evening. But I shouldn't have--"

"Tracy, don't panic."

"Don't panic?" She squeaked. "I'll ruin any chance we have by cooking. The way to a man's heart is through his stomach. Ha! Not if I'm doing the cooking, it's not. I think I'll call and cancel. He'll never want *me* again anyway. I broke his heart, and he's still hung up on his dead wife. Zack just wants a roll in the hay--"

Mom let out a sigh. "What time is he coming over?"

"Five. I didn't want him to think it was a date. So, I told him, if he came over early, Amanda and Bobby would have time to play."

"Good."

Tracy stopped pacing and looked at her mother. "Mom, am I making a mistake? I don't want him to think I'm a slut..." She shook head and started pacing again. "Mandy really likes me. She's such a little spitfire."

"She needs a mother."

"Yeah, but her father doesn't want that woman to be me."

Her mother came around the counter and took Tracy into her arms as if she was still a little girl. "Tracy, Zack Cartwright is a good man. He's honest and grounded--now that he's not risking his fool neck by riding wild horses. He loved you once, sweetheart. No man forgets his first love--not completely. He may have loved his wife, but she's dead and gone. And for a year now, the two of you have gone from avoiding each other to eating together, and setting the dance floor on fire." Her mother paused. Tracy met her blue eyes, and her mom took a deep breath. "Zack will come around. Just don't underestimate yourself."

"Mom, what if I can't make him fall in love with me again? What if he can't forgive me?" *What if I'm not what he's looking for?*

"Sweetheart, you just be yourself, and Zack will fall head over heels in love with you."

"Who else would I be?" But she knew what her mother meant. She had to show Zack the rumors and the mistakes were not who she really was. But telling him wasn't going to work. Zack had to see that she wasn't a cheater or vindictive. He had to figure it out on his own that she had believed a man like Zack Cartwright couldn't love a woman like her.

"You know what I mean," her mother softly said.

"Yeah, I guess I do." Tracy thrust out a long breath between her teeth. "Okay, but I still have no idea what to do about dinner. I just know I can't grill steaks. I guess I could pick something up or order a pizza."

Her mother stepped away and shook her head. "You do know if you'd paid attention when I tried to teach you how to cook--"

Tracy's glare cut her off. Her mother chuckled and headed back to the stove and her big, bubbling pot. Tracy followed her and looked in as her mom stirred the contents.

"Is that your special chili?"

"Yes. Tom Miller brought me a whole bushel of tomatoes and a bunch of different kinds of peppers from a garden the ranch hands have over at the bunkhouse. He asked if I could make them some of my famous chili."

Tracy stared at her mother. "How on Earth could anyone know about your chili? You've only been here for two months?"

She shrugged. "Probably Tom's uncle, Jesse Riley. I've been making this recipe since I was a girl." Her mother winked. Jesse was a handyman who worked on the ranch and her mother's girlhood sweetheart. "I have an idea about your dinner. Plan to eat about six-thirty. Make a salad and throw some potatoes into the oven. Get some strip or T-bone steaks."

"Okay." Tracy smiled and nodded. "That sounds easy enough."

Her mother chuckled and moved away from the pot. She opened a spice cabinet and rummaged around for a few moments, picking up bottles of spices to look at them. "Ah. Good. We have everything I'll need." She looked at Tracy again. "Get a piece of paper and a pen to write this down. I'm going to give you a simple recipe for a marinade that is to die for. Then when Zack gets here, you mention about grilling the steaks outdoors, and I'll bet my secret chili recipe he'll jump right in and want to cook them." She winked and together they said, "Because grilling steaks is a man thing."

* * * *

After Zack tucked Mandy into bed, he went out into the living room. It was late, but he knew sleep wouldn't come easy. Lunch that afternoon had proved to him just how attracted he was to Tracy.

He wanted her.

And after denying the fact to himself for the best part of a year, he was finally ready to admit he had to have her.

He stood before the floor-to-ceiling window and looked out over the darkened beauty of his ranch. Rain pelted the window while thunder sounded over the distant ridge. Lightning flashed lighting up the land. Beyond the yard and pasture was the lake where so many of his memories had occurred, where so many of his dreams had been born. In every one of those dreams, Tracy stood beside him. Back then, he'd wanted to eventually take over his share of the ranch and raise cattle. His father and uncle had thought the idea was crazy. He was only eighteen. What did he know about anything?

Nothing.

As the thunder chased the harsh light from the sky, he turned away from the window. Logan had given him a shoebox full of crap, explaining he'd found it when he'd cleaned out his condo in Dallas. Zack hadn't asked what was in the box; he'd simply tossed it amongst the clutter of Mandy's play dishes, and his latest ranch and law enforcement magazines on the coffee table.

Picking up the old box, he sat down on the couch. He stared down at it. Would opening the lid bring chaos like the fabled Pandora's Box?

Chuckling, he mumbled, "You are becoming way too introspective, Zack, my boy."

Taking a deep breath, he lifted the lid. The world didn't stop spinning, and as far as he could tell, no demons were unleashed, but his heart missed a few beats and breathing was impossible. He thought he'd thrown out all this stuff. How the hell did Logan get his hands on it?

The first thing on top was a snapshot of him and Tracy standing before the Christmas tree at his parents' house. It was taken on Christmas Eve at a party. He picked it up and stared down into the image of them, smiling, hugging, two teenagers with big chips on their shoulders. Tracy had been shy about the 35mm camera his younger brother had pointed at them at every turn. He remembered what had happened later that night.

His grandparents had been out of town, and he'd stayed in the old log house to keep an eye on things for them. His grandfather knew Zack loved the old house and just wanted his own space; so, every time he and Grandma went to Palm Springs, the old man let Zack stay over.

Following the party that Christmas Eve, Zack had brought Tracy here, and he'd told her about his dreams after making love to her. She must have found his ideas boring, because she'd fallen to sleep. At the time, he'd found it endearing. After all, he'd made love to her several times before he spilled his guts.

Beneath the Christmas picture was a large professionally done photograph of Tracy. Taken senior year, it was the one in their yearbook. Her hair was permed and curled high, sprayed stiff with too much hairspray. Her makeup was a little overdone, but she took his breath away.

He slowly laid it beside him on the couch and picked up the next picture--a blown up snapshot of them on graduation day. As lightning flashed and thunder rattled the glass in the big windows, he went back in time. They were dressed in their caps and gowns, proudly holding their diplomas--and each other. Around her neck was the sash of an honor student, and a corsage of white roses was pinned to her breast signifying her as the class salutatorian. He'd been just happy to get through school. He hadn't cared about being valedictorian, so he'd gotten rid of the trappings as soon as he'd finished the speech and his diploma was in his hand.

"Is that you and Miz Tracy?"

He started and looked up to Mandy standing before him in her nightgown. She hugged the stuffed rabbit Lisa had given to her, and sucked on her thumb. She only did that when she was afraid.

He set aside the past and reached for the little girl he loved more than anything. As he pulled her onto his lap, he asked, "Can't you sleep, baby girl?"

She moved her head in the negative against his chest and snuggled close. "You didn't answer my question."

He chuckled low in his chest. Amanda Jean Cartwright might only be six years old, but she was nobody's fool. "Yeah, that's me and Miz Tracy. We were graduating high school."

"Was Momma there?"

"No." He sighed. "I hadn't met your momma yet."

"Oh." She shifted away and looked into the box sitting beside him on the couch. The next photo was of him and Tracy kissing by the barn. He hadn't even known the picture was taken until Logan had tried to blackmail him with it. "Did you like her?"

"Yeah, Mandy, I did." How did he tell a six-year-old about the kind of betrayal he'd suffered? "But she decided she liked Bobby's daddy more."

Mandy lay back against him again. "I wish she liked you again. Miz Tracy could be your friend and my substitute momma if she did. She could give me a baby sister and Bobby would be my big brother."

"Amanda Jean." He breathed and held her close. The picture of the passionate kiss drew his attention, and he was painfully reminded how much he missed Tracy Quinn.

And how much he wished he could fulfill his daughter's wish.

Chapter 9

Bobby hung up the old wall phone in the kitchen and sulked into the living room where Jake sat on his new leather recliner. Bobby bit on his bottom lip--an annoying habit he'd inherited from the bitch. Something had him thinking.

"Hey, T-Rex, what did she say to you?" Jake muted the Thursday night football game on TV.

Bobby sat on the edge of the couch and shrugged a shoulder. "Mom's dating another guy again."

"And that surprises you?" Jake didn't even try to keep the sarcasm from his voice.

"I guess not, but I never met any of those other guys." Bobby took a deep breath and looked up at Jake. "It's the sheriff. She said they're coming over to ranch for supper tomorrow night."

"They?"

"Sheriff Cartwright and Mandy."

Ah, yeah, the daughter. "How do you feel about your mom and the sheriff together?" Jake took a drink from the bottle of Coors in his hand. He tossed the remote onto the table beside his chair as he regarded Bobby over the tilted bottle.

"I don't know. I like Mandy. She's okay for a girl." Bobby played with his fingers by entwining them, then straightening them. "The sheriff's okay, too, I guess."

Jake lowered the bottle. "Except he yelled at you when he has no right to. He's not related to you in any way that matters."

Bobby hesitated and then nodded. "Yeah, I guess. But Mom said he didn't really yell."

After setting the beer down beside the remote on the messy end table, Jake sat forward and peered at Bobby. "Don't let your mother talk you into believin' something that didn't happen, Bobby." Damn, how he wished he could change the boy's name. He hated that, in a weak moment after his birth, Tracy talked him into naming his son after her arrogant father. "Cartwright can't be trusted."

"What do you mean?" Bobby fidgeted on his seat.

"He's the reason I wasn't able to play professional ball." When Bobby's face pinched in a pretty good imitation of a question mark, Jake explained, "Back in high school I was on my way to playing the best ball around. I was scouted out and given a scholarship to Texas A and M to play for them at the end of the season of my junior year. But because I trusted that--" He caught the word *bastard* just in time. "Trusted Zack, I tore up my right knee and couldn't play at all my senior year. I lost the money and the chance to go to school. Unlike your mom, I wasn't born with a silver spoon in my mouth."

"How did Sheriff Cartwright make you hurt your knee?"

"I hated horses. Still do. Zack knew that, but he demanded we go riding. That's why I never want you on a horse. You have the chance I never did. Anyway, we were going along the cliffs that cut into the ranch when my horse slipped and threw me. My foot got caught in the stirrup, and the horse dragged me. If Cartwright hadn't insisted we go riding on one of the most dangerous trails on the CW, I'd be playing in the NFL right now."

Jake watched Bobby chew on what he'd told him. Before he could ask the questions Jake saw forming, he added, "Zack is no one's friend, T-Rex. He'll try to win you over to his side, then he'll hurt you just like he did me."

* * * *

"Don't worry," Tracy said, drawing Zack's attention back to her. "They'll be fine. Thanks for the football. Bobby liked it."

Zack watched Amanda run up the gleaming, curved, stairway after Bobby. Eileen Quinn's two Yorkies yipped and barked as they bounded up behind the kids. "I hope so. I don't think I made a great impression on him at the wedding. I was a little harsh." Tracy had been right about their kids. Despite the difference of four years in age and being of opposite sexes, Bobby and Amanda were becoming fast friends.

Bobby would be my big brother.

He forced the memory of Mandy's comment to the back of his mind and looked at Tracy.

"Bobby needed someone to show him he was being a butthead. You did that. Don't worry about it."

Zack's gaze drifted to her bright smile. "Sorry we're late." He removed his hat then ran his fingers through his hair. "I was stuck at the office again."

"Another rustling?"

"No. There was an accident on Highway Six." He shook his head as images of the mangled mess of the car involved flashed in his mind.

She started moving down the hall. "Bad?"

"Yeah." As he followed her into the kitchen, his boots thumped on the Italian tiles. "The driver was drunk and wrapped himself around a telephone pole."

She pushed the kitchen door open and grimaced. "Oh, no. Not someone we know? Is he okay?"

He swallowed and shook his head. "He's dead. No, he wasn't anyone you'd know. He was just passing through from Crawford to Palo Pinto County."

"Oh."

She stopped by the island and leaned against the marble edge as if waiting for him to speak. Problem was he couldn't. She looked great dressed in white jeans and a bright electric blue, lightweight sweater, which seemed to bring out the light blue of her otherwise gray eyes. Her hair was pulled over her shoulder and held in place with one of those fat ponytail things Mandy called a scrunchie. Then he noticed the bangs hanging over her forehead.

"You cut your hair."

She seemed startled he'd noticed. "Just the front and trimmed the ends. This style seems to be the trend in Hollywood these days. Thought I'd give it a try. Melissa cut it for me." Brightening, she added, "Thanks for noticing. Most people never would."

Unsure of what else he could say that didn't make it obvious he'd notice even the slightest change, he said, "It's the bangs. You didn't have them before."

"True." Her smile quivered a little. "Well, it's getting late, and I have to get the grill going."

He nodded and looked around the large kitchen. The room was huge and warmly decorated in a fruit theme, all maple wood cabinetry and stainless steel. But he didn't see many personal items around. The sand-colored granite countertops were virtually bare. "Still unpacking?"

"Not really. I moved in the stuff I had and bought a few things. But the house is still pretty empty. Mom and Dad are bringing their furniture with them when they come home next week."

"How do you like the house?" He asked when the silence stretched too long. Then realized how lame the question was. She'd lived in this monster maze of rooms as a teenager.

"I'm still getting used to it. But right now, I'm trying not to get lost going from my bed to the bathroom. I've never slept in the master bedroom before. Mom and Dad took the guest suite."

Zack chuckled. "Well, I hope you drew a map. Otherwise, you could have dire consequences if you end up somewhere else."

A grin lit up her face. "Oh, so very true."

There were absolutely no signs of supper, but he smelled potatoes baking in the oven. Tracy's mother was a chef. What kind of cook was his hostess?

As the lag in the conversation stretched uncomfortably, he twisted his hat in his hand, wishing he'd left it in the truck. She must have noticed his fidgeting and jumped away from the island. "I'm sorry. You can stow your hat in the closet through here. I really need to get a rack for the entry." She led him into the mudroom and slid a door open. The coat closet was big and nearly empty. Reaching past her shoulder, he laid the old Stetson on a shelf. When she turned toward him, he brushed her breast with his upper arm, causing a flame to shoot through him.

Her thin sweater tightened over her pert breasts as she sucked in a deep breath, providing proof their proximity to each other affected her as powerfully as it did him. He pulled his gaze from her chest to lock with her eyes. They had darkened to a silvery blue, made more intense by the brilliant color of her top. Her breath hitched, and her eyes lowered to his lips. He knew what she wanted, because he wanted it even more.

Without thinking about exactly what he was doing, he lowered his lips to hers. His heart slammed into overdrive when she lifted her hands to his chest and moaned his name. He wrapped his hand around her nape and tilted her face to allow him better access to her mouth. When he traced her upper lip with his tongue, she drew in a breath and opened her mouth under his. He took the invitation by thrusting his tongue deeply into the warm sweetness.

As their tongues dueled, she wrapped her arms around his neck, bringing her body in full contact with his. She sucked on his tongue when he pressed his hard-on into her lower belly. Sweet mercy, he wanted to strip her right here and have his way with her on the cold tile floor of her mudroom. Damn the danger to his pride and self-respect.

And damn the alarm warning him to be careful.

But he couldn't forget their kids were upstairs. Somehow, somewhere, he found the control to back off and eventually break the kiss. Tracy opened her eyes and peered at him, dazed. She blinked a few times as he ran the back of his fingers over her cheek. He couldn't hold in the raspy laugh.

"What's funny?"

"You had that exact same expression on your face the very first time I kissed you." His voice seemed to come from his toes as he remembered their first kiss. He'd had no idea how innocent she was until that night. How could she still have that virginal look of awe?

Her cheeks turned a darker pink and embarrassment replaced the wonder, making her appear even more naive. "Is that a good thing?"

He continued to caress her cheek. "I don't know."

Her hold around his neck slackened as she slipped her hands from around his neck. She smoothed his shirt where her earlier kneading had wrinkled the chambray. Looking at her hands, she winced. "I'd better get the grill started. The potatoes should be done in thirty minutes."

She moved away without looking at him, leaving him feeling bereft. What the hell had happened to put such chill in the air? Wishing he could take her back into his arms, he swallowed as she moved through the kitchen.

Had she sensed the battle going on within him? Had reminding her of their early past upset her? Or was she expecting more than he could give? She couldn't expect him to simply forget about how she'd betrayed him, and he was a fool for giving in to the lust. But as she opened the French doors leading to the patio, he knew one kiss hadn't been enough. Whatever her motives were for getting involved with him again, he now had his own. He wouldn't stop until she was in his bed, but he'd never love her again.

He couldn't.

However, before anything could happen, they had to get through supper with their kids. "Tracy, wait."

She turned, and he crossed the kitchen to the open door. He saw the uncertainty in her expression. "Let me grill the steaks. That way you can finish with the rest of the meal."

He had no idea what he'd said, but her face beamed as she patted him on the chest and passed him to return to the kitchen. "That would be fantastic! There's the grill."

* * * *

"What's their names again?" Mandy got down on her knees in the middle of Bobby's bedroom to play with the dogs.

"The darker one is Ginger and the lighter brown one is Cinnamon. They belong to my grandma."

As Ginger licked her face, Mandy giggled. "We have a dog, too. Her name is Bailey. I want a kitty, but Daddy won't let me have one. Says we have too many barn cats already. I really like kitty-cats. Grandma Jackie has three."

Bobby liked Cinnamon and Ginger, but he'd like to have his own dog. The only pets he had were in a glass aquarium. "Hey would you like to see my frogs?"

"Sure." Mandy stopped playing with the dogs. She peered through the glass of the aquarium sitting on a stand by the windows of the big room. "Cool!"

"You like frogs?" He never played with girls, but Mandy was different. She didn't act like a girl. When they'd played at Uncle Dylan's wedding, he'd expected her to be a sissy. But he'd never forget what she looked like in that frilly dress when she followed him into the lake to play in the water--until her dad yelled at them to get out.

She looked over at him with a big gap-toothed grin. "Oh, yeah. Once I found one in Grandma's garden and picked it up." She shrugged and giggled. "I thought she'd scream her head off when I showed it to her. It was so funny."

Bobby matched her smile. "My aunt Charli hates 'em, too. She doesn't like snakes either. There's lots of snakes in the lake over on Butterfly. She wants Uncle Dylan to get rid of 'em, but he won't 'cause they eat mice and stuff like that."

"Do you like to ride?" Mandy asked after a few moments more of watching the three tropical frogs hanging on to the side of the glass.

"I--I never went riding." He wasn't going to tell her his dad didn't want him to learn to ride. "But Uncle Dylan is gonna teach me and give me a horse." He wanted his mom to get him a horse. His uncle Dylan had told him he'd teach him if his mom wouldn't. "I bet you have a pony."

She turned and leaned against the aquarium stand. "I have a horse, too. My daddy gave me Holly for Christmas last year. I got my pony Poppy for my birthday after we moved to Texas. Daddy's teaching me how barrel race on him. I'm gonna be in the rodeo at the fair next summer."

"Oh, wow." Sure, she could probably get whatever horse she wanted. The Cartwrights owned a horse ranch and her dad had been a rodeo cowboy. "Where'd you live before moving here?"

"Wyoming."

"Why'd you move?"

He watched Mandy lose her smile. "My momma went to live in heaven with Jesus."

"Oh. You mean she died?" She nodded, and he said, "I thought your dad and mom were divorced."

She shook her head. "But your momma and daddy are, right?"

"Yeah, they're divorced, and they hate each other. I live with my dad every other week. He's great." He thought about the football game when the other team was winning. His dad wasn't so great then. He'd threatened to take away all of his video games and told him he was playing like a baby. He hated when his dad got like that.

Mandy puckered her mouth as if she was thinking really hard. "I don't remember much about Momma anymore. We have pictures of her, but sometimes I forget things. I remember she'd take me to the park and play with me. I didn't see much of my daddy. He was a Marine and fought in the war."

"My uncle Dylan was in the Army, and Granddad Quinn was a general." Bobby couldn't imagine not being able to remember his dad, or never seeing him again. Or his mom. He'd really miss his mom if she ever went totally away. It made him sorry for the little girl. When she only nodded and continued to stare into the frog tank, he asked, "How old were you when your mom died?"

She glanced at him. "Almost four. She died in a car wreck. But now she's an angel in heaven and helps God take care of sick people. She was a nurse and that's what she does in heaven."

He didn't know much about angels. His mom took him to church on Sunday mornings when he was with her, but his dad didn't go to church. He didn't think Dad even believed in the stuff the preacher talked about. Bobby liked to think there was a heaven, but sometimes it all seemed too confusing.

Before he could show her his new Xbox game, she asked, "Do you think your momma will be my daddy's girlfriend?"

He sharpened his gaze on the girl. "What do you mean?"

"I think me and Daddy need a substitute momma. You know, like a substitute teacher. She could do my hair and teach me about girl stuff and play with me like my real momma did. My grandma tries when I'm with her and so does Amy--my other babysitter--but I'm not with them much when Daddy's at work. I'm in school or at the daycare."

"You want my mom and your dad to get married?"

"Yeah, I guess someday. I like your momma lots," she said softly after a while and turned toward the frogs again.

"I'd like my mom and dad to get back together. I don't like your dad."

She looked at him. "Why not? My daddy is nice. He gave you a football."

Bobby had expected Zack to ignore him, but Zack talked about the game at which he and his mom had sat together.

"You said your momma and daddy hate each other," she reminded him.

Bobby moved over to where his games were stored and wouldn't look at her. His mom wouldn't let him have his gaming system in his room, but he kept his favorite games on a shelf by his bed. Someday when his dad and mom got married again, he'd have a TV in his room like he did at Dad's house.

"I think my daddy likes your momma." Amanda's quiet voice broke into his thoughts. "I caught him looking at pictures last night. They were of him and Miz Tracy from before he and Momma were married."

"Yeah, I think they were boyfriend and girlfriend back when they were in high school or something." He didn't want to think about having Zack in his mother's life. "Let's go down to the lake out front. Maybe we can find some other neat stuff."

Mandy looked up at him and smiled toothlessly again. "Maybe we can find some more frogs."

He grinned and hoped her dad never found a substitute mom to teach her about girl stuff. He liked her exactly the way she was. "Yeah. Let's go before Mom gets dinner ready. Hopefully, she doesn't burn the steaks. She usually does."

Mandy giggled.

"You know my mom can't cook, don't you?" he asked as they left his room. Maybe then she'd see his mom wasn't right for the job she wanted for her.

"That's okay. My daddy's the best cook ever."

* * * *

Dinner was fantastic, despite the simple fare of baked potatoes, salad with store bought dressings and steak. Her mother's marinade, which Tracy had found relatively easy to make, and Zack's skill with the grill, made the steaks perfect. The night turned out pleasantly warm, and they ate on the wide flagstone patio by the pool.

Once they were finished eating, Bobby announced, "Mandy and me are going swimming."

Tracy finished her sweet tea and shook her head. "Not until you wait a little while."

"Maybe we can go find more frogs?" Mandy looked up at Bobby with hopeful, big blue eyes.

Bobby grinned at her and jumped out of his chair. "Okay!"

"Hold up there, you two." Zack gave Mandy a pointed look. "Miz Tracy has made a great dinner. I think it would be only fitting for us to clean up the dishes."

"Oh, Zack, you don't have to do that." Tracy stood and started gathering dishes.

Zack laid his hand over hers to cease her actions. The jolt it caused brought her up short, and she snapped her gaze to his. He must have felt it, too, because he smiled, causing even more frissons to quake through her. "It won't hurt them to help, and then we *all* can change and go swimming. By then the requisite half hour should be up."

She didn't miss the emphasis on the word all. Gulping at the thought of changing into her ratty old bathing suit, she could only nod. He continued to rest his hand on her forearm, the thumb making a slow circle on the inside of her arm. A mischievous glimmer showed in his eyes as if he could easily read her discomfort.

"Go change, Tracy. We've got this."

While the kids carted in the dishes from the patio table and Zack loaded them into the dishwasher, Tracy changed. She stared at her reflection and groaned. Her friend Mary Estrada, who after three children had packed on the weight, didn't understand Tracy's hang-ups over her skinny figure. Charli had pretty much said the same things Mary had when she'd tried to talk Tracy into wearing one of her skimpy dresses to the Fourth of July ball. Somehow, her new sister-in-law had managed to talk her into wearing a similar dress for the wedding.

How could they not see what Tracy saw when she looked in the mirror? The sharp angles of her face that made her nose too pointed and her cheeks too high. She only wore a double A cup bra--when she chose to wear one. Then there was the boyishness of her hips. They didn't know how relentlessly she had been tormented by the other kids while she lived in Germany, and how they'd called her names because of her crossed eyes.

She'd had several treatments for her eyes. For several months, she'd worn an eye-patch. Oh, yes, that had been fun. Then while in Germany, she'd had her first surgery because the eye-patch hadn't worked. For a year, she'd lived in relative normalcy, until the right eye had pulled to the inside again, then the left followed.

She'd undergone one more surgery after moving to Texas; fortunately that fixed her eyes.

After that nightmare, another had started. Her mouth was too small, the orthodontist had told her and her mother. Braces had been the only alternative to fix the overbite and make room for her permanent molars. She'd gone from being Wall-eyed Quinn to Metal Mouth in the space of three months.

All this on top of being cursed as the tallest girl in her junior and high schools. It hadn't helped she was also skinny, which had earned her the lovely nickname of Olive Oyl.

She'd been poked and prodded by several doctors over the years, but the conclusion had always been the same. Her thyroid worked just fine, but her mother was tall and thin, as was her maternal grandfather and his father. She'd never forget a more recent visit to the doctor when the nurse had told her she should stop complaining; most women would kill to have her skinny genes.

During the summer between her freshmen and sophomore years, she ate ice cream by the gallons, but it didn't help. When she'd mentioned to the wrong group of girls about her predicament, they'd turned on her, becoming jealous of her *unfair, supercharged metabolism.*

Girls were jealous of her for being skinny, while the boys thought she was too skinny.

She shuddered at the cruel memories. Her only salvation had been her brother. After he'd beaten a boy for making fun of her, kids weren't as loud about their taunts. However, they'd still made them, especially after Dylan, who was four years older, headed off to college.

She'd had one boyfriend before Zack. Derrick Marino had been a year older than her sixteen years, a junior, and had been very shy. Everyone considered him a geek, but he'd been nice to her, and she'd given him a chance. He'd taken her to the drive-in and seemed too nervous even to hold her hand. By their fifth date, he'd eventually kissed her. She'd been infatuated with Derrick and often daydreamed that he was *the one*.

For weeks, she'd practiced writing her name, Mrs. Derrick Marino, over and over along with little hearts in her notebooks. She'd imagined their wedding and their babies. He'd become an engineer, she'd be a doctor, and they'd live happily ever after.

The happily-ever-after had ended one very painful night at the drive-in.

"I've been meaning to ask." His voice cracked the way it did when he was nervous.

She smiled and nestled closer. Here it comes, she pathetically thought, he's going to ask me to wear his class ring. *"Yeah?"*

"Why don't you get a boob job?"

"What?" *She pulled away to stare at him.*

"You know what I mean. All the actresses are getting them nowadays. You could get one. Your family's rich enough."

Tracy bit her lip so hard she tasted blood as the memory played out to its terrible end. That had been the last date with Derrick. He'd called several times over the next few days, but she'd refused to talk to him. He'd tried to explain that he was sorry.

Yeah, right.

She was glad that he was balding, had gained a paunch, and at last report, had just divorced his second wife. But he'd become a petroleum engineer. He worked in Dallas and lived in the swanky suburbs, while she'd gained a reputation of being a cheater and gone nowhere in Colton.

She'd thought about having her breasts enlarged, but never had the money to go through with the surgery. Now, maybe she should think about it. Then she thought about some of the women she'd known who had boob jobs. Did she honestly want to look like them? No, she couldn't say she did. Besides, if she did have her breasts augmented, her already shaky reputation would be shot to hell and back.

She'd dated men since leaving Jake, but not seriously. In fact, most of them were nothing more than friends she'd meet up with when she'd go honky-tonk hopping. Of all the men she'd known over the years, only a handful had suggested more than a good time on the dance floor, but she'd always refused them.

Partly, because she wasn't that kind of girl, despite her earlier mistakes, and in part, out of fear of rejection once they saw her without her clothes and padded pushup bra.

A knock on her bedroom door startled her. "Mom?" Bobby's voice sounded from the other side. "Are you ready? We're waiting on you."

She swallowed down the bitterness caused by the years of feeling inadequate and ugly. "In a minute," she choked out and wiped at the moisture on her cheeks. "Go ahead and get in with Zack."

Turning away from the mirror, she glanced one last time at the image of her unremarkable body in the black one-piece. Suddenly, a different memory snuck up on her. Zack laid her down on an old quilt over the soft grass on a starry, warm, mid-September evening.

The golden-haired boy over her had promised not to hurt her as he slowly undressed her. He'd seemed to worship every uncovered area of skin, causing a plethora of new and exciting sensations with his hands and lips. When the time had come for him to enter her, he'd whispered in her ear, *"I'll never hurt you."*

And as he'd gently taken her to a place she'd never known existed, she'd almost believed he thought she was pretty.

"He loved you, Tracy! He wanted to marry you!" Logan's voice echoed in her mind from the day he'd come to her door with evidence of how much Zack had, indeed, loved her.

"No!" she said and held her baby boy against her breast. *"If he loved me, he'd have told me. He wouldn't have cheated on me!"*

"Cheated on you?*"*

"Jake caught him with Dawn Madison."

"Tracy, Dawn Madison is only a friend. Zack has no interest in her. Jake lied to you. Zack came over to the ranch to give you this, that day he caught you and Jake together." Logan pulled the most beautiful diamond ring from his pocket. *"My brother loved you. But you threw him away for a no-good grease monkey who publicly criticizes you and has done nothing but held you back."*

Taking a deep breath, she turned her back on the mirror and the ghosts it conjured. But two questions still rattled around in her mind like the chains of a phantom in a corny old movie.

What did Zack see in me to make him fall so deeply in love?

Can he still see it?

* * * *

Although he was thoroughly in the middle of the splashing, the dunking, and other pool antics with the kids, Zack somehow managed to take a long, hard look at his hostess. She walked from the French doors to the edge of the pool and slowly dropped the cover-up onto a chaise lounge.

The plain suit she wore would never be featured in *Sports Illustrated*. But there was something about the fluid motion of her willowy body slipping into the water and the swan-like grace of her strokes as she swam out to them that had Zack thinking about her without the suit.

Don't go there.

She stopped and straightened several feet from him. Water sluiced off her, and she wiped a hand over her face. She'd pulled her hair back into a ponytail and water glistened on her high cheeks and dripped off the point of her chin. She gave him a slight smile, then looked over at the kids.

"What are we going to do?"

"Let's play volleyball!" Bobby yipped and swam to the edge to grab the net setup.

Tracy smiled and looked at Mandy, who was treading water with the help of a Styrofoam noodle tucked under her arms. "Is that what you'd like to play?"

"Yeah. Can I be on your side, Tracy?"

"I'd love it if you were." Tracy gave his daughter a winning smile. "We girls gotta stick together."

"I can't get it." Bobby struggled with the end of the net. Zack swam over to the edge, and within moments, had it attached to the other end.

"Looks like it's you and me, buddy." Zack smiled at Bobby. He'd gotten the impression all evening the boy was less than happy at having him here.

"Okay." Bobby looked up at him. As Tracy retrieved a big beach ball from the diving end of the pool, he asked, "Did you really ride rodeo?"

"Yep. I've been riding horses since I was two years old."

"Not by yourself?" His hazel eyes--Jake's eyes--grew wide.

"I had a little pony that wasn't much bigger than a shepherd dog. My dad would lead me around on him. By the time I was four, I was riding on my own horse."

Tracy was back and spoke with Mandy, but her gaze surreptitiously met his.

"When I was about your age, I started riding broncos. About the same time, I started working for my dad and granddad, learning how to saddle train horses."

Bobby's brow pinched together as if he was deep in thought.

Zack said loud enough to ensure Tracy heard, "Maybe you could come over to the ranch sometime. You and your mom. We could go riding."

Bobby shook his head, looked at the surface of the water, and mumbled, "I don't know how to ride."

Zack glanced at Tracy, who was biting her lower lip. "That's okay. I could teach you. It's not hard."

Bobby met his grin with a wobbly smile. "I don't know."

"I think we'll need to think about it," Tracy chimed in and looked from Bobby to Zack. "Thank you for the offer, Zack."

"No problem." Zack shrugged. What the hell? Bobby didn't know how to ride? Tracy was an accomplished rider, and she'd always had access to the Ferguson horses even when Leon owned the place.

"Let's play!" Mandy chirped. "We girls are gonna beat the pants off y'all!"

Zack and Tracy both laughed, and Bobby teased, "No way, little girl."

Then Tracy served ball and the game began.

* * * *

After the very cutthroat volleyball game, which the girls won by one point, Tracy suggested the kids play Marco Polo. She and Zack got out. She made coffee and carried out two mugs to the wicker chair, where Zack settled in to watch their children frolic in the water.

Amanda's swimming ability had surprised her during the volleyball game. When she jumped into the deep end and swam across the pool chasing Bobby, Tracy commented, "Wow. She's quite a swimmer."

Zack sipped from his mug and nodded. "Yeah, she's part fish, I think." He sat the mug down on the small table between their chairs. "I'm glad Lance has a pool, or she'd be bugging me to put one in. Lisa had taken her to swimming lessons since she was a baby."

"I did that with Bobby, too." Tracy hugged her hands around the hot cup she held. Lisa...she always seemed to come up. Tracy knew Zack still missed his wife, but she wanted to know if he still loved her. Accepting that he wanted her only for sex was one thing, but if he was still in love with another woman, even a dead one, she'd never have a chance. "What was she like?"

He pulled his gaze from the kids and studied her. "Who?"

"Lisa."

"She was outgoing," he said in a low tone and looked back out at his daughter. "She was a nurse and a fantastic mother. She had to be--I was gone most of the time. I wasn't even there for Amanda's birth or the time she got her appendix out."

"That was when you were wounded, wasn't it?" She'd spent all evening trying not to let her gaze settle on the silvery puckered scar on his mid-abdomen where he'd been shot.

He looked at her again and nodded. "Yeah, Lisa had called me and told me she was taking Mandy to the hospital because she was afraid her appendix had burst. Mandy had woken up screaming her belly hurt." He paused and looked down at his hands in his lap. Tracy watched as he fisted one of them. "I wanted to be there so badly, if it had been possible, I would've gone AWOL. I'd already missed so much of her life. I hadn't been there for her birth because I was on a training mission. I missed her first words and steps because I was deployed to Iraq. Now, she was sick, and instead of being home, I was watching supply trucks roll through the checkpoint at Peshawar on the Afghan-Pakistani border.

"Finally, one rolled in and exploded. Guerrilla soldiers swarmed us, and I was shot in the gut. Dennis, one of my fellow Marines, pulled me to the safety of a rock. But we had been followed, and that Taliban bastard shot Dennis in the chest. The only good thing out of it was Dennis got a shot off, too." Zack paused and took a long draw on his coffee cup. She flinched at the haunted shadows in his blue eyes. "If he hadn't risked his life, I'd be dead."

Zack looked out at Mandy again playing in the pool and murmured, "I wish I could turn back time. I'll never..."

She wished she could give all those early experiences with Amanda back to him. She understood, because her father hadn't been around for so many of her milestones. "Zack, you're here now for her when she really needs you."

"I know." He shook his head. "I should never have re-enlisted after my four years were up. I wouldn't have been there. Dennis wouldn't be dead, and... Well..." His smile looked pasted on. "Nothing will change the past."

No wonder Zack understood Dylan's post-traumatic stress so well. "True."

He looked away and murmured, "I just wish I'd realized that years ago."

As she watched the way his jaw clenched, something else he'd said to her from a meeting a year ago in his office when she'd gone to pick up Dylan came to mind.

"For me it was an IED packed in a supply truck. I blamed myself when I came home for not checking out the truck better. Then an argument over stupid stuff from the past and a drunk driver crossing a double yellow line killed my wife. I can imagine what Dylan is going through. I was wounded and came back only to have my wife killed six months later, leaving me a single father of a four-year-old baby girl. I blamed everyone and anyone while I tried to crawl into a bottle of whiskey, but I could never bring Lisa back."

Tracy looked out at the pool. Bobby tagged Mandy in their Marco Polo game. The floodlights had long ago come on, with a mass of moths and gnats swarming around the bright bulbs.

She turned back to Zack and found him staring down at his fisted hands. Although she wanted him to open up, she knew now wasn't the time, nor was he ready. "That was really nice of you to invite Bobby out to the ranch."

He seemed to pull himself from some dark place and looked at her. "The invitation was for you, too. I'm hoping you'll let me reciprocate the time we had tonight. I don't have a pool, but I think Bobby would have fun. I can't believe he doesn't know how to ride. I could teach him. I still have old Grasshopper. He's the gentlest horse in Texas."

Tracy ached at the realization Zack wanted to spend time with her and Bobby, but she couldn't risk Jake using the invitation against her in his ridiculous custody case. "I'll have to get back with you. I'm not sure about Bobby's football schedule." She told a boldfaced lie and hated it.

He stared at her for a few moments, as if searching for something. "Okay. The invitation is open. Maybe some time you'd like to come over and go riding--without Bobby."

Her heart slammed against her ribs so hard she figured he had to hear the thumping. "Okay," she heard herself say.

His eyes burned under the dim lighting reaching them from the floods. The left side of his mouth twisted upward. "Good. Perfect."

They drank their coffee and found a safe topic in talking about the kids and the return of Dylan and Charli from their three-week honeymoon--which had undoubtedly been more like a family vacation since they had their teenage ward, Annie, with them.

When Mandy and Bobby finally got out of the pool, Zack sat his empty cup on the table. "Mandy and I should be heading home. I have to work tomorrow."

The evening had been too magical. Tracy didn't want Zack and Mandy to go.

After they changed back into their clothes, Tracy walked Zack out onto the front porch. While the kids ran off toward his truck, chattering about what they would do during their next visit, he held back and turned to her. "Thanks for dinner. We had fun."

"We did, too."

"You know what's happening here, don't you?"

A thrill ran through her, so electrifying it curled her toes. Did she dare hope? She hadn't missed that he hadn't told her much about Lisa; in fact, he could have been talking about anyone with his few words. "I think so."

Zack feathered her cheek with the backs of his fingers. The porch light couldn't hide the blaze in the dark depths of his blue eyes. He leaned in and kissed her lightly on her lips, instantly igniting Tracy's own need.

"I don't think you really do, Tracy. I'm not looking for another wife. I had one. I'll never fall in love again. Ask yourself if you can live with that because I can't--I won't--give you more than sex."

His husky words extinguished the fire as effectively as being dunked into a pool of icy water.

Tracy couldn't respond. He turned and took the porch steps two at a time. Bobby came back up the steps and looked up at her. She watched Zack drive the big truck down the driveway and over the bridge that straddled Oak Springs Creek.

"Mom?"

She turned from Zack's disappearing taillights. "Yes, sweetheart?"

"Are you and Zack gonna get married?"

Rattled by Zack's proclamation, Bobby's question only turned the shock into an ache. "It's too soon for questions like that, Bobby."

"Mandy likes you."

She nodded and ruffled her son's brown hair. "Yeah, I know. Do you like Zack?"

He wavered for a moment, then nodded as he bit on his bottom lip in a perfect imitation of her. "I guess."

She turned away from him and thought about Zack's painful words. It would hurt too much to be with him.

"Zack didn't care that I didn't win the volleyball game. Dad would've been mad as heck."

"Oh, sweetheart." She took him into her arms. Zack was a wonderful father. He provided prudent guidance where it really mattered, he praised accomplishments, and he cared, but he never held his acceptance and approval over a child's head.

Zack was the kind of father Bobby needed.

"Mandy wants a mother," Bobby said when she let him go.

"What do you mean?"

With his head down, he shrugged and bit his lower lip again. She got the impression he wished he'd kept his mouth shut.

She didn't push. Tracy already knew what he'd meant.

Two children caught in Fate's vicious games and people's stupid mistakes. How far was she willing to go to get back what had been taken away?

Did she honestly believe she had an ice cube's chance in the center of the sun of making Zack fall in love with her again?

Maybe there was only one way to find out.

Chapter 10

Zack poured his second cup of coffee and prayed the day would be a good one. He hadn't slept the night before. Instead, he'd spent the night thinking about the evening with Tracy.

What kept him up wasn't the amazing time he'd had sharing a meal and playing in the pool, or even the fireworks that had gone off when he'd kissed her. The things plaguing him were his parting words and the reason he'd said them.

I'm not looking for another wife. I had one. I'll never fall in love again.

They went far deeper than letting her know where she stood because he'd never forgive her. Maybe if they had been spoken for that reason, he wouldn't feel like a fresh pile of horseshit. He'd said them to remind himself that he could never feel more than lust for Tracy.

He carried his cup from the kitchen into the living room. The room, like the rest of the house, was large, but the design and the decor weren't fancy or formal. The house was over 140 years old and made of logs and limestone. The interior was white painted plaster, exposed ceiling beams, and solid oak and stone floors so old his great-great-great grandparents had walked on them.

He stopped at the floor-to-ceiling windows overlooking the land making up his share of the CW Ranch. In the distance, Oak Springs Creek cut through a pasture and acted as the boundary between his and his cousin's half to the south. The sun was coming over the massive oak trees lining the creek. Bordering Lance's half of the CW was Oak Springs Ranch; Butterfly Ranch bordered his. Originally, the tract of land had covered about one hundred-twenty-thousand acres, nearly one hundred-ninety square miles. All the land of Forrest County, Texas.

He sipped his coffee, looking out over more pasture and past the barn. Out there was the lake where he'd first made love to Tracy, probably his favorite spot on the whole ranch. Yet, he'd never taken Lisa to the lake during the times they'd visited his family. Nor had he ever considered moving her into this house after his grandfather's death when he'd inherited it.

He'd never told Lisa much about Tracy, but she knew he'd loved her. His late wife had been jealous of the woman who had stolen his heart when he was nothing more than a boy. What about Tracy had always intrigued him so damned much? She wasn't centerfold gorgeous--far from it, but something about her made her beautiful, an inner brilliance that out-shined many of the Hollywood sex goddesses.

When he'd first fallen in love with her, she'd been as skittish as a range-raised filly. To his surprise, in many ways she still was. Tracy had never been like the girls and women he'd dated--or the one he'd married. It had taken him months of making love to her before she'd finally believe him her small breasts, bony hips, or *spaghetti* legs, as she called them, hadn't repulsed him. To his surprise, Lisa had been a virgin, too, when they'd first made love, but he'd never had to convince the former pageant queen of her beauty.

He turned away from the windows, and the mantle on the adjacent wall caught his attention. A painting of the founder of CW Ranch, Cole Cartwright, and his wife Isabelle, hung on the rough river rock chimney. Dressed in a dark suit of the time, Cole made an imposingly tall image. Seated in the foreground was a beautiful blond woman in a deep blue gown that matched her eyes. Cole and his wife sat with their backs to the pasture he could see out the windows. Not much had changed in the landscape since 1867, except that it had contained countless longhorns. Now some of his horses grazed on that grass.

Zack had heard their story since he was a toddler. He'd even believed he could follow in the footsteps of his famous ancestor and learn to love his wife after the wedding. It was no secret in the family that Cole and Belle hadn't loved each other when they'd married. Cole offered her marriage instead of hanging her on the old oak tree in front of the present day courthouse for robbing the stagecoach. Somehow, they'd eventually fallen in love and had eight children by the time they'd died after the turn of the twentieth century.

He looked from his ancestors to a photograph of Lisa holding a place of honor next to numerous shots of Mandy on the oak plank mantle. He picked up the frame and looked down into the face of the woman who'd loved him with all her heart.

However, he could never give her more than a tiny part of his.

He set the mug on the mantle and gingerly ran his fingertips over her face. She'd been so beautiful and full of life. He would never forget the argument that took that life away.

"Your aunt Winnie called today." Lisa placed a plate of pork chops on the kitchen table of the small house they'd purchased in Cheyenne after he'd left the Marines.

After shaking the snow off his coat, he shucked out of it and hung it on a peg by the door. "What did she have to say?"

Lisa flitted over and straightened the collar of his police uniform. He had to bend to receive her kiss on the lips. "She just wondered how we were. Asked if we were coming home for Thanksgiving. Apparently, she's planning some shindig. The whole family will be there. I think it would be good to go to Texas this year. I don't see enough of your family. She also said your dad is thinking about retiring and wants to discuss your taking over the ranch with you. I really think you should consider it. I'd love to move there. My parents will have a fit, but--"

He moved past her and tossed his keys on the kitchen counter, but instead of sitting down to eat the supper his wife had prepared, he headed into the small bedroom they'd converted into an office. For his bottle of whiskey.

"Zack?" She followed him. "Supper's ready. Where're you going?"

He pulled the bottle from a bottom drawer of the desk and poured a tumbler three fingers full. "I'll never live in Texas. Logan can have the ranch. I don't want it."

"Why not?" Lisa demanded and moved into the dark room.

The only lighting came from the streetlight through the window and the rectangle of the open door. She switched on the desk lamp. The harsh light made him squint, and he turned away.

"You hate living here," she said to his back. "I worry about you. The nightmares are getting worse. I think it's your being a cop. It's too much like being an MP and reminds you of the war. I can get a nursing job anywhere, and Mandy would be better off in that little town than here."

He downed the whiskey and poured another, then stared out at the snow falling in the small front yard. He didn't need more liquor and was already halfway drunk from stopping at the beer joint on the way home, but he had to have it. These days the whiskey was all that got him through the day and night.

"Zack?"

"*Leave me the hell alone, Lisa.*" He turned on her. "*I'm not moving to Texas. So, forget it. I don't care what happens to the ranch. After what happened with her--*"

He realized what he'd said a second too late. Lisa flinched as if he'd slapped her. At last, she put her hands on her hips. "*Fine. Are you going to eat tonight or are you going to drink all night?*"

Zack slammed down the glass so hard on the desk, whiskey sloshed all over the sides. He was as irritated with himself as he was with her. Tracy never kept poking and prodding like Lisa did. Tracy had known when to leave him alone and when he needed to talk. Tracy. She was coming to mind more and more these days, especially after he'd heard from his brother she'd been divorced from Jake for almost two years. "*Dammit! Can't a man come home from a crappy day at work and have some peace and quiet?*"

"*No!*" she'd yelled back. "*Zack, I can't go on like this. I know something's changed in you.*"

"*Yes, something changed. I watched my friend get killed as he saved my life. I should be the one dead!*"

"*It's been six months and you're still blaming yourself for something you couldn't have prevented.*" She'd moved around the desk to stand before him. Her voice softened. "*Maybe you shouldn't have taken the job with the police force.*"

"*You're the one who talked me into it!*"

"*I know, but maybe it was too soon...Maybe moving back to Texas--*"

"*What the hell do you want? I told you I will never go back there. I can't. Not while she's--*"

Lisa stepped back and stared up at him. "*What kind of hold does she have over you? I forgave you for calling out her name when you woke up in Germany...*" Her eyes widened and her voice shook. "*You're still in love with her, aren't you? Have you ever loved me at all? I believed when you didn't say the words first that was just who you are. You'd only say them back to appease me. But you've never said them first because you never really felt them.*"

The stricken expression and the tears she was trying to hold back twisted his gut. But he didn't deny the accusation, because he knew she was right. He'd never stopped loving Tracy Quinn.

She stepped away and straightened her shoulders. "*I love you, Zack, but I can't compete with a memory anymore. I've been doing it for too long. Mandy is afraid of you. That's why she stays with Mom so much.*

You come home and sulk in here, drinking whiskey until you pass out. I'm leaving until you decide what you want--me and your daughter...or her."

Lisa packed a suitcase, got into her car and headed for her parents' ranch sixty miles north of Cheyenne.

All Zack remembered thinking, as he'd watched her taillights disappear in the gloom outside the office window, was how relieved he was their marriage was finally over.

Banging at the door jolted him out of the agonizing memory. He put the frame back and went out to the entry. Expecting one of his ranch hands, he was surprised to find Lance when he opened the door.

His cousin gave him a solemn look. "We've got trouble."

"What kind of trouble?"

"I think it's better if I show you."

"Okay, but I can't leave Mandy alone." Zack headed into the big, open kitchen.

"Aunt Jackie's on her way, along with Uncle Luke." Lance followed Zack.

That got Zack's attention. His parents lived about a mile down the road in a house one of his other ancestors had built. They never came to his place in the morning. He didn't press Lance on the matter. He didn't want to know what other disaster had befallen the ranch. "You want some coffee?"

"Sure." Lance helped himself and looked Zack over from head to toe. He lowered his mug after sipping from it. "Have a rough night?"

Zack sharpened his gaze on him. "What makes you think that?"

Lance raised a brow. "Well, for one thing, you didn't shave, *Sheriff.* Second, you're wound too tight to look this bad from a night of wild sex."

"I think you need to mind your own damned business." Zack crossed the kitchen to return to the living room where he'd left his mug. His family didn't know much about his marriage to Lisa, and he wanted to keep it that way. Lance's footsteps echoed across the stone floor and through the archway onto the wood floor of the living room.

"She was a beautiful woman."

Zack hadn't even realized he was staring at the picture of his dead wife until Lance's comment pulled him back. He glanced over his shoulder to find Lance standing behind him. "Yes, she was."

A comforting hand landed on his shoulder. "You miss her."

Zack wanted to shake off his cousin and tell him he didn't need his comfort or his sympathy.

"Zack, if you have a chance at happiness again, take it. Tracy's a good woman."

Tracy. She was the reason everything had happened.

"Lance." He shook off his cousin. "Let it alone."

"No, I can't." Lance set his mug on the coffee table and stepped in front of Zack. "You loved that girl. She ripped you up one side and down the other when she cheated on you, but you bounced back eventually. You found another woman who loved you, and who you would've given up everything for. But she's gone. You've grieved for two years. It's time to move on."

Zack's back teeth clenched tight enough his jaw hurt. He gritted out, "Whatever happens between Tracy *Parker* and me is my damned business, understand? I'm not in the market for another wife. So, drop it."

He walked away from Lance, heading for his office.

"I can't."

Zack turned at the archway and glared at his cousin.

Lance tucked his thumbs into the pockets of his designer suit pants. He'd obviously been on his way to his Dallas office. The lawyer never rested. "Because for almost a year, you've been doing everything you can to avoid the fact you're lonely. You have no life outside of Mandy, the ranch, and playing lawman. You're a workaholic, but the stress is starting to show. Mandy's with your mom more than she's with you. You're over your head with the mess Leon Ferguson made, and now we have a rash of cattle rustling. I'm not going to mention the half-assed attempt you're making at running this ranch. You aren't happy. We all see it. And we have all seen the flames. You want Tracy. Go after her before it's too late."

Zack turned to walk away. He'd heard enough.

"Twelve years ago, I almost threw away a chance at having a wonderful life. I was playing one sister against the other. I knew they both were in love with me, and I was living it up. It took Audrey getting pregnant to make me see what I almost lost."

"Do you have a point to all this?" Zack asked without turning. He wasn't about to mention how his cousin broke Rachel McPherson's heart by choosing her older sister over her.

Or Lance's own half-assed running of the CW. If Audrey didn't manage his share, he'd have gone belly-up years ago.

"We all make mistakes. Don't let something Tracy did fourteen years ago cloud your decisions now."

Zack didn't respond. He couldn't tell Lance he had every intention of getting involved with Tracy, but not as a possible a wife. She had something he wanted, although he could never give her more than what he was taking.

When the front door opened, Zack's parents rushed into the front entry.

"I hope to hell you finally got those fillies out there on the north pasture branded," Zack's dad said and ripped his hat off his head.

"No, Tate and I are planning on doing it when I get the time." A feeling of dread settled deep in Zack's stomach at the red creeping up his father's weathered neck.

"Luke, remember your blood pressure." His mother rested a hand on his arm.

He shook off the hand and scowled at her, then he slapped his old straw cowboy hat on his thigh. "Goddammit, boy! As if that fence being down wasn't enough to get your ass in gear. No need for branding those fillies now, 'cause they're gone."

* * * *

Crouching so he could get a closer look, Zack stared at the tire tracks and wondered how no one had seen or heard anything. As best he could determine, the thieves had used two full-sized livestock trucks to steal the mares. The fences that he and Logan had spent all day last Saturday replacing were cut, as was the one on Estrada's side. The mares had been herded through the fences and a break in the fencerow where he and Logan had cut down a lightning-damaged mesquite. The horses had then cut through the pasture of the Estrada ranch. At the road, they were loaded into the trucks.

Dawn Madison headed toward him, and he stood. She'd spent the past hour interviewing the Estradas' only ranch hand.

"Did Billy see anything?" he asked.

Zack expected what the answer was before she even spoke. "No. He claims he was over at Jesse Reilly's, playing poker all night. And the Estradas were in Albuquerque looking at condos. They just got back, and Luis was fussing up a storm about his cut fences and the mess the front yard was in from the thieves driving the trucks over it to load the horses."

Zack glanced away from the deputy. Thunderbolt, the big paint stallion, watched from a distance. His ears pointed up, and every once in a while he'd toss his head. Three other horses watched them as well, although they didn't seem as brave as Thunderbolt. They were well-trained quarter horse geldings, but Zack knew they would have been worth almost as much as any one of his young mares.

He narrowed his eyes on his neighbor's four horses. "Notice anything strange?"

"Yeah, the thieves didn't take Estrada's horses." Dawn bobbed the brim of her tan Stetson at the paint. "That old horse there is worth a small fortune. My brother Talon said he was a rodeo bronc."

"Possibly the thieves didn't know. Hell, I didn't know that until recently."

Dawn smiled and shrugged. "You only had to ask Luis."

"Well, that doesn't help me figure out who stole my horses." He looked over the pasture his horses had been driven through. Estrada's hundred-acre ranch had originally belonged to the CW, but had been chiseled off as a wedding gift to one of Zack's female ancestors. Mrs. Estrada was distantly related to Zack in some convoluted fashion.

He studied the hoof prints in the loose dirt of the yard, but he wasn't a skilled enough tracker to determine much of anything.

"We'll have to call the Rangers," Dawn said after a few moments. "Let them get someone in here. I'll also get a team together to comb this place for evidence."

"Yeah." Zack took off his hat to beat against his thigh, instantly reminding himself of his father, and set it back on his head. "I'm the damned sheriff! Things like this aren't supposed to happen to me."

Dawn laughed. "I'd beg to differ. When Daddy was the sheriff he had cattle rustled all the time. He also had his hunting dog and an old Buick stolen."

He looked at her and grinned. "Your brother Talon and his other brother Darryl Blackwell rustled the cattle. They sold them and used the money for a wild time up in Dallas. The dog ran away. And Jake Parker and I *borrowed* the Buick. Your dad got it back..." He added with a wince at the memory. "In almost the same condition as we'd borrowed it."

"Suppose this isn't related to the cattle rustling. Maybe someone just wanted to pull a prank on you. Besides, as you pointed out, Estrada still has his horses."

"Deputy Madison, if you really believe that crock of bullshit, I think you should turn in your badge right now."

A slow grin curled her lips. "Of course I don't, but someone wanted to get back at you for something." She held up her hand in a good imitation of a traffic cop, to forestall his retort. "Look. I haven't forgotten the other rustlings. But you have to admit something about this sinks of rotten eggs." She pointed to the horses in Estrada's pasture. "If they weren't just targeting you, Estrada would be four horses short today."

"Maybe they didn't have any room on their trucks. Twenty horses are a lot for two trucks," he countered. "Or they wanted my thoroughbreds instead."

She shrugged, and before he could gather enough steam to explode, added, "You weren't playing Texas Hold 'Em again, were you?"

He glared at his deputy--and friend. Dawn always teased him when they were alone--and when he started to lose perspective, which meant he was starting to act like a jackass.

They had known each other since they were both in diapers. In some ways, she was the sister he'd never had. Her grandmother had worked as a housekeeper for his grandparents until they'd both died. Her grandfather, *Chief* Madison, had been his grandfather's unofficial adopted brother and his head foreman for forty years, until he retired. When Zack's great-grandfather had died, he'd deeded off five thousand acres to him. Dawn's father, the former sheriff, had raised fine Angus cattle on the grassland, and when a heart attack forced him to quit ranching, he divided the place up among his three children.

Besides their families being close, they had spent years riding the same rodeos together. She'd been a champion barrel racer back then. Her older half-brother, Talon Blackwell, and younger brother, Hunter Madison, still rode the circuit. However, Dawn had lost interest in the rodeo. She'd studied criminal justice at college, and after graduation, gone to the police academy in Austin. She'd wanted to be a cop like her dad, who'd been the first Native American to ever be elected sheriff of Forest County. Dawn made it no secret she'd like to not only be the next Indian to get the job if Zack chose to leave it, but also be the first woman to be elected as well. However, she wouldn't run against Zack; he was positive of that.

He'd be the first to admit, she was more qualified for the job than he was, and he valued her opinions. She'd worked as a vice cop on the Dallas PD for a while until a drug bust went sour and she'd been shot. Now, she was Zack's lieutenant.

"I haven't played poker in years," he said, going along with the taunt. "But I was called out to break up a fight your granddad started at a high stakes game at O'Donnell's Bar and Grill a few weeks ago. He swore retribution."

"If you think Chief had anything to do with this, you should turn in *your* badge, Sheriff," she said smugly. Everyone in the community called the old Comanche *Chief*, including his grandchildren.

The paint curiously watched them from only a few yards away.

Zack laughed and put his hands on his sides above his service belt. "I don't understand it. Rustlers usually steal either cattle or horses, but seldom do they mix what they take."

"I've noticed something else." Dawn looked in the direction of the Estradas' home and barn off in the distance. "Whoever did this must have been watching the Estradas. Otherwise, how would they have known they'd be gone, and Billy, too? As serious as these guys are, I can't imagine them risking being heard. Driving those horses through that pasture would've made some noise."

He considered what she'd said for a moment. "I've also seen a pattern. They're taking livestock that has only recently been purchased or haven't been branded." Damn, he'd had plenty of time in the past month to freeze-brand his horses. He'd simply procrastinated too long, and now, he was branded a fool.

"That's probably the real reason they didn't take Estrada's horses. Or the fortune my cousin and I have grazing over by the cliffs off Gambler's Folly." He and Lance had three hundred head of Santa Gertrudis breeding stock in a pasture near the county road bordering the entire front of the ranch. The rustlers could have easily pulled up near the fence, cut it and herded them in. However, those cattle were registered, branded and had been owned by them for over a year.

"Good point. But the cattle taken off Oak Springs weren't newly purchased."

"No, but those steers have changed hands. They went from belonging to Leon Ferguson to being jointly owned by Dylan and Charli Quinn under their new brand--Butterfly Springs Cattle Company. It might be to our benefit to stake out some of the locals who have bought livestock within the past six months. Put Kennedy in charge of getting a team together. If they follow their pattern, they won't strike again until later in the week. And let Herb know what we've discovered."

She acknowledged the order and looked over his neighbor's pasture. "Have you contacted the Quinns about their cattle yet?"

"No. Tracy and her parents asked me not to, and since they haven't had any other cattle stolen, I decided to let it ride until they return."

Dawn frowned and wouldn't look at him.

"What is it?"

She took a deep breath and met his gaze. "If you get involved with Tracy again, you're crazy. She ripped you apart."

"Well, it's a good thing that's my damned business, then, isn't it?" What the hell was wrong with everyone butting into his life? Halfway to his horse, he turned. "Call in the Rangers, Deputy Madison. I want my horses back." Zack pushed his hat back and swung up into the saddle, gave the big Appaloosa stallion some rein, and took off at a run.

Chapter 11

Zack entered the reception area of Tracy's salon late Monday morning. At the tinkling of the bell over the door, Tracy's voice chimed from a room on the right. "I'll be right there."

He removed his hat. "Okay."

Turning around, he looked over the fussy room. Prints of Victorian ladies, most of them seated before mirrors, hung in a grouping on one wall. Gilt framed mirrors hung on another. Frilly curtains dressed the windows. Cabinets held knick-knacks and styling supplies. Even the tops were covered with fake ivy with white Christmas lights strung through it. One of those obnoxious smelling jar candles burned on the edge of the antique desk she used as a reception counter. He wrinkled his nose at the cloying scent.

Damn, the place reminded him an old-time bordello. A scene flashed through his mind of him ambling in like some gun-slinging sheriff of the Wild West. Tracy, dressed in a black and red corset, garter belt and silk stockings, lounged on the old desk. All long legs and wanton invitation. Her hair was done up in big curls and held high on her head, just waiting to be set free to tumble down around her shoulders.

Laughter from the inner room scattered the vision like a bullet to a mirror, leaving Zack grasping for reality.

Shacking off the last shards of the fantasy, he twisted his hat in his hand in front of him, glad he had it. The only place to sit was a fancy couch with big pink roses on the delicate-looking fabric. He sat and heard another voice in the inner room. "Thanks so much, my dear."

"I'm glad you like it, Mrs. Pratt," Tracy replied. "And thank you for the contact at the college. I'll give them a call."

Zack groaned. Aida Mae Pratt was as notorious a gossip as his aunt. He glanced at the door. Could he sneak out before she knew he was here?

"You do it, dear. That little apartment upstairs would be perfect for college students," the old widow and boarding house proprietor said. "Well, I'll be going. I think that was the sheriff I heard out there."

Too late.

When the women came out of the room, which Zack figured must be where Tracy worked her magic on the hair of the county's women, he stood and pasted on a smile. Unable to bear the hopefulness Tracy couldn't quite mask, he tipped his head to the older woman. Her too-blonde hair was piled high on her head. "Mrs. Pratt, how're you doing?"

"I'm fine, Sheriff. Thanks for asking. I heard about those rustlers taking your horses."

Good to see the Grapevine was working just fine. He glanced at Tracy, who was busy ringing up the service on an antique cash register. "Yes, well, the department has it under control." He looked at Tracy again. "In fact, that's why I stopped by. I wanted to make sure everything was secure out on Butterfly and Oak Springs."

He watched the hopeful glint brighten in her eyes. If he was a smart man, he wouldn't touch her ever again. He'd never used a woman. He'd had his share of flings and one-night stands, but those women hadn't been looking for hearts and flowers out of the encounters either. It didn't take a brilliant strategist to determine Tracy was shooting for much more out of this, whatever the hell *this* was, than he could give her. But just what did she want? The question was like an echo off the limestone cliffs that cut across the eastern edge of Lance's half of the ranch. Over and over again it kept bouncing back at him.

Tracy finished cashing in Mrs. Pratt's twenty. "Yes, I think Tom and the boys have everything under control."

Mrs. Pratt watched them intently enough to make Zack tighten the grip on his hat. "I was tickled pink when Charli and Dylan got together. Amazing how things worked out."

Zack's brow shot up, and he cocked a lopsided grin when he noticed the furrowing of Tracy's brow as she narrowed her eyes on her customer. Aida Mae made it no secret that she disliked Dylan Quinn.

"Well," Aida went on as she put her change away into one of those fanny packs attached to the leather belt of her tight jeans, "I've got to get going and get the noon meal on. Go ahead and schedule me with Melissa for the next time. I always thought Buck got the bastard's end in his divorce to that gold-digger he married. Glad to see at least one of his girls hasn't forgotten their daddy in his hour of need."

"I'm glad you're giving Melissa a chance. Will one o'clock on Thursday be okay?"

"Yep, works for me." Smiling broadly, she looked from Zack to Tracy again and waved as she headed out the door. "Y'all have a great afternoon."

Tracy wrote the appointment in her book and called a farewell. She crossed her arms over her chest, then uncrossed them. After clearing her throat, she asked, "How many horses did they take?"

"Twenty. Those thoroughbred mares I told you about. They drove them over Luis Estrada's place to get to them to their trucks."

"I'm so sorry. You were planning on breeding them, weren't you?" She bit her lower lip and her eyes took on a silvery color.

He nodded, moved around the end of the desk, and tossed the hat on the top beside the register. Her breathing caught and then sped up as he invaded her space.

"Do you have any more customers?"

* * * *

Tracy's body reacted to the possibility of him coming on to her the moment she'd heard his husky voice. She swallowed hard and shook her head. "I don't. Melissa will be in at one. I usually take Monday afternoons off to do my books."

"I was hoping you could keep me company this afternoon." He skimmed his fingers over her cheek.

Her insides, heating up like lava under the surface of the earth, pooled in her low belly. Her lips parted.

Against her lips, he whispered, "Tracy, I want you."

She had thought of little else since he'd left her standing on her porch Friday night. He was asking her to enter into a sexual relationship without any hope of a future--without love.

But she was already in love with Zack.

Both of their kids would benefit from them being together. Hadn't that been what she'd decided while she tossed and turned in her big, empty bed?

With her gaze locked on his, she murmured, "I want you, too, but I have a stipulation."

He leaned back. "What is it?"

"I'm no one's fuck-buddy, Zack. I know what my reputation is in this town, but it's all wrong." She swallowed her rapidly thumping heart back into place. "I'll only go through with this, if you promise to treat me as a serious girlfriend. That means we date, we visit with our families and we share our kids." When his expression hardened, she quickly added, "Mandy likes me. And I adore her. I'd like to bring her here, to the shop, for a few hours and play. And take her shopping. I know your mom tries, but she's busy with her foundations and charities she does for the Junior League."

The breath she sucked in was full of Zack's scent of sage and leather. "Meanwhile, you can teach Bobby how to ride and maybe take him to the sheriff's department and show him around. Jake won't like it, but I'll deal with him." Having laid her demands out on the proverbial table, she held her breath, waiting for him to tell her what she could do with herself. After all, a man of Zack's caliber could have any damned woman he wanted. Tracy was just handy, and according to the gossip of her ex-husband and mother-in-law, she was easy.

He studied her for a few moments. "That's more than one stipulation."

"Take it or leave it."

"Tracy, it won't change what I told you Friday night. I'm never getting married again."

His words stung as much now as they had the other night, but she didn't show him how much. She kept her face determined, as if she were haggling over one of his horses, rather than her body and soul.

"Fine. But I'm not a floozy. Yes, I've made mistakes. But I have my son to consider. And I'd hope you'd feel the same about Mandy. They're bound to see us together. What do you plan on telling your six-year-old daughter when she asks about me? That I'm your friend with benefits? I know that *isn't* what I want to be teaching my son." Moreover, she didn't want to give credence to Jake's claim that she had no sexual morals.

"Okay," he said at last. "We'll play the game your way." He pressed her against him. "Luck would have it I'm off this afternoon, too. I've already put in sixteen hours."

When his lips captured hers, she knew she'd made a pact with the devil, but she couldn't stop the elation surging through her. There was something he wanted from her. Sex was a big portion of it, but something else kept Zack from walking away and hooking up with any one of the many available women in town.

He tilted her head with his hands on either side of her face, and she opened completely to him. He plunged into her mouth, drank in her will to fight along with her breath, and left her trembling and weak-kneed.

Breathing harshly, he pulled back. "When do you have to get Bobby to his practice?"

"Five-thirty." She somehow managed to breathe out.

The sexy grin sent a quake through the heat building pressure in her lower regions. He caressed her cheeks with his thumbs. "Let's go out to the ranch. Mandy goes to the daycare after school, and I don't need to pick her up until five. I can drive you back to get your car."

"I'll follow you."

She was too far gone not to go through with this, but she wanted her own car so she could leave when she wanted to.

He kissed her nose and chuckled. "Alright."

"Zack, there's something you..." She paused to search his eyes and bit hard on her lower lip.

"Tracy, if you don't want to do this now, I'll understand."

She shook her head. "It's not that. I'm not taking anything. Birth control, I mean."

The furrow of his brow told her he was surprised. He heaved in a long breath. "Well, I guess I'd better stop for condoms then. I'll run over to Hamilton, because I can't get them in this county without everyone knowing about it before you even have your first orgasm."

Heat burned her cheeks at the picture he presented.

He produced a ring of keys from his pocket, removed one of them and held the key toward her. "This will open the mudroom door, beside the garage. Go in and make yourself at home."

Yeah, right.

She gingerly accepted the key as if it was a poisoned dart. "Okay."

He picked his hat up from the desk, but before setting it on his head, he drew her to him again with his free hand on her waist. This kiss was lighter, teasing and promised delights to come. When he pulled back, he left her wanting to strip him right there and have her way with him. Without saying a word, he smiled, settled the Stetson on his head and left.

Tracy watched the door close, the tinkling bell giving a cheerful good-bye. To her it was the harbinger of doom.

What the hell was she doing?

* * * *

Tracy slowed down as she came to the turn-off for Oak Springs Road. She should just go home and forget this whole crazy thing. Her heart was bound to be broken.

She stared at the sign for the county road named for the creek running parallel to it and the ranch to which it led. A beep sounded, and she looked in the rearview mirror to find a pickup truck behind her. When had she stopped? Shaking her head, she took her foot off the brake and hit the gas, zoomed right by the turn-off and over the bridge. At the fork in the road, she turned onto another county road, aptly named Gambler's Folly.

Yep, this was a gamble alright, and it definitely was folly. She stopped again on the road when she came to the Zack's gate--the original gate to the CW Ranch. The arch over the driveway was made of wood and showcased the cattle brand the Cartwrights had used for nearly a century and a half--a connected C and W. Beside the brand were painted a pair of aces, representing the winning hand in the poker game in which Cole Cartwright had won the original land in 1865.

The story went that his cousins, Dylan Ferguson and Elijah Blackwell, had pooled their money together and insisted Cole play in the Dallas game only months after they'd returned from the Civil War.

Taking a deep breath, Tracy stared at the aces. "I'm betting one heart and my dignity. What will you raise me, Zack?"

She parked her car next to the garage, added since Zack owned the house. A porch ran the length of the sprawling ranch house. Several rocking chairs sat in the shade, along with a jumble of large toys, including a bright pink battery operated toy car. In the side yard, under a large oak tree was a wooden swing set, complete with tower and slide. A sandbox nestled under the floor of the loft.

Tracy imagined Zack sitting on the porch watching Mandy play in the yard. She wasn't prepared for the longing to be there beside him watching *their* kids playing.

Rather than give into the hopelessness, she found courage and opened her car door. She fished the key Zack had given her out of her slacks pocket and opened the first door she came to. As promised, it opened into a mudroom. To the left of the kitchen, a huge dining room opened through an impressive timber arch. She turned away from the exhilarating view of the pastures provided by the wall of windows and looked around the kitchen as she thrust out a sigh.

"Make yourself at home. Right."

She set her hobo purse and the key on the top of the black marble counter of the island, over which hung an assortment of copper-bottomed pots and pans. The appliances were state-of-the-art and stainless steel. This kitchen belonged to someone who knew how to cook. Her heels sounded hollow on the stone floor, reminding her of a big empty castle. A stone fireplace divided the kitchen and the parlor. A long, heavy trestle table with a bench on either side took up the space before the cold hearth. On either end were antique high-backed Spanish chairs.

She turned toward the mudroom door, thinking it might be a good idea to just leave while she could. She caught sight of the counter closest to the door. It was a muddle of newspapers, magazines and a few toys. The tiny naked arm and a head with badly cut blonde hair poking out from among the daily news made her laugh. Most of the time, she felt as if she was drowning in the bad news of the world, too, just like Barbie.

The allusion helped her relax enough to continue exploring. She felt the pulse of history in the home, much as she did at the house at Oak Springs. However, unlike her mother's childhood home, here she didn't feel so overwhelmed by the formality.

As she wandered around the large dark wood table in the dining room, gently running her fingertips over the dusty surface, she remembered the time Zack had brought her over to this house the Christmas Eve they'd stayed here while his grandparents were away. Zack and she had attended the family gathering at his Uncle Paul's, then instead of taking her home, Zack had brought her back here. She smiled at the bittersweet memory.

"This house will be mine someday." Zack showed her around. "Do you like it?"

"Yes." She looked around at the table and hutch full of old dishes. "It's a really neat place."

"It is. Some of this stuff has been in my family for well over a hundred years." After taking her into his arms, he said, "C'mon, there's something I want to show you."

He led her to the bedroom at the end of the long corridor. The master suite was as massive as the rest of the house and as primitive, although it had been added recently. Zack left her long enough to light the candles he'd placed around the room. "You aren't really thinking of doing what I think you are. Not here. In your grandparents' bed!"

He laughed and kissed her on the nose after wrapping her up into his arms again. "I changed the sheets and even laundered the comforter. Besides, they don't sleep in here anymore. Granny sleeps in one of the other rooms in a special bed. And Granddad sleeps in a twin bed beside hers. He didn't like being in here without her. Claims the bed's too damned big."

He'd made love to her most of the night. At the memory of his touch, anticipation sizzled through her.

As if a ghost whispered in her ear, she heard his words as they'd lain together, wrapped up in a glorious afterglow. *"I want to ride rodeo after graduation, while you go to school. I'll take some ag-business classes*

*between rodeos, and by the time you're done with med school, I should be
done with what I need to know to run this place. Then we can move in..."*

Tracy gasped as the meaning of his words burned through her brain
like a rocket. She'd been too tired to listen to the rest of his words and
fallen to sleep.

"He was talking about our future." The pain of the realization rocketed
through her. She had to make Zack fall in love with her again.

With renewed determination, she decided to look around the rest of
the house.

She made her way to the living room, again taken aback by the mix of
modern and antique furniture, the amazing view from a wall of windows
and the clutter of toys mixed with Zack's magazines and books. It was
such an intimate view into his life. She could see him relaxing in the big
leather chair reading his magazines or watching the big screen TV hanging
on the wall, while Mandy sat on the floor playing with her Barbies in the
giant pink dollhouse in the corner.

Suddenly, a chill tickled down her spine, and she hugged herself against
the shiver. She didn't believe in ghosts. But she figured with the history
this place had, if they did exist, there had to be a ghost or two wandering
aimlessly around the wide halls and big rooms.

Tracy looked toward the fireplace separating the living room from the
formal dining room, and her heart stuttered over a few beats when she
saw the photographs lovingly displayed. No, the ghost she felt wasn't
Cole Cartwright coming back to check up on his poker winnings. This
ghost was far more real, and a lot harder to exorcise.

"You must be Lisa," she whispered, but her voice echoed in her mind
as if she'd screamed the words.

The stunning woman stared back at Tracy with her full lips frozen
forever in a bright smile. She'd been a beauty queen and she looked the
part. Long black hair framed a heart-shaped face. Her intelligent, brown
eyes were set wide with a pert nose between. Amanda, indeed, looked a
great deal like her mother.

Tracy turned her attention away from the woman who'd taken the
heart she'd so carelessly broken and made it her own, to the other photos.
The next photograph was of Zach in full dress uniform before the flag.
The insignia on his uniform was that of a private first class. He looked
so young in the picture. She'd seen it before; his aunt had shown it to
her years ago. Carefully, she picked up the frame and gazed down at the
stranger in the picture chronicling a chapter in Zack's life she knew very
little about.

"That was taken before I went to Afghanistan the first time."

She almost dropped the frame when she spun to look into the somber face of the live, older version of the man in the picture. The uniform was different, but he resembled the soldier more than the scruffy-haired cowboy she'd fallen for in high school.

Staring into his blue eyes, she saw an unfamiliar shadow. Maybe Zack was more a stranger than she liked to admit. How much of the cowboy she'd hopelessly loved was still in there? Or had his beautiful wife and the life of a Marine fighting in the war completely changed him?

She was ready to find out.

Tracy returned the frame to its place on the mantle and forced herself to look at the pictures of Zack's life. There were several of Lisa and Amanda as she went from infant to toddler, and a few of Zack with his family. But the one that stopped her cold was obviously a wedding picture. He had Lisa tucked under his arm. Lisa had been the complete opposite from Tracy--average height, busty and curvy. Zack was dressed in a suit and Lisa wore a simple white dress. Lisa practically glowed, and Tracy wasn't sure she'd ever seen Zack look so happy.

She turned away from the depiction of the life that could have been hers. "Lisa was so beautiful." Her voice sounded as if she'd dragged it out of her over sandpaper. She hated herself for reminding him of how much she would never measure up to his dead wife.

"Yes, she was." He held her gaze as if looking for the secrets of the universe.

"Zack..."

She gasped when he pulled her to him. "And so are you," he whispered against her lips and swallowed her will to disbelieve with his blazing kiss.

Much as he had on that Christmas Eve a lifetime ago, Zack led her down the hall to the open heavy wooden double doors of bedroom at the end. They stopped by the bed, and he deposited a small plastic bag holding a box of condoms on the bedside table.

Anxiousness like nothing she'd ever felt before smacked into her like a tornado when she looked at the king-sized bed. The bed wasn't made, but the dark green and tan comforter and plain white sheet were pulled up to the pillows.

"Sorry about the mess." He reached for the buckle of his service belt. "I never entertain company in here."

She bit her lip as he removed the belt holding various gear, including a holstered Glock, and gently laid it on the couch in front of a red brick fireplace. He didn't date and probably hadn't had sex since his wife's death. The prospect of being the first since Lisa both thrilled and scared her to her core.

When he stood before her again, she met his gaze. "Shouldn't you lock that up? Because of the gun?"

The grin tugging on his lips had invisible tentacles attached to the pit in her lower belly where she felt its pull. With his hands on the buttons of his shirt, he said, "Are you afraid of my gun?" He opened more buttons, revealing his chest was bare underneath.

As with the night they'd played in the pool, she found it hard not to stare at the muscles moving under the tanned skin and the scar marking the wound that had nearly killed him.

He shrugged out of the shirt. "I wasn't planning on shooting off *that* particular gun."

He sat down on the edge of the bed and unlaced his boots, pulled them off, then his socks. Such a simple act, but the exhaled breath caught behind her heart somewhere in her throat. He stood, held out his hand to her. "Come here."

And despite every warning bell in her going off, she took his hand and let him pull her to him. He wrapped her up in his arms.

"This is crazy. It's the middle of the afternoon. You should be at work trying to figure out who stole your horses. Or sleeping. You said you worked all night."

A grin lifted the corner of his lips. He hadn't shaved, and the day's growth of beard darkened the angle of his jaw and planes of his cheeks. A troublesome lock of hair fell over his forehead. He looked just like the picture of the bad-assed rodeo cowboy she'd ripped from a friend's calendar and kept folded up in her underwear drawer.

"Yeah, we probably are crazy, but I don't care." A hairsbreadth above her lips, he murmured, "Tell me now if you don't want to do this, Tracy."

He gave her an out. She should walk away now, before she completely lost her heart, but her body had other ideas. She pressed her lips to his and licked the full upper lip. When he pressed her pelvis into his, she felt the hard, long steel of his erection. Parting his lips, he let her tentatively explore his hot mouth. He tasted so good, sweet and spicy. His tongue stroked against hers, and her hands, caught between their bodies, splayed over his hard six-pack and inched their way upward. Only a sparse dusting of hair tickled her fingers in their blind exploration. As she stroked over the points of his masculine nipples, he sucked in a heavy breath and caressed his tongue against hers and turned up the passion of the kiss to *toe-curling.*

He slipped his hands under her top, and she shuddered as he caressed up her spine, pushing the thin material up, breaking the kiss to remove her t-shirt. After tossing it on top of his uniform shirt, he reached for the belt of her pants. Before any semblance of sanity returned, she was stepping out of her sandals and kicking off the slacks pooled around her ankles.

She couldn't meet his gaze. Tracy knew he was peering at her, dressed in her plain white bra and panties. She didn't want to see what she'd find in his eyes.

"Tracy." His voice was low and gentle. Using his finger and thumb, he lifted her chin to bring her eyes to his. He smiled and ran the backs of his fingers over her cheek, down her neck to the small rise above her padded push-up bra.

She wasn't sure what she'd expected to see in the midnight pools, but an inferno wasn't it. He curled his other hand around her hipbone, and he turned her to lay her on the bed. He stretched out beside her, and his lips followed the blazing trail his fingers had made only moments before.

For several moments, he teased the flesh above the edge of her bra. His hand splayed over her belly; the heat warming, tantalizing, making her want so much more. Now that she was committed to going through with making love with him, she ached for him. She squirmed under him, and he rewarded her by flicking open the front closure of her bra and uncovering her breasts.

The cool air on the puckered nipples sobered her a little, made her uncomfortable with being so exposed to him. She opened her eyes to him smiling at her. He leaned over and kissed her, while he covered her entire breast with a hand, gently kneading, caressing the tender skin and supersensitive nipple with a work-roughed palm. When she gasped and arched into the sensations, he moved his lips to her ear and huskily whispered, "I've always loved your perky little breasts, Tracy. Let me show you how much."

His words excited her more than she could explain. She fisted her hands in his hair while he moved his mouth to the nipple he'd been teasing with his hand. With the kind of attention only he'd ever shown her, he encircled the areolas, of first one breast, then the other. Then he sucked, nibbled, and teased the nipples with his fingers. She writhed under his ministrations while fire burned through her veins, sending a shudder through her that could have been the first quakes of orgasm. By the time he moved his fingers down to her heaving belly, she was a trembling mess, so close to exploding, desperate for his touch.

When he reached her panties, he cupped her and lightly caressed her through the cotton. She arched against him, reaching for more, wanting him. She touched every inch of his shoulders, back and arms she could reach, but it wasn't enough. He wouldn't do more than lightly touch her. She groaned in as much delicious frustration as in pleasure.

He nipped the flesh above the edge of her panties. She moaned and pressed her pubic bone into his touch. He pulled his hand back, not letting her find the pressure she so frantically wanted. She whimpered, begged, "Zack...please..."

He again rewarded her with a little more, but not enough. He slipped his thumbs under the edge of her cotton panties, slid them over her hips, down to her feet. He caressed up her legs to the apex, burrowed his fingers into the nest of curls, and caressed the hungry bundle of nerves hidden within. She gasped his name again and clawed at the bedding when his fingers encircled her clitoris, around and around, but never quite close enough.

Then his mouth and tongue replaced his fingers. The fire turned her insides to lava, building, bubbling. She rolled her hips into his touch. When he suckled her and pressed a finger into her, she blew apart, erupting into a million flaming pieces.

Once the splinters burned out and the ashes cooled, congealing back into place, she opened her eyes to him leaning over her. He kissed her, then stood beside the bed and undid the fly of his pants. He gave her a sexy grin and pushed the trousers down his muscular legs. He was as magnificent as he'd been all those years ago, but maturity had been generous. Slowly she moved her gaze up his body and met his. The hunger there was unmistakable and the pressure in the pit of her belly built again.

He kneeled between her legs and unfurled a condom over his erection. Her eyes drifted closed, waiting for him to thrust into her and find his own pleasure. Instead, he leaned over her, his breathing rapid, his voice smoky in her ear. "Look at me, Tracy. Watch me love you."

Despite knowing what he meant, his reference to love caused her heart to jump into her throat. He used his knees to spread her legs farther to accommodate him. He kissed her thoroughly and lightly touched, probed, but didn't enter her deeper than his tip. Although she tried to impale herself on him by wrapping her arms and legs around him, he held steady, while she undulated lustfully under him. When he broke the kiss, leaving her breathless and shaking, he slipped his hands under her hips, thrusting forward, claiming her with one swift move.

He moved within her in slow, powerful strokes meant to fan the flames into raging blazes within both of them. The brows over his passion-darkened eyes lowered, and the lock of golden hair hung over his moist forehead. She pushed it back, held it there as he kissed her in a soulful kiss.

She felt a sensation of being lifted, but hadn't realized what he'd done until he broke the kiss and was kneeling with her wrapped around him and his hands grasping her hips. Her head lolled back when he increased the pace by guiding her over his shaft. He kissed her neck, the stubble of his beard adding tantalizing tingles over her sweat-slickened skin. Their bodies entwined as one, moving in perfect rhythm like a well-oiled machine. He caught one of her nipples in his mouth and suckled. Seismic waves of pleasure danced over her sensitive nerves, turning up the heat on the pool in the center of her being.

"Oh, God, Zack," she may have said, or merely thought. He was so deep, and the friction so sweet. "I'm..."

The rest was lost on a long, breathy exaltation as the climax shattered her. She clung to him as he slowly moved her over him, dragging out the ecstasy. Then he laid her down onto her back again, never breaking contact. He lifted her hips off the bed and pulled almost out to plunge into her with fast, deep strokes.

She had to be spent, but to her fuzzy astonishment, the bubbling heat was back, quickly building in pressure and energy with each hungry thrust.

"Tracy." He groaned and took her with him when he found release.

Chapter 12

"What's going on?" Zack asked Dawn after she picked up on her end. He had no idea what he'd tell her if she questioned him for the reason his cell was off. He'd told her to call him if they found anything, after all. Figures that during the one time he'd turned his cell off, she'd try to call him. She never called.

"Finally." The irritation in Dawn's voice poked at Zack's sense of responsibility. "Nice of you to call me back, Sheriff Cartwright."

"Somehow my phone was turned off." He watched the flat landscape speed by. There was no *somehow* about it; he'd turned it off right before entering the house with newly purchased condoms in hand.

He drove back to town like a wild man. Not exactly speeding, but he definitely pushed the envelope, just as he had with the trip to and from Hamilton. Not only had he missed Dawn's calls, but the daycare closed in five minutes. How could he have been so carried away he'd completely lost track of time?

Had he actually made love with Tracy three times in five hours? The last time had been hot and slick in the shower, which was why they both were now racing to town to pick up their children. Tracy'd run out first, her hair still damp and her lips swollen from his kisses.

He shook his head and ran his hand through his hair. Dear God, one look at her and everyone in town would know exactly what she'd done with her afternoon off. Maybe that wasn't such a shocker regarding Tracy. But it wouldn't take a genius to add up the tally. Zack Cartwright *never* took a day off no matter how many hours he spent at the job, and he *never* turned off his cell phone.

Something about his assumption about what people thought of Tracy bothered him. She hadn't acted like a woman who routinely had wild, steamy sex in the middle of the afternoon. She'd been shy and nervous until he'd aroused her beyond nervousness. If he hadn't known better, he'd bet she hadn't had sex in a very long time.

Dawn's voice jerked him out of his ponderings. "You may want to check your messages a little more frequently."

Annoyed with her as much as with himself, he tightened his hold on the phone. "What the hell is so important, Madison?"

Huffing, she smoothed her feathers. "My team just finished combing the area, and I found some evidence, Zack. Blood on a mesquite branch, and a few drops near the first set of truck tires. I don't know how we missed them until now. I've sent it off to be analyzed. The Texas Ranger may have also found a witness."

"That's the best damn news I've heard in a while." Zack slowed as he passed the first clump of houses leading into town where the speed limit took a drastic drop from forty-five to twenty-five. The classic small town speed trap.

"I've called everyone in who's involved with the case. Hope you don't mind, boss," she added a beat too late.

He smiled and turned on the right signal. "Pat yourself on the back. You saved me from giving the order."

She laughed. "So, when can I expect you to show up?"

He turned on to Main Street as the light changed from green to yellow, and cringed as a car full of teenagers, who had stopped in the opposing lane, saw him coming toward the light without slowing and watched him go through the caution signal.

"I'm on my way to pick up Mandy. The daycare closes in..." He glanced at the clock on the dash. "In two minutes. I'll be in as soon as I figure out what to do with her."

He parked along the empty curb. Damn, Mandy was the last to be picked up, which meant Beth was the only adult around. "Dawn, I gotta go. I'll be at the office within the hour."

Disconnecting the call, he reached for the door handle and wondered where Mandy could stay for the evening. His parents and uncle and aunt had gone to Dallas for some charity function. He thought about calling Audrey, but quickly squashed that idea. Lance's comment about Mandy's care still irked him. And he never called Amy Jackson when an all-nighter was in the cards, especially on a school night.

Not for the first time, he thought about how much easier things would be if he hired a nanny or a housekeeper. And quickly threw out that idea, too. The last thing he wanted was a nanny raising his daughter.

So, pawning her off to whoever is available is better?

Pulling open the door to the daycare, he gritted his teeth at the answer. He hated his conscience sometimes.

"Daddy!" Mandy squealed and made a running leap toward him. He kneeled to catch her and wrapped his arms around her. "Where were you? I was getting worried. Miz Beth said you didn't call. You always call when you're late."

The very real concern in her voice tugged at something deep within him. Mandy wasn't a baby anymore. She understood that, despite the lack of rabid crime in the county, her father's life was in danger every time he strapped on his gun and pinned on his star. He pulled her against him for a moment, closed his eyes and murmured close to her ear, "I'm sorry, baby girl. Did you have a good day?"

She stepped away and nodded. "Today was fun. We went on the fieldtrip to the museum in Dallas, remember?"

"Yeah, I remember." Vaguely. He remembered signing a permission slip among the pile of papers she'd received her first day of school. He'd forgotten the trip was today. "Well, go get your bag and let's get going."

Watching her scamper off, he became aware of the woman standing before the reception desk. He looked over at her and gave her an apologetic smile. "Sorry, Beth, I should've called."

The youngest daughter of Aida Mae Pratt, Beth was twenty-nine and had been close to marriage twice, but had been dumped by the prospective grooms only days before both ceremonies. She'd moved back to Colton three years ago and opened Little People Daycare and Preschool. She lived in the remodeled carriage house behind the old house, which she'd converted into her daycare. Taking a page from her mother's book, she'd redone the upstairs into two apartments and rented them to college kids during the school year, offsetting her loss of income when the kids went back to school. The short blonde smiled. "No problem. I heard about those rustlers hitting up your place. I'm sorry. Hope you soon catch them."

"We will." He glanced back to the hall down which Mandy had disappeared.

"I know you will." Beth shifted and took a deep breath, pushing out her sizable chest.

Inwardly, he groaned. She was going to ask him out again. Beth had been asking him to come with her to picnics and street fairs for the past six months. It wasn't that he didn't find her attractive; he did. But she wasn't his type. Besides, Logan had dated her in high school. She was Logan's type--blond, bubbly, big breasts. He and Logan had never fought over women because they had completely different tastes, and they'd never dated each other's castoffs even when the lines between types became blurred.

At last, she must have found her gumption and said with a bright, inviting smile, "I was wondering if you and Mandy would like to come with me to a barbeque after the roundup at my brother's place on Saturday."

Her blue eyes brightened with hope, and he hated turning her down. But he despised the idea of getting tangled up with Beth Pratt even more. He pasted on a smile. "I'm sorry, Beth. I can't."

"Oh, that's okay. Maybe next time." She clasped her hands in front of her.

He glanced toward the back room, hoped Mandy didn't return at that moment, and cleared his throat of the sudden lump. "I'm seeing someone."

"Ah, yes, I heard about you and Tracy Parker. Momma mentioned you came into her salon this morning."

"We had lunch together," he lied. He knew Aida Mae would have told everyone she knew about him being at Tracy's salon. Not exactly the way he wanted it to come out, especially since he'd been turning Beth down for six months straight. She deserved an honest answer as to why he didn't want her.

Why was that, anyway? If any woman would do, Beth was more than willing. Despite the daycare and the respectability she had now, Beth Pratt had been wild in her younger days. Even he didn't buy the bullshit about her and Logan going at it like two dogs in heat way back when being the reason either. He remembered the afternoon with Tracy naked in his bed and a hot knot formed deep in the pit of his stomach.

"Daddy, I'm ready."

Amanda's voice drew him out of his contemplations.

"Okay, let's go. Tell Miz Beth thank you." He smiled apologetically at Beth.

Mandy took hold of his hand. "Thanks for staying late and watching me."

Beth's smile appeared stiff. "That's okay. Have a good night, y'all."

"You too." He tipped his hat and turned to leave.

He buckled them both into the truck, climbed in behind the wheel, and looked over his shoulder at Mandy, dreading the whole time what he had to say to her. "I have to work tonight, baby girl. I'm hoping Josie can take care of you." His parents' old housekeeper loved having Mandy around, but she was pushing seventy-five and had bad arthritis.

Mandy's face fell. "But you were working all day and all last night. I thought you said we'd have your special tacos for dinner and ice cream later."

He took a deep breath and let it out slowly, put the truck into gear, and moved away from the curb. "I wasn't at the office this afternoon. I had something I needed to do. But I have to go in tonight. We might know who stole our horses."

"Oh. That's good." Mandy loved horses and had cried Saturday morning when she found out about the theft.

When he was almost at the intersection, he pulled out his phone to call Josie, praying she could keep Mandy that night.

"Daddy, can I stay with Miz Tracy tonight?"

Mandy's question stopped him from pressing the connect button.

"Miz Josie always smells funny." She wrinkled her nose.

Addicted to Ben Gay, Josie loved to use the stuff on her arthritic joints. He remembered her smelling of it even when he was a boy. But letting Mandy stay with Tracy seemed unfair to Mandy. He knew she was bonding with the woman, but despite what he'd promised Tracy that morning, he had no intention of allowing Mandy with her for long periods of time. He trusted Tracy with his daughter; however, Mandy would suffer when they called it quits once the lust burned out. He had to protect his baby's fragile heart. It was only now whole again from her mother's death.

"Please, Daddy. I know she's at Bobby's football practice. Call her."

"Okay," he thrust out, drawing the word from somewhere around his ankles. "I'll call her."

Five minutes later, he pulled into the parking lot of a McDonald's by the mall where Tracy had taken Bobby for a quick dinner. Mandy's face lit up when she noticed Tracy waiting for them on the sidewalk. Tracy had pulled her hair back into a ponytail and the wild-afternoon-sex glow had dimmed. When their eyes connected, he felt the familiar pull of the woman he vowed he'd never let get to him.

How the hell had his life suddenly become so complicated?

* * * *

Bobby ran off with the rest of his team, and Tracy smiled down at the little girl beside her. "So, did you want to stay here and watch a bunch of boys beat up on each other or would you like to go over to my shop and we'll play?"

The big smile on Mandy's small face touched Tracy's heart. The love she felt blooming for the little girl was a dangerous thing. When Zack finally got tired of her, Tracy would suffer doubly.

"Let's go to your shop!"

"Let me tell Coach Parker I'll return to get Bobby after practice."

Mandy nodded and took Tracy's hand. Jake watched her approach with his arms crossed over his Junior Cowboys white and blue t-shirt.

They stopped before him, and Tracy said, "I'll pick Bobby up after practice."

Jake studied Amanda, and she tucked in closer to Tracy's side. He gave her a smile, but Tracy saw it for what it was. His eyes gleamed with resentment. "My, you are a pretty little girl. You must have gotten your looks from your momma."

Nice, jerk. Two for one. Hurt me and her with one seemingly innocent off-handed compliment. Tracy unlocked her teeth. "I'll see you later."

Before she could turn, Jake unfolded his arms, and Tracy noticed a gauze bandage on his hand. He put the hand against his thigh. "I know you switched lawyers."

She narrowed her eyes on him. "I'm not talking about this now, Jake."

"Fine. But don't think it will change anything. Your million-dollar lawyer isn't changing my mind. Or are you just screwing him?"

Before Tracy could wrap her mind around a suitable PG-rated retort, Mandy asked, "What did you do to your hand?"

Jake jerked his attention to Mandy and fisted the hand around the bandage. "I cut it working. Unlike you Cartwrights and Quinns, some of us actually have to work."

He walked away, leaving Tracy fuming.

"C'mon, Mandy, let's go."

They were almost to the car when Mandy said, "He's not really a nice man."

Tracy glanced down at the girl and smiled, awed by her insight. "No, he's not. And I have a rule."

"What's that?"

"We don't talk about grouchy people." She opened up the backdoor of her Taurus.

Zack had made sure Mandy's booster seat had been installed correctly before he headed off to the sheriff's department. She'd talked him into having a fast food dinner with her and the kids before he ran off. They hadn't had lunch and she assumed he wouldn't get a chance to eat supper if he didn't eat before he walked into the office. They wolfed down their Big Macs, chicken nuggets, and french fries, then went their separate ways. The whole time, Tracy envisioned being married to Zack, them raising Bobby and Mandy, and maybe someday having a few together.

Dreams like that were going to make it even harder when he cut her loose.

"That's a good rule." Mandy climbed into her seat and buckled the belt across her. "Let's go fix my hair."

Tracy pulled into her spot next the Dumpster behind the shop. She helped Mandy out of the car and unlocking the door, and they entered into the back of the building. Flipping on the lights in the hall and her office, she dropped her keys and hobo purse on the desk, and tried to figure out what she and Mandy could do for the hour of Bobby's practice.

She'd asked Zack at the restaurant while the kids raced each other to the trashcan if he minded her trimming Mandy's hair.

"You're not going to cut it short, are you?" he asked as they followed the kids out the glass doors. "Mom threatened to cut it short a couple of times."

Tracy shook her head. "No, I won't give her a dreaded bowl cut or make her look like a boy. Just a little shorter. Cut all those uneven ends off. She hasn't had a cut in a long time."

Zack looked at Mandy and pursed his lips. "I can't remember ever getting her hair cut. I guess I never gave it a thought, and I wouldn't let Mom take her because I didn't want her hair to be short. Mandy was bald when she was born, and it took forever for her hair to grow. I'm not sure if Lisa had ever had it trimmed either. She'd always dreamed of the day when Mandy's hair would be long enough to do something with, as she put it." He shrugged and added, "I think that's why I keep it long. Because that's what Lisa would have wanted."

For a long moment, she thought he was going to tell her to mind her own business and to let his daughter's hair alone.

"Okay." A slow smile touched his luscious mouth. "Surprise me. Aunt Winnie calls you an artist. Show me your stuff."

Tracy had groaned at the reference to his imperious aunt, but inside she was thrilled. She'd seen the play of doubt on his face. Had he been wondering what Lisa would have done?

"Miz Tracy?" Mandy's voice jarred her out of the reverie.

Tracy smiled at Mandy's wide-eyed wonder as she looked around the small office. "Come on." Tracy held out her hand. "Your daddy gave me permission to give you a trim."

"You mean cut my hair?" The trepidation in the little girl's voice didn't surprise Tracy. Most kids were afraid of their first haircuts. However, usually little girls were easier to reason with than boys, simply because they were often older than boys when they received their first ride in her chair.

Tracy kneeled down before her, took both of Mandy's hands, and gave her a reassuring smile. "I'll only do what you want me to, Mandy. If you're afraid of getting your hair cut, then we won't do it. But I think it would be a good thing to have done for school. Maybe give you some bangs." Tracy gently pushed flyaway hairs out of Mandy's eyes. "That way you wouldn't always have to wear your hair in ponytails or in barrettes."

Her eyes brightened, and she reached out and gently touched Tracy's bangs. "You mean like you have?"

"Yep. In fact, that was the reason I cut my hair. I was getting annoyed at it always being in my face."

"Alright," Mandy chirped after careful consideration.

Tracy led the girl to the styling chair before a workstation and a large gilt-framed mirror. She got her settled on a booster chair, removed the elastic band holding Mandy's long, black locks, and picked up a brush.

As she began to gently stroke it through the silky strands, Mandy said, "I think Daddy likes you."

Tracy paused in her brushing and met the girl's gaze through her reflection. "Do you think so?"

"Yeah, he looks at your picture a lot."

He had a picture of her?

"Really?" She managed to get out of her constricting throat.

"Uh-uh. It's a picture from before he and Momma were together."

Of course it was, but what was Zack doing looking at a picture of her?

"Miz Tracy?" Mandy turned her head. "Do you like my daddy?"

Tracy swallowed hard and began to brush the girl's hair again. "Do you think I don't like your daddy?"

"No, not that." Mandy looked into the mirror again, watching.

Tracy sectioned off some of Mandy's hair and clipped back the excess.

"I wish you could be my new momma."

The little girl's words almost brought Tracy to her knees.

She stared at the deep blue eyes of the daughter of a woman she had never met, had never wanted to meet, and at times had even despised, but in that heart-wrenching moment, she wished she'd known Lisa Cartwright. If Mandy was truly similar in personality to her mother, no wonder Zack had fallen so far so fast for her.

She remembered hearing the stories about his whirlwind romance with the Wyoming pageant queen-turned-nurse. At first, she hadn't believed Zack could have possibly fallen for her so fast. Logan hadn't believed it either. He'd wanted Tracy to leave Jake and go after him, but no matter how much she'd loved Zack, she couldn't have taken Jake's son away from him.

When she'd heard the news Zack had joined the Marines, she had a hard time accepting the Zack she had known and loved could have been happy giving up rodeo. She'd blamed Lisa for forcing him into doing it. Tracy wondered for years if she'd made the right decision by not going after him, especially when he'd been wounded and near death in the military hospital in Landstuhl, Germany.

Now she knew she'd done the right thing. However, in realizing her acceptance of the other woman in Zack's life, she became more determined than ever to go after him with everything she had. Not only for herself, or to give Bobby a father figure who could teach him right from wrong, but for this little girl who had unwittingly stolen her heart.

When she finally found her voice, Tracy said, "I like you, too, Mandy. As for being your new mommy, how about we just try being friends. I could be like an aunt. Would you like that?"

Mandy nodded and smiled, but Tracy saw the sparkle go out of it. "Okay. But Daddy is a little lonely. I think he could use the company."

Remembering his reference to wanting her to keep him company that afternoon, Tracy burst out laughing. Mandy watched her, then matched Tracy giggle for giggle, although Mandy had no idea why she was laughing.

Getting her composure back, Tracy patted Mandy on the head. "I say let's make you beautiful."

Mandy grinned and clapped her hands. "Yippy!"

Chapter 13

The conference room in the sheriff's office was full to the max, not an uncommon phenomenon these days. When had Forest County, Texas, become such a hotbed of crime? Dawn stood at the front of the room, having what appeared to be a heated conversation with the Texas Ranger. Besides five other sheriff's deputies, TSCRA agent Herb Milroy was also sitting at the table.

Feeling out-of-place dressed in jeans and his usual chambray shirt instead of a uniform while working, Zack nodded toward the other men as he headed for the front of the room. "Wyatt, what are you doing here? Last I heard you were over in Midland."

Wyatt McPherson held out his hand and Zack shook it. "I just transferred to Waco. Sorry to hear about your fillies."

Zack shrugged and tucked his thumbs into his front pockets. "We'll find the bastards who took 'em. So, you're replacing, Mathes? What did his wife have?"

"Yep, the captain sent me, partly because I'm from Colton." Wyatt grinned. "Mathes is the proud papa of a new baby boy."

The eldest son of the town's fire chief and twin brother to Lance Cartwright's wife, Audrey, Wyatt had been Dawn's partner while they both worked for the Dallas PD. After she'd been shot in the line of duty, Wyatt had joined the Texas Rangers, and Dawn came back to Colton.

Dawn had her arms crossed over the beige uniform blouse and the naturally tan skin over her high cheekbones pulled taut. She always looked impeccable and professional with her long black hair pulled back and bound in a bun at her nape, but a few loose strands fell over her forehead, like she'd been playing with it, as she had a habit of doing when she was nervous or upset. Nothing usually ruffled her feathers, but by the way her brown eyes were narrowed, she didn't look at all happy about Wyatt being here.

Perplexed, Zack raised a brow at Dawn's obvious cold shoulder and Wyatt's attempt to act as if she wasn't affecting him. Most police officers developed close friendships with their partners that never went away. Besides, they'd all practically cut their teeth on the same brandy-dipped teething ring.

Before Zack could ponder that situation more, Wyatt ran a hand through his chestnut hair and his blue eyes sobered. "Hey, I just wanted to say, I'm sorry about the crap my shithead little brother put you through. I hope I'm never in the same room with the idiot. They'll be locking me up in his place because I'll wring his damn fool neck."

"Don't worry about it. No one holds your family responsible for what he did." Zack reached out and patted the other man on the shoulder. He was well aware of the curious audience. Everyone in town had wondered if Kyle McPherson would receive some special preference after his arrest for the arson of Charli Quinn's barn and poisoning her cattle. The McPhersons were an extremely respected family in Colton--and second cousins to Tracy and Dylan Quinn.

Before Zack could begin thinking about the amazing afternoon he'd spent with Tracy, Wyatt gave a nod of his head. "Kyle's always been coddled. He was Mom's baby."

"What do you say we get started?" Zack asked to change the subject. "It's already been a long day. And promises to be an even longer night ahead of us."

A few moments later, Dawn was standing at the head of the table and debriefing the rest of the group on what she'd already told Zack over the phone.

"When do we expect to get the DNA back from Austin?" Zack asked.

"Within the next two weeks."

"If the culprit has no DNA on file, the information will be next to useless," Wyatt pointed out from where he leaned against the wall beside a large map of Texas.

Dawn shot him another glare. "Most people don't wake up one day and decide to become cattle and horse thieves. This guy has a record. I'd stake my reputation as a cop on it."

Pushing off the wall, Wyatt raised a brow and smirked. "Well, for the sake of your esteemed reputation, Deputy Madison, I sure hope you're right."

Dawn stiffened her already poker-straight back and scowled at Wyatt McPherson in a way Zack had never seen her do in all the years he'd known her. What had gone down between these two?

Several of the other deputies around the table began to snicker. Obviously, Zack wasn't the only one wondering the same thing. Zack cleared his throat and said, "Lieutenant McPherson, what do you have to report?"

Wyatt slid in beside Dawn. With a bolo tie at the neck of his white Western shirt, black jeans and polished boots, he looked more like a cowboy than a police officer. However if the *cinco peso* coin star pinned to his shirt didn't prove otherwise, the Colt .45 secured in a shoulder holster would do so. He bracketed his waist with his hands.

"Alright, gentlemen...and lady." Wyatt glanced at Dawn.

She turned and sat down in a vacant chair by one of the other uniformed deputies. Zack was so intent on watching Dawn he almost missed what Wyatt said next.

"Before Mathes ran out of here earlier this afternoon, he was following up on possible routes the thieves could have taken. As all of you know, livestock theft is on the rise, as are the number of shady packing plants and livestock auction houses willing to buy questionable stock and horses. Agent Milroy..." He nodded toward the TSCRA agent. "Has some leads on a few such butcher houses in Texas, Western Oklahoma and Southern Colorado. However, theft of horses is a different game. Usually they're sent to Mexico and slaughtered. When I was in Midland, the Rangers along with the sheriff's department of Gaines County were tracking a ring of horse thieves operating near Seminole. We suspected them of selling not only stolen horses, using bogus papers, to buyers from mostly back East and even overseas. We also suspected the same ring to be connected to one in New Mexico that has been rounding up wild Mustangs for the same purposes. I believe our boys are headed for this ring."

Wyatt cleared his throat and rubbed his clean-shaven chin. "Since the twenty horses stolen were not branded and were young thoroughbred mares, they're the perfect target for this ring."

Zack shifted uncomfortably in the hard wooden chair when every eye looked his way.

With a grin, Larry Simms, the oldest of his deputies teased, "Just how much were those fillies worth again, boss?"

Zack squared his shoulders. "Enough for me to learn not to ever pasture horses again without branding them."

Everyone laughed at his expense. He supposed he deserved the ribbing. He'd known the dangers and ignored them. "Okay, how much are the horses worth on the black market?"

Shrugging, Wyatt said, "Anywhere from two to five thousand a head."

Now a few whistles accompanied the laughter. When the group finished their teasing, Deputy Kennedy asked the question Zack was sure was on everyone's mind. "Despite what the horses are worth to this ring, what makes you think our boys went that direction? We're a heck of a long way from Seminole. The Mexican border is a lot closer. Or, if it's the same guys rustling the cattle, they could've just taken them to the same slaughterhouse."

Wyatt paced the front of the room. "I hit possible pay dirt when I followed up on a lead Mathes found, and contacted a truck stop in Stephenville. At approximately four AM, Saturday, two livestock trucks pulled into the Texaco. The driver got out of only one of the trucks and went into the convenience store." Wyatt turned to the state map and picked up the pointer from the top of a file cabinet in the corner. Using the slender piece of plastic, he pointed to Stephenville. He slid the pointer along the line representing a state road. "As you can see, State Route 108 intersects with I-20 and that leads west." He paused, and with a smirk, glanced at Dawn. "I bet my reputation as a Texas Ranger that our boys headed to Seminole."

Dawn huffed and closed her notebook. "I'll call for a warrant for the security tapes."

"I already have." Wyatt replaced the pointer on the cabinet top where he'd found it.

Zack finished writing in his notebook. "Have you talked to the clerk?"

Wyatt looked his way. "No, she apparently works the graveyard shift. I was hoping to talk to her tonight."

"Good." Zack stood, indicating the meeting was at an end. "I'll go with you. Let's get back to work, folks. Dawn, Grant, contact the Gaines County sheriff and find out if they've had any increased activity in the sale of horses within that ring they're watching. Kennedy, Timmons, and Simms, you hit the patrol. Stick close to the ranches we discovered have recently bought livestock. I don't expect any trouble, but we can't leave our guard down." As the deputies listed got up and started to gather their notes, Zack turned to the remaining two deputies. "Griscom and Abbott, you guys are off tonight." Before they could show their jubilation, Zack added, "I want you here to assist Herb in his investigation at oh-six-hundred."

Zack waited for the deputies to acknowledge him and then turned to Wyatt and nodded. "Let's go."

* * * *

Tracy and Mandy returned to the ball field just as practice was ending. With Mandy holding Tracy's hand tight, they headed to where the boys gathered around Jake.

"There you are. You know I don't go chasing down all my clients like this."

Tracy stopped when Logan strode up beside her.

Mandy let go of Tracy's hand and launched herself into Logan's open arms. "Uncle Logan, what are you doin' here?"

He let go of Mandy and raised a brow at Tracy. "I'm here to talk to Miz Tracy. What are you doin' here? Is your dad around?"

"Tracy's watching me tonight. Daddy's got to work."

Logan looked at Tracy. "That so?"

Before Mandy could respond, Tracy said, "Zack was called in and asked if I could watch Mandy tonight. Now that *that*'s all settled, what *are* you doing here?"

Logan sniggered at the abrupt change. "I've got some news."

"What is it?"

Logan pulled a letter from the inner pocket of his suit jacket and held it out to her. "After tomorrow, you can start signing my checks as Tracy Caroline Quinn."

Tracy stared at him as his meaning sunk in. When it did, she snatched the envelope and bounded into his arms. "Oh, Logan. Thank you!" Then she kissed his cheek, and Logan laughed as he hugged her back.

"Hey!" Mandy exclaimed. "I thought you liked my daddy."

Tracy pulled away and met a pair of narrowed blue eyes. She laughed and stepped out of his embrace.

He swung Mandy up into his arms as if she weighed nothing and tickled her sides until she giggled. "Don't you worry your pretty little head, firecracker. I know Tracy likes your daddy, and I think your daddy likes her."

Tracy looked sharply at him, but he was focused on Mandy.

"Well, if this isn't a heartwarming little scene." Jake drew Tracy's attention. His lips twisted upward, but it was more grimace than smile. "Hello, Logan. You sure do like stepping in and taking over another man's family, don't you?"

Logan simply smiled at Tracy as he set Mandy on her feet again. "Tracy, I'll be in touch before we go to court Friday."

"Okay. See you then."

"Don't worry. I'll call you tomorrow." Without even acknowledging Jake, he kissed Mandy on the forehead, and walked away with his hands in the pockets of his designer suit pants.

Bobby rushed forward, and the two kids headed off toward the bleachers, chattering up a storm about what they would do once they got back to the ranch.

Tracy made sure they were out of earshot, then fisted her hands until her nails bit into her palms, and glared at him. "You bastard. You know nothing has ever happened between Logan and me."

He shrugged and leaned forward. "Maybe not, but I know someone who would believe it had. You do have a reputation of being a cheater, after all. Remember what I said, Tracy. I don't want Zack Cartwright anywhere near my son. You got it?"

"You can't dictate to me. And you only have a trumped up account that can't ever hold any credence in court. Zack is a good man, and a respected member of this community. And no one in this town would ever call Zack a bad father."

He snorted and crossed his arms over his wide chest. "I know for a fact, Zack Cartwright has a temper and a mean streak. He didn't want me to succeed in football, so he made sure I'd never be able to play again. No one but him and I were out on the trail that day. It would be my word against his. I've also heard he and his wife had a fight before she left the house during a snowstorm. Then she was hit head-on by a drunk driver. The story goes that Zack was passed out on the floor when his sister-in-law found him to deliver the news." Jake's smirk broadened as he added, "Interestingly, his in-laws gave him an ultimatum--either stop drinking or they were taking Amanda away. He moved to Texas right after that and hasn't been back once in two years. Who knows if he's stopped drinking or not. He puts on that holier-than-thou show when he's in public, but he's admitted he hasn't completely stopped drinking."

She wasn't playing into his mind game. "Good night, Jake." She turned away and then faced him again. "Oh, by the way, I'm no longer bound to you in any way. Logan just informed me that he put the paperwork in for my name-change. It was time to get rid of that last bit of garbage. I've toted it around long enough. Good riddance."

She spun away, squared her shoulders, and headed to round up the kids.

* * * *

"Lucinda Tritt?" Zack asked as he approached the clerk at the counter of the convenience store of a Texaco station in Stephenville.

The clerk pushed her thick glasses up on her nose and looked from Zack to Wyatt and back again. "That's me."

Zack guessed the woman to be about forty-five as he and Wyatt held out their identifications. "I'm Sheriff Zachery Cartwright of Forest County and this is Lieutenant Wyatt McPherson of the Texas Rangers. We understand you were working Saturday morning when two livestock trucks rolled in here." He opened a small notebook to take notes. "We need you to tell us everything you can remember about the drivers."

She gave Zack a small smile and pushed a mass of frizzy gray-shot brown hair from her face. "There ain't much to tell." She shrugged and looked at Wyatt. "Two trucks drove up. A guy got out of the first one and came in around four in the morning."

"Can you describe him and tell us what he bought?" Wyatt prompted when she paused.

"He was a big guy--not tall, but heavy-set, stocky. His hair was long and dark." Lucinda pushed at her own hair as she remembered. "He got a bottle of Dr. Pepper and a bag of potato chips. And two candy bars, I think. Oh, and a First Aid kit and a bottle of Motrin."

Wyatt asked, "Did you see the other men at all?"

The clerk shook her head. "They parked out past the light. I couldn't see much except that they were livestock trucks."

"Do you know if the trucks were carrying animals?" Zack finished jotting down her descriptions.

She puckered her brow as if that would help her memory. "Yeah, I'm pretty sure I heard horses."

Zack smiled and put the notebook into his back jeans pocket. "Thank you, Miz Tritt, for your cooperation. We'll get in touch if we need to talk to you again."

She smiled, nodded, and headed back to work. "Wait." She turned toward them. "I did see one of the guys when they drove past. He was a passenger in the first truck. I think I could recognize a picture of him, too."

Wyatt grinned and held out his hand for her to shake. "Thanks, ma'am. You've been a lot of help."

The manager of the store stepped forward and held out a CD to Wyatt. "Here are those security tapes from the other night. So, you think these guys are cattle rustlers?"

Zack smiled inwardly. Stephenville was nearly a hundred miles west of Colton, but the thefts had gotten a mention on the evening news after the rustling at Oak Springs Ranch. The media considered it a way to keep the prominent Ferguson-Quinn clan in the news. Not to mention making light of the sheriff falling victim to the thieves again on the eleven o'clock report.

"There's a possibility they are connected," Zack said.

"Well, I hope you catch 'em. My uncle had cattle stolen from him years ago, and it about broke him. You gentlemen have a good night."

Wyatt looked at Zack and smiled. "Are you thinking what I'm thinking?"

Zack opened the front door. "Yeah. Let's get back to Colton. I suddenly have a hankering to watch TV."

* * * *

The sun rode high on the eastern horizon as Zack drove through the elaborate wrought iron gate of Oak Springs. He drove over the concrete bridge spanning the creek and looked around the manicured front lawn. Everything about the place reeked of money. The Cartwrights were as rich as the Fergusons, but his family never flaunted their wealth the way Tracy's family had. That wasn't exactly true. It hadn't been her entire family, but Jason Ferguson's second wife and her son, Leon.

He stopped by the garage and got out of the truck. He hadn't been this tired since his early days in the mountains of Afghanistan as a new Marine.

After speaking to the clerk at the Texaco, Zack and Wyatt came back to the office to watch the surveillance footage. Unfortunately, the man's face wasn't visible in the grainy black and white frames. The cameras were angled all wrong or set too high. He also had worn a wide brimmed hat.

Now, he had to hope the thief had DNA on file. However, he still had no idea who the other men in the trucks were. Nor could the authorities prove Zack's horse theft was connected to the cattle rustling. As he knew, with police work nothing was ever cut and dry. Often one clue only answered half the riddle and produced a whole slew of other possibilities and questions.

With a sigh, he rang Tracy's doorbell and waited. When the door opened, he expected to find an anxious Mandy. She would be late for school at this rate. Instead, Tracy stood there looking beyond great in a pair of jeans shorts and a t-shirt with a large flower over her chest.

"Hey." He pulled his hat from his head.

"Come in." Tracy moved away from the door and smiled. "I have coffee on. You look like you need some."

"I do, but I have to get Mandy to school. Then I'm going home and crashing for a long, long time." He looked around. Where was the little tornado?

Tracy clasped her hands before her. "When you were so late, I decided to take her to school. The principal had a fit because I wasn't on her pickup list, and I tried to explain I wasn't picking her up, but dropping her off. I swear sometimes Mrs. Longoria takes the rules a little overboard."

He reached out and pulled her to him. Her surprised gasp as she came up against him brought a chuckle from his throat, which ended on a groan as his lips touched hers. She opened under his questing tongue as he drank her in.

She moaned and threaded her fingers into his hair. The need for air forced them apart, and they gasped for oxygen. He held her to him and rested his forehead on hers.

"Good morning to you, too." Her voice was a sexy purr that had him wishing he could strip her and have his way with her.

"It is now. Thank you for taking care of Mandy. I'll have to make sure Mrs. Longoria knows it was alright for you to bring Mandy to school. I was worried she'd be late."

She moved away, but took his hand. "C'mon, I have fresh coffee, and I can make you something to eat. Melissa can open the shop."

He stopped short when they entered the kitchen at the end of the entrance hall. The other night when he'd been here, the kitchen had seemed so sterile. This morning, bits of multi-colored construction paper, crayons and markers covered the table and artwork that could have come from only Mandy decorated the refrigerator. As Tracy headed for the coffee maker by the sink, he went to the stainless steel door and stared at the homemade frame around a picture of Mandy. Her hair cut in a style similar to Tracy's with bangs and her face framed by long dark locks.

"I want you to know I loved having Mandy. We had so much fun."

He glanced up from the picture to Tracy.

She held two mugs of coffee and smiled. "I hope you don't mind. I got my digital camera out and took pictures of her and Bobby last night. Then this morning she wanted to make frames for the pictures. You'll be getting one tonight. I put it in her book bag. Oh, and I helped her study for her spelling test."

His throat swelled shut. He hadn't even given her homework a thought. Before he could speak, he had to swallow down the lump. "Thanks for helping her. I guess this is her first spelling test."

"Yeah. She's a smart little girl, so she caught on quick. Bobby has a test today, too. I made a game of it and they studied together. It was a hoot, her trying to spell his words."

He looked down at the photo with its gaudy frame of pink and blue construction paper and crayon-colored purple flowers. "I like her hair. It's cut just like yours."

Tracy glanced down at the coffee mugs in her hands. "She wanted it like mine, so that's what I did."

"I like it."

"I'm glad." She looked up with her bottom lip caught between her teeth, so damned unsure of herself.

After a moment, she said, "Let me make you some eggs and bacon. I'm not much of a cook. I'll admit that right now. But I can fry eggs and bacon."

He put the paper frame back under its magnet on the fridge door and grinned as he took the cup she held out to him. He'd let her take care of him, just this once. "That sounds good. I'm starving."

Forty minutes later, he'd devoured his breakfast and drank a half a pot of coffee loaded with sugar. The two excited Yorkies had come in from outside, yipped themselves out over his arrival, and now lay in the sunlight by the French doors. Tracy had to get going to her shop, and he had to go home and sleep, but neither of them wanted to leave the kitchen.

She set her cup on the countertop of the bar. "Wow. I just thought of something."

He chuckled and arched a brow. "And we blondes are the brunt of all the jokes."

She poked him in the side with her elbow. "If I ever hear a blonde joke about a ditsy blond *guy*, I'll make sure I remember to tell you about it. But what I meant was today I can officially start calling myself by my maiden name again."

"You had your name changed?"

"Oh, I guess I didn't tell you." She tilted her head and looked at him. Her hair fell over her shoulder, and the sun shining through the windows picked out the highlights she'd added to her brown hair. "When I talked to Logan about taking on my case, I asked him to file the paperwork to change my name. I guess it's not official--I don't have the documents from the state and Social Security office yet--but he said I could start using Quinn again. I can't believe he was able to get it done this fast."

He glanced away before he lost something to her he could never give her, and finished his coffee. "My little brother is a good lawyer."

"Well, I'm not really sure why I ever kept Parker. I told everyone it was because of Bobby, but I don't think it was really for him."

"Sentimentality makes us do strange things."

She snorted and shook her head. "Trust me, Zack, there is nothing about Jake Parker that I'm sentimental about. I haven't even kept a single wedding picture. So, my keeping his name was really a joke--on me."

He studied her with his breath caught in his throat. "What do you mean, you didn't keep any wedding pictures?"

She met his gaze again and shrugged. "I burnt them." She sipped her coffee, and instead of explaining more, she shook her head. "Did you find anything out last night?"

"Yes, but nothing concrete." What the hell did Jake do to her?

"Can't talk about it?"

He shook his head and winced at her wide eyes, but he couldn't discuss the case with her. "No, I can't."

She surprised him again by not pushing, and simply changed the subject. "I wish Bobby didn't have a game tonight. I'd love to have you and Mandy over for dinner again." She then let out a giggle. "But this time we'll order pizza."

He smiled at her. "You really can't cook?"

"Nope. Mom tried to teach me when I was a teenager, but I never took much interest in it. And after we moved in here with Granddad and Maddie while Dad was overseas, Maddie wouldn't allow Mom anywhere near the kitchen. She considered it beneath Mom to want to be a chef. I was a kid and thought maybe Maddie was right." She blushed and glanced away. "Maddie was one of the most glamorous women I knew. She took me under her wing, in a way, and... Well, she helped me. But I never learned to cook."

He remembered Madeline Ferguson, the daughter of a Houston oilman and only two years older than her stepdaughter, as mostly a bitch on wheels. However, Tracy had been close to the woman who was more like an aunt than a grandmother.

"Josie insisted on Logan and me learning to cook. You remember Josie, Mom and Dad's housekeeper when we were kids?" Tracy nodded, and he went on. "I'm glad she taught me something. Mandy would've starved otherwise." He looked at his watch. "Let me help get the dishes cleaned up, then I'd better get going. You still have to drive to town."

When the kitchen was spotless, she walked him to the door, and he turned toward her. "You'll be at the game tonight?"

"Yeah, it's in Valley Mills."

The thought of Tracy and Bobby away from home, and Jake coaching a whole team of little boys made his blood run cold. "Let's go together. Before the game, we can stop and get pizza. Afterward, we can get ice cream to celebrate Bobby's big win against the Valley Mills Bulldogs."

"That sounds great." Tracy smiled and stepped closer to him, slipping her arms around his neck. Unable to resist her closeness, he pulled her to him. Her kiss was soft and tender, but it tingled clear to his toes. "Now, go home and get some sleep."

* * * *

Despite it only being four-thirty in the afternoon, Angelo's Pizzeria was busy. Zack held onto Amanda's hand on one side, and Tracy had entwined the fingers of his other hand. Bobby led the way into the pizza joint in the Mills Plaza Mall along Highway 6 not far from the ball field the Colton Cowboys would take on the Valley Mills Bulldogs in an hour.

A teenage girl, wearing her uniform of red polo shirt and black jeans much too tightly, flashed them a cheerful smile and led them to a booth in the corner. Once they were seated and she rattled off the specialty pizza special of the evening, she took their drink orders.

"So, what do y'all think you want?" Tracy asked as soon as the waitress scampered away.

"Extra cheese and pepperoni!"

Zack glanced up from his menu, amazed at the perfect chorus from the kids.

"You like the same pizza I do." Mandy looked up with near worship in her big blue eyes at Bobby. Zack's heart twisted at the thought of how hard the end to the farce with Tracy would be on Mandy.

"Yeah." Bobby glanced at Mandy, then looked around the restaurant.

"Well, then I guess we're gonna have extra cheese and pepperoni." Tracy closed her menu. The waitress returned with their drinks and took the order for a large, extra cheese and pepperoni pizza.

"I wish everyone wasn't looking at us," Bobby said with a deep furrow in his forehead.

Mandy lifted her child-sized drink with both hands and giggled. "That's because you're the only Colton Cowboy in here."

"I know. I wish we ate in Colton."

"This place has better pizza than we can get back home." Tracy sipped her sweet tea.

"I don't care." Bobby continued to frown at the other boys peering at their table. "I don't like being stared at."

Zack shifted in his seat. Tracy's thigh pressed against his. Was she sitting so close simply because she knew how it affected him? "Ignore them. They're only trying to intimidate you."

Bobby turned his narrowed hazel eyes on Zack. "What does that mean?"

Zack shrugged and picked up his Coke--and nearly dropped it when Tracy's hand landed on his thigh only a few inches from his groin. He snapped his gaze on her, but she seemed focused on her son. When he reached down to remove her hand, she entwined her fingers through his. Fighting the sudden knot of desire that seared though him, he cleared his throat.

"When I rode rodeo, other cowboys loved to do the same things before someone went out. At first, it would affect me. When a horse is doing its crazy best to buck you off, concentration is essential."

"So, they're trying to psych me out so I can't play as good?"

"Yep." Zack leaned back as the server paced the pizza on the table. After she served each of them a slice, Zack thanked her and picked up his piece. "The best thing you can do is to ignore them. That way they'll think you aren't bothered by them." He winked at the kid as he reached for the shaker of red pepper at the end of the table. "And that will psych them out."

* * * *

Tracy looked over at Zack, amazed by his advice to Bobby. She remembered the time shortly after she and Jake had started dating when they'd gone to a football game in Crawford. Brent had been a high school linebacker for the Colton Mavericks. The Crawford Pirates had always been Colton's biggest rival. After the game, Jake and she had run into some of the opposing team's players. One of them had made a smart comment about Jake, and she'd begged him to ignore them, but he wouldn't. He'd brushed her off and ended up in a fight. Jake never backed down from something he considered a challenge. She could imagine if Jake were here instead of Zack, he'd have made a scene by now.

Bobby sat a little straighter and squared his shoulders under his jersey, which mimicked that of the Dallas Cowboys. His number was ten--the same as Jake's in high school--and his name was printed on the back. He ate his pizza and drank his chocolate milk with as much pride as she imagined he could muster.

"You really rode broncos?" Bobby asked between bites.

Zack wiped his mouth on a paper napkin and nodded, but it was Mandy who answered. "Yep. My Daddy has tons of silver buckles from all of the rodeos he's won. He has a couple from the National Finals Rodeo, too."

Bobby's eyes widened. "Wow! I like to watch rodeo, but Dad hates it. He doesn't like horses." He took a bite of his pizza, and his brow lowered pensively as he chewed. "Were you ever hurt by a horse?"

Zack sipped his drink, and his expression turned somber. "I was hurt a few times. Nothing too serious though."

Mandy wiped her face on a napkin, smearing more pizza sauce than she removed. "Daddy was hurt really bad the last time, though. That's why he quit. Momma wouldn't let him do it anymore."

"You quit for a girl?"

Zack shrugged and glanced at Tracy.

How would he answer Bobby's question?

"It was time to give it up and settle down. I'd always said I'd only ride for a few years."

"My dad said that he was thrown off a horse and hurt his knee real bad, and that's why he couldn't play football anymore. He said you made him ride the horse."

"Bobby." Tracy knew the story. Zack and Jake had gone riding, and when Jake's horse had thrown him, his foot caught in the stirrup, causing major injury to Jake's knee. She also knew Zack had blamed himself for the accident for a long time afterward because Jake had been unable to play football their senior year and lost his scholarship.

"I asked him if he'd like to go riding that morning. He could have said no. I knew he didn't like horses, but he often went riding with me. I'm not sure what happened, but I think his horse saw either a rattlesnake or something else spooked it. I felt really bad about what happened to your dad, Bobby. Still do."

Bobby furrowed his brow again as he picked at the crust of his pizza slice. What had Jake said to him about that morning the two weeks before the start of their last year of high school? She'd bet it wasn't the same as what Zack had told him.

The pizza devoured, Zack looked at his watch. "We'd better get going."

Zack scooted out of the booth and wiped Mandy's mouth. Tracy watched the gentle way he took care of his daughter. The task finished, Mandy stood on the seat and wrapped her arms around his neck. He pulled her to him and kissed her forehead, before setting her on her feet beside him. Tracy didn't miss that Bobby watched the exchange with something akin to longing in his eyes. Not that he'd wanted the same treatment from Zack, but Bobby had never had it from his own father when he was younger and would have appreciated the reassurance of being cherished.

They reached the cashier, and Zack pulled out his credit card. Tracy still wasn't happy he insisted on paying for the tab. He claimed it was his way of paying her back for the meal last Friday night.

Once they arrived at the community park, Tracy, Zack and the kids made their way to the area where the rest of the team gathered on the side of the field. Jake was barking instructions as he normally did before the game. Bobby joined the edge of the circle of boys, and Jake turned. When he saw she was with Zack, his expression became wary. Zack's hand tightened on hers, before he dropped it and slid it around her waist. Mandy's fingers clasped around Tracy's, and Zack laid his free hand on Bobby's shoulder.

The picture perfect family, Tracy thought wryly.

Jake strode toward them, his arms folded over his wide chest. "About time you showed up. I was wondering where my quarterback was."

"Sorry, Dad." Bobby shuffled his feet and fiddled with his helmet. "We stopped for pizza."

"Jake." Zack's grip around Tracy's waist tightened, pulling her into his side. Jake stiffened and scowled at them, but what delighted her more was when Zack ruffled Bobby's hair and said, "Good luck, buddy. We'll see you later."

Bobby smiled up at Zack and nodded. "See ya later. We're still going for ice cream, right?"

"You bet." Zack winked at him.

"C'mon, we have a game to win." Jake laid his hand on Bobby's shoulder, turning him away from Zack and Tracy.

After they found an area to spread her blanket, Tracy, Zack and Mandy settled down. She expected Zack to put some distance between them by pulling Mandy down between them, but she shifted to the other side of Tracy. He had no option but to sit next to her. She suspected he'd only held her earlier to send a message to Jake. Maybe he hadn't even been aware of his actions. Or maybe he was like a stud staking claim to his mare. She didn't know what to make of it, but she knew she aroused him and that encouraged her.

He loved me once. She hoped everyone was right, and he could love her again.

Chapter 14

The Cowboys trailed by a touchdown, and his dad paced the sideline. He wouldn't be happy if the Cowboys lost.

Bobby stood on the sideline, gripped his helmet under his arm, and bit his bottom lip when the Bulldog's quarterback tucked the ball in and ran for the goal line. The Valley Mills crowd went wild. Bobby sniffed and his gut rolled. He should have played better. He knew that; he wasn't looking forward to his dad pointing out his mistakes in front of the team.

Maybe if he 'fessed up to his mistakes, Dad would go a little easier on him. He dragged his feet over to where his dad stood by the end of the bench watching the rest of the team come off the field.

"I'm sorry, Dad. I know I screwed up big time when I threw that interception. I'll do better the next game."

His dad looked down at him. "Yeah, you better win next time."

Bobby flinched at the ugly scowl and the harshness of his dad's voice. He kept his head down because he didn't want to see the rest of the guys watching him. "I will, Dad."

"Hey, T-Rex."

Surprised by the change in his father's tone, Bobby looked up at him, but his dad was looking over his head. A muscle jumped in his jaw. Bobby glanced over his shoulder. Mandy ran toward him, and his mom and the sheriff were holding hands following her.

He still wasn't sure what he thought of the sheriff. He seemed nice enough at the restaurant. "Yeah, Dad?"

"Do you think you can tell me if you hear the sheriff tell your mom anything about me?"

Bobby frowned and shrugged. "I guess."

"That's good. I'll see you Friday." Dad patted his shoulder. "After the court hearing, you'll be moving in permanently." Dad walked away and past the rest of the guys. He rounded the end of the bleachers to the parking lot.

"Yeah," he murmured even though Dad wouldn't hear it. He never took losing a game this easily. Something had to be wrong. His dad usually yelled at the team, trying to get them to figure out why they'd lost the game, and when that was done, would blame the loss on Bobby.

"Bobby!" Mandy's call drew his attention back to his mom and Zack. Mandy hugged him around the waist. "I'm sorry you lost."

He looked down into her face and shrugged, aware the guys were all watching him. "Stop hugging me. That's for babies."

She stepped back. "No it's not. My daddy hugs me all the time. I just thought you'd be feeling real bad right now."

"Well, I'm not."

His mom came up and patted his shoulder. "You did well, Bobby. I hope your dad didn't say too much about the loss."

He shrugged again and looked around. Other parents were picking up the other guys and leaving toward the parking lot. His dad's pick-up sped past the ball field. "I think he had something else on his mind." He turned back to the sheriff. "I'd like to go home. I guess we aren't stopping for ice cream now."

Zack smiled and ruffled his hair. "Of course we're stopping. You can't always win, but it doesn't mean you still didn't do a good job."

* * * *

Lucinda Tritt looked up from the photographs. "Yeah, that's the guy who came into the store last Saturday morning."

"Are you positive?" Zack let out a breath he hadn't realized he was holding and fisted his hands under his desk across from the convenience store clerk.

Lucinda nodded and looked from him to Wyatt McPherson and Dawn Madison standing behind him. "Yeah. I'm positive. This is the guy in the truck. Is there anything else, Sheriff?"

"No, we'll be in touch, Miss Tritt. Thank you for coming in this morning." He stood when she did. She met all three gazes again before nodding and leaving Zack's office.

Once she was gone, Zack said, "I think it's time we question the Parker boys."

"Brent's working out at Johnny Blackwell's place," Dawn provided. "I'll take Kennedy and head over there."

Zack nodded as he shuffled his notes and the photos he'd shown the clerk into a pile on his desk. "Jake's at the courthouse today. He's trying to get custody of his boy from Tracy."

Wyatt, who was a second cousin to Tracy, chuckled. "So, he wants a cut of her money, now."

"Yeah, something like that." Zack remembered the previous night at the football game and stopping for ice cream afterward. He'd promised to teach the boy how to ride when he got the chance. Regardless of the outcome of the custody case today, Jake would have Bobby for the coming week.

He'd taken a real liking to Tracy's son. Zack had no idea what Jake had told the boy about him, but he sensed Jake must have said something to cause Bobby not to fully trust him. "Let's go and get that bastard."

* * * *

Logan waited for Tracy outside the Forest County courthouse. She looked up at the old limestone building that never failed to intimidate her. In 1895, the original two-room building was built on the site where Cole Cartwright, Elijah Blackwell and her great-great-great grandfather Dylan Ferguson played judge, jury and executioner of a gang of cattle rustlers who had stolen longhorns from their herd. The massive oak tree they'd hanged the thieves from still grew strong and tall in front of the court of law.

Those rustlers hadn't been the only criminals hanged from the tree in the wild days. Cole Cartwright's wife had been saved from a long drop on a short rope by marrying her prosecutor.

"You ready for this?" Logan asked when Tracy reached the top of the stairs.

She smiled and nodded. "I think so. How do you feel about this? I still can't believe you got ready so soon."

Logan held one of the thick wooden doors open for her. "I told you your case will be a breeze to win."

"I would have preferred a little more time to prepare."

Dressed in a designer suit, Logan looked every bit the perfect picture of the successful lawyer. He grinned and put his free arm around her shoulders. "Stop worrying. That's my job, and I'm not, so you shouldn't be either."

"Easier said than done."

As they made their way to the front of the courtroom, he asked, "How're things going with Zack?"

"I guess okay. We had a great evening last night."

"Good." He laid his briefcase on a table. "Keep it up. Have you slept with him yet?"

"Logan! I can't believe you'd--"

He laughed and shook his head. "I think I know the answer just by the look on your face."

She closed her mouth, swallowed hard. Hoping the heat in her cheeks hadn't turned them bright red, she looked away. "I can't believe you'd ask me such a thing."

Logan leaned over and said near her ear, "It's okay, T.C., hot, sweaty monkey sex between you and my big brother is *exactly* what you both need."

She jerked away and glared at him.

He shrugged as he opened his briefcase. "Now, you need to keep reminding him what he's missing when he's not with you."

Before she had the chance slug him, Jake and his lawyer entered the courtroom. Logan's smile faded away, and he became the intimidating attorney she'd hired.

Judge Martha Delaney entered not long after Jake. When she wasn't wearing the black robe of justice, Martha was the mild-mannered wife of the pastor of the Colton Baptist Church--wife of the same minister who had married Jake and Tracy and baptized Bobby. Jake's lawyer had tried to claim Judge Delaney had a conflict of interest since Tracy--and Logan when he chose to go to church--belonged to her husband's congregation. However, Logan didn't fail to point out that Jake's family belonged to the same church. Judge Delaney had also presided over Jake and Tracy's first custody battle following their divorce, in which she'd proven to be impartial, so the claims were considered unfounded.

After the judge brought the court to order, she asked Jake's lawyer to open the proceedings. The slick-looking middle-aged man stepped forward and flashed Tracy and Logan a predatory smile of perfect white teeth. His face was too orangey to be tanned by anything other than a spray bottle. The word *shark* fit Preston Tilley perfectly. "Your Honor, my client, Jacob Parker, is concerned about the welfare of his son and asks the court to grant full custody of him, along with child support."

"I'm going to cut to the chase and say I've read over the affidavit. For the record, why does your client consider Ms. Quinn an unfit mother?"

Tilley squared his shoulders. As he told the judge the standard line of bull that had been on the lips of gossipers for years, Tracy looked over at Jake. He was dressed in a white Western shirt and dress pants. He'd cut his dark hair and was clean-shaven.

Tilley glanced over at her and glowered at her in the way a self-righteous matron might a street tramp. "She has subjected my client's son to possible dangers when she allowed her brother to live with her in a small two-bedroom apartment. My client's not degrading the sacrifice Captain Dylan Quinn made for his country, but following his return, he had a documented case of post-traumatic stress disorder. He became an alcoholic and often resorted to violence. Now, Ms. Quinn is romantically involved with Zachery Cartwright, who also has PTSD and has publicly admitted that he suffered from a drinking problem."

"Objection," Logan shook his head and stood. "Neither Captain Quinn or Sheriff Cartwright are here to verify or deny these claims."

"Granted." Judge Delaney leaned forward on a bench that dwarfed her petite frame. "Mr. Tilley, you have said nothing that would make me believe for a moment Ms. Quinn is an unfit mother. Has she neglected Bobby?"

"Ma'am, on Monday of this week, she allowed her son home alone with a babysitter after school while she met with Zachery Cartwright for a sexual liaison. My client feels this is the type of behavior that is the most destructive to his son. Especially, since he already has problems with authority."

Tracy narrowed her eyes on Jake, not sure which made her angrier--that he knew about her and Zack, or that he would have the audacity to blame her for Bobby's problems with authority.

"Your Honor." Logan made his way around the table. "Whether or not my client met with Sheriff Cartwright isn't the concern of this court. Mr. Tilley has brought up Ms. Quinn's dating history. I'd like to bring up Mr. Parker's. He has actively dated several women, whom he's brought to his home while Bobby was there for overnight stays." Logan paused and consulted his notes. Tracy glanced at Jake, who glared at her. "On July 16, Mr. Parker brought a Miss Jasmine Pritchett, a recently convicted Waco prostitute, to his home while his son was under his care. Ms. Quinn has never brought any of the men she's dated home, nor has Bobby ever met any of them, except Sheriff Cartwright."

"Is this true, Mr. Parker?" The judge turned her hard dark eyes on Jake.

Jake scowled at Logan.

"Answer the question, Mr. Parker."

"Yes, but I didn't know she was a hooker."

Tracy raised a brow.

Logan smirked. "Interesting. When I spoke to Miss Pritchett, she related she told you her price before you brought her home from the bar.

You told her she had to come to Colton with you because you had to pick your son up from your grandmother's, who is ninety-one years old."

"Objection." Tilley stepped closer to the bench. "Hearsay."

Judge Delaney sat back in her chair and sighed. "Granted. Mr. Cartwright, please refrain--" She stopped as the doors of the courtroom opened.

Tracy turned and gasped when Zack and Wyatt entered the courtroom. Both men were tall and handsome in their determined walks and set jaws. They removed their hats simultaneously, and Tracy suddenly felt like she was transported back a hundred years. Despite how handsome the Texas Ranger was, the sheriff outshined him.

"Sheriff Cartwright." Judge Delaney didn't hide her displeasure at having her court disrupted. "Please explain this disruption."

"Your Honor," Zack said as he and Wyatt stopped beside Tracy's table. "May we approach the bench?"

"This had better be good."

"I object to this," Tilley whined with his hands gesturing. "This is highly irregular, considering Ms. Quinn is having an illicit affair with the sheriff."

* * * *

Zack shot Tilley through with a glare. The lawyer looked like a weasel. Zack walked to the judge's bench. Martha leaned forward with impatience thinning her lips into a tight line, which did nothing to hide her multitude of wrinkles.

"Alright, Zack, what the heck is going on?"

Zack cleared his throat and spoke in a low tone. "I just wanted to make sure you know Jake Parker is our prime suspect in the rustling that's been going on. We're here to take him in for questioning."

Martha sat back with her eyes wide. Not much surprised her anymore, but obviously, this did. "Well, now, that certainly throws a wrench into the fan. Alright, Zack, Wyatt, do what you need to." As they stepped away, she said, "Mr. Cartwright, Mr. Tilley, approach the bench, please."

Zack ignored his brother's questioning look and Tracy's wide eyes as he headed toward Jake. While Martha informed the lawyers of what was going on, Zack and Wyatt stopped before Jake. His jaw was set and beads of sweat formed on his brow. Jake's hazel eyes were two cold amber stones as he glowered up at Zack. "What the hell is going on?"

Wyatt leaned forward with his hands on the table. "We'd like to ask you some questions regarding your whereabouts last Friday night into

Saturday morning. We'd also be interested in you telling us about just how you got that cut on your hand."

Jake shifted his eyes from Zack to Wyatt and a bead of sweat ran down the side of his temple. If he hadn't known Jake since they were kids, Zack would have chocked it up to the custody case. Jake stood and glanced at the lawyer, who came to stand beside him.

Zack unlocked his back teeth. "You can come with us on your own, or we can take you in by force. The choice is yours."

Jake shrugged. "I have nothing to hide, but I want my lawyer there. Mr. Tilley?"

The way the lawyer's eyes widened was almost comical, but he covered his surprise with puffing out his chest and nodding. "I agree. My client has nothing to hide."

Zack suppressed a chuckle, but Wyatt wasn't as reserved as he snickered. "We'll see about that. Let's go."

As they turned to go, Tracy caught Zack's attention. She was biting her lower lip, and her eyes were still wide with disbelief. Once Jake, Tilley, and Wyatt were out of the room, he stepped over to stand beside her.

"You think Jake stole your horses?"

Zack shrugged and twisted his hat in his hands. "It looks like it."

Logan stepped in behind Tracy and laughed. "Well, I have to say this is a first in four years of practicing law. Thanks, big brother, for upstaging me."

"Anytime." Zack matched his brother's grin.

"So, what happens now?" Tracy glanced between the brothers.

"We ask for this ridiculous custody suit to be thrown out, for one thing." Logan gathered his notes. "And you have some fun. Hey, I'm doing a show tomorrow night at the Longhorn. Probably my last before I head off to Nashville. Why don't you two show up, have fun, and do some dancing?"

Tracy locked gazes with Zack. He knew he shouldn't, but he couldn't stay away from her. "Okay. I'll be tied up all day with the case, but tomorrow night sounds good."

She smiled and touched the hand holding his hat. Her fingers were soft and hot and reminded him of how she touched him in other places. "Would you like me to pick up Mandy this afternoon? I can bring her back to Oak Springs with me when I pick up Bobby. I think it's a safe bet he won't be going to Jake's tonight."

He hesitated for a long moment, but his mother was playing bridge that night, and he hated dumping Mandy on Lance and Audrey. "I'll call the school and let Mrs. Longoria know you're picking her up."

Logan smirked as he closed his briefcase. He winked at Tracy and thumped Zack on the shoulder as he passed by. Zack met her gaze, and he was well aware that they were suddenly alone, until Logan whistled the *Wedding March* as he went through the door.

She laughed, until the gales of mirth turned breathy. "He isn't very subtle, is he?"

"Tracy." He sobered, caught for a moment in the spell she wove with her innocent eyes and inhaled breath. He broke the trance by looking away. "Don't think any of this changes how I feel. I'll never fall for you again."

Unable to bear watching the hopefulness in her pewter eyes turn to regret and hurt, he turned and plopped his hat on his head. As he hurried down the aisle to the door, his heart reminded him with each beat he was the biggest fool around.

Because he'd never stopped loving her.

* * * *

"I have no idea what y'all are talking about. Last Friday night I was in Waco." Jake leaned back in the wooden chair.

Zack paced the floor of the conference room. He'd agreed to let Wyatt and Dawn question Jake. Wyatt suggested for sake of preventing a conflict of interest--on more levels than just the fact Jake was the prime suspect in stealing Zack's horses--that could jeopardize the case.

"Who were you with?" Dawn asked and leaned over her arms on the table.

"I've told you four times. Angela Duran. I met her for dinner at her place and didn't leave until seven the next morning. Call her. She'll verify it. Dammit, I'm not the guy you're lookin' for."

"How did you cut your hand?" Wyatt sat forward in his chair and leaned over the table to look Jake in the face.

Jake shifted in his seat and shrugged. With a chuckle sounding more forced than real, he said, "Angie is a bit of a klutz. She broke a wine glass, and I cut my hand picking up the pieces. I probably should've got stitches, but I was havin' too much fun to care. Y'all know what's it like when you've got a willin' woman around. Isn't that right, Zack? Is Tracy still a wildcat in the sack?"

Zack jerked to a stop and took a step forward. Only years of discipline and Wyatt and Dawn's warning looks stopped him from punching the smirk off Jake's face.

With his hands fisted tightly, Zack turned away and stared at the wall.

"Do you know where your brother Brent was on Friday night?" Dawn asked.

"Nope. I'm not his keeper. But isn't he next door? Why not ask him."

"Okay, folks, I think my client has answered all the questions he needs to. He can't be the person you're looking for." Preston Tilley scraped his chair against the floor as he stood. He'd remained rather quiet throughout the four hours of redundant questioning, which surprised Zack. Then again, Tilley was a divorce lawyer, not a criminal attorney.

With the warning for Jake not to leave the county, Wyatt and Dawn allowed him and Tilley to go. Zack turned and let out a breath. "He's lying through his teeth."

"Brent told me and Kennedy the same thing when we questioned him. I'll check out their alibis." Dawn headed for the door with Wyatt watching the gentle sway of her backside as she left.

Zack poured them both a cup of coffee from the stained, old Mr. Coffee in the corner. "So, what's going on between you and Dawn?"

"Nothing." Wyatt sat down in the chair Jake had vacated and sipped his cup.

"Uh-huh." Zack sat across from him. "How come I believe you even less than I do Parker?"

Wyatt ran a hand through his reddish-brown hair. "She drives me crazy."

With a laugh, Zack set his mug down. "No kidding. What's really going on?"

Wyatt took a deep breath and leaned back in his chair. "When we were partners on the Dallas PD, we crossed a line that should never be crossed by a female and a male partner. Especially when that partner was a friend for almost thirty years," he added more to himself then to Zack.

"Let me guess, she wanted more than you were willing to give?"

Wyatt shook his head. "The other way around." He stood and picked up his mug. "It's all water under the bridge."

"Until it floods my department. I've never seen Dawn so uptight in my life, and she's been my friend since we shared the same bath water in her grandmother's kitchen sink. She may have been your friend, but she's always been like a sister to me. And I don't like seeing her like this."

"I've tried to talk to her." Wyatt drank more coffee and turned toward the large framed map of Texas on the wall. "I'm not the one who ended it. She did. What else is there to say?"

Then Wyatt faced Zack again. "Enough about me and Deputy Dawn Madison. What the hell is going on between you and my cousin?"

Zack took a gulp of coffee and shrugged. He wanted to say nothing was going on, but that wasn't exactly true. He'd promised Tracy he'd treat her like a girlfriend. "Tracy and I are dating."

"That so?" Wyatt grinned and sat down again. "I seem to remember you swore you'd never speak to her again."

"True. But then Dylan came back from the war, and I couldn't let him continue to beat himself up over something outside of his control." He stared into his coffee mug at the black brew. "I needed Tracy's help since he's her brother and he was living with her." He shrugged and drained the cup. "Who knows if anything will come of us dating?"

He couldn't let anything come of it. He owed that to Lisa. She was dead because he couldn't love her more than he'd loved a memory.

"Tracy's a good woman, Zack. I know she hurt you, but I think you'd be wise to give her a second chance." He shook his head. "I know her life with that idiot Parker sure as hell wasn't a bed of roses. I'll never understand what she saw in him, because he treated her like shit. Tracy's too good-natured for her own good."

What was with everyone? His friends and family were free with their opinions on his love life lately. He was about to tell Wyatt that whatever went on between him and Tracy was none of his damn business, when Wyatt's cell phone began playing Toby Keith's *Beer for My Horses*.

Wyatt set his cup onto the table and pulled the phone from his belt. A moment passed before he spoke, and as he listened, his forehead furrowed. "It's okay, Ma, I'm finished for now. What's going on?" It didn't take Zack too long to realize the news wasn't good. Wyatt's tanned face lost most of its color and his voice was rough. "Yeah, Ma, I'll be right over. Have you called Audrey?" He paused to listen. "No, I'll stop by the CW, then come over. Love you, too. See you soon."

Zack waited for Wyatt to slip the iPhone into the holder on his belt. The stricken look on his face told Zack something terrible happened in his family.

Wyatt swallowed and looked at him. "That was my mother. She and Dad just got a call from an Army chaplain."

Zack was instantly on alert. Wyatt's younger sister, who recently deployed to Afghanistan, was a registered nurse and Army major. "Rachel?"

Wyatt nodded. "Yeah. Ma didn't know much, except Rachel was injured today and is being airlifted to Germany. I have to go. I need to stop by Lance and Audrey's place to tell them." He paused at the door but didn't look at Zack. "I hope my twin sister can forgive herself if our little sister dies over there."

As Wyatt left, Zack leaned back in his chair and silently sent a prayer to heaven for a fellow soldier and one of his friends.

Chapter 15

"Zack." Tracy opened her door a little after one AM, instantly wishing she wasn't wearing the rattiest t-shirt she owned as a nightshirt. "I wasn't expecting you until morning."

He walked across the porch as if his shoes were made of concrete, and stepped into the entry, removing his hat. "Is Mandy sleeping?"

Tracy glanced up the stairs. "Yeah. I was headed upstairs myself when I saw your headlights in the driveway." He nodded and looked around. She got the impression he was trying not to look at her. She clasped her hands together in front of the old University of Texas t-shirt. "Want something to drink? I usually drink tea at night, but I can make coffee. You look like you could use some."

He met her gaze, and the ghosts haunting his eyes took her aback. "That would be good. How long has Mandy been asleep?"

Shrugging, Tracy led him down the dimly lit hall to the kitchen. "Oh, since about nine. She and Bobby played in the pool after supper and that tired them both out."

Her laptop and American History text lay on the counter where she'd left them after finishing her paper that was due tomorrow. He touched the book cover. "So, the classes going okay?"

"Yeah. I'm getting back into the groove and already decided I'm going to try going full time next semester." She went about making coffee while Zack sat at the island bar. His gaze caressed her every move, heating her skin. "It will be tough, but I also would like to get into med school before I'm forty."

"I have faith in you."

She looked at him and smiled, her heart swelling. "I'm glad."

"Bobby in bed, too?"

As the coffee brewed, she leaned against the sink. "Yeah."

His brow lowered as he studied her for a moment. "Where'd you get that shirt? It obviously isn't new."

Surely, he didn't remember it, did he? "Where do you think?"

He shook his head and laughed, but it was choppy and short-lived. "That's not the shirt I gave you for your eighteenth birthday, is it?"

Tracy turned and poured two mugs of coffee. After dumping four heaping spoonfuls of sugar into his and milk into hers, she headed for the island. With his brow furrowed and his kissable mouth twisting in puzzlement, he looked more handsome than any man had a right to. She took the stool next to him. "Yes, it is." Before he could comment, she asked, "How did the questioning go?"

For a moment, Zack stared at her, then shook his head and picked up the steaming mug. "As I expected. Brent and Jake denied everything. Dawn checked out their alibis tonight. Jake's appears to be watertight. He was in Waco last Friday with a girlfriend." Zack glanced at her, as if he were waiting for a reaction.

Tracy didn't even blink at the news. "How about Brent?"

"Colleen Stryker provided him with a story, too."

"Johnny Blackwell's mother?"

"Yep." Zack sipped from his cup. "Brent was with Johnny Blackwell and his son Matt all night playing poker at Colleen's place."

"Damn, I was hoping they were the culprits. If for no other reason, just to have the rustling stopped. Good people are being hurt badly by this."

"I know." Zack looked into his mug, his brow low over dull eyes.

Tracy lightly rubbed his shoulder and leaned forward for a better look of his face. "What's wrong? Somehow, I don't think it's only the case bothering you."

He met her gaze. "Wyatt got a call this afternoon."

She pulled back. "My cousin?"

He nodded. "Rachel was wounded today and airlifted to Germany. I don't know much more than that, but I know from personal experience only the seriously wounded get sent out that quick."

The breath whooshed out of her and her hand flew to her mouth. "Oh God, no. She came home just this past May. We went honky-tonk hopping one night, and she told me she was hoping this would be her last deployment." She jumped off the stool, spun away from him and paced the tile floor. Her heart ached with the news of her cousin. Rachel McPherson had been one of her closest girlfriends after she moved to Texas. "Dear Lord, how many more people, who shouldn't even be over there, will get hurt?"

"What do you mean?"

Halting in mid pace, she stared at him. Unable to stop the tears, she let them slide down her cheeks. "You, Dylan, and now Rachel. She only joined the Army because Lance decided he wanted her sister instead of her. Dylan was over there because Leon forged Granddad's will and stole Oak Springs Ranch out from under him. And you..." She stepped closer and took a shaky breath. "You were only there because of--of what happened between us."

* * * *

Zack's gut twisted when she covered her face. He got off the stool and pulled her to him. "Shhh..."

He held her tightly against him as she sobbed into his neck. Her arms wound tightly around his waist, and he buried his nose into her hair at her temple. She was too tall for him to rest his chin on top of her head as he'd always done when he'd held Lisa. The thought of his dead wife brought him up short. He tried to ease out of the embrace, but Tracy clung to him tighter than before.

"I was so afraid, Zack, when I heard about you getting shot."

She looked up at him with rivulets of tears running down her cheeks. Pain and fear reflected in the depths of her eyes and his heart twisted. Had she cared so much about him?

"Then the news came that you were in a coma and the docs weren't at all sure if you'd live. I prayed every day, every minute, that God would let you be okay." Her lips twitched as if she was trying to smile, but never quite worked up the effort. "I even made deals with Him."

She shook her head and laid it on his shoulder. As she trembled in his arms, she held on to him so fiercely the shudders ricocheted through his own body.

"I know if--if things had been different, you wouldn't have joined the Marines. I'll never forgive myself for you enduring all that you did while over there. It was my fault, and I would have given up anything and everything..." She hiccoughed on a sob. "I knew you could never be mine again, but the world would be a much darker place without you in it."

Her confession and raw emotions rattled him. He rubbed her back and sucked in a breath, catching the light scent of flowers and honey. Tracy had always smelled this way. Her unique fragrance had haunted his dreams while he slept on the hard desert sand a half a world away.

"Aw, baby, I joined up because it was the right thing to do. As cliched as it sounds, I joined out of love for my country, not for any other reason."

He was surprised at how right that answer was. He couldn't blame Tracy's betrayal or Lisa's hatred of the rodeo any more.

Tracy looked up at him again with shimmery eyes. He stroked her wet cheeks, drying her tears with his thumbs. How many times had Lisa cried for him? But never had her tears ripped him apart as much as Tracy's did now. "It may not have been the Marines, but I would've joined something after Nine-eleven."

"Zack...I..."

Her voice trailed off, and she held him captive in her gaze. When she leaned in, he met her lips. He responded to her and caressed her upper lip with his tongue. She opened her mouth under his and they drank each other in. He needed her, wanted her.

She yanked his uniform shirt out of his pants and unbuttoned it, all the while kissing him with desperate passion. Her hands slid between them and up his chest. When her soft fingers found the sensitive buds of his nipples, he hissed and eased out of the kiss.

With a smile, she simply took his hand and led him upstairs to the master bedroom. He didn't protest the invitation, despite her son and his daughter sleeping down the hall.

As she locked the door, he shrugged out of the shirt and took stock of the dim room. Only a small lamp was lit on the dresser between the windows. His impression of the room was a mismatch, an indication that she hadn't done much redecorating after her step-uncle vacated the house. The walls and carpeting were masculine shades of tan and blue, while the bed was piled high with lacy white pillows and feminine floral linens.

Her turning to him to caress down his chest to stop on his belt had him forgetting everything but her. He'd taken off his service belt and locked it in the truck, which reminded him of the last time they'd been together and his feverish trip to the drugstore. "Are you sure about this? I don't have any condoms on me."

She swallowed and glanced away. "I bought a box the other day after you were here to pick up Mandy. If you hadn't been so tired, I would've dragged you upstairs then. The only thing that stopped me from doing so anyway was the fact I didn't have condoms." Her cheeks pinked slightly, and she shrugged as she slid the zipper down and pushed the pants and briefs over his hips. "But now I do." Her wicked smile was completely at odds with the soft blush. "And I intend to use 'em."

"Good, because I'm up for the challenge." He leaned in and captured her lips again.

His pants tangled around his boots, and she pushed on his shoulders until he sat on the bed. She stood before him as he caressed her smooth, silky legs from her knees to her hips, lifting the hem of the old t-shirt to reveal plain blue cotton panties. No woman had ever fired his blood as she did, and though he hated to admit it, that was the real reason he hadn't sought someone else out after he'd recovered from his grief after Lisa died. The guilt he'd never get over.

He pulled the shirt over her head and dropped it to the floor. All thought evaporated from his overheating mind like rain on the hot pavement of Highway 6 in mid August. His mouth went dry and his groin ached with need. Cool air kissed her skin, tightening her nipples into hard raspberries ready for devouring. He pulled her to him and flicked his tongue over one of the points, while he plucked at the other with his fingers. With his other hand, he stroked up and down her spine.

She moaned, and he watched her long lashes veil darkened pewter eyes. He teased until she pulled back and knelt before him. After undoing the lacings of his work boots, she pulled them off, then tugged off his socks, and removed his pants. She slid between his legs, her fingertips scorching him on their slow trek up his legs to his groin. Anticipation kicked his heart into high gear, as she closed her warm, smooth hand around his erection and gently stoked. He held his breath when she leaned in to place a kiss on the tip, then she slid her lips along the length. The feathery touch was blissfully excruciating.

She looked up at him. "Remember the very first time I did this?"

His breath hissed out between clenched teeth, and his hands tangled in her hair when she took him completely into her hot, soft mouth. Fighting for control, he gasped for air and rasped, "Yeah. You told me...it was my... Christmas present." His head lolled, and he struggled with wanting her to continue and wanting her to stop. "Tracy...damn... It's too much. Stop, baby."

She caressed his sac as she sucked him. Watching her was almost as hot as what she was doing to him.

"Tracy...I'm..." He groaned and was lost. Tightening the grasp on her hair, he held on and growled a curse as light exploded through him.

At last, he slowly opened his eyes and met her gaze. She wiped her mouth and the cum off his belly with her discarded shirt. When she stood, slowly pushed her panties over her hips, and stepped out of them, she amazed him by how sexy she was without ever trying to be. She placed her hands on his shoulders and peered deeply into his eyes. A fire burned deep in her gaze, but also an emotion he didn't want to analyze blazed in the depths of her gray eyes.

"This time it was for coming back to me."

He wanted to argue that he hadn't come back to her, but she applied pressure to his shoulders. He lay back with his head on her pile of pillows and with her in his arms. When she straddled him, he huskily said, "It might be a while. I'm not eighteen anymore."

She leaned over him, her breath hot on his ear as she purred. "We have all night, Zack."

She kissed him, thrusting her tongue against his. A shudder quaked through her body when she pressed and ground herself into his spent cock. He moaned because she felt so good, hot, and soft--and wet.

He broke the kiss and shifted her over him until she was over his face. "Better hang on. You're in for one hell of a wild ride."

She put her hands on the headboard and let out a long breathy moan when he took her into his mouth. The first orgasm came fast. The second was slower and more powerful. She bucked on him with each shudder. He looked up to her face. She bit her lip to keep the squeal from escaping. He nibbled on the inside of her thigh. Then he ran his tongue over her clit again before circling it. When he stroked up her belly to her engorged nipples and plucked them between his fingers and thumbs, she shuddered.

"Zack, I--I need you in me now."

And he couldn't have agreed more. With a little maneuvering, he had her on her back and kneeled between her legs.

"The condoms are in the drawer," she rasped.

He ripped the package open and suited up. Entering her to the hilt, he groaned and his eyes fluttered closed. He kept the rhythm slow while he caressed her flat belly to her breasts. At first, he kneaded the small mounds, then plucked at the puckered nipples.

"Oh, that feels so good."

"One of these days, I'm gonna make you come by playing with your breasts."

She lazily smiled and opened her eyes. "That's not possible."

He knew his grin was cocky and didn't care. "Oh, I think it is, and I'm more than willing to try." He kissed her and then dragged his lips down her neck to one of her nipples. He licked the bud, and she wrapped her legs around him and tried to move against him. She begged him to take her where she wanted to go. He held himself still, filling her but not thrusting for as long as he could, but his own need was too much. Soon, he brought his mouth back to hers, pulled out only to plunge back in, and set a pace that would give them what they both wanted.

He stared down into her glazed eyes and clenched his teeth to keep the growl contained as his release boiled through him. She moaned his name as her own orgasm quaked through her.

And he lost his heart to her all over again.

She'd always had his soul.

* * * *

Tracy woke with her head on Zack's shoulder and his arms around her. Was she dreaming? Soft morning light glowed around the heavy drapes at the windows. Then the past night came back to her. She'd sensed a subtle change in him when she broke down; the wall he'd built around himself began to crack. If she hadn't felt it, she'd never have been able to seduce him as she had.

He shifted beneath her, and before she knew how it happened, their positions switched. Smiling, he leaned over her and said in a sexy, deep Southern drawl, "Good mornin', gorgeous."

She patted the upper arm on which he supported himself. The muscle was a solid mass. She may not have been born and raised in Texas, but she was Texas bred and could drawl out her words as well as the best Southern belle. "You already have me in bed, sir. And I'm more than willin', so there's no need to flatter me."

He laughed; the deep rumble skittered across her senses. "You have no idea, do you?"

"About what?" She held her breath, unsure of what she was expecting. Her pulse fluttered as he skimmed the backs of his fingers up her arm.

"I think you are the sexiest, most beautiful woman I've ever known."

A tremble shook though her, and she stared up at him with wide eyes. Did he honestly believe that? Could she believe it?

With a lopsided grin and a shake of his head, he leaned over her and kissed her senseless. When she thought she'd succumb to either asphyxia or desire, he pulled away, leaving her achy with want. "As much as I'd like to stay in bed and show you exactly how damned sexy you are, I think we'd better get up. I'd like to be dressed and down stairs before the kids are up."

She smiled up at him, and her heart swelled with so much love it hurt. Even while her body protested the idea, he was right. "Forever the voice of reason."

"That's me." He nuzzled her neck, then sat up on the end of the bed. "Do you think you can find a sitter for Bobby tonight?"

She sat up, pulling the sheet up to cover her chest. "I don't know. Why?"

"I was thinking we could go to Logan's gig at the Longhorn if you can find a sitter. We did kinda promise him."

"I suppose I could call Mary Estrada. Her son Andy and Bobby are best friends."

"Call her. I'm sure I can get Amy Jackson to babysit Mandy. We can't stay out long, but I want to take you out on a proper date, even if it is just to the Longhorn Saloon."

* * * *

"Bobby."

He groaned and covered his head with the blanket. The sun was up, but he wasn't ready to get out of bed yet.

"Bobby, wake up."

More awake after she shook his shoulder, he peeked out from under his warm covers and came face to face with Mandy. Man did she have one awful mess of bed-head. Her black hair was all tangled and the bangs his mom had given her stuck up on one side. "What are you doin' in my room?"

She pushed a clump of hair from her face and climbed up to sit on the edge of his twin bed. "I woke up and had to pee. I was on the way back to my room when I heard my daddy's voice coming from Tracy's room. Then I heard them laugh. I think he and your momma had a sleepover, too." Mandy giggled and covered her mouth. "I didn't think grownups had sleepovers. Wanna go surprise 'em?"

Bobby pushed himself up to a sitting position and stared at her. He considered her one of his best friends, until she said stuff like that. She was such a baby.

His Dad had women stay over all the time when he stayed with him. And he knew what went on when the bedroom door closed, especially after he snuck in one time and caught them wrestling together naked. He had never seen his dad as mad as he was that time, nor had he ever been so afraid of him either.

He'd promised Dad never to tell Mom about what he'd seen. His dad said his mom wouldn't let Bobby come to stay with him anymore if she knew about it. Logan had asked Bobby if he'd ever seen his dad with a girl a few days ago, and he told him the truth. He liked Logan, even though Dad hated his guts.

"No. Don't ever go into the bedroom when grownups are together. They're probably doin' sex." Bobby grimaced at the thought of kissing a girl and touching her while they were naked.

Mandy scrunched up her brow and tilted her head. "What's that?"

He groaned again and shook his head. "Don't you know anything? Sex. It's like where babies come from."

Her eyes got so big he thought they would pop right out of her head. "Babies! My daddy and your momma are gonna have a baby?"

"Shhh!" Bobby ran a hand through his hair. "No. It doesn't always work." He didn't know exactly how it did all work or all that much about the subject. He only knew what his uncle Brent had told him when he'd asked him about what his dad did with those girls he brought home. "I just know a guy and a girl have to do a lot of kissing and touching to make a baby. I guess they have to practice a lot to get it right."

"Are they gonna get married? My daddy said people should be married before having babies."

"Who knows?" He shrugged. The more he got to know Zack, the more he liked him. Zack didn't get mad at him, not like Dad did at times. The other night after the game, Zack had bought him ice cream and told him he didn't care that the team lost the game. *The important thing is you had fun and gave it your best.*"

Bobby had been mad when his mom said he couldn't go to his dad's last night. Dad had told Bobby he'd soon be living all the time with him, but he didn't want that either. He'd miss his mom too much. And he'd miss Mandy.

"Do you think your dad will be off work today? Since it's Saturday?"

Mandy shrugged and pulled at the bottom of the t-shirt his mom had given her to wear as a nightgown over her knees. "I donno. Sometimes he's off. But usually he's workin'. He's tryin' to catch those bad guys who stole our horses." She puckered her brow again. "Why?"

He swallowed and looked down at the Batman comforter covering him. "Well, since my mom has to work at her shop today, I was wonderin' if I could come over to your place and he could teach me how to ride a horse. I liked it the other night when we got ice cream and he talked about his days in rodeo. He must've had lots of fun."

"He must like you, because he never tells me anything about when he rode broncos. I think he's afraid Momma won't like it."

"You said something like that before. That your mom wouldn't let your dad ride in the rodeo anymore. Why not?"

"I donno." Mandy sighed and averted her eyes to her hands lying in her lap. "I don't remember much about Momma now. Just things like her singing to me. She had a pretty voice. And us goin' to the park by our house before it got too cold. I remember more of bein' afraid of Daddy when he came back from the war. He always yelled at Momma and made her cry. I didn't like bein' at home when he was there. I liked staying with my Grammy and Pappy. They live on a ranch and have cows and horses and chickens."

What kind of person was Zack? Bobby remembered his dad's warning about Zack acting nice when he really wasn't. Maybe Dad was right. "How's your dad now?"

She perked up and smiled her gap-toothed grin. "Oh, now he's a lot different. He's real sorry about how he yelled at Momma and that I got so scared. He had that--that P...P...D--something or other."

"P...T...S...D." He said each letter slowly so he wouldn't mess it up. "My uncle Dylan had it, too."

"That's it. Anyway, Daddy was real messed up after coming home from the war. He almost died. At least that's what I heard my Pappy tell someone once."

"My Uncle Dylan almost died, too. He was blown up. I've heard my granddad talk about it. Lots of soldiers get PTSD. I guess when they get over it they go back to being happy again. Uncle Dylan did after he met Aunt Charli."

"Daddy did when we moved here. I don't think he liked Wyoming."

"Why?"

She shrugged and pulled on her t-shirt again. "Donno. I don't think Pappy and Grammy liked him. And I don't think Grandma--Daddy's momma--liked my momma much either. She called her a bad name one day to my Aunt Winnie. They didn't know I was listenin'. Grandma said, 'Lisa's still controlling Zack even beyond the grave.'" She tilted her head and met Bobby's gaze. "I don't know what she meant, but that's when Aunt Winnie said Daddy needed a girlfriend."

Bobby didn't comment. What kind of marriage did Zack and Mandy's mom have? He knew his granddad and grandma didn't like his dad. If no one wanted her parents to get married and they fought all the time, maybe they had the same kind of marriage his mom and dad had. His mom seemed so sad before she divorced his dad. Now since Zack started coming around, she'd hum to herself and often smiled even when no one was around as if she was thinking of something she liked.

Maybe no one should get married at all. But then there was his granddad and grandma Quinn. They'd been married forever and still seemed to like each other. He caught his granddad kissing his grandma the day before they left to go back to Washington. Dylan and Charli always held hands, just as he'd seen his mom and Zack do the other night at the football game. He'd never seen such things between his mom and dad, even before they got divorced.

Did that mean his mom and dad really didn't like each other? But then why did they get married?

Mandy broke into his confusing thoughts. "Hey, do you wanna make 'em breakfast? Daddy likes Cheerios."

"Mom likes them, too." At the thought of Mandy and him making bowls of cereal and coffee for his mom and Zack like he'd seen in TV shows, he smiled. Maybe he could pretend Mandy was his little sister. He'd always wondered what having a little sister or brother would be like. "Yeah. Let's go." As they headed out the bedroom door, Bobby warned, "Oh, don't mention anything about what I told you. Kids aren't supposed to know about what grownups do. So, let's keep it our little secret. Okay?"

She took his hand and squeezed it as she pulled him along the hall to the stairs. "Okay."

* * * *

The clanging of dishes echoed from the kitchen as Tracy and Zack descended the stairs. She turned and faced him. "Well, I think the kids are already up. Now what?"

He stopped in the foyer and glanced in the direction of the kitchen. "I could always go outside and ring the doorbell and they'll think I just got here."

With a raised brow, she laughed. "Zachery, that has to be the craziest thing you've ever come up with. How do you explain your wet hair or the fact you're holding your boots in your hand? It's almost as bad as the whopper you told my dad Christmas morning after bringing me home when we spent that night together."

He chuckled and shrugged. "I never figured he'd call my parents to check our stories. I only figured, if you called and told your dad and mom you were spending the night with my cousin Faith, they'd never question it. When he cornered me the next morning, I just spouted the first thing that popped into my mind, which was my truck broke down."

Amusement of the old memory brightened the stubble-rough face, and small crinkles creased the corners of his eyes. The light coming in the entry windows played over his damp hair and picked out gold highlights.

Darker honey-colored ringlets curled at his ears. She remembered a younger Zack standing in this very same foyer and facing down an angry Bob Quinn. "What did Dad say to you, anyway? You've never told me."

Zack groaned and he lost the smile, but not the humor in his bottomless blue eyes. "He pulled me into the parlor and gave me the same speech he'd give to a new recruit."

Her eyes widened. "The safe-sex--AKA condom--lecture?"

"You got it. That had to be the most embarrassing conversation I've ever had."

She covered her mouth, but the snort escaped, and she laughed so hard tears came to her eyes. She leaned her forehead on his shoulder.

"Sure, laugh at my expense. It was damned embarrassing enough when my old man told me that stuff--a year too late, mind you. But to have my girlfriend's father do it was excruciating to say the least."

She wiped her eyes and looked into his contorted expression. "I'm sorry. If it's any consolation, my mother gave me a similar lecture about birth control pills. She was all ready to make an appointment at the doctor until I told her I'd been on the Pill since that September. I swear, I thought Mom was gonna fall off the chair. She had no idea I'd lost my virginity long before that Christmas Eve."

He chuckled and wrapped his free arm around her waist. His boots dangled at his side from his other hand. "No wonder your mother watched us like a hawk for a month of Sundays after that day. When will the general and your mom be home?"

She groaned and laid her head on his shoulder again, drinking in the easy, comfortable feeling. "They were going to leave Washington yesterday. She called me last night from Bristol, Tennessee. She said they should be here sometime Sunday afternoon, same day Dylan, Charli, and Annie are flying home."

"You don't sound happy about the return of your parents."

"I don't know how I feel. When Mom's here, she takes over. Not in a mean way and not even in a bad way, but she suddenly cooks every meal and does all the laundry and all the cleaning."

Zack snickered. "I figured you'd be loving that. You hate to cook, and I've never met a woman who likes to clean and do laundry."

"That's what I meant by not in a bad way. I do hate doing those things, but when she takes over it makes me feel--"

"Inadequate?"

She pulled back and met his gaze. "Exactly. Like I don't already have enough to feel inadequate about. I love my parents, but sometimes I wonder how this living together is going to work. Sometimes I wish I'd just stayed in my apartment."

He lowered his brow in thought, but before he could speak, the kitchen door down the hall swung open. Zack jumped back as Mandy came running out. She was still dressed in a pink t-shirt Tracy had given her to wear. Mandy took their hands and pulled them into the kitchen.

"Hey, you sleepyheads, we made you breakfast!"

"Hi, Mom. I'm making toast and brewed coffee." Bobby stood on a footstool and bent over the counter to peer down in the toaster. "You'll have to pour the coffee, then I think we can eat." When the toast popped up, Bobby put it on a plate already piled high. He jumped off the stool and moved around the island to the table with the plate of golden toast. As he passed them, he looked at Zack. "Morning, Sheriff."

Her eyes stung at the scene of him setting the plate on the table set with bowls of cereal, orange juice, and a jar of grape jelly.

Mandy pulled on her hand. "You sit here." Tracy obeyed and sat at the end of the table. "Daddy, you're here."

Zack put his boots beside the chair at the other end of the table. He looked across the meal their children had prepared and slowly sat in the chair. She sensed he was as overwhelmed as she was.

"This is really great," Zack said after clearing his throat, but his voice was still thick.

"Thanks, Daddy." Mandy beamed with pride. "Did you have a nice sleepover with Tracy, too?"

Across the table, Bobby narrowed his eyes on Mandy and shook his head. What was *that* about?

Then Mandy leaned toward him and said in a loud whisper, "I didn't say anything about sex. But when the baby comes, I get to name her."

Bobby groaned and covered his face with his hands. "Oh, Mandy..."

Tracy's mouth dropped open, and she caught Zack's mortified expression. At long last, he rubbed back of his red-tinged neck and let out a long breath. "I stand corrected. *This* is the most embarrassing conversation I've ever had."

"Yep." With her cheeks burning, she glanced at Bobby. "I think you and I need to have a talk, young man." Dear Lord, she hadn't planned to have *that* conversation for a few more years. Bobby's cheeks were red, and he stared at the table. Needing to do something, Tracy jumped up to pour coffee.

She returned with steaming cups and set one before Zack. His brows furrowed as he looked at his daughter. "Mandy, there isn't going to be a baby."

When her little face melted, Tracy felt the disappointment in her own heart. Mandy brightened almost instantly and shrugged. "That's okay. But I want a baby sister soon."

Tracy met Zack's gaze across the table as he swallowed hard enough to make his throat move. He looked at Mandy again. The warmth from earlier completely sucked from the room as surely as if an arctic breeze blew through, leaving it as cold as the empty spaces in her heart.

"Mandy, there isn't going to be..." His husky voice drifted away with the bitter wind.

Tracy forced a shaky smile and laid a hand on Mandy's small shoulder. When the little girl turned bright, hopeful eyes on her, she fought the burn in her sinuses. "Why don't we talk about something else?" She pulled her hand away and glanced at Zack. "I was hoping we could have a barbeque Sunday night after my family comes home."

Zack shrugged and picked up his cooling cup of coffee. "Sure. Sounds fun."

An uneasy silence settled over them for a few moments and no one seemed interested in breakfast.

"Hey, Sheriff, do you have to work today?" Bobby flicked a glance at Tracy.

Zack shrugged and sat his mug on the table. "I was planning to. At least for a few hours this morning. Why do you ask?"

Bobby's shoulders slumped, and he picked up his spoon, but he only played in his cereal by stirring it. "It's nothin'."

Mandy reached for the sugar bowl and dumped two spoonfuls on her Cheerios. "Bobby wanted to come over to the CW so you can teach him how to ride."

"Mandy," Bobby chided again.

"Well, you did. I figured you could ride old Grasshopper since he's nice."

Zack glanced at Tracy before saying to Bobby, "You'd like to go riding?"

Bobby shrugged one shoulder and kept on stirring his cereal. "You're busy, so don't worry about it."

* * * *

Zack swallowed hard, besieged by so much emotion he wasn't sure what he felt. Despite the embarrassment of a moment ago and the tension afterward, he couldn't deny he didn't want the time this morning to end. Somehow, he belonged here with this woman and their children. He wanted to take this little boy and tuck him under his wing.

"Daddy, do you really have to work today? I want to go riding with Bobby. I want to show him Holly and how I can ride around barrels on Poppy," Mandy whined, referring to her mare and pony. "Please, can't you take today off?"

Mandy never complained about him working. He knew she didn't always like it, but she hadn't ever asked him to stay home. He glanced at Bobby--his face pinched in disappointment. When Zack lifted his eyes to Tracy's, he saw the hope in them. Did he really have to go in? Dawn, Wyatt, Herb, and the rest of his deputies had the investigations covered. At least, for a few hours.

"I suppose I don't have to go in to work today. I can check in later. Do you have to work this morning?"

Tracy sighed and nodded. "Unfortunately, Melissa and I have to do all the hair for the Oberton-Garcia wedding. Eight attendants, the bride and both mothers. They're coming in at nine and have to be done by one. I normally only work on the Saturdays Bobby's with Jake." She looked at Bobby. "Sorry, sweetheart, but I guess you've got to spend the day with me at the shop. Maybe later we can go over to the CW--"

"You know I hate sittin' there! Why can't I just go with Dad? What happened yesterday at the court? Dad said you'd say anything to make him look like the bad guy."

The mix of anger and pain in Bobby's voice tugged at something in Zack's gut. He hated Jake Parker more than ever before. How could that bastard play on his own kid's emotions?

But it was the pain in Tracy's voice that clenched his heart. "Bobby, you don't understand everything that's going on. Your dad couldn't..."

Zack reached over and ruffled Bobby's hair. "How about you come over to the ranch with Mandy and me while your mom's at work?"

Bobby pulled away from Zack's touch and looked at Tracy.

She smiled and met Zack's gaze, then said to Bobby, "It's okay with me if you want to go with Zack."

"But Dad doesn't--"

"Your dad isn't making decisions for you," Tracy interrupted. "I think it's high time for you to learn to ride, and Zack is the best rider I know."

Bobby looked up at him. The boy's apprehension was almost palpable, but so was his anticipation. "You'll teach me how to ride?"

"You bet, buddy."

"Yay!" Mandy jumped up and down, clapping her hands.

"Well, then. I think we should start eating this great breakfast you two made." Tracy reached for the milk carton and poured some over her Cheerios.

Zack caught Tracy's gaze, and his heart skipped a beat. What would life with her be like? Damn, he wished he could allow himself to find out.

Chapter 16

Zack and Tracy made their way through the packed barroom. They found a small table in the back when another couple got up and left. Zack wished the stage was easier to see, but it was the best they could do.

On the stage, Logan sang one of his own songs about a brokenhearted rodeo cowboy. His deep voice had the usually rowdy Longhorn crowd mesmerized, and the dance floor packed with couples two-stepping.

When Tracy sat in the chair he held out for her, Zack was hit with her perfume. The light flowery scent hit him hard in the pit of his gut. He took the seat beside her and draped his arm over the back of her chair.

Julie Larson approached, took their drink orders and collected the cover charge for the live entertainment. Although he saw curiosity in the waitress's smile, she kept the conversation short when he handed her his credit card. She headed off to give the order to her older brother behind the bar.

The day had turned out to be a good one. While Tracy had gone to her shop, he'd taken Bobby and Mandy back to the CW. There he, with Mandy's help, had taught Bobby how to sit a horse, and how to ride around the same corral where Zack had learned to ride his first pony when he was still a baby. He'd been surprised at how easy the kid caught on, and how well he'd done in the saddle. The three of them eventually had gone for a ride through the pasture near the barn.

After a supper of hamburgers and potato salad at the ranch, Amy Jackson had come to sit with Mandy, and Tracy had taken Bobby to her friend's place to spend the evening. Logan was done at eleven o'clock, which was perfect so she could take Bobby home.

As much as Zack wanted to spend the night tangled in the sheets with Tracy, she'd said that she couldn't leave Bobby with a friend while she spent the night with him. She didn't want to give Jake that much advantage in his custody case by doing exactly what he'd been accusing her of. Even though the devil would be ice fishing in the bowels of hell before Jake Parker ever won a custody case, Zack humored her. Besides, hearing his little girl say the *S* word that morning was enough to dunk his libido into a bucket full of ice.

Julie brought their drinks. He took a sip of his Coke and sat back to watch Tracy. She looked every bit a cowgirl in tight jeans, tailored white Western shirt with red roses embroidered across the yoke and red lace at the collar and cuffs. But the sexiest things she was wearing were her red cowboy boots and a doe-colored Stetson. Would she ever agree to have sex with him wearing only her boots and hat and nothing else?

When Logan started the next song--a cover of Restless Heart's *I'm Still Loving You*, she turned to him. "Want to dance?"

"Sure."

Hand-in-hand, they found room at the edge of the dance floor and fell into an up-close dance. Logan and his band sang about how he'd need his lover until the sun didn't shine and time stood still. Was his brother trying to tell him something?

Could he just walk away from her in a few weeks? Or was it too late?

Could he go back to endless days of work and trying to raise his daughter without a woman around? Would Amanda's bedtime prayers go from wanting her momma to come home from heaven to wanting Tracy back in her life?

The song ended and she looked up at him when he moved her into the next step after the last note. He sucked in a breath.

Before they could move off the floor, the next song started with fiddle and steel guitar in a classic old Texas swing melody. Logan sang about finding love again and never learning to live without that one special woman. Where the hell had the boy come up with the lyrics? As far as he could remember, his brother had never been in love.

His body responded to Tracy's closeness, and he was damned glad the tail of his Western shirt was tucked into his jeans, which fit well, but fortunately, weren't skin tight.

She laid her head on his shoulder and hummed along with the melody. "How do you know this song?"

Tracy shrugged and looked up at him. "The CD Logan cut a few months ago. He gave me one before he started selling them after his shows."

He let the topic drop, but a memory wiggled its way to the surface of his mind while he danced with the woman he'd never learned to live without.

"Oh, maybe that's why she's back with Logan, then." Fifteen minutes after Brent Parker had made that puzzling statement the day Zack had stopped him for speeding, he'd caught Tracy and Logan in a close hug. Had he missed the kiss, or had he interrupted before it could happen?

The song wound down, the band broke into a faster tune, and the line dancers took over the worn wood floor. He and Tracy headed back to their table, which they'd saved by leaving her Stetson and their drinks. Once they were seated again, she drank some of her sweet tea and swayed to the music, completely focused on the man on stage.

Zack took a sip of his Coke. "I didn't realize you and Logan were that close of friends."

"What?" She looked at him with a puckered brow.

Her hand rested on his thigh, and his arm was around her chair. They appeared to be the perfect dating couple, but he knew better. He and Tracy had a gulf between them as big as the state of Texas, and he couldn't see any way for them to close it.

She'd still be the one who'd cheated on him, and his lack of love for his wife, because he'd never let Tracy go, had been the reason for Lisa's death.

Was Tracy now sneaking around behind his back with his own brother?

"I just find it surprising. I knew you and Logan were friends, but he hadn't given me one of his CDs until I asked for it." He didn't give a shit he sounded like a jealous husband. But, damn, he was pissed that he was jealous.

If she was seeing Logan, wouldn't that be the perfect way to break it off and never see her again?

She looked at him, but he tilted his head under his hat brim to hide his face. "I told you Logan became my best friend over the years."

"No, you never told me."

She sipped her drink. Without looking at him, she set the glass on the table, shrugging. "Over the past few years he's filled some of the gap left when Dylan went off to the Army. Whenever I've needed a friend, he was always there." She turned her attention back to his brother on stage. When the set was over, she clapped and whistled through her teeth. "Damn, I just know he'll knock somebody's socks off in Nashville."

"Yeah."

"Well, well, if it's not the happy couple." Jake grinned and bracketed his waist with his hands, elbows out.

The gauze wrapped around Jake's right hand looked fresh. How deep was the wound, to warrant such a bandage a week after the supposed accident with a broken wineglass? Wearing a dinner-plate-sized silver belt buckle, the boots and hat, Jake looked like he'd finished the day punching cattle and cleaned up for a night on the town. New York City wasn't the only place with rhinestone cowboy-wannabes. Jake hated horses and grew up in the middle of town. At least Zack had earned the silver buckle he was wearing the old-fashioned way--by winning it. He'd bet Jake bought his at a pawnshop in Waco.

"What the hell are you doing here?" Tracy asked before Zack had the chance to.

Jake shrugged. "Decided to have a few beers. Question should be what the hell are you doing here? And where's my son?"

"My business is my business. And *my* son is spending the evening visiting with his best friend." Tracy stiffened in her chair.

"I wonder what Judge Delaney would think about you pawning our boy off to your friends so you can cat around town with your latest fling?"

Zack stood and glowered at the other man. "I think you should move along, Parker."

Jake dropped his hands to his sides and sneered. "Or you'll what? Arrest me on some other trumped up charge? I wonder if that dog and pony show yesterday in the courtroom was just so you and my whorin' ex-wife could drag my reputation down and make me look bad in front of the judge? My lawyer thinks that might be enough to get another judge on the case."

Zack didn't want a bar brawl, and he sure as hell didn't want to be the one to throw the first punch, but he didn't take to Jake calling Tracy a whore, despite his own concern over her relationship with his brother. He bunched up his fists and leaned toward Jake.

Tracy stood and touched his arm. "Zack, don't. He's not worth it."

Jake snarled and his face turned red. As he stepped closer to Zack, he shook his left fist at him. "You fuckin' Cartwrights and Fergusons think you own this county."

Zack caught sight of Sam Larson moving from around the bar, billy club in hand. The Longhorn didn't have a bouncer at the door. It didn't need one. Sam could smell a fight and have the instigators out the door before the first punch was thrown--usually. If he couldn't handle it, Julie pulled a sawed-off shotgun from behind the bar and backed up her brother with enough redneck grit to stop a freight train.

Zack felt every eye in the place on him, Tracy and Jake. Most of the patrons were quieter watching them than they had been watching Logan gyrate over the stage in the front, singing a cover of Johnny Cash's *Ring of Fire*. The music abruptly stopped, but Zack didn't take his eyes off Parker to see what his brother was doing. "Before you decide to throw any punches, Parker, just remember I'm still the sheriff. I'll arrest you and throw the book at you."

Jake grabbed the end of the table and sent it flying. Tracy screamed as she jumped out of the way. Zack blocked the punch and spun away, grabbing hold of Parker's wrist. Jake landed with a *thunk* and a grunt face-first against the back wall of the bar. The memorabilia of old signed photographs of country singers and rodeo riders of long past rattled. Zack held Jake's wrists behind his back. Too damned bad he didn't have a pair of handcuffs.

Tracy stood back, glaring at Jake, and Logan moved in beside her. He slipped his arm around her shoulders, and she didn't push him off.

"Zack, don't do anything you'll regret," Logan said.

"Tell me, Zack." Jake's voice was muffled from being pressed against the wall. "Has Tracy told you just who she left me for, yet?"

"It's a lie!"

Zack glanced over his shoulder at Tracy. Her face flushed, and her hands clenched into tight fists on her hips. Logan still had his arm on her shoulders, but he looked mad enough to eat his guitar.

"Why don't you ask your little brother?" Jake asked. "They'd been goin' at like jackrabbits for years. I bet she's still fuckin' him when you aren't around. One man has never been enough for her--as you should know, old buddy."

Zack didn't want to react, but the stab in his heart was too much. He spun Jake around.

Sam Larson brandished his billy club. "Damn it, you boys take this outside, or I'll bash both your fool heads in, and I don't give a tinker's damn that one of you's the sheriff."

Zack fisted his hand, determined to pound the smirk off Jake Parker's smug face. Logan grabbed his arm before he could let the punch fly. "If you believe that pile of shit, Zack, you're a fool."

"Go on, ask him who paid the rent for her and got her a job in Waco when she filed for divorce. Hell, he even paid for the divorce!" Jake snickered.

Zack glared at his brother, shook him off, then looked at Tracy. Despite his best intentions, he'd fallen in love with her again, and she'd lied to him. Again.

She shook her head and tears ran from her gray eyes. "Zack...I never..."

The burn in his gut was too much like the first time she'd cheated on him. He let go of Parker with a shove and scowled at his brother. Too drained to do anything else, he grabbed his Stetson off the floor and pushed past his brother, leaving them and the stunned bar crowd behind.

* * * *

Tracy stared at the old-fashioned saloon doors as they moved back and forth from Zack shoving them open. A flash of movement and the patrons' exclamations drew her attention to the men behind her. She turned, and Logan threw a punch knocking Jake into the same wall Zack had.

"Logan!" Tracy screamed the same time the crowd took sides and either cheered or booed. While Sam Larson rushed forward with his billy club held high.

Jake pushed away from the wall, pulled back his arm and let go with a left hook that landed on Logan's jaw. He stumbled back, and Jake rushed him, using his shorter stature and bulk to ram Logan in the gut with a shoulder, linebacker style. The couple sitting at a neighboring table grabbed their Mason jars of beer a second before the two men fell onto it. The flimsy table crashed to the floor when its legs gave out on one side. Tracy was too upset to watch who got punches in.

Logan's band members stood next to her watching and cheering on their lead singer. Sam Larson was yelling for the two men to stop or he'd bash in their brains and even got a few whacks in, but the men continued to throw punches.

The cocking of a shotgun in the midst of the fray was like flipping a switch. The room went quiet, and Julie Larson pointed a sawed-off shotgun at the men locked in battle on the sawdust and peanut shell littered floor. "That's enough ruckus, or I'll fill both your sorry asses with enough lead to sink y'all to the bottom of Gambler's Lake."

Logan was the first to move to his feet. His left eye would be swelled shut by morning, and his lip was split and bleeding; his jaw was already purpling. He moved his bloody right hand to his midsection. Guitar picking would be impossible for a few days.

Jake followed to his feet, and with his right hand, wiped at the blood on his mouth where his lips bled. The bandage was nearly torn off, and he shook the hand as if it was numb. His plaid Western shirt was torn, and he seemed to be favoring his right knee--the same one he'd injured the summer before his senior year of high school.

Sam tapped both men on the shoulder with the baton. "Now get the hell out of here."

"Hey, we paid good money to hear Cartwright sing," a cowboy shouted from somewhere within the crowd.

With shotgun still in hand, but now safely pointed toward the ceiling, Sam's sister turned around. "Too damn bad. I'll give y'all a beer on the house and call us even. He only had another half-hour anyways."

"None of that cheap swill either," someone else called.

"Y'all will take what you get or leave it," Julie replied and turned back to Tracy. She shook her head. "Damn, woman, your love life's more excitin' than those soap operas I watch. I don't care which one of these stallions you leave with, but get one of 'em the hell out of here."

Tracy turned and headed for the door. She wasn't leaving with either one of them. The one she wanted had already left. She fished her cell phone out of her purse to call Mary Estrada and ask her to come to take her home. When the doors swung open, she turned to Logan sucking on a cut on his bruised knuckles.

"Let me get you home, and then I'll go talk some sense into that moron I call brother." Not waiting for her response, Logan took her by the elbow and led her to his car in the back of the parking lot. He helped her inside the BMW Roadster and got in behind the wheel of the sports car.

"What about the band? Your equipment?"

"The band will take care of it." He clipped his seatbelt. "You haven't told Zack anything, have you?"

She looked over at him as he started the engine. "I'm not begging him to forgive me, Logan. Either he can figure out on his own I'm not the person he seems to think I am, or he can go straight to hell."

Logan backed out of the space. "Y'all are two of the biggest pigheaded idiots I've ever known. You love him, and he's got it so bad for you that he goes up in flames every time you're around."

"Yeah, but sex isn't love." She wrapped her arms around herself in a tight hug.

"That's not what I meant." He pulled out onto the street and headed southwest out of town. "He loves you, Tracy."

She looked up at him and hated the hope his gruff voice sparked to life in her bruised and battered heart. Then she remembered Zack's words from when they entered into this charade. "He still loves Lisa. All he wants from me is sex. He told me as much. I was foolish to agree, but told him we had to act like we were in a relationship." She looked at her lap in the dark interior of the car, glad that the dim light from the dashboard wasn't bright enough for him to see her tears. Not that Logan hadn't seen them before. "I was foolish to believe I could make him love me again. That he'd forgive me because he loved me."

She bit her lip so hard she tasted blood. Despite her efforts to keep it inside, a sob broke loose from the depths of her being.

"Oh, T.C." He reached over and laid his injured hand on her shoulder. She gently took it from her shoulder and held it in her lap. He let her cry as the miles between town and the turnoff for Oak Springs flew by her window.

He turned onto Oak Springs Road and glanced at her. "Tell Zack what happened, Tracy. Then ask him about Lisa."

"What about Lisa?" She used the handkerchief he'd handed her to wipe at her eyes and blew her nose.

They passed the gate to Butterfly Ranch. Then the one on opposite side of the road, the Broken B Ranch, which was still owned by Buck Blackwell. Risking wrecking his fancy German convertible on the windy road, Logan looked at her, his expression solemn. "Ask him what happened before she died."

* * * *

When Zack got home, he paid Amy Jackson for babysitting and walked her out to the old red Honda she drove. He turned off the movie she'd been watching and checked on Mandy. He stared at his sleeping daughter. How was he going to break the news about him and Tracy breaking up? Hard to believe only that morning he'd been fantasizing about them being a family.

He hit an open palm against the doorframe and pulled the door closed. Damn it all to hell, he'd known there was no future for him and Tracy from the beginning. Why hadn't he left well enough alone and stayed away from her?

The front door opened while he headed toward the kitchen to snag a much-needed beer.

"You look like shit," Zack said as Logan moved down the darkened hallway into the light coming from the living room.

"Yeah, so do you. Someone had to beat the hell out of that son-of-a-bitch." Logan tossed his Stetson on the kitchen table and faced him. "You couldn't afford the possible assault charge for police brutality or some other shit, but I could. Besides, I've wanted to pound on that bastard for a very long time."

"What are you doing here?" Zack opened the refrigerator door and retrieved a bottle of Coors. As he popped the top, he said, "Go back to Tracy."

"Tracy's fine. Or she will be as soon as my big brother gets his head out of his ass and stops trying to come up with reasons to dump her."

Zack lowered the bottle and took a step toward Logan. "Get out."

Logan spread his hands and smirked. "Dear God almighty, Zack, do you really believe I'm having an affair with Tracy--or that I ever have? It would be like sleeping with our cousin Faith."

"Kissin' cousins isn't unusual. Not in this town."

"I'll never... This is getting us nowhere." Logan shoved his left hand through his dark hair. "For the last time, I have no interest in Tracy. She's like my sister. Now, let's get to the real problem. You think if you admit to yourself that you love her and want a future with her, you've dishonored Lisa. So you're looking for any reason to run--even if you know damned well it's a lie."

"I'm not talking about this." Zack passed Logan and headed into the living room. He pointed down the hall toward the door with the beer bottle. "You know where the door is."

"I know what you said when you woke up from the coma in Germany."

Zack spun around and stared at Logan as if he was the devil come to life. No one but Lisa had been in the room when he woke up. And Logan and Lisa had never been close; she'd disliked him as much as he had her. She'd been the wedge that had driven the brothers apart. There was a time they'd been close.

Logan ambled around the room. His boot heels kept time with the ticking of the antique grandfather clock in the corner and sounded as loud as thunder in the silence. He stopped in front of the mantle and picked up the frame holding Lisa's picture. "I always thought she looked a little like Tracy." Looking up, he smiled. "In an if-I-was-out-of-it kind of way. Maybe it's just the long dark hair." Logan squinted his eyes almost shut and held the photo this way and that in front of him before setting it back on the plank mantel.

"You were in the room?" Zack sat down on the couch.

Logan faced him and shoved his hands into the pockets of his jeans--or at least tried to. He shook his right hand. "Ouch. That bastard has a hard head."

Zack nodded toward the swollen and bruised knuckles. "You've probably got a boxer's fracture."

"If I do, I'm taking it out of Jake Parker's sorry hide." Logan sat in the recliner across from him and leaned over his legs. "Look, you know the whole family was over in Germany those two weeks you were in the coma. Hell, we didn't know if you'd live or die. I was standing in the doorway when you woke up. I was going in to check on Lisa to make sure she didn't want anything to drink or eat. I realized while she held vigil over you just how much she truly did love you." He sighed and sat back in the recliner. "When I opened the door, she was bent over you calling your name, and then I heard you call her Tracy. I knew then you were still in love with her. And to hell with whatever you wanted the rest of the world, and probably yourself as well, to believe."

Zack closed his eyes and leaned back into the soft leather of the couch. With his head against the couch, he opened his eyes to look up at the rough-hewn beams and white plaster ceiling. He should be mad at his brother for making such an assertion, but he couldn't gather up enough energy.

"Zack, do yourself a favor and let Lisa rest in peace. She wouldn't want you punishing yourself over something that wasn't your fault."

He looked at Logan and took a deep breath. "But it was my fault. If we hadn't been fighting about moving back here... If I hadn't--"

"If a rock star's boyfriend hadn't dumped her at a bar in Las Vegas during the National Finals Rodeo, a rodeo cowboy from Central Texas wouldn't've met her and neither one of us would be having this conversation," Logan said, referring to their parents' first meeting. Zack glared at his brother, who went on, "My point is we can't control Fate and we sure as hell can't control the actions of others. You didn't kill Lisa, Zack. A drunk driver did. Don't you dare say you're the reason she was out there, either. Bullshit. She's the one that left, and she's the one who got behind the wheel of a car. So unless you held a gun to her head, you are not responsible."

Zack stared at him for a moment, then lifted the Coors to his mouth. Before drinking the entire bottle, he muttered, "Shit happens."

"Yep." Logan stood, walked around the coffee table, and patted him on the shoulder with his left hand. "Now, go and tell that woman you forgive her and you love her, and don't you ever believe a thing Jake Parker says again."

As Logan headed toward the kitchen, Zack said, "I can't leave now. Mandy's here."

Logan turned at the doorway and arched an eyebrow. "Uncle Logan isn't qualified to babysit? I'll camp out in one of the spare bedrooms. This damned monster of a house has six of 'em." Logan looked around the living room. "I'm damned glad I didn't inherit this place."

Zack smiled. "Why's that?"

Sara Walter Ellwood

"Because then I'm not the one who has to fill all those bedrooms with little Cartwright brats. I'm never getting married."

"Yeah, right." Zack laughed and stood. "You've always been a hopeless romantic. I'll bet within a year some Nashville starlet snags your heart." Sobering, he stepped forward and put his hands on Logan's shoulders. "You know why Tracy did what she did, don't you?"

"Yeah, I do. But it's not my place to explain it to you. Just like it isn't my place to explain to her your reasons for holding her at a distance. Y'all need to talk this through, and then you can move forward. You and Tracy Quinn belong together. Now, get. I'll see you in the morning." He tried to smile, but it looked more like a grimace. His jaw was swollen, so was his eye. "Or whenever. Right now, I'm gonna get a glass of sweet tea, take a half-bottle of aspirin, and get ice on my hand and face."

Zack pulled his brother into a hug. "You're a bonehead most of the time, but I don't know what I'd do without you."

Logan stepped back and grunted. "Love you, too, knucklehead." He pointed to the mudroom door as he went into the kitchen. "Will you go, already? Oh, wait." He pulled something from the pocket of his jeans. "I stopped by my cabin before coming over here."

When Zack noticed what Logan was holding out for him, he gasped.

"You might need this someday."

Zack stared at the three-carat diamond platinum engagement ring. He'd bought it with the money from his rodeo wins and some of his trust fund from his grandfather. He met Logan's gaze. "I told you to sell it and to keep the money."

Logan shrugged as put the ring in Zack's hand. "I decided not to. I've been the keeper of this thing for fourteen years. I think it's high time the danged thing should go to its rightful owner, don't you?"

Chapter 17

"What are you doin' here?" Jake asked as he looked up at his brother entering his trailer.

"Whoa! What happened to you?" Brent asked instead of answering the question.

Jake tossed the damp washcloth he'd used to wipe the blood off his face onto the counter separating the kitchen and living room. "Logan Cartwright. Now, answer my question."

As Jake pulled a beer from the fridge, Brent shuffled his feet. "I got a call from Johnny."

Jake straightened and faced his brother and scowled, which hurt like hell. He didn't want to deal with this crap now. "Why would he call you?"

"Because he got a call from the owner of the slaughterhouse in Breckenridge. Jake, he called to warn us. The TSCRA raided the place today. They confiscated all their records, and the owner is talking to save his ass." His voice rose in pitch and became more breathy as he spoke. "He's told the cops about buying stolen cattle from us, and their faking the brands and paperwork for the inspectors. They're gonna figure out we've been stealing the cattle 'round here!"

Jake set the unopened beer on the dirty-dish-cluttered counter. "The law can't know for sure." His tone didn't sound any more convincing than he felt. Cartwright and McPherson already suspected him of the crime. And he knew the bitch in Waco would change her story about him being with her last Friday night when Cartwright's horses were stolen if cornered by the Texas Rangers. She'd already warned Jake his money wasn't enough to keep her quiet if the cops threatened jail time.

"What are we gonna do, Jake? I don't wanna go to jail."

With a sharp glance at his brother, he rushed past him. "Well, I for one am not stickin' around waitin'."

"Jake? Where you goin'? Why are you limping?"

Jake ignored the asshole and headed for the bedroom, cursing not only the situation, but also the sharp pain in his knee. Logan's kick had probably undid the repaired ligaments. He threw a couple changes of clothes into a duffle bag, then went into Bobby's room. He grabbed clothes for him and stuffed them into the bag, too.

"Why are you taking Bobby's stuff?"

He turned to Brent standing at the door. "Because we're headed to Mexico, and I'm taking my boy with me. Now, get the hell out of my way."

"I don't think that's a good idea." Brent moved toward him. "That's kidnapping on top of everything else."

Jake grabbed Brent by the shirtfront. "He's my boy! I'll be damned if I'll leave him here for fuckin' Cartwright and the bitch to turn against me."

He let go of Brent's shirt and headed for the gun safe in the corner of the living room. After undoing the lock, he grabbed the Colt .45 he'd inherited from his father, a hunting rifle and enough ammunition to shoot his way out of anything.

After tossing the Remington .300 and a box of ammo to Brent, he loaded the pistol. Brent shifted the rifle in his beefy hands. "Jake, that's plumb crazy. Let's just get out of here. We'll go down to Monterrey where Granny Blackwell's cousins live. Aunt Colleen, Johnny, and his boy have already skipped town and headed there. Johnny wanted me to go with them, but I had to warn you. I was with them when the call came in from Breckenridge."

Jake jammed the pistol into his belt under his shirt behind him. "Bobby's with Mary Estrada. Tracy and Cartwright were at the Longhorn--"

Brent whistled between his teeth. "I thought she was screwin' Zack. So, she's really seein' Logan."

"No."

"But you said Logan beat you up."

"I wasn't beat up by that asshole or anyone else. She was there with Zack. Logan was singin', and I decided to have some fun with the happy couple. It worked. Zack left her there, but Logan decided to play hero." He grabbed the duffle bag off the couch. "Let's get the hell out of here. I'll drive. So give me the goddamn keys."

Outside, Brent climbed into the passenger side of his truck and handed over the keys. "Why don't we take your truck?"

"You sure as hell ask a lot of questions. What are you, two years old?" Jake started the engine, but before he put it in gear, he glanced at the garage door of his service shop. "Wait here. I have an idea."

Jake punched the code into the opener and ducked in before the big door crawled the whole way upward. He removed the license plates from the old Ford Ranger pickup sitting in the bay and waiting on the part that was supposed to be in on Monday. Once he returned to Brent's new truck, Jake switched the plates and then quickly put the Silverado's tags on the Ranger.

While Jake climbed behind the wheel again, Brent said, "Wow. That's sure to confuse the law."

"Let's hope long enough for us to get to the border."

* * * *

With his mind filled with questions and doubts, Zack neared the entrance to Oak Springs Ranch. He had no idea what he was going to say to Tracy when he got there, but he hoped she'd let him say something before she slammed the door in his face.

When his cell phone rang, he let it go to voicemail. Immediately, it rang again, and he knew it had to be someone at the station. He pulled it out and answered it.

Dawn didn't bother with a greeting or a smart remark about him not answering the first time. "We need you here ASAP. Jake and Brent Parker, Colleen Stryker, Johnny and Matthew Blackwell have been implicated by a sting operation at a slaughterhouse in Breckenridge."

He stopped at the end of Tracy's driveway. The house couldn't be seen from here; it sat back another half-mile. He imagined her lying in bed, crying and thinking of him as the biggest jerk in the world.

Resigned that duty had to come first, he put the truck into reverse and turned around. "Okay. I'll be there in less than a half-hour."

* * * *

Tracy stared at her friend, not believing what she was hearing. "Jake told you I wanted him to pick up Bobby?"

"Yeah." Mary shifted her weight and puckered her brow. "He told me you'd called him. I knew it was his week to have him, so I just figured..." She sat on the couch in her living room.

Tracy continued to stand in the entrance of the small house a few doors down the street from her beauty salon. She and Mary Estrada had been friends since Tracy moved to Colton. Their sons had been friends since they were toddlers.

When Mary looked back at Tracy, her rotund face was red with anger. "He lied to me. I wondered why he seemed--I don't know--nervous, and Bobby looked at him funny, like he didn't believe his ears. Of course, that could have been because he looked like someone beat the shit out of him."

"Logan should've knocked off his head."

"Logan? What does..."

Tracy shook her head. "A story for another day." She didn't intend to dredge up the reason for the brawl at the Longhorn. She'd spent the past hour crying over Zack Cartwright. When she'd dried her last tear, she'd decided to go over to the CW and tell Zack exactly what had happened, and either he'd forgive her or not. But she was done chasing him. However, when she called to ask Mary if she'd mind keeping Bobby all night, she'd told Tracy Jake had come and taken him home.

The thought of Zack's lack of trust in her and Jake's interference had her temper catching fire, and she paced across the living room. "I never called Jake. I decided not to let Bobby go to him this week. Jake was taken in for questioning yesterday for stealing Zack's horses. Zack and my cousin Wyatt barged into the courtroom during the hearing. It was like something out of an old movie."

Mary smiled. "With two of the sexiest lawmen around, I'm sure it did look like a movie." Then she lost the grin. "So, Zack thinks Jake's involved with all the rustlin' goin' on?"

"Zack did think that, but Jake has an alibi. Some bimbo from Waco, though if you listen to Jake tell it, I'm the one who has no morals. I intend to give Jake Parker a piece of my mind." She adjusted her purse strap on her shoulder and headed for the front door.

At the entry, Mary touched Tracy's arm. "I'm sorry, Tracy. I had no idea about Jake. I just assumed you and Zack decided to spend the night together... If I'd really thought about it, I would've known you'd never call Jake."

Tracy stepped forward and hugged the much shorter and rounder woman. "Don't worry about it. I didn't tell you about Jake, so you had no way of knowing." She stepped out of Mary's embrace and opened the door. "I'll call you to have you come bail me out of jail after I kill the idiot."

Mary laughed. "Naw, we'll dump the body in Gambler's Lake. Remember that Dixie Chicks song? Instead of Earl, we'll be singing about Jake."

They shared a laugh and another hug before Tracy left to head straight across town to her ex-husband's.

Flashing red and blue lights of police cars and bright spotlights had her heart racing the moment she turned down Blackwell Drive. The sheriff department Tahoe parked across the street forced her to stop. Ben Timmons approached as she scrambled out of the Taurus. Sudden fear frosted up the blood which anger had set to boiling only seconds before.

The deputy held a flashlight on her face, blinding her until she shut her eyes and turned her head with a hand blocking the beam. "Ben, get that damned thing out of my face."

"Sorry, Tracy. What are you doin' here?" The deputy turned off the light.

She looked back at him, blinking the spots from her eyes. "I'm here to get my son from Jake. What are y'all doing here?" She looked past the deputy. Several Tahoes and unmarked SUVs crowded the street. Her former mother-in-law sat in a chair on the porch of her house across the street from Jake's trailer and appeared distraught as she wrung her hands and shook her head. Wyatt McPherson, Dawn Madison, and Herb Milroy were standing before her and obviously asking questions. She swung her gaze over to the trailer across the street. Zack paced the gravel drive in front of the garage doors of Jake's service shop. His hands were splayed on either side of his waist, elbows pointed out. She recognized the signs of agitation easily. Still dressed in the same clothes he'd worn to the Longhorn, he had his gun tucked into a shoulder holster and a badge clipped to his belt. He turned and the bright spotlights highlighted the harsh lines of his face.

When she saw Jake's pickup still parked off to the side and that the windows of the trailer were dark, she turned back to Timmons.

"Where's Jake? Where's my son?" Panic painted her words with a higher than normal note.

The man's pockmarked face blanched at her growing hysteria. "Neither one of them are here, ma'am. We're waitin' on the search warrant. Judge Delaney was in Dallas--"

Not waiting for the rest of the explanation, she ran across the yards of Jake's neighbor and that of the trailer to the front door. After ripping open the screen door, she banged on the dented aluminum door, calling Bobby's name.

"Tracy, what's wrong?" Zack asked from her side. "What's this about Bobby?"

She stared at him and laid a hand over the pain in her chest. She couldn't get enough air no matter how fast she tried to breathe. She let the screen door bang closed and took a step toward him. "Jake took Bobby from Mary's tonight! Where is he? Where's my baby?"

He laid a hand on her arm. "Jake has Bobby?"

"Yes! Dammit, where are they?" She bent over when a sharp pain ripped through her chest, and she couldn't breathe. Gasping, she wrapped her arms around herself. "I have to..."

"Tracy, calm down. You're hyperventilating." Zack took her by the arms and guided her to sit on the step of the stoop. He sat down beside her and pressed his hand on her back. "Now, bend over your knees and take slow breaths."

"Can't."

"Shhh. Yes, you can." He rubbed soothingly over her back. "Take a breath. That's it. Let it out slowly. Now another." His voice was soft, gentle, and she found herself complying.

After a few slow breaths, the pain in her chest eased and she sat up.

"Now, what's this about Bobby?" He continued to rub her back. He turned to face her and his thigh pressed against hers. With his free hand, he reached up and used the pad of his thumb to wipe away the tears on her cheeks.

She peered into his blue eyes and instantly felt more at ease. He pulled a clean white handkerchief from his pocket and handed it to her. Much calmer now, she wiped her nose, then cleared her throat, but her heart was still painfully stuck. "Jake took Bobby from Mary's before I got there. They aren't here, are they?"

"No." He narrowed his eyes and his jaw twitched. "We received evidence tonight implicating Jake, Brent and Johnny Blackwell and a bunch of other people in the cattle thefts. Since we can't find Brent's truck anywhere, we're assuming they got away in it. You're sure Bobby's with Jake?"

"Yes!" She struggled to stand, panic seizing her again.

He held her in place. "I just had to make sure. How long ago?"

"Sometime within the last hour. Zack, I'm scared. What if Jake hurts him? He's my world." A new wash of tears gushed from her eyes, and she bit her bottom lip.

"Shhh." He hugged her close to his side and murmured, "Bobby'll be fine, baby. We'll get him back." He held her away slightly to peer into her face. "I'm going to call the FBI and get an Amber Alert out. Do you have a recent photo of him?" She nodded and immediately retrieved her wallet from her purse. After he took the wallet-sized school picture from her, he stood and brushed his work-roughened thumb over her cheek again. "You stay here. I'll be right back, baby. After I get everything settled here, I'll take you home."

She nodded absently and stared up at him, not at all sure how to interpret his touch or the pet name. She didn't get a chance to puzzle it through for too long before he leaned down and brushed his lips over hers. She blinked a couple of times in surprise as he took off at a jog toward two deputies watching from the street.

* * * *

Bobby peered out of the back seat of Uncle Brent's truck and watched as the long miles of dark road passed by. He'd gone to sleep not long after his dad picked him up from Miz Mary's. He and Andy had just fallen asleep after playing video games in the family room. Dad had woken him, and Bobby hadn't considered anything strange was going on until he woke up a few moments ago.

This wasn't the way home.

His uncle spoke over the low country music from the radio. "How far do you think we need to go before we can stop?"

"I'm not stoppin' until we need gas. If you have to piss, you have two choices--either go in that empty soda bottle or aim it out the window."

"I'm good. I was just wonderin' that's all."

Why wouldn't his dad stop?

"How are we gonna get over the border?" Brent asked.

His dad laughed, and he shook his head in the dim dashboard light. "You really are stupid. We can't come from the same gene pool. How the hell do Mexicans cross the border? It can work both ways."

Mexicans? Border? Were they going to Mexico? His mom would never have let his dad take him that far away. Or would she? Now that she and Zack were together, maybe she didn't want him around anymore. Did Zack not want him around and talked his mom into his dad taking him?

The memory of the day at the CW with Zack and Mandy came to mind.

His heart raced when Zack helped him up into the saddle for the first time and gave him the reins. "Hold on to these. Not too tight, and don't yank on them. The bit will hurt the mouth of the horse and will confuse him. He'll follow me as we walk around the corral. We'll start out slow to get you used to the feel of the horse moving under you. Okay?"

Bobby nodded, and they were off. He was riding a horse! After a few times around the fence, Zack showed him how to use the slight movements of the reins to steer the old dappled gray gelding, Grasshopper.

"Don't kick him either. That will make him run," Mandy warned from her perch on top of the white rail fence.

"I want him to go faster." Bobby laughed from the saddle.

He expected Zack to tell him no, but instead, he said, "Okay. Touch his sides with your heels. Not hard, just a soft touch. He'll respond."

Bobby touched the horse's sides, and Grasshopper went from an easy walk to a jog. Zack kept up with the horse, but Bobby didn't need his help. With a whoop, Bobby hung on to both the reins and the saddle horn. He leaned forward and kept his head down like he'd seen the cowboys on Oak Springs Ranch do.

The warm breeze felt good on his face, and he'd never been freer than he was that morning while in the saddle.

"I want to run!"

Jogging beside Grasshopper, Zack caught hold of the horse's rein, looped at his neck, and the horse stopped. "You have to learn a lot more and be more secure in the saddle before that can happen. Besides, Grasshopper is too old for doing much more than a fast trot."

"Okay. I don't want to hurt him."

"But we could take him for a short ride in the pasture. He'd like that."

Bobby nodded and smiled. Zack saddled his big Palomino, Wild Aces, and helped Mandy with her sorrel mare, Holly. They mounted up, then headed out into the pasture behind the big barn.

Zack told him all sorts of things about horses and answered his questions about rodeo, including how he'd gotten Wild Aces.

"I got him my last year of rodeoing. While I was away with the Marines, he stayed at my in-laws' ranch in Wyoming."

"He's really old," Mandy chimed in.

"Not really. Not as old as Grasshopper. He'll be thirty-two on his next birthday."

"Wow!" Bobby looked down at the gray mane. He held the reins, which lay on the edge of his saddle on either side of the saddle horn.

"I remember old Jock Blackwell had a horse that was about thirty-five before it died. It was an old rodeo horse."

"My great-uncle Jock rode in the rodeo before he took over the oil business with my great-granddad Jason Ferguson."

Zack smiled over at him. "Yep, and your great-grandfather Ferguson was a champion cutting horse rider, and your real great-grandma trained his horses. That's how they met."

"Really? I didn't know that. I always thought he was just an oilman."

"Before he took over the Ferguson's share of the oil business with your uncle Jock, he was a cowboy. My dad says he never knew a better horseman than Jason Ferguson. Your mom is a good rider, too. It's in your blood." He nodded toward Grasshopper. "You're good on him. You aren't afraid at all."

"No." Bobby looked out over the waving grass and the big, red, wrinkly cows grazing in the pasture. "But Dad said horses are dangerous. That's why he hates them and never wanted me to learn to ride."

Zack took a breath so deep that Bobby heard when he let it out, over the distance separating their horses. "Your dad just never understood horses. They sense fear and distrust and he had both. I thought his feelings for them got better, but it never happened. Then--" Zack paused and Bobby looked over at him.

"What?"

Zack met his gaze. "He got hurt and blamed me for it. I should've known he still disliked horses. But he insisted on riding one of the more spirited horses instead of his usual mount, Grasshopper."

Bobby looked down at the horse's neck again. Grasshopper was gentle and had let Bobby pet him for a long time before Zack had shown Bobby how to saddle him. The horse had stood still and never even moved his tail when Zack helped Bobby mount onto his back. How could anyone not like the old dapple gray?

They'd ridden for a long time through the pasture. He'd been to ranches all his life, but he'd never been able to go back into the depths of the open land. Cattle and horses ate the grass, but there were also rabbits, squirrels, prairie dogs, and a small herd of deer eating not far from a bunch of trees.

But, it was the sense of belonging that struck Bobby. Zack told him about the land. About the history of the Cartwrights, which included Bobby's own families--the Blackwells and the Fergusons. Zack made him feel at home when they got back to the house. He'd made them ham sandwiches and baked beans, and let Bobby and Mandy help make the potato salad they'd eaten for supper. Afterward, they played Monopoly out on the deck until Mom came over after she closed her shop and she joined the game. He'd never had so much fun.

But never once did Zack make him feel unwelcome.

So why would Zack and his mom suddenly decide they didn't want him?

"Fuck. There's a cop behind us." Dad's sharp words startled him.

Brent turned and looked out the back of the truck, and Bobby quickly closed his eyes. Maybe it would be better if he pretended to be a sleep.

"Do you think they're checking the license plate?"

"Probably. Austin is up ahead. I'll get off the beltway and go through the city, then get back on I-35. Hopefully, that'll throw 'em off the trail."

"Maybe we should get off the interstate and take the back roads."

Bobby opened his eyes enough to see his dad glance at Brent and reach over to whack him on the side of the head with the back of his fingers.

"Ouch." Brent rubbed the place Dad had hit him.

Dad snorted. "I think you do have a brain rattling around up there after all, because that's actually a damned good idea."

"Then why the fuck did you hit me?"

"Because I don't want you to forget who's in charge here."

They were quiet for a while. Bobby stared out the window at Austin's city lights speeding by as the truck turned off the interstate and onto a main street, then headed down side streets, weaving through the city. He'd only been to the Texas state capitol once, last year for a school field trip.

He closed his eyes to go back to sleep as the radio filled the quiet darkness with a constant stream of old country music. A lady was singing about standing by her man when a buzzing broke into the song.

After a few beeps, an announcer guy said, "This is an Amber Alert for missing eleven-year-old boy, Robert Allan Parker, who goes by Bobby. Last seen at a friend's home late Friday night in Colton, Texas. Suspected abductors are the boy's father, thirty-three-year-old Jacob Parker and twenty-eight-year-old Brent Parker, both of Colton. Driving a late model tan Chevrolet Silverado..." The announcer went on with giving the license plate number and what Bobby, his dad, and Brent looked like. "The abductors are to be considered armed and dangerous." Bobby sat up, forgetting he was pretending to be asleep, and stared at the colored lights of the dash. Dad and Uncle Brent were dangerous? "They are the main suspects in a rash of cattle and horse thefts--" The announcement suddenly died as his dad turned off the radio, and Bobby stared at his father.

"Fuck! That's what that cop was checking out. Cartwright figured out the license plate switch." Dad slapped the steering wheel. "Damn you, Brent. He got the info from when he stopped you for speeding."

"But how did he find the number for the truck in your garage? That's the number the alert gave."

"That's my point! You really are an idiot. He called that old biddy great-aunt of his and got the information. It's Ethel Cartwright's truck. We'll hookup with a back road to get to US-90 east of San Antonio. They won't be expecting that."

"Dad?" His mother and Zack hadn't told Dad to take him. He stole him. "What's goin' on? Did you steal Uncle Dylan's cows and Zack's horses?"

Dad looked back at him with a dark scowl. "Shut the hell up and stay down!"

Bobby leaned back in the seat again and drew up his legs to wrap his arms around his knees. He wasn't supposed to cry, Dad would be mad if he did, but he couldn't keep the tears from slipping down his cheeks--or one recurring thought from his mind.

Mommy, I'm scared.

Chapter 18

"Come on. Let me get you home."

Tracy looked from her clasped hands to Zack as he got into his Tahoe. She'd sat in the passenger seat for the past hour stiff as a rail and with tears in her eyes while he'd searched Jake's house and garage after the warrant came through. He'd hated leaving her there alone, but he had no choice. If that bastard had Bobby, he had to find Jake before he took the boy out of the country.

He'd been about to leave when he noticed the license plates on the old Ford Ranger sitting in the garage. Something wasn't right. The plates were too new to belong on the twenty-year-old vehicle. On a hunch, he ran the tags--they belonged to a Chevy Silverado registered to Brent Parker, with a traffic citation for speeding still pending.

Jake had switched the plates. Finding the number for the Ranger was easy enough. He'd simply check the registration in the glove box. The truck belonged to his great-aunt Ethel.

Before he turned the key in the ignition, he reached over and stroked at the stream of tears running down her cheek. A blade twisted in his gut when he thought about how he'd feel if someone ever took Mandy from him. "Baby, we'll get him back. The Amber Alert has sounded and every cop in Texas--in the whole country--will be looking for him. I know Jake won't hurt his own boy."

He hoped she believed his last statement more than he did.

She sniffed and wiped her nose on a soggy tissue. "I'm scared. If I lose Bobby, it'll mean I've lost everything. He's the only good thing ever to come out of the charade that was mine and Jake's marriage."

He glanced at her as he pulled away from the curb in front of Jake's trailer. What did she mean by charade? He remembered the evening at the bar when Jake approached and manipulated the situation until he believed the lie.

He got hurt and blamed me for it. Zack's words to Bobby while they'd gone riding whispered through his mind. After that summer, his and Jake's friendship was strained at best. They continued to do things together, but when Zack and Tracy started dating, he and Jake did less and less together. Then the week before the rodeo in Houston, Jake started coming around again. He wanted to know how serious Zack was about Tracy.

"I'm gonna ask her to marry me," he told Jake one day as Zack worked *in the barn. "I'm hoping to win the money so I can afford the ring I picked out."*

"I thought Tracy was goin' to college."

"She is, and I'm going to ride rodeo for a little while. Go professional. But that doesn't mean we can't be married or engaged while she goes to school. Maybe even get a place together. Our parents won't be thrilled, but, hey, it's our life."

Jake smiled and shrugged. "I guess. She means that much to you?"

Zack stopped mucking the stall and leaned on the pitchfork. "More than you'd ever know."

A couple of days later, he left for the rodeo, and when he came home, two weeks later, he'd found Jake and Tracy going at it like two dogs in heat in her barn. He shoved the pain the memory brought to the recesses of his mind as another floated in from the first Pee Wee football game he and Tracy had watched together.

"Jake saw you as having it all. He's only ever taken care of number one. Trust me, I know."

Her abject gaze met his, and in it, he realized a horrible truth.

"Jake manipulated you into thinking I--I didn't love you. How?" he choked out.

Tracy couldn't hide her surprise. "Yes," she whispered, her voice so hoarse he almost couldn't hear it. "He--he told me you were cheating on me with Dawn Madison and that..." Her voice broke and she sniffed. "That he loved me and would never hurt me."

He let out the breath he'd been holding and turned the key.

They were nearly at the town limits when he asked, "How could you believe him?"

She sniffed again, and he glanced at her. "He swept me off my feet at first. I won't lie to you, I liked Jake--not romantically--but as a friend. I guess I wanted to get back at you. I loved you--I still do... How could you really be interested in someone like me?"

Tracy's voice cracked on the last word, breaking Zack's heart.

She wiped her nose on the tissue again. "I don't understand it any better now than I did back then. Dawn is beautiful. I believed Jake's lies that you were only playing with me."

He gripped the steering wheel so tightly his hands ached. He pulled to the edge of the street and closed his eyes. Bitter hatred burned through him, but he pushed back the urge to vent his rage. Tracy didn't need his anger; she needed his love and support.

He unclamped his jaw. "You don't have any idea just how beautiful you are, do you?" Wishing the console wasn't in the way, he twisted toward her. He released his hold on the wheel to caress her face. With only the greenish glow of the dash illuminating the interior of the SUV, her face was in shadow, but he couldn't miss her eyes widen with surprise and pain that went much deeper than her son being kidnapped. His voice husky, he said, "I love you, Tracy. I think I fell in love with you the very first day you sat beside me in homeroom in sixth grade."

"I was cross-eyed and bucktoothed. All knobby legs and spaghetti arms. You mocked me with the nickname Olive Oyl."

He winced and lowered his chin to his chest, regretting one of the stupidest things he'd ever said. He remembered Logan's tirade the morning they fixed fences together and felt as disgusting as a fresh pile of cow shit.

His thumb continued to caress her soft cheek. When he met her solemn eyes, he saw into her soul, and what he saw twisted his gut. How could he have hurt her so badly? How could he have missed it?

"Oh, God, Tracy, I'm sorry." He swallowed and fought the sudden burn in his sinuses. "I didn't fall in love with your looks. Not at first. I fell in love with your kindness--your heart and soul. No matter who made fun of you, you never held any ill will against them--including me." His voice broke and he had to swallow again.

He'd been lucky enough to be loved by two fantastic women, and he'd destroyed them both. Lisa's death might be laid at his feet come Judgment Day, but long before her, he'd helped destroy Tracy's fragile self-esteem. How could he blame her for jumping at Jake's golden words? Lord knew he'd never offered them.

"Remember in seventh grade when I forgot my history book and we were having a big test the next day?"

She jerked her head in a shaky nod.

"I called Jake first, but he didn't have his either. He could've cared less about school, but I knew Mom and Dad wouldn't let me ride rodeo if I let my grades slip. So out of desperation, I called you. I never expected you to have your granddad drive you all the way over from Oak Springs to my parents' house. But you did, even though only days before I had you in tears by calling you that stupid name." He sniffed back the shame and the ache in his heart at the pain his cruelty had caused her.

He shifted more in the seat, cupping the side of her face in his hand. "I hated World History, but you made it come alive when you started telling me about all the places you visited while your father was stationed in Germany. Rome, Greece, England, France. Places I'd never seen. You helped me, not only pass that test, but I learned to like history by seeing things through your eyes."

Her eyes grew wide and her mouth slightly opened.

He laughed, but it came out more like a croak. "You're a better person than I'll ever be. If it had been me, I would've told myself to go jump off a bridge and would've laughed when I failed the test. Instead, you helped me. You became my friend."

"Zack..."

He leaned over the console and brushed his lips over hers. Above them, he whispered, "Even Popeye thinks Olive Oyl is beautiful, and I hope you give me a chance to show you just how beautiful you are to me--inside and out."

"You forgive me?" The words were as shaky as a blade of grass in a twister.

"Yeah. I do." He slid his hand along her nape. They leaned in at the same time, and he kissed her. She wrapped her arms round his neck as he wrapped her up. He cursed the console between them and Jake Parker for a multitude of sins, least of them being kidnapping her son.

When the gentle kiss ended, she pulled away, biting her lower lip. Her eyes locked on his. "I love you, Zack. I never stopped loving you. I would never have married Jake, if I hadn't..."

He touched her lips with a finger to forestall her words. "Later. We'll talk about this later. Just know I love you. And I forgive you. I have some confessions to make, too. But first we need to get Bobby back."

Before she could question him, the police radio buzzed to life. He let her go and answered the call, thankful for the distraction. The coward in him didn't want to tell her just how ruthless he'd been to his dead wife by marrying her when he'd never completely given her his heart. Clearing his throat, he spoke into the handset. "What is it, Madison?"

"Just got a call from the Austin PD. They spotted the suspects heading south on I-35."

He glanced at Tracy. She worried her lower lip again. Taking her hand into his, he squeezed it. "Ten-four, I need to drop Tracy off at the ranch, and I'll head to Austin."

"Come back to the station. Wyatt says you can go with him."

"Ten-four, I'll be there ASAP. Keep me posted." He signed off and put the Tahoe in gear.

When they passed the turn off to Oak Springs fifteen minutes later, Tracy looked at him. "Where are you going?"

He glanced at her. "I'm taking you over to the CW. Logan's there with Mandy. I don't want you to be alone tonight."

"You don't mind Logan and me... After what Jake--"

"No. I know he's your friend, but it's more than that." He thought about the diamond ring in his jeans pocket. "I think he's appointed himself our own personal cupid."

He looked at her in time to see her weak smile. "I think you're probably right. Logan came to me the day you announced you were engaged to Lisa." Her smile faltered as she clenched her hands in her lap. "He wanted me to leave Jake. To come after you."

His heart stuttered a few times. "Why didn't you?"

She was quiet for so long, he didn't expect her to answer. A few minutes later when he turned onto his road, he looked over at her and captured her gaze for as long as he could hold it.

"I just had Bobby and I couldn't take my baby away from his father." Her voice came from the depths of her soul, dragged over jagged and broken pieces. "How could I ever expect you to raise Jake's baby without resentment? How could I ever ask you to forgive me when I hardly forgave myself?"

He had to make up for all of the wrongs he'd done. It may be too late for Lisa, but he'd been given another chance to have a future with Tracy. First, he had to deal with Jake Parker. "If it's the last thing I ever do, I'll bring Bobby home." *And be the best father possible to him.*

Chapter 19

The middle-aged Hispanic man peered from Zack to Wyatt over his thick glasses, suspicion almost palpable in his dark eyes. Zack knew they both looked like horses that had been ridden hard and put away wet. A day's worth of beard darkened their faces and neither of them had changed from the clothes they'd worn the previous night.

Zack was certain the manager wondered if they were really who they said they were, despite the badges pinned to their Western shirts and the IDs they'd flashed.

Enrique Ramirez, the manager of the McDonald's in San Marcos, took only a moment to study the pictures of Jake and Brent. "*Si.* They were in here about a half hour ago. That's why I called the police. I saw the Amber Alert come over TV before I came to work last night."

Zack met Wyatt's gaze. They were close. When the police call came in, they'd been just south of San Marcos. They were close enough to turn back and check out the lead.

"Was the boy with them?"

One of the hardest things Zack had to do was let Wyatt ask Ramirez the questions. Wyatt had jurisdiction, since he was a Texas Ranger. Despite Zack's personal reasons for wanting to find the boy who had slowly stolen his heart and the man who had stolen the only woman he'd ever loved, Zack was just along for the ride. With a hand that he consciously had to steady, Zack handed the manager the wallet-sized photo Tracy had given him earlier.

"No, *Señor.*" Ramirez handed the picture back, but held onto the other two and tapped Jake's photo. "This one looked like he was in a fight. He seemed mad that the drive-thru was closed. He kept pulling on his hat brim. You know, as if he was trying to hide his face. But I recognized it. And this one..." He pointed to Brent's picture. "He stood back and let the other man do all the talking. But he couldn't stand still and kept looking around. They got gas from the station next door and left. I never saw the boy."

After thanking the man for his time, they headed back to Zack's Tahoe. Zack turned the key to start the air conditioning flowing. Not even six AM, but the day promised to be hot. He glanced at the Texas Ranger. "I don't think they stayed on I-35."

Wyatt looked around before meeting Zack's gaze. "You know Jake better than I do. What do you think he'd do?"

Zack stared out the windshield. The McDonald's was close to the interstate and Guadalupe Street, a main street through the city of San Marcos, but off the beaten path enough not to be the first choice of an investigating team. Most criminals would have gone straight for the border, the fastest route to freedom. Jake would manipulate the system by doing what wasn't expected.

He looked back at Wyatt. "Open the glove box and get that map out of there." Once Wyatt had the state map open and folded to a manageable size, zeroing in on the south-central half of Texas, Zack pointed to the junction of I-35 and Guadalupe Street. He tapped on the line representing State Route 123. "He'd take this south. We know the Blackwells have distant cousins in Monterrey. It would make sense for him to head there."

"Yeah." Wyatt tilted his head to study the map. "Mrs. Parker told me last night she was afraid he'd go there."

Zack tapped the map again. "I think we should let the state boys and the FBI chase down I-35 in case I'm wrong. But we should take this hunch and head down 123 to I-10 or US-90. I'd bet the ranch, he'll hit Seguin and then take US-90 across…" He slid his finger over the wrinkled map. "To meet up with US-83 then US-57 on the other side of San Antonio. It would keep him off the major interstates and make it easier for him to find a way across the border. I'll call the Guadalupe County sheriff and give them a heads up."

"Sounds like the logical thing for him to do." Wyatt stared at the map a little while longer before he folded it back up. "Do you suppose Johnny Blackwell would have gone to these distant cousins, too?"

Zack shrugged and put the SUV into gear. "It's possible. But my biggest concern is finding Bobby." When he slipped out onto Guadalupe Street, he looked at his friend and forced between clenched teeth, "Then you'll have to make sure I don't kill that lying bastard Jake Parker."

* * * *

The sun shone through the windows of the truck when Bobby woke up. Brent drove the truck, and his dad was asleep in the passenger side. The aroma of breakfast sandwiches and coffee filled the air, reminding him that he was hungry even before his belly growled.

"Hey, T-Rex." Brent looked at him through his reflection in the rearview mirror.

"Mornin', Uncle Brent." He peered out the side window. The two-lane road wasn't the interstate. Miles of open ranchland stretched ahead of the flat strip of road. "Where are we? And what time is it?"

"Heading south. It's just a little past six." Brent glanced at him again. "You hungry? We stopped for gas in San Marcos, and I talked your dad into getting breakfast."

Bobby nodded, but Brent had already looked back at the road. "Yeah." He moved to the middle and leaned between the seats. The bright sunlight glittered off the gun lying on the console. "Why are you taking me with you?"

Instead of answering, Brent dug around in a McDonald's bag. He held up a sandwich. "Here. You better eat. Hard to tell when we'll get a chance again."

Bobby took the wrapped egg and sausage sandwich. Brent then handed him a large soda. As he took a sip, Brent turned to look at him. "Don't drink too much. Stopping to piss ain't gonna happen anytime soon, if your dad has any say."

He nodded and sat back in the seat again. He placed the cup in a beverage holder, greedily unwrapped the sandwich, and took a bite of the cold egg and spicy sausage on soggy English muffin.

Surely, they'd have to stop if he had to go to the bathroom bad enough. Brent would, as long as Dad was still asleep. He laid the sandwich back on the wrapper in his lap and picked up the drink.

Ten minutes later, Bobby couldn't sit still. "Uncle Brent, I have to go to the bathroom."

Brent looked over his shoulder at him. "Aw, shit, Bobby. I told you not to drink it all."

"I didn't." He hadn't needed to drink the whole soda; he'd only a few sips before he had to pee. He held up the large paper cup to prove his point. "But I haven't gone to the bathroom since last night and I--"

"Alright." Brent shoved a hand through his hair and glanced over at Dad. He was still sleeping in the reclined front seat. "We're goin' through Seguin. A diner is up ahead and they look open. You can go there."

Brent pulled into the parking lot of the family restaurant. Bobby glanced anxiously at his dad as he eased open the door. Dad shifted in his sleep, but didn't wake up. Bobby jumped out of the truck, leaving the door open a little. He didn't want the slam to wake up his father. Brent followed him out of the truck and grabbed his arm.

"Stay behind me. Keep your head down and don't look at anyone or say anything." As Brent looked around and tugged at the bill of his baseball cap over his forehead, he muttered, "Jake's gonna kill me."

As they headed across the parking lot, a man and a woman got into a SUV. The woman turned to talk to the little kid on her hip and glanced his way. She met his gaze, and Bobby was close enough to see the woman furrow her brow. When her eyes widened, she said something to the man. He stopped opening the driver's door and looked over at Bobby. When the man pulled his cell phone from his pocket, Bobby nodded and smiled.

The must have recognized him from the news.

He followed his uncle into the diner with a silent prayer on his lips.

Zack, if you're looking, please come get me.

* * * *

The truck had stopped moving. Jake sat up and peered out the window at the bright yellow wall of a building. He cursed and looked around for Brent and Bobby. Neither of them was in the truck. The stink of fry grease was definitely not from the lingering scent of Egg and Sausage McMuffins and strong coffee.

Both doors on the driver's side were open enough to let in the noise of the busy street and the tinny sound of Mariachi music piped through a sound system into the parking lot. Jake grabbed the .45 from the console and shoved it into his jeans.

Hot rage replaced the stiffness and pain from Logan's beating and from driving all night as he got out of the truck. His knee was swollen from where Logan had gotten a kick in, and he cursed the bastard again. He limped around the corner, warily keeping his hat brim down as he looked around at the few vehicles in front of the building. The sign out front proclaimed it Rosalita's Family Restaurant.

Jake entered the glass door and blinked a few times to help his eyes adjust to the darker interior of the restaurant. Brent stood in a hallway behind the salad bar. The frilly sign above said, "Restrooms."

An older woman approached and asked cheerfully in a strong Mexican accent, "Just one?"

He ignored the question and pushed past her to head for his brother. With widened eyes and a gapping pie hole, Brent took a step back when he noticed him. "Jake."

"What the fuck do you think you're doing?"

Brent spread his hands and stuttered, "B-bobby had to piss. He begged me to stop."

"You're an idiot," he snarled and headed into the door marked *Mens*.

He found Bobby standing at the sink washing his hands. The boy jerked with shock when he saw him. "Dad. You're up."

The brat was up to something. He grabbed Bobby by the shoulder and yanked so hard the kid yelped in pain. "C'mon, we're getting the hell out of here before someone calls the cops."

"Oww. Dad, you're hurting me," Bobby cried out again as Jake pushed him into the wall beside the sink. The boy turned and looked up at him with fear and tears in his eyes.

"You think you're pretty smart gettin' Brent to stop, don't you?" Jake clenched his fists, then released the tension as he slapped Bobby hard enough the boy fell into the side of the sink. He bawled louder and the sound served to grate on Jake's nerves. He lifted his hand again to hit the sniveling brat. "You will know who's the boss when I'm done with you. I am, and you will never do something like this again."

"Dad, please don't hit me." Bobby sobbed as Jake's hand landed on his face again.

"Jake, what are you doing? We gotta go. I think the cops are coming."

Jake turned his fury on his brother. He pulled the gun out from his belt. "And whose fault is that?"

Brent's eyes widened so large it was almost comical. He backed up with his hands, palms out, held up on either side of his head. "Wh--what are you doin'?"

"I told you never to double cross me, Brent.

* * * *

"Where do you want to start?" Wyatt asked as Zack drove through the morning traffic of Seguin.

Zack shrugged and kept his eye on business route US-90 otherwise known as West Kingsbury Street. He and Wyatt had disagreed about which way Jake would go. He had no reason as to why anyone would choose to go through the city and stay away from the faster by-pass, but he'd won the argument when they heard chatter over the police radio that put two county sheriff deputies on the I-10, not to mention the Guadalupe County Sheriff's department was off the interstate.

"They won't stop again. But I know we're not far behind them."

"Back there a little ways, you said Jake was a lying bastard. What did you mean?"

Zack spared the Ranger a glance. "Why do you want to know?"

Wyatt shrugged and rubbed the dark auburn stubble on his chin. "I'd like to know how likely you are to snap and try to kill him."

Sucking in a deep breath, Zack let it out slowly. "Jake lied to Tracy. I'm not getting into the gory details, except to say his lies are the reason Tracy cheated on me."

He knew it was irrational to lay blame for his shaky marriage to Lisa and her ultimate death on Jake Parker's head, but it was hard for him to remain that rational. If Jake hadn't broken his heart by leading Tracy on, Zack would have never wanted to find solace in another woman's arms. And if he had never led Lisa on, she wouldn't have married him. She wouldn't have been killed after she found out he never fully loved her.

He couldn't tell Wyatt all that. It was crazy to blame someone else for his mistakes. However, thinking everything had happened because of happenstance and no one, including himself, was to blame for the mess into which his life had turned was hard to believe.

"I see." Wyatt's quiet words had Zack looking at his friend when he stopped at a four-way stop. When Wyatt had his attention, he said, "You found an easy target to blame, but remember taking all of your hate and anger at what had happened out on Jake Parker won't change a damned thing."

"No, you shittin' me?" Zack snorted. "Are you done, Dr. Phil?"

"No, I'm not done. If you go off half-cocked and do something crazy where Parker is concerned, it can destroy your future."

Zack looked back at him. Wyatt was right.

"You and Tracy have a chance, Zack. Yes, I know it hurts like someone ripped your heart out because you've missed so much. That she's been with someone else. But think about what you wouldn't have if Tracy and you had gotten together all those years ago. You wouldn't have your little girl if you hadn't met your wife, and Tracy wouldn't have Bobby if she and Jake hadn't been together."

Zack focused on the road as he eased through the intersection. Before he could respond to his friend, the police radio buzzed to life. "Calling all units in the vicinity of West Kingsbury and Eighth Streets. Missing boy, Robert Parker, was seen entering Rosalita's Family Restaurant..."

Wyatt picked up the handset and glanced at Zack as he called in their proximity to the suspects. They'd just crossed Sixth Street. Zack's heart kicked into overdrive. He was close.

Hang in there, buddy, I'll get you.

* * * *

Zack and Wyatt weren't the only police to respond. Two Guadalupe County sheriff deputies also pulled into the small parking lot. Brent's truck sat in a space beside the brightly painted stucco building.

He and Wyatt got out of the Tahoe and introduced themselves to the two deputies.

The lieutenant of the two smiled. "I know this boy's from Forest County, but it's unusual for the sheriff to go hunting outside of his county."

Zack took one look at the young man and the deputy lost his cocky grin. "I have a personal reason for wanting Bobby found."

Wyatt took a step forward as the front door shattered when a bullet hit it. Zack dropped to the ground the same time as Wyatt and the two deputies, all of them with pistols aimed at the restaurant.

Jake's voice boomed through the opening. "I have ten hostages including the boy. If you don't let me go, I'll start shootin'."

Zack's heart sank into his stomach when Jake stepped into the line-of-sight of the shot-out door window with a middle-aged Mexican woman. He held her to him with an arm around her ample waist, and with a Colt .45 pressed against her head. She was crying and muttered something in Spanish.

Jake wiggled the gun at her temple to make his point. "You have ten seconds to put your guns away."

"Jake, you can't get away," Zack said from beside Wyatt as he lay prone on the cracked, hot macadam. "Half of all the law in Texas is looking for you. The Border Patrol have been alerted to your plans to cross into Mexico."

"Shut up! Just shut the fuck up!" Jake raged. "You have five seconds or Rosalita here meets her maker."

Wyatt glanced at Zack and the deputies before voicing the order. "Stand down."

The deputies reluctantly obeyed the Texas Ranger, but Zack continued to aim his Glock at a man he'd once considered his best friend.

"Zack?" Wyatt spoke with determined authority. "Don't make me regret bringing you along."

Zack eased back and crawled behind the front fender of the Guadalupe Sheriff's department Crown Victoria with the other three men. Wyatt pulled out his iPhone and called in the situation to his boss, who would notify everyone else involved in the manhunt.

Jake stood with the frightened woman, staring out at Zack with a hatred he didn't understand.

"Johnny, his mother and his son Matt were caught trying to get over the border. They're in custody in San Antonio." Wyatt slipped his phone back into the holder on his belt. "The captain has a hostage negotiator and backup on their way. He wants me to find out what he wants."

Zack slowly nodded, then called across the pavement, "Jake, what do you want?"

"You can't give me what I want, Cartwright."

"Try me."

"Fuck you!"

"Zack, don't agitate him," Wyatt said. With a snort of derision, he added, "I'm beginning to think there's something wrong with all the Blackwells. First Leon and now Jake."

Zack didn't respond, just stood up.

"Zack, what the hell are you doing?"

Zack ignored his friend and the cautions of the deputies as he held his hands high. "Let the hostages go, Jake. It's not them you want to hurt. It's me. You blame me for taking away your chance at playing football. And for it you've made me pay dearly. You took away the woman I loved."

"Yeah, I got the bitch away from you, but then you went off and got richer riding rodeo, then married a damned beauty queen. I was stuck in fuckin' Colton with nothing."

"My life was far from glamorous. I may have married, but I never stopped loving Tracy. I spent a total of six years fighting in the war, Jake. I watched men I called friends injured and killed. I watched the man who saved my life take a bullet in the chest that should've been mine." Zack swallowed hard. Framed within the broken window of the door, Jake still held the gun at the sobbing woman's head. "I came home and suffered depression and watched my marriage fall apart. Then my wife died. I've suffered plenty for my part in the injury that prevented you from getting a football scholarship, Jake. Don't you think it's time to stop?"

"You haven't suffered anywhere near enough." Jake spat, and his tone became high pitched and wild, proving to Zack that he was clearly unstable. "I don't want my son anywhere near you. I'll kill him before I let you turn him against me, Cartwright. You hear me?"

* * * *

Brent stood back and listened to Zack's admission and the vow made by his brother. He had to act, despite his own fear of Jake and his lack of weapon. Bobby clung to his side and turned his face into Brent's belly as he shook with the violence of his silent sobs.

He'd never been the brave sort. Hell, this whole rustling operation had scared him shitless from the beginning. But as he had his entire life, Brent followed Jake's orders and took his abuse.

He was done being Jake's sheep.

Brent took hold of Bobby's shoulders and held him away from his side. He tried to offer the boy a smile, but he knew it was pitiful at best. One of the customers stood beside him. It was obvious she was scared, but seemed to have it somewhat together. Dressed in jeans and a green button shirt, she was pretty, with blond hair, big blue eyes, and a nice round ass and enough tits to get lost in. Brent let himself wonder what she did for a living. She was exactly the kind of woman he'd have liked to settle down with someday. She met his regard with narrowed eyes. Of course, she was afraid of him. He was this madman's brother, after all.

Brent looked back down at his nephew, a boy he loved with a heart only an uncle could have. He forced a slippery smile again. "Whatever happens, T-Rex, remember that I'm not like your dad."

He pushed Bobby into the pretty blonde beside him, who reached for the boy and held him, steadying herself as she was knocked off balance. Brent immediately took off on a jog and came up behind his brother.

Jake must have heard him coming and turned, with his gun swinging around. He let go of Rosalita, and she fell to the floor with a scream when the gun went off. Brent held his breath as the bullet hit him in the chest, but he didn't stop. He hit Jake with enough momentum to knock him through the door of the restaurant.

Jake tried to shove him off. When the second gunshot sounded, Brent wasn't sure if it hit him or if the bullet aimed for Jake, but *bang* was the last sound he would ever hear.

* * * *

Bobby clung to the woman as she held his face against her heaving chest. Too many sounds swirled around him. Gunshots. A scream, sirens, shouts of men, running feet. The woman's rapid breathing and heartbeat.

"Bobby, are you okay?"

He turned and looked into Zack's face. He crouched next to him and held out his arms. Bobby immediately fell into them and held him close as Zack wrapped him up.

"I was so afraid, Zack. Dad started talkin' crazy. He pulled the gun on Uncle Brent and made everyone stand in the corner." He pulled away and met Zack's gaze. "Uncle Brent, is he okay? How about Dad?"

Zack pulled him close again and said near his ear, "I'm sorry, buddy. Brent... Brent didn't make it."

"He's dead?" His voice cracked. He couldn't believe his next question, but he had to know for sure. "He killed...Uncle Brent?"

Zack swallowed and nodded.

Bobby couldn't hold in the sob, then croaked, "Dad?"

"He's being taken to the hospital."

Another sob ripped through him. How could Dad kill his own brother? He hiccoughed. "Did--did you...?"

Zack's voice was deep and husky at his ear. "I had no choice, Bobby. After he shot Brent, he might've hurt someone else or you. I couldn't let that happen. You mean too much to your momma--and to me."

Chapter 20

Tracy ran off the porch as soon as she heard a vehicle come up the long driveway. Her family followed close behind. Dylan, Charli and Annie had landed in Dallas just that morning. When they arrived home, Tracy called them to alert them to Bobby's kidnapping and they came to Oak Springs immediately. Her parents had been called and hoped to be home that night. Logan hadn't left her alone since last night and was by her side now, with Mandy in his arms.

Thank God he was here. The phone--calls from concerned neighbors, friends, far-flung family and the media--hadn't stopped ringing since the Amber Alert had been posted.

She caught her lip between her teeth as the Tahoe came to a stop in front of the house. Her heart raced like a captured bird beating its wings against its cage. Zack had called, and she knew her baby was alright, but she had to see him. She wouldn't believe it until she held him to her.

By the time she reached the side of the SUV, Bobby scampered out with Zack and Wyatt right behind him.

"Momma!" Bobby lurched himself into her arms as she fell to her knees on the pavement.

"Oh, my baby," Tracy sobbed and clung to him. She placed kisses all over his face, and he even kissed her back. She dried his tears with her lips.

"Momma, I was so afraid. I thought I'd never see you again." He buried his face into the side of her neck. His body shook with the force of his sobbing relief.

Tracy looked up and met Zack's gaze. With Mandy in his arms, he smiled and kneeled beside her and Bobby. She tried to swallow past her swollen throat and whispered, "Thank you."

Mandy let go of her dad to hug Bobby while Zack encircled all of them within his arms and held on with a force that set the caged bird in her chest free.

* * * *

Two days after Bobby's return, Zack decided it was time to get on with the rest of his life. He stood before the mantle and stared at the photos of Lisa. He'd pack them away soon, to give to Mandy when she got older.

He picked up the middle picture of his dead wife and rubbed his thumb over her lips. "I'm sorry, Lisa. I'm sorry I never was able to give you my whole heart. You deserved so much more than I could give, but I can't go on living in the past or blaming myself for what happened." He leaned over and placed a soft kiss on the lips of the photograph. When he replaced the frame, he laid it upside down and turned away.

The horses were saddled and the picnic supper of fried chicken and peach cobbler packed in a saddlebag. He'd changed one of the items from that first time he'd packed a picnic lunch for today's purpose. Instead of a bottle of homemade wine from his grandfather's cellar, he sprang for a bottle of Dom Perignon. Now, all he needed was to get Tracy.

He'd called ahead, and she waited on the porch. She jumped into his truck and smiled. "Where're we going?"

Zack shrugged and put the Dodge into gear. "I thought we'd go riding out to our special spot and go camping. I've already talked to your Mom and Dad. They'll take care of Bobby.

"I hate leaving him alone." She fidgeted with her seatbelt. "He's still afraid his dad's going to come and take him away."

"Understandable, but this can't wait any longer." He pointed the truck up the driveway. "I talked to Bobby. He's okay with us going camping."

"Well, then what are we waiting for?"

Twenty minutes later, they'd mounted their horses and headed toward the interior of the CW. He rode his stallion, Wild Aces, while Tracy sat upon an Appaloosa mare he'd recently purchased from a business associate.

They dismounted in the grove of trees next to the lake. She loosened the cinch on the saddle and slid it from the mare's back. "She's a beautiful horse. You never told me her name."

He set his saddle under one of the live oaks and turned to remove the bridle. "She is a fine horse. I haven't given her a barn name yet. I figured since she's yours, you'd like to do the honors."

Tracy turned on him and gasped. "Mine? I can't--"

"You said so yourself you didn't have a horse of your own. Well, now you do. There's only one thing I'd like in return."

"Anything?"

Zack smiled and raised a brow. "You let me mate her with Wild Aces here." He petted the stallion's long black and white splotched face.

Tracy stared at him with her mouth slightly open before closing it and nodding. "Okay. I'll have to think of a name I guess."

"Yep. C'mon." He set her saddle beside his and picked up the saddlebags. She retrieved the sleeping bag and the quilt she'd untied from behind her saddle and followed him to the water's edge.

Zack spread the patchwork quilt over the ground and then went about setting out the picnic supper. As they ate the chicken and salad, he kept the conversation light and focused on their kids, although he was aware of the questions in Tracy's eyes. They hadn't had a chance to have the talk he'd promised her Sunday night. She was more than ready now.

They finished their supper, he opened the champagne, and gave her one of the plastic cups.

She smiled. "What's the occasion?"

"I think it's time we consider where we go from here."

"Oh."

"But before we get too serious, I thought we'd have a toast." He held his cup up and she followed suit.

"What are we toasting?"

"Love. And forgiveness."

She smiled and tapped her cup on his. "To love and forgiveness. I love you, Zack."

After taking a gulp of the fizzy wine, he set his cup down and took her hand. She set her champagne aside, settled herself next to him and waited for him to speak.

He cleared his throat and squeezed her hand. "Tracy, I love you. I told you the other night I had my own confessions." He looked over the calm water of the lake. Cattails and other water-loving plants competed for what sunlight the trees allowed filter through along the water's edge.

He met her soft gray eyes again and swallowed so hard it hurt. "Here it goes. I don't deserve you. I never have, but I can't live without you anymore. I've never stopped loving you. Lisa and I..."

She sighed and reached up to lay her hand over his cheek. "Oh, Zack, I don't have to hear this if it hurts you this much to say it."

He nodded and covered her hand with his free one. "Yeah, you do, and I need to get it out. When I heard you had a baby with Jake, something died in me. I had hoped that after you lost the first pregnancy you'd leave him, but only a year later you got pregnant again."

"I should have left him after I lost the baby, but he kept telling me how much he loved me, and that he wanted a family with me." She shook her head and looked down at their clasped hands. "I was such a fool."

He tightened his hold on her hand, and she looked up again. "No, you weren't."

"I broke up with Jake after you--you found us in the barn. And when I started school, I had every intention of transferring that spring to University of Texas. But Jake started coming around. He'd meet me after classes, and we started going out again. I hadn't known then it was all a plan to keep me away from you. I learned later that he was afraid I'd go off to find you. So, he started up his lies. He swept me off my feet--again--with words of love and how much he couldn't live without me." She made a sound of disgust in her throat and shook her head. "I'd stopped taking the Pill when I started school." She smiled ruefully. "I had no reason to continue taking it--I wasn't dating anyone. And I started getting headaches and my doctor thought it was from the birth control pills. Instead of switching brands, I stopped taking them. Then Jake seduced me. I still don't know how exactly I got pregnant. We always used condoms." She shrugged. "But I did. I've often wondered after I learned the truth if he'd done something to make it happen." Again she shrugged and looked away. "The rest is sad history."

He sighed, pulled her into his lap, and held her against him. "I met Lisa and it was instant lust. I know this is probably hard for you to hear, but I think you should know."

She looked over her shoulder at him. "Zack, I know you loved her."

"No, Tracy, I never loved Lisa--not enough anyway. I never loved her as I've always loved you."

She turned in his embrace. "What?"

"I was in lust with her. I was jealous of you." He couldn't meet her gaze. "I took her virginity, and she told me she loved me the third time we were together. Despite her title as a pageant queen, she was so naive. I asked her to marry me just two weeks after meeting her. I liked her and we--" He cut himself off, Tracy didn't need to know their sex was great. "When I was with her, I could forget you. At least, for a little while. I hoped I'd learn to love her." He snorted. "You know the history of our families as well as I do. Everyone knows the first Cole Cartwright didn't love his wife when they married, but he grew to love her. I figured if it worked for my great-great-great granddad, it would work for me. Maybe if I hadn't spent so much time away from her, I would have. But each time I'd come home from a deployment, I'd find something else I just didn't like. Her laugh started to annoy me. Her nagging about me not going places with her. Her bossiness. I began regretting letting her talk me out of my rodeo career. I hated the way she'd talk for me when we visited her friends or people we'd just met, as if I was some bumpkin because I didn't have a college education."

The warm September breeze fluttered through her hair and he smoothed the silk back behind her ear. "If she hadn't gotten pregnant, I seriously considered asking for a divorce. Then she had Amanda and I couldn't leave her, so I reenlisted, although it made her furious. I was almost relieved when I was sent off to Afghanistan that last time."

Her eyes widened and she opened her lips as if to speak. He smiled and caressed her bottom lip with his thumb, stilling whatever she had to say.

"When I woke up from the coma, I called your name, Tracy. Lisa had realized years before I was still in love with you. When we came back to Cheyenne, she and I fought all the time. Not all of it was a result of my PTSD. I felt I was being suffocated. I had no drive to be a big city cop. All I ever wanted to do was raise cattle here. When I'd heard you divorced Jake, I started wondering what it would be like if--"

He cut himself off and swallowed. "She was leaving me the night she died, and I was glad it was finally over."

"You blame yourself for her death."

"I think I always will. But punishing myself isn't bringing her back or necessarily good for my daughter--or for me. Mandy loves you. I love you--and I love Bobby."

"Zack, I love you with all my heart." She swallowed, and her pewter eyes shimmered. "And Mandy, too. She's a wonderful little girl, and I'm thankful you had her with Lisa. The world would be a darker place without her."

"I've always had this dream that you and I would have a bunch of kids and fill that big house my great-great-great grandfather built. We'd live here and bring the Cartwright legacy full circle. We'd raise cattle and kids and dogs and horses and live happily ever after."

She blushed. When she spoke, her voice cracked. "Me, too. I love Oak Springs, but it's not my house, not my home. I've always dreamed of living here and having a family with you."

Zack smiled. "I'm not running for reelection. In fact, I'm resigning as sheriff. Dawn can take over until the election in November. She'll make a fantastic sheriff. I'm a cowboy, not a cop. What about you?"

"I want to finish my degree, but I'm thinking that becoming a physician's assistant might be more realistic. I'll still be able to treat people and work as a medical provider."

"If that's what you want, you know I'll support you the whole way."

"Who knows if I'd be a good doctor?"

He chuckled and laid her down on the old quilt. "Bullshit. You are one of the kindest, most compassionate people I've ever met."

She wrapped her arms around his neck. "You know what my ultimate dream is?"

He ran his hand down her side. Her breathing kicked up a notch. "Nope."

"I'd much rather be a cowboy's wife someday."

His body fit perfectly in the cradle of hers. She lifted his Stetson off his head. After tossing it to the side, she threaded her fingers through his hair. He kissed her, but with a gentle teasing of lips brushing lips. When his erection pressed against her, she licked along the seam of his mouth, and he let her explore his mouth.

The heat built and passion caught fire. He took over the kiss and plunged into her mouth in direct imitation of what he wanted to do with her. She moaned and found the buttons of his shirt. When her hands pushed the open halves away, brushing his chest, he shrugged out of the shirt without breaking the kiss. Her hands touched him everywhere, and he eased out of the kiss as he lifted away her t-shirt.

She'd forgone a bra, and her nipples stood taut. He took one of them into his mouth and suckled until she clutched at his back, her nails biting deliciously into his skin. She arched into him as he moved to the other one, while his fingers teased and plucked at the moist pebbly nipple he'd left, alternating between sucking, nibbling and caressing. Her breathing quickened and her moans became more insistent. She wrapped her legs around his waist. The torture of her thrusting and rubbing herself against his hard-on nearly had him giving up and finish undressing both of them and burying himself inside her. However, he was determined to have this, to give her this.

"Zack...Oh...I'm..." The words were lost as she shattered beneath him.

When she opened eyes full of wonder, he smiled down into her face. "I knew I could make you come by playing with your breasts."

She laughed and shifted against him, eliciting a groan from him. "I think it's time we get naked, don't you?"

"In a second. But first..." He reached into his jeans pocket and pulled out the engagement ring. "I think this belongs to you."

She furrowed her brow, and he kissed her nose. When he pulled back, he held the ring before her face.

She gasped. "My ring." Then her face flushed a deeper red. This time from embarrassment, not passion. "I mean. The ring you--"

He knew Logan had shown the ring to her, but he hadn't known she'd always considered it hers. "What do you say we change your last name?"

"I just got my last name back." She laid her left hand on his cheek and grinned. "I could opt to keep it."

"True."

He took her hand from his face and slid the diamond ring he'd bought for her fourteen years ago onto her finger. As he peered into her luminous eyes swimming in unshed tears of joy, he huskily asked, "Tracy Caroline Quinn, will you marry me? Become this cowboy's wife?"

"Yes," she breathed and pulled him to her and kissed him so deeply it took his breath away. When she finally pulled away, she rasped, "I think we're both a little overdressed."

He toed off his boots and shucked his jeans, and then helped pull off her boots and jeans. After he sheathed himself with a condom, she lay back pulling him over her again. As he kissed her, he pressed into her one inch at a time. She moaned and then broke the kiss. Her eyes opened and she gasped as he seated himself completely inside her.

"Oh, God. Zack..." She met him thrust for passionate thrust, and he couldn't remember anything except that he loved this woman.

Always had. Always would.

Sara Walter Ellwood

Although Sara Walter Ellwood has long ago left the farm for the glamour of the big town, she draws on her experiences growing up on a small hobby farm in West Central Pennsylvania to write her stories. She's been married to her college sweetheart for nearly 20 years, and they have two teenagers and one very spoiled rescue cat named Penny. She longs to visit the places she writes about and jokes she's a cowgirl at heart stuck in Pennsylvania suburbia.

She also writes paranormal romantic suspense under the pen name of Cera duBois.